St. Martin's Paperbacks Titles by
Caris Roane

ASCENSION

BURNING SKIES

WINGS OF FIRE

WINGS OF FIRE

CARIS ROANE

St. Martin's Paperbacks

This is a work of fiction. All of the characters, organizations, and events portrayed in this novel are either products of the author's imagination or are used fictitiously.

WINGS OF FIRE

Copyright © 2011 by Caris Roane.

For information address St. Martin's Press, 175 Fifth Avenue, New York, NY 10010.

ISBN: 978-0-312-53373-1

Printed in the United States of America

St. Martin's Paperbacks edition / September 2011

St. Martin's Paperbacks are published by St. Martin's Press, 175 Fifth Avenue, New York, NY 10010.

10 9 8 7 6 5 4 3 2 1

ACKNOWLEDGMENTS

Many thanks to my agent, Jennifer Schober, for all the wonderful conversations about the Guardians of Ascension.

To Rose Hilliard—lady, you rock!!!

Danielle Fiorella—thank you so much for the best covers in publishing!

Laurie Henderson and Laura Jorstad, again thank you so much for taking care of my beloved Antony and Parisa.

I am once again so very grateful to Anne Marie Tallberg and Eileen Rothschild for continuing to bring my winged vampires to market.

And as always, many thanks to Matthew Shear, Jen Enderlin, and the amazing team at SMP.

My Beloved

In the twilight I think of him
He sees me in the wonder of his eye
I allow the air to breathe
He does not move with swift feet

His thoughts turn to me imagined
I wait beyond the faint boundary of time
He does not rush
My steps are measured

I have known his love from the beginning
I perceive his beauty angled, firm
He is earnest in his movements
Love rises on wings of fire

—Maria Medichi (AD 707–732),
translated by her husband, Antony, 1845

The search is futile
When carried out by the avenging heart.

—*Collected Proverbs,* Beatrice of Fourth

CHAPTER 1

In the last three months, since the abduction of his woman, Antony Medichi, out of Italy in the late Roman era, had become a killing machine. He had steel for bones and molten iron for blood. He rarely slept. He battled death vampires at night, sending to perdition any who crossed his sword. But during the day, when most of the pretty-boys were asleep, Antony bled his wrists on his altar and hunted rogue vampires on Mortal Earth, searching for the woman he'd lost.

Those hunts also ended in death. Not his.

He stood on the rim of the Grand Canyon, Mortal Earth, looking down, tracking a death vampire flying in the shadows. Even though he was far from the touristy areas, he still cloaked his presence with a heavy concentration of mist, a preternatural creation designed to confuse the average human mind. Most mortals simply couldn't see him, and right now he didn't want to be seen.

Antony stared into the abyss. The profound silence across

the canyon formed a strange juxtaposition to the visual feast. The Grand Canyon was all for the eyes, not for the ears. But he hadn't come to admire the view or embrace the quiet.

His predatory gaze followed the death vampire flying below, legs straight back, glossy black wings glinting in the early-morning sunshine. He'd been hunting this particular bastard for weeks now. All clues had led here. This pretty-boy had known both Eldon Crace and Rith Do'onwa, two sons of bitches who had harmed women belonging to the Warriors of the Blood. Both vampires deserved death. Crace had already gotten what he deserved, and within the depths of Medichi's mind Rith Do'onwa, the fiend who had kidnapped his woman, was a death waiting to happen, nothing more.

Three months ago, Medichi had served as Parisa Love-joy's Guardian of Ascension. She'd entered his world as an anomaly, a mortal-with-wings, a woman of extraordinary pre-ternatural power in need of protection from the enemy. No one, except the first ascender, had mounted wings on Mortal Earth. But Parisa had. She'd also arrived with the ability to voyeur, a power that allowed her to focus on an individual or a place and *see* what was happening in real time, even in an entirely separate location, or a different dimension.

So much power, and beauty, and a strong analytical mind.

But all these immense gifts and abilities paled in comparison with the call of the *breh-hedden,* the myth of vampire mate-bonding, that had proved as real as the air he breathed. She was his *breh,* his mate, the one destiny had selected for him, the one he *craved.*

He hadn't asked for a mate. He hadn't wanted one and he sure as hell didn't deserve one, but she'd come, he'd served as her guardian, and she'd been abducted on his watch.

So here he was, a wrecked shell of a warrior, struggling to find his way back to her.

When Rith had abducted Parisa, he'd not only blocked his trace—which indicated an enormous amount of power—but also deceived Medichi with a hologram of Parisa that lasted for at least half a minute. Medichi didn't know anyone, not even any of his warrior brothers, the powerful Warriors of the Blood, who could create a hologram. So, yeah, Rith had power, which made him a clever, dangerous opponent.

But the death vampire working the airstreams of the Grand Canyon had known Rith. He had answers, and Medichi meant to have them. Right now. This morning.

His heart pumped hard in his chest.

The death vampire flew close to the canyon walls as though trying to hide in the shadows. Medichi smiled the hard smile that tended to work his jaw at the same time. Did the death vamp actually think to hide in a place this size?

Medichi bound his hair not in the ritual *cadroen* as he was supposed to, but with a narrow leather strap over his forehead, tied at the back of his head so that his long warrior hair flowed free. He was uncivilized now, a wild beast hunting for what was his by right, for what had been taken from him.

He had his wings at close-mount, tight to his body; any breeze would send him off the canyon's edge otherwise. But now it was time to take care of business. With the practice of thirteen centuries, he spread his wings to full-mount, adjusting with infinitesimal shifts to balance the air currents, then launched into the empty airspace over the canyon.

A rush of pure adrenaline shot through his heart then sent dizzying endorphins into his head. There was nothing like flight, nothing like falling off a cliff and knowing that spreading his wings to their farthest span would catch, hold, then carry him where he wanted to go.

With a slight adjustment, the barest drawing back of his wings, his body shifted at an angle that meant *down,* and down he started to fly. Down and down, into the varying degrees of cool shadow and warm light as the canyon walls jutted and receded.

He was close now, his quarry an eighth of a mile away, less, less, a hundred yards now.

The bastard looked up. Shit. Maybe Medichi's shadow had crossed him.

Panic seized the pretty-boy's eyes and he banked left,

then drew his wings into close-mount. He threw his arms forward as though diving, his body now aimed in the direction of the Colorado River.

Medichi didn't hesitate. He folded his wings close to his body and, instead of flying in long pulls through the air, became a missile and headed with fierce intent after his prey.

The bastard was good and he was old, which meant he had power, speed, and lots of fucking skill.

But then so did Medichi. He had never mounted his wings during battle, but he flew, a lot. He practiced, a lot. And now he smiled, his jaw twitching.

The mile-deep canyon walls sped past him, the striated layers of rock blending into an orange-beige fusion as he jetted toward the blue-and-white ribbon below. Closer.

He could almost touch the bastard's foot.

Closer.

If he could wrap a hand around his ankle.

Closer.

The waters rose up and up.

Shit.

The death vamp leveled off just three feet above the water but Medichi took a huge risk, kept his missile shape for a split second longer, and just as the death vamp started to plow air Medichi caught his ankle and jerked him down, straight into the frothy rapids of the river below. At the same time, with the steel of his bones, the molten iron of his blood, and a swift mental command, he snagged his levitation ability and threw his wings into parachute mount, cupped at the top, to keep from plunging into the frigid water.

The death vamp wasn't so lucky. His wings went under, and he surfaced screaming because the water had trashed them. The mesh superstructure that held the feathers in place was fairly fragile, and the smallest injury hurt like a bitch. This tumbling in wild waters would be a form of torture. As the current dragged him in a heap, tossing him over and over, the death vamp screamed each time his head breached the water. He landed back-first against an enormous rock. Medichi heard the crack as well as another shriek.

Medichi flew after him. When the pretty-boy would have slid into the heavy currents that swirled at the base of the rock, the warrior grabbed him by his long, dark hair and hauled him out of the water. He threw him facedown on the rock. How many mortals had this motherfucker drunk to death? How many ascenders? Death vamps didn't differentiate when it came to dying blood. Any human, ascended or not, would do.

Medichi wafted his wings slowly to keep his balance against the air currents that streamed through the canyon.

God, the bastard's wings were a mess. The vamp shook hard, maybe from the icy water but probably from shock and a mountain of pain.

"Where's Rith?" he asked. Time to keep the questions simple.

The death vampire shifted slightly to cast one dark, beautiful eye up at Medichi. Calling death vampires "pretty-boys" was more than accurate. He was exquisite, chiseled features shaped by the effects of dying blood, porcelain skin with a faint bluish cast, enhanced no doubt by the freezing water. Medichi felt the pull of attraction, an allure that created a swelling of ease within his chest. Fuck. Even shaking with pain and approaching death, the bastard was trying to enthrall him.

Medichi punched back with a shot of mental power that acted like a blow, pushing the death vamp's face into the rock. "Even at this hour," he shouted, "when you face death, you'd try to enthrall me?"

A smile curved the side of the pretty-boy's mouth. Blood dribbled from his lips onto the wet black rock beneath his face. "Fuck you," he whispered.

"Where's Rith?"

The death vampire just smiled. Yeah, questions would be futile, but he always gave them a chance because what he intended to do next would hurt like hell.

He retracted his wings then dropped to his knees beside the death vamp. A bone jutted from the bastard's thigh, shiny and white. Blood ran in a rivulet down his ruptured skin, but the water, still shedding from the nearest feathers of his broken wings, kept washing it away.

"You sure you don't want to just tell me?" Medichi asked. One last chance.

The same reply returned, this time a much stronger "Fuck you."

"Fine," Medichi said. "We'll do it the hard way." He put his hand on the vamp's forehead.

The struggle began as the pretty-boy's mind bucked against Medichi's touch as though trying to cast him out of his head. He put up a good fight, too, but more than just Medichi's body had grown tougher over the forced separation from Parisa. He'd been working his mental powers as well, trying to find his woman telepathically. In doing so, he'd gotten stronger.

He shoved hard, and the vampire's mind gave way. The death vamp screamed but Medichi ignored him and began the real hunt.

He cast aside memories like batting at flies until Rith's strange face emerged, the Asian cast to his features, the broad forehead and wide nose. He focused on those memories and gained a portrait of the man as a powerful servant of Commander Greaves—but then what else would he be? Greaves was the acknowledged enemy of all that Medichi held dear on Second Earth, in this beautiful dimensional world. Darian Greaves had ambitions to rule both Second Earth and Mortal Earth and was creating a powerful army of death vamps to back up his efforts. Rith was a favored servant.

Within the death vampire's mind, he saw Rith's lairs, sometimes in great caverns, sometimes in tents, sometimes in suburban homes, but all in separate geographic locales. He kept picking through them, trying to *feel* the presence of his woman. All the while the death vamp screamed at the invasion.

Medichi came across the memory of one of Rith's properties that was shrouded in a mental shield. What the fuck was that? This death vampire didn't have enough power to create a deep mental shield like this, which meant that Rith had done it himself.

He tried punching through the shroud but couldn't and then the preternatural sensation stole over him, of simply *knowing*. He knew. He could *feel* that this was where Rith held Parisa captive, cloaked even from Central's advanced high-tech grid system, which could locate anything on two earths.

Parisa.

Parisa.

Sweet Jesus. He felt light-headed. He struggled to breathe.

At last. He'd found a connection to her at last. He focused on breathing for a moment. He had to get command of himself if he had any hope of extracting the information he needed.

When he was calmer and while he was still inside the pretty-boy's mind, he moved around the shrouded entity as though walking a mental circle. The death vampire sobbed now, but Medichi didn't give a rat's ass. He'd witnessed too many of the bastard's memories, those that involved securing dying blood, and the women he'd killed to get to it— always women because they were easily subdued physically.

So, yeah, let the bastard feel some pain. Let him feel a lot of pain because it wouldn't be even a fraction of the devastation he'd created in the women he'd killed and the families left behind to deal with all those losses.

He focused once more on the shrouded dwelling and from deep within the death vampire's mind a location at last came forth: *Burma, Second Earth.*

Medichi couldn't quite grasp the sensation that plowed through him, but it popped a firework in his mind until glitter rained in his head. Relief flowed, pure exhilarating relief. After three long horrible months of hunting, he had just limited his search to a single country, located on only one of two dimensional earths.

Finally.

His entire body sagged and his throat tightened. He had a chance now of finding her, his woman.

Parisa on Second Earth and in Burma.

Even so, given Rith's level of preternatural power it would take a few days to find the lair that held her captive. With Rith's ability to create shields, no doubt the dwelling in which Parisa was kept was under some crazy-ass mist. The grid would have to search for an anomaly, something nonspecific and unidentifiable—in other words, something vague that didn't belong.

But what were a few more days after searching for three long months and finding nothing? Yeah, he could wait for the grid to uncover an anomaly.

He closed his eyes. He took a long, long moment to offer thanks to the Creator, lifting his face to the heavens, his heart almost floating in a chest that had been constricted from the moment when the hologram of Parisa had disintegrated in front of his eyes.

He felt the pretty-boy's life fading. He withdrew from his mind. The death vamp vomited blood, a lot of it.

Medichi sat down beside the creature that had once been a proper vampire youth. He put his hand on his shoulder, and kept it there. His touch calmed the shaking.

Medichi lowered his head to his knees. He despised what the death vamp had done, but he'd also seen that as a young ascender, a Twoling born on Second Earth, he'd tried dying blood on a dare, offered not from a body but from a goblet at a party. He'd been promised no ill effects, just pleasure. Well, pleasure he'd gotten, but he'd also gotten about three centuries of addiction, killing, despair, and no way back from a stupid teenage mistake. He hated all this shit, the treachery of Greaves and his forces, the resulting mortal victims. Still Medichi remained close to the vampire, as much a victim as those he'd killed, until he felt the final breath.

Stillness overcame the broken body. Medichi looked up. How far away the rim of the canyon seemed. The rush of water was loud in his ears and dominated his impression of the space. Above, complete silence. Below, all this rushing noise.

With his hand still on the death vampire, he repeated the

words that had been his ritual for centuries. He was a man of faith if not a believer in structured religion, so in certain situations, like this one, he did what he thought was right, even necessary.

He looked at the now empty shell beside him and spoke against the hurtling water: "May the Great Spirit help you atone for these your terrible sins. May you be forgiven and may you find peace in the arms of the Creator. Amen."

He released a heavy sigh.

So much death in their ascended dimension when it wasn't necessary. Vampires were essentially immortal, or had the potential to live forever. But the addictive nature of dying blood, which seduced every death vampire who partook, made it necessary to kill mortals and ascenders alike for more.

In turn, Commander Greaves, bent on the domination of two worlds, used dying blood as one of his weapons. He not only encouraged the creation of death vampires, but built armies made up of them. There were even rumors that he provided the blood not just to his armies but to those High Administrators around the globe that he'd persuaded to join his faction.

Medichi had no qualms about being the sword of justice.

He left forgiveness to God.

Still sitting, he pulled his phone from the pocket of his black leather battle kilt and held it to his ear. He thumbed it. The phone was the size of a credit card and was a direct line to Central. For all other calls, he had a BlackBerry.

"Hey, Warrior Medichi," Carla said. "Did you get him?"

"I got him."

He heard a whoop and a shout and then Medichi smiled. Thank God for the women at Central. They were chosen for their calm tempers and positive outlooks even in the face of nightly death. They also did clean-up through a sophisticated inter-dimensional process that was more technology than preternatural power.

"Has Jeannie gone home for the day?" Carla and Jeannie overlapped their schedules. Carla had the day shift, while her best friend, Jeannie, had the night shift. The women were gold and served seven days and nights a week, just like the Warriors of the Blood.

"Yeah," Carla said. "I kicked her out an hour ago. She has a brunch this morning with a Militia Warrior."

He bristled. As a Warrior of the Blood, his protective instincts were always in overdrive, even where Jeannie and Carla were concerned. The Militia Warriors, though less powerful than the elite Warriors of the Blood, were still strong hombres and carried a shitload of testosterone in their own right. "Is he treating her good?" he growled.

"He'd better if he wants to stay alive," Carla responded, but she was chuckling. "Hey, don't worry. Not only can Jeannie handle herself after so many centuries as a vampire, but our Militia boys aren't stupid. They know the Warriors of the Blood would be all over their asses if either of us got hurt."

"Damn straight," he cried, but more softly he added, "You still dating your man?"

She giggled then sighed.

"I take that as a yes."

"He's gorgeous," she cooed. "Almost as pretty as you."

Medichi found himself smiling all over again even though he was exhausted and had a torn-up and really dead pretty-boy beside him. Yeah, this was his life, finding small measures of comfort while sitting next to a corpse.

"I need a little cleanup action," he said.

"I see him. What a mess. Oh, God, look at those wings." In recent months, satellite imaging had enhanced the grid's capacity as well. Medichi wondered if Carla could see the scars laced down his back, although right now his hair hung almost to his waist. Well, if she'd seen his scars anytime in the last three months, she hadn't said anything. One more reason to love her. "Close your peepers."

Medichi let his eyelids fall. Damn, he was tired, because it felt good to shut down like this, on a wet rock in the middle of the Colorado River. "Ready," he murmured into his phone.

He saw the flash of light behind his lids. He felt the air

move beside him. He opened his eyes. The death vamp was gone as well as any traces of blood, bone, or other feathered debris. "Clean as a whistle as usual, Carla. Thanks."

"I know you've been after this death vamp for weeks. Please tell me you have some news for me? Anything I can use to find our girl?"

Our girl. That's why he loved the Central staff. They made everything feel like a team effort; no matter what you went through, you had backup.

Relief flowed through him again, like a cool breeze on a hot day. "Actually, I have the best news." He explained getting inside the pretty-boy's head and finding the shrouded dwelling.

Carla squealed several times in the telling. He could hear her tapping on her keyboard. "I'm reconfiguring the grid to Burma, Second Earth, even as we speak. If I find so much as a flyspeck out of place I'll call you. Just remember that this will probably take two or three days. Jesus, this country is so frigging big. Did you know it's the size of Texas?"

"Do what you can do," he said.

"If we were looking for a power signature, it would be different, but we've already searched both worlds and didn't find one, so expect some near-misses."

"Hey. Trust me. I know the drill."

"I know you do but oh, how I want this to go fast and it just can't but holy shit—" Carla rarely used profanity. "Burma, Second Earth. This is fantastic news. Have a limoncello on me. Now head home, Warrior, and for the Creator's sake, get some sleep. You've earned it."

Aw, hell. Carla was such a sweetheart. "Can't. Not yet. I'm heading over to the Cave. Some of the brothers might still be there having their morning bullshit session, and I'll want to talk to Thorne. I'll let him know about the shift in grid coordinates." Thorne was in charge of the Warriors of the Blood, including all communications with Central. But once the warriors had checked in from a night of battling, searching for Parisa took priority.

Medichi wasn't alone in his despair. All the warriors had

been wrecked by a disappearance on their watch. If it could happen to Medichi, it could happen to any of them.

Carla's voice dropped to a whisper. "And you'll let us know about . . . well, you know."

"Of course."

"Good. Now give me a second to reconfigure the grid." The tapping started.

He sighed as his heart pulled into a hard knot.

Every twenty-four hours he had contact with Parisa, and everyone knew it. What they didn't know was the personal way in which it happened. And like hell would he ever reveal that truth, because it was like having phone sex without the phone. Once a day, and always in the morning after he'd battled all night, he'd go home, shower up, and sit on the side of his bed. That's when he'd hear Parisa's voice in his head, only once, *Antony.* A sweet telepathic whisper that fired his heart and kept hope alive.

That was the only form of communication he had with her. She wasn't even ascended, so not all of her powers were developed. And for whatever reason, even though she was a mortal with wings, she couldn't communicate with her mind, at least not yet.

Despite this critical lack, she had another preternatural power that was considered a Third Earth or third dimension ability—that voyeur's window she could open. If she was indeed in Burma, she was halfway around the globe when she sent her single telepathic communication. It would be night to his day.

If that were true, then she had enormous telepathic capacity. She just hadn't learned how to use it yet.

Whatever.

It still meant that in half an hour or so, he would go home, get ready for bed, and discover whether his woman was still alive.

His heart tightened a little more. He both dreaded and longed for the experience because honest to God he didn't know what he would do if he didn't hear her say his name today within the depths of his mind. If he thought for even a minute that she might be dead, he'd go mad.

Carla's voice came back on the line. "The grid's on Burma, Warrior, and you're in my prayers."

His eyes burned. "Thanks," he said, but his voice sounded hoarse. "Later."

"Later."

He thumbed his phone and with a thought, folded to his villa to change out of his kilt and weapons harness. He still hadn't revealed his scars to his brothers. Only Marcus knew that his back was covered in a basket weave of silver scar tissue, and he'd promised his silence. There was no way he was going to the Cave to meet with the brothers while wearing only a kilt and a weapons harness. The latter, though broad enough in the front to support two daggers, had only a heavy narrow strip of black leather running down his spine.

Shit. He knew the time had come to reveal this hard truth about what had happened to him and to his family thirteen centuries ago, just before his ascension. But he dreaded speaking about the *why* of his scars. Dreaded letting anyone get that close to him.

Well, he wasn't ready to talk just yet.

He changed into his usual: a black tee, black cargoes, and steel-toed boots. He thought the thought and headed to the Cave.

Parisa Lovejoy had run out of time.

She didn't know the how or why of it, but something in Rith Do'onwa's demeanor toward her had darkened. When she was around him now, shivers chased down her neck and shoulders.

She stood outside on the lawn, barefoot, a few feet away from the enormous tamarind tree in Rith's large side yard. She stared up at the double dome of mist and as usual, was amazed.

She could see both layers. The exterior dome was the usual fine crochet-like composite, but the interior swirled in

beautiful colors of aquamarine, sea green, blue, and gray . . .
magnificent. The mist kept the master's home invisible to
Central's electronic surveillance grid. She had learned at
least that much in the three months she'd been held captive:
The Warriors of the Blood couldn't find her because Rith
had concealed her location under not one but two powerful
domes of mist.

Two exquisite domes that meant she couldn't count on a
rescue.

Yesterday, Rith had treated her with his usual indifference, but when she had awakened this morning and met him
over the breakfast table, displeasure, perhaps even hatred,
had rolled from him, a living writhing thing. And just like
that she knew she had run out of time. Whatever mantle of
grace had kept her safe in his home these past three months
had just been obliterated.

She had to escape. She just didn't know how to get the job
done.

She had struggled with the question all day. Now night had
fallen and she had a decision to make. Should she take flight
and bust through the double dome of mist that protected the
property, or should she take her chances and stay put? She
knew that the nature of mist would allow her to easily reach
the sky beyond, but her flight skills were untested. It was one
thing to practice in the gentle environment of the garden
protected by the mist, but another to be in the open air where
unpredictable wind shears could turn her upside down.

She truly didn't know what to do—but just in case inspi-
ration struck at the last moment, she had begged for one last
flight before bed.

She hadn't expected Rith to allow it. He kept a very strict
schedule for her throughout any given day. To her surprise,
however, he'd agreed to her request. Given his attitude toward her, she'd found his acquiescence suspect.

As she stared up into the inner domes, swirling with a
pattern of blue-green mist, her heart hammered in her chest.
Should she take her chances and fly through both domes,
right here, right now?

Even as the thought entered her mind, she felt tendrils reaching toward her, whispering for her to do it, to go, to leave, to break through.

She looked around. Was she hearing Antony at long last? Had he found her? Was he encouraging her to leave? Did he wait for her beyond the mist?

She trembled. She wanted to leave. Oh, how she wanted to leave. More than anything in the world, she longed to see Warrior Medichi.

Again, the whispers drifted over her: *Go, leave, run away, now.*

Antony, she sent from her mind. Nothing returned to her.

Was it possible he had found a way to reach her telepathically?

She wore a long halter gown of beautiful amethyst silk, the same color as her eyes. From the beginning, Rith had kept her in beautiful clothes. But in this case, the halter meant that her back was bare and she could mount her wings. She knew that if she took to the skies she might get her legs tangled up in the skirting, but she believed Rith had wanted her hampered. Rith always had a reason for every action. He was the most careful man, or rather vampire, she had ever known.

She stepped farther away from the enormous tamarind tree, away from Rith, away from his three Burmese slaves who had come to watch the show. The women loved to watch her fly. As far as she knew, none of them had wings—yet they'd been ascended for centuries. She found the absence of wings very strange for second dimension vampires, unless of course Rith had found a way to prevent them from gaining normal flight capability.

Whatever.

Rith was a monster, a quiet, dedicated, harmless-looking monster. He had ways of hurting her, and probably his slaves, that left no marks: His torture skills involved the piercing of the mind with his superior mental power. If she escaped his home tonight and he caught her, at the very least he would fill her mind with the equivalent of whirling knives. At the most, he would find an excuse to take her life.

So what was she to do? Take her chances and attempt to escape the mist or remain and risk staying one more night in the power of a man who now radiated a desire to kill her?

Her arms trembled as she prepared to mount her wings. She closed her eyes and drew in a deep breath, forcing herself to relax, an exercise that required a full minute of firm concentration.

She took a final deep cleansing breath, leaned forward slightly with her hands on her waist, then released her wings. She couldn't hold back the moan of pleasure. Her nipples drew into hard beads. For whatever reason, mounting her wings had always been for her an experience akin to sexual release.

The feathers flew in perfect balance through the small weeping apertures in her back and at the exact same moment joined with the mesh superstructure that also emerged and held the incomprehensible mass together. She would never understand how her body produced the glory that was her wings, but then how could she open the windows of her preternatural voyeurism and see what others were doing? How could the ascended vampire dematerialize? How did Rith create the extraordinary mist that appeared in visible domes over his home? Power then more power.

These were the mysteries of her world, her new world, the world of ascension.

She moved in a slow circle, wafting her wings up and down, practicing the combined movements of her back, her arms, and her wings. She was new to flight, having flown for the first time three months ago, though she'd had her wings over a year before that. Her friend Havily Morgan, an ascended vampire, had been teaching her to fly before the abduction. In one early session, Parisa had almost gotten herself killed by launching into the air without enough training, but Havily had pulled on her feet and brought her out of a deadly forward roll.

Because she was alone here in her garden prison, all her practice had been done with great care. She feared falling and breaking her wings more than anything. She didn't heal at lightning speed like normal vampires did, which was part of the reason she feared attempting an unsupported escape. One huge gust of wind would probably throw her into an uncontrolled spin or roll; she could easily fall to the ground. In her mortal state, she didn't want to think what that would feel like. She could end up paralyzed or even dead.

Yeah, this really wasn't a simple decision.

She looked up into the swirling dome and drew her wings back. She launched into the air, brought her wings forward, caught air, and began to fly. A collective gasp came from the three women on the porch. She flapped her wings and smiled. She understood their delight. She had seen Havily fly. It was a sight to behold.

She had seen all the Warriors of the Blood in flight at one time or another, all except Antony, of course. She knew the reason why he didn't mount his wings. She had voyeured him for over a year, so she had seen the secret he kept hidden from those closest to him. What she didn't know was the *why* of it.

Antony.

Now she was here, struggling to find a way to escape. The truth was, even if she did escape she still didn't know which path she would choose: to stay on Mortal Earth or ascend.

She tilted her wings slightly to the left and began a turn. She had to keep her movements small or she would start a rolling maneuver from which she would have a hard time recovering. Maybe impossible.

Her heart pounded as she approached the upper reaches. She flew in an arc and raised her arm straight over her head, carefully controlling the shape of her right wing as she dragged her fingers through the blue-green mist. A wonderful ripple of power flowed up her arm. The women below applauded since the dome reacted to these movements by swirling in enormous patterns to reconfigure over and over again, an oversized kaleidoscope.

Parisa dove toward the ground. Yes, her skills had improved. The women gasped again but at the last moment, she fluffed her wings into parachute position, brought her feet up, and floated to earth. She touched her toes to the grass, bent her knees, drew her wings close to her body, then once more launched upward.

The whispering grew louder from deep within her mind. *Yes, leave now. Make your escape.*

Antony? she sent, hoping. Was her guardian warrior communicating with her? The whispers were so faint, she couldn't tell.

Antony?

But nothing returned.

She drew close to the top of the tamarind tree and once more assumed the parachute position. This time she stared down at Rith. He had moved to the edge of the porch, his fists clenched at his sides, his eyes dark and glittering as he stared up at her. She wafted her wings slowly to maintain altitude.

She met his gaze.

Fly through the mist. Hurry. Escape now!

Then she knew and her heart plummeted. She wasn't hearing Antony's whispers at all. Rith was in her mind. These were his words, his commands, and he had but one purpose—he wanted her to make a run for it. If she did, she knew she would die.

She understood now that though Rith wanted her dead, he couldn't kill her outright. He must be under orders to keep her alive, which meant he'd have to make her death look like an accident. His master, Commander Greaves, was the one truly in charge of her. Rith was just her keeper.

What better way to create *an accident* than to hurt her high in the air, beyond the mist, and send her into a deadly spin?

Yet what exactly had changed for Rith that he now wished for her death?

Her heart sank farther, a rock dropping into a pond. She turned slowly and wafted her wings, gliding down to the lawn below. She didn't look at him or the women. Once she felt the grass beneath her feet, she closed her eyes and retracted her wings.

She ignored Rith as she made her way onto the porch then into the house. The female servants followed her.

Time for bed.

She showered and slid on a soft white cotton nightgown trimmed with lavender lace. Yes, everything of the finest quality had been provided for her since the first day of her captivity.

The women put her to bed because that was one of their duties, even though she was perfectly capable of pulling back the patchwork silk coverlet and sliding between the sheets all by herself. Ridiculous. But Rith insisted that they tuck her in, like a child, every night, which was of course more about control than kindness. Shortly after her arrival, she'd become aware that the women were as much captives as she was. To her knowledge, they never left the house, and they were forced to sleep on mats in the hall outside Parisa's bedroom. It sickened her.

Once she was alone in her bed and she could hear the women rustling on their mats, she glanced at the clock on her bedside table. The hour was too early for her to voyeur Warrior Medichi. He would not come to her for at least half an hour, perhaps more.

Over the course of three months, he had developed a routine of hunting down rogue death vampires on Mortal Earth—but not until after dawn. He did this searching for information about Rith and following leads to places she might be held captive. But he couldn't engage in these solo hunts until after a night of battling death vampires at one of the Mortal Earth Borderlands.

Her guardian warrior was utterly exhausted. The only contact she had with him occurred when he'd completed his final runs to Mortal Earth in pursuit of whatever leads he'd garnered the previous afternoon. He rarely slept, just a four- or five-hour block that crossed the noon hour. The afternoons prior to his night's usual work were spent pursuing rumors of rogue vampire lairs on Mortal Earth.

She turned on her side and stared at the slim brass Buddha on the table near the door to her private bathroom. She sighed heavily. She opened her voyeur's window, then thought of Antony. When she saw that he was in conference with Warrior

Thorne, she closed the window quickly. She had set certain rules for herself in order to preserve her sanity. She didn't voyeur anyone but Antony, and only when she could be with him in the privacy of his bedroom.

So she waited. Every fifteen minutes, she opened her window again, until she saw him at last showered, naked, and sitting on the side of his bed, waiting for her.

Antony had been her Guardian of Ascension, assigned to protect her during her rite of ascension to Second Earth. Not everyone who began a rite of ascension needed a guardian, but she had been a mortal-with-wings, something that had apparently happened only once before on Mortal Earth.

Though she had been voyeuring him the entire year preceding her rite and knew what he looked like, meeting him for the first time had been an extraordinary experience. She had been standing in the kitchen of his villa, chatting with Havily. He had appeared in the doorway, like a god, dripping wet from the shower, his muscled chest on display, and only a black towel around his hips.

The towel had been completely inadequate to disguise that he'd been in a full state of arousal. His scent, a beautiful, musky, sage fragrance, had already been heavy in the house, but at that moment clouds of sage had billowed toward her. As always, the scent had teased every tender place of her body to a ripeness she'd never experienced before. Through her voyeurs, she had been completely attracted to him, but standing in the same room her attraction had turned into an inferno of pure sexual need and desire.

Then he had done the unthinkable: He'd dropped the towel. Her gaze had wasted no time in sliding down his chest, down and down, until her eyes found what she needed. She remembered putting her fingers to her neck and stroking her vein. In her voyeurs she had seen him take women into the booths at the Blood and Bite, the club the Warriors used for R&R. She'd been just voyeur enough to stay and watch as well, which meant she'd seen him take blood.

She had wanted nothing more, standing there in that

kitchen, than to take Antony somewhere private and give him what he needed.

Havily, bless her, had rescued the situation. Marcus, too, since he'd arrived and punched Antony in the jaw with a solid right hook. Parisa had wanted to go to him, but Havily had taken her outside until she could calm down and think things through.

She'd done a lot of thinking over the next few days, while death vampires were after her. She'd also seen the war up close, and it had frightened her. The whole experience, however, had led her to believe that despite her insane attraction to Antony, despite the tender feelings he aroused in her, she didn't want to complete her ascension. She wanted to return to her Mortal Earth world, to her cloistered job as a librarian, to her solitary life, to peace and serenity.

She knew Antony would be sad, even angry that she'd decided against ascension, but her choice was made. She'd just been about to tell him when Rith intervened and changed everything.

She couldn't help the tears that leaked from her eyes, slid over the bridge of her nose, joined with more tears, and splashed into the hair on the side of her head. At least she would be with him again soon, but she couldn't even share with him that when it was morning for him it was evening for her. Surely he could have found her by now if he'd had that one scrap of information.

And right now, she wished more than anything that she could tell him of her present danger, ask for his advice, his help, anything.

Oh, God, would she even be alive by morning?

But no matter how hard she tried to create a telepathic link with Antony, she simply couldn't. Only at the point of release, when she would touch herself and experience an orgasm, could she whisper his name in her mind and know that he heard.

She had tried countless ways to talk to Antony short of standing on her head. She had attempted to scream his name inside her head, scream it aloud and in her head at the same time, whisper his name, cry out his name when she was having an orgasm all by herself. Nothing worked. Only in this one special moment, when they connected through her voyeur's window, could he hear her, and then only once. Everything else had failed.

She hated that she was so weak in this way. She hated that she was a prisoner. She hated that she still knew so little about ascended life and her powers. The only thing she had accomplished in three months was improving her flight.

Be wise and do not judge what creates love for others,
since shoes often travel to unsuspecting feet.

—*Collected Proverbs,* Beatrice of Fourth

CHAPTER 2

Rith was not an original thinker. He never had been. For that reason he relied on the future streams to guide him, all those beautiful ribbons of light that prophesied forthcoming events.

He reclined on the dark blue velvet chaise-longue in his small private room adjacent to his office. He clasped his hands loosely over his stomach. He stared at the mahogany ceiling. His facial muscles felt strange and lax, almost burdened, and his throat was tight.

He'd just emerged from the future streams and was devastated all over again. The same prophecy from last night had returned even stronger just moments ago, while the shower had been running and Parisa had been going through her nightly ritual.

Parisa Lovejoy was to share a bond with Commander Greaves.

It couldn't be true. It just couldn't.

Parisa's unspecified yet critical role in the war against the Commander had already been foretold numerous times. Rith had recommended her death to his master over and over, but for whatever incomprehensible reason, Greaves tended to play fast and loose with Seers' prophecies. He couldn't be entirely faulted for this, since the prophecies didn't always come to pass. And Greaves preferred to work every angle of a prophecy before acting, and often succeeded in his rather daring ventures.

But where the mortal-with-wings was concerned, the Seers' predictions had been constant, and increasing in intensity in recent days. Rith had developed a sense of near-panic where Parisa was concerned. He was, himself, a man of power, perhaps more than the Commander realized, and of late he had developed a real *knowing* about just how dangerous Parisa was both to himself and to the Commander. He had several times urged Greaves in the proper direction, to get rid of the woman, but the Commander would not be moved.

However, even with all Rith's *knowing,* even with the numerous prophecies and their intensity, what had finally pushed Rith over the edge was this latest future stream about a bond-forging event. A sense of deep despair and of jealousy now devoured Rith whole. He could forgive the predictions about Parisa's danger to the Coming Order—but not that she would become so intimately connected to his master.

He could not imagine, even on a prophetic level, how Greaves could allow this travesty when even he, Rith Do'onwa, the master's most favored servant, did not have such a bond.

Earlier, when Parisa had asked to fly one last time before nightfall, he saw an opportunity to kill her himself. If she left his artfully crafted domes of mist, he could follow after her and cause a most unfortunate but very fatal accident.

But she hadn't left. She had floated above the tamarind tree and somehow read his mind. So now she was safe and secure in her bed and he had no means of taking her life.

Were all his centuries of service to be thus rewarded?

He knew only one thing: He must prevent this bond.

He loved Greaves as no one could love him. Greaves was his master; he would lay down his life for him. He wanted a bond, a link with the Commander. He deserved such a bond. Why should Parisa be allowed to forge one?

It was obscene.

Rith took deep breaths. He had to focus. He must find a way to counteract the event.

As he breathed, his mind settled. After a few minutes, his fierce jealousy abated.

He focused on the ribbons of light. Whenever a change in destiny was imminent, ribbons would glow. As he mentally reviewed all the critical people involved in the Coming Order, on both sides of the equation, he found a burnished bronze ribbon that grew so brilliant with light, even though his eyes were closed he felt the light burned through his eyelids.

He mentally picked up the ribbon, which belonged to Warrior Medichi. He slid his mind along the future streams and came to an image that caused his heart to seize, in part because of the nature of the vision but also due to its location. He saw the warrior trapped in a dark space, one made of oversized terra-cotta bricks. He knew this particular Second Earth temple in Bengal Two. He had built it himself, modeled on Mortal Earth structures, but with a very convenient basement designed just for his purposes.

He smiled now. Even though he wanted the mortal-with-wings dead, the sure knowledge that one day very soon he would have within his power a Warrior of the Blood changed everything. If the Creator was good and shined his favor upon Rith, he would fulfill this prophecy. Perhaps then his standing with Greaves would increase to include a forged bond as well.

Was Parisa still alive?

Medichi sat on the side of his bed, sleep-deprived and on edge. He was in the master suite of his villa, a retreat that had become a prison because the woman meant for him was missing . . . gone . . . taken. But in a few minutes, he would know if she still lived: She would come to him as she always did at this hour.

He'd been to the Cave, arriving later than usual, so that only Thorne remained. Thorne had been slumped on a stool in front of the bar, a bottle of Ketel One at the ready, his fingers sliding up and down a full tumbler, his gaze fixed on nothing in particular. Medichi had told him of the death vampire at the Grand Canyon and what he'd learned in the pretty-boy's mind.

The news had brought a little life into Thorne's red-rimmed hazel eyes. He'd even smiled and clapped Medichi on the shoulder. "We'll find her and don't worry, Carla will keep me up to speed. Jeannie, as well, when she comes on later today."

Medichi had nodded.

Thorne had nodded.

Medichi had headed home and now here he was, sitting on the side of his bed, ready to complete his morning ritual, ready to hear Parisa's voice in his head once again, ready to be assured that she was still alive.

Oh, God, please let her be alive.

He'd just showered and his long hair dripped at the ends, forming rivulets that tracked down his abdomen and down his back. He loosed the black towel from around his waist and laid it in a heavy loop across his knees.

At least he had privacy. The first time this had happened was three days after Parisa's abduction. Both Havily and Marcus still lived in his villa. They were his closest friends, his strongest support, but that day Hav had brought tangerines home from the market without thinking what it would do to him, without remembering that for Medichi, Parisa smelled of tangerines, her special scent meant only for him. For Parisa, Medichi smelled of sage.

Havily should have known better. For her, Marcus's special scent was like earthy grasses and fennel combined.

But Havily hadn't remembered, and Medichi had been left aroused as hell with nowhere to go. Naturally, he'd complained of not feeling well and had retired to his suite of rooms at the south end of the villa.

The tangerines had acted as an aphrodisiac. He hadn't wanted to pleasure himself but that was the curse of his situation: Because of the *breh-hedden,* the scent of tangerines meant Parisa, and Parisa meant pure hot-blooded sex.

Damn the *breh-hedden.* He'd been struck down the moment he'd smelled Parisa's lovely pheromone-riddled tangerine scent.

The *breh-hedden* was a terrible mate-bonding ritual that occurred only between preternaturally powerful women and Warriors of the Blood. Before Warrior Kerrick had found his *breh* in Alison Wells, all the warriors had thought the ritual a myth. Then Marcus had bonded with Havily in exactly the same way. No more myth. Just hard agonizing reality.

So, yeah, the *breh-hedden* was alive and well among the Warriors of the Blood.

God, how he loved the smell of tangerines.

So it was that Medichi had pleasured himself. And for whatever reasons, at that same moment Parisa had found him with her voyeur's window. But only when he'd released, his fist pumping hard, had he heard her beautiful voice in his head, a soft, melodic *Antony.* Several times before the abduction, he thought he'd heard her voice in his head, the emergence of her telepathic ability. So when he heard the sound again, he knew he had not been mistaken: He had heard her voice, and she was alive.

He'd rejoiced. He'd cried out. He'd wept because that's when he'd felt her presence, very faint but very real and he knew she was still alive. He'd spoken to her for an hour afterward, even though she still couldn't communicate mind-to-mind with him. He'd talked and talked about all that they were doing to try to find her, he encouraged her to stay alive, he promised her he'd never stop looking for her. He'd only stopped talking when he felt her drift away and finally end the communication.

From that moment until now, he'd repeated the ritual with her every morning after hunting down rogue death vampires.

He would return to the villa, shower, and ready himself to meet his woman.

Right now, with the towel looped over his lap, only one question was in his mind: Would he hear her voice, feel her presence today? Was his woman still alive?

Jesus, his fingers trembled around the small silver bowl he held in his hands. In it, nine small Satsuma tangerines were piled one atop another, tempting him with the forbidden as though he stared at the apple from the Garden of Eden.

Time to get on with his morning ritual. He'd never been one to limit himself to the use of his fist. If he needed a fuck, he went out and got one. He'd worn out a lot of velvet in the booths at the Blood and Bite getting the release he needed. Mortal women flocked to the vampire club every night and kept the warriors of Second Earth satisfied—both the Militia Warriors and the Warriors of the Blood. The club had been designed just for that purpose and even sanctioned by Madame Endelle, the Supreme High Administrator of all Second Earth. But from the moment he'd met Parisa, the club had lost all appeal.

He set the bowl on his nightstand. Holding one tangerine in his hand, he plunged his thumb hard into the center, breaking the loose skin apart. He pulled the skin back. Juice flowed. He kept peeling until the wedges were exposed. He thrust his thumb into the middle once more, breaking up the wedges. More juice.

He shuddered. The smell penetrated his brain, and his eyes rolled back in his head. Yes, he was hard. What else would he be? From the moment he had first caught Parisa's scent, the one thing he could count on was a fierce demanding erection when she was near.

The hairs on the nape of his neck rose and relief poured through him.

Now he felt her. Yes. He closed his eyes. He could tell she was near, just a strange rippling vibration along his back, now across his shoulders, now over his neck. She was here.

The terrible tension inside his chest, the frightful worry

that she was dead, eased. For the first time in twenty-four hours he could breathe.

"I'm here," he said aloud. "I'm ready for you."

He put his mouth to the tangerine, suckled the juice, and groaned.

Parisa's heart ached, a low throb deep in her chest, a pain that had become so familiar it was now a comfort.

She still lay on her side on her large four-poster bed, the window of her preternatural voyeurism open.

She could see Antony now. Like a good director, she could move her window to any position she desired. Tonight, thirteen-plus hours ahead of him, she panned her vision so that she could face him, as though she were standing right in front of him.

She drew a ragged breath as though her throat had shriveled. Yes, he was handsome—strong cheekbones and a sharp angled jaw—but to her he would always be *beautiful*. His hair was black, thick, straight, and long, almost to his waist now. He'd showered and his hair was damp, even dripping in spots. He took long, steaming showers after a night of battle. Many times she arrived early enough to watch him in the shower. He was lean and muscular, all warrior.

Yes, so *beautiful*.

She moved closer, until she was a few inches from his face. She watched his tongue nestle within the tangerine, making small sucking noises. She knew that he was imagining his tongue inside her body. He'd told her that as well. *Desire* was too small a word for what she felt for this man, this warrior. She would be the tangerine for him and he could devour her.

Tears rolled down her cheeks as her need for him grew, her thighs trembling. She had to keep her voice quiet or the servants would descend on her.

She leaned in and kissed the air an inch or two away from him. He groaned, as though feeling how close she was. She watched his hand glide lower, sliding down his chest. She pulled the window back to watch. His abs were rippling, taut, rolling hard mounds she wanted to touch, to lick, to savor. His forefinger touched the narrow erotic line of hair that led down. Lower. Lower.

In her mind she spoke to him. *Yes, touch yourself for me. I'm here. I want you to know pleasure. Antony, hear me.*

His groans thickened the air. With one hand he held the tangerine to his mouth, his tongue working feverishly. With his other hand he held himself in a firm grip, pumping now. His hips moved, jerking forward.

She panted and the core of her spasmed. She rolled onto her stomach and slid her hand between her legs. She pushed, pulled, pressed. Her hips bucked off the mattress as she watched him. His groans were loud in her ears. She could tell he was close. He opened his mouth, and the groan turned to a shout as he came.

She came with him, the core of her body rippling and tugging, streaking pleasure up through her tender flesh. She imagined him inside her and the sensation intensified. She withheld the gasps and moans that wanted to erupt for fear the servants would hear. *Antony. Antony,* sped along the telepathic highway.

All movement on his bed ceased, as it always did just at this moment. "I hear you," he said aloud to the room. "You said, *Antony, Antony.* Twice tonight. I feel you near me, Parisa. I know you're here and I know you're alive. Thank God."

Antony, she cried out with her mind. More tears slipped down her cheeks. She shifted back onto her side, still looking at him. *I'm here,* she sent. *I'm here.* If only her telepathy would improve. At least he'd heard his name twice. That was something. Not much, but something.

"Parisa, I have a piece of information about you, but getting some usable results from the grid might take a few days. I found a rogue death vampire in northern Arizona, Mortal Earth, this morning. He knew Rith. He was connected with the underbelly of Mortal Earth rogue life and he knew of you. I searched his memories and discovered that you're in Burma on Second Earth. Carla's already moved Central's grid in place. We know your signature doesn't show up, so we're hunting for an anomaly, anything that seems out of the ordinary. I swear I'd dematerialize to Burma and start hunting for you myself, but the damn place is as big as Texas."

She heard his frustration but her mind whirled with the new possibility that Central could locate her in a day or two, maybe three. Oh . . . God . . . yes!

"If only you could communicate better telepathically. Can you try? Please try. I heard my name twice tonight. That has to mean something."

Her own frustration rose until she was kneeling in bed, beating her fists against her pillows. Had she tried? Only a thousand times. *Of course I've tried,* she sent.

"You can do this. I know you can. If I can feel your presence like this, I know you can talk to me." He flopped back on the bed and shifted his hips to bring his legs straight out in front of him. His cock lay half thickened on his groin. He was very big and so damn beautiful. She watched tears fill his eyes, spill over, then run down the sides of his face and into his long warrior hair. She moved in close and pretended to touch his hair, run her fingers through it.

"The minute we find an anomaly, I will come for you. We'll all come for you. All the brothers."

I'm near Mandalay, she sent, but she knew it was useless. She had tried a hundred different ways to communicate, but all he'd ever been able to hear was his name at the moment of her release.

She had tried different locations as well, moving from room to room while she called his name, changing the time of day, the time of night, beneath the tamarind tree, away from the tree, shouting the words in her head, then calling them softly. Nothing had worked. When she opened her voyeur's window, that strange preternatural gift she possessed, she could find him anywhere. She just couldn't communicate her thoughts to him.

He slid his hands behind his head, his gaze fixed somewhere on the ceiling. "I love that you're here with me," he whispered. "And I can feel you near."

Good. I'm here.

"Do I disgust you? Please understand, it's the only time I can hear your voice. I wouldn't do this otherwise."

You could never disgust me. I know you, Antony. I've listened to your warrior brothers as well. They speak of you with such respect and they turn to you for advice, for approval. I love your kindness and that you've never stopped searching for me.

It was almost a conversation.

Almost.

"Last night before my tour at the New River Borderland, Jeannie and I spent hours scoping South African Territory for your sign." He smiled faintly. "Now we know you're in Burma. It's hard to stay here—I want to fold right now to Burma. But what good would that do? I'll wait here, but I don't have to like it.

"I don't think I told you this but yesterday afternoon, Jean-Pierre and I hit a rogue vampire lair in Mortal Earth Sweden. That's when we learned about this rogue in fucking Sedona, Mortal Earth. Remember how Thorne has a house in Sedona?" He sighed. "I love talking to you and feeling you close."

Me too, she sent.

"I chased that bastard north all the way to the Grand Canyon. That motherfucker had one set of wings on him—pardon my French or as Jean-Pierre says, *my Italian.* He's so funny. He's been with me every afternoon, hunting beside me. He's as wrecked as I am. No warrior ever had a better brother. I owe him everything. Do you believe me that I haven't stopped looking? That I never will?"

I believe you.

He sat up suddenly. "You must do one thing, Parisa. Promise me this, that you'll stay alive for me. Please . . . stay alive."

I will try.

"Don't just try, either." Yep, almost a conversation. "Do whatever you have to do to stay alive, no matter how horrible your current situation. Know this: I will come for you."

She moved in close once more, toward his lips. She tilted

slightly and pretended to kiss him. He gasped. "What did you just do?"

She moved in again, and kissed him.

He put his fingers to his lips. "Did you just kiss me?"

"Yes," she whispered aloud into her room.

"Parisa. Do it again."

She leaned forward once more. He stayed very still. She drew back. His eyes opened. "I didn't feel anything. If you tried again, I couldn't feel it." He flopped back on the bed once more and threw an arm over his forehead. "Oh, God, how I miss you. I ache for you."

She panned back and looked at the full length of him again. He had a faint dusting of black hair over his pecs angling to his stomach. She loved the distinct line of hair that traveled his lower abdomen, showing the way. His hair was curled over his groin, a healthy animal. His cock was still half erect—it always was so long as she was near, even after he'd come. The same fine black hair covered his legs. She loved the way he looked, so masculine. She had always liked hair on a man. She wanted to sift her fingers through all of it, from his toes, up his legs, around the base of his cock, up that sexy line, over his chest, his arms . . . but mostly she wanted her hands in his long warrior hair.

Long hair meant something to the Warriors of the Blood. In a ritual that went back several millennia, the warriors faced battle by binding their hair in the ritual clasp called the *cadroen,* symbolizing strength of will and purpose.

Yes, Antony had told her many things during this time he shared with her. Though he couldn't hear her, he knew she was listening so he talked.

Antony's voice continued softly. "Did I tell you that the first time I used my wings after my ascension, I fell flat on my back? I couldn't breathe for a good minute, and the pain was almost unbearable. I'd crushed some of the feathers. Three healers worked for hours to put me back together. When the wings are broken like that, you can't retract them. Remember that when you fly. Be careful."

She got very close and rubbed her fingers over his lips.

I almost did the same thing. Do you remember? I'd ended up in a forward roll the first time I flew and Havily tugged on my feet and saved me. Later, she told me privately that you'd been watching us. She often shared things even though he couldn't hear her.

Havily Morgan had been a good friend to her and had saved her life more than once during the short time she'd known her. She missed Havily. She missed all of them.

"Remember how you almost crashed that first day flying with Havily? Did you know I was watching you? When you almost fell, I dropped a plate of pasta. I was afraid for you but Havily kept you safe."

Oh, why couldn't he hear her? She pressed a fingers to her lips.

"I will always be grateful that Havily took care of you that day and taught you so much about flying. I wish I could have been the one but . . ."

You never mount your wings in front of anyone.

". . . I never mount my wings except in private. I just can't. They'd see my back. Marcus knows the truth but I trust him to be discreet." His chest rose and fell in a heavy sigh. "When I ascended and understood how quickly I could heal in my new vampire state, I thought my back would change, but it didn't. I'm . . . scarred, Parisa. Forever."

Parisa could tell by the way he whispered the words that whatever had scarred his back had wounded him more deeply in his mind, maybe even in his soul.

I've seen your scars, Antony. Don't you realize that? How could I be so close to you all these months and not have seen your scars?

"Shit," he muttered. "You've already seen them, haven't you? Of course you have. Shit." He sounded so ashamed.

She wanted to comfort him, to tell him it didn't matter, but she couldn't. All she could do was keep wiping away her tears.

She was drawn back, deep into her memories of Antony. He had comforted her once, held her while she wept. Three months ago, at the Ambassadors Reception, a bomb had been used in place of fireworks and set the skies afire. Marcus, one of Antony's best friends, had been severely burned and a death vampire had abducted Havily. Antony had begged Parisa to make use of her voyeur window. The thought of it had been overwhelming to her; she feared what she might find. But Antony had held her and supported her. He'd gotten her through, and as a team they'd brought Havily home.

He was still getting her through by being with her every night like this, talking to her, making love with her in this odd but beautiful way.

Her mind began to drift in and out now. It was past ten o'clock in Burma and Rith roused his household early, at precisely five in the morning. He kept a strict schedule for his servants. Her fatigue was intensified because she was so sad and because, after three months, she wasn't very hopeful. Rith was a clever vampire. If he even suspected his home was in danger, he'd remove her before anyone had a chance to get to her.

"You're getting sleepy, aren't you? I can always tell. It's as though your presence starts pulsing in waves, going away from me, coming back. Please don't go."

He always said that.

"If you go, I'll have to wonder for another twenty-four hours if you're still alive."

I'll be here for you, Antony. I'll be here. She released a sigh. Sleep claimed her.

Beloved, take the glass to your lips,
I will hold your hand
Drink and be eased.
Beloved, let the wine of your creation,
From the vineyards of your soul,
Give you peace.

—*Collected Poems*, Beatrice of Fourth

CHAPTER 3

Medichi felt Parisa depart—or probably fall asleep. It was close to ten o'clock at night for her.

He rolled onto his side. At some point, the remnants of the tangerine had fallen from his hand and now lay face-down on the bottom sheet. The hunger he knew for Parisa crawled through his belly. Wasn't this just like the *breh-hedden*, creating all kinds of irrational behavior. Like sucking tangerines and talking out loud to a woman he couldn't see.

But he felt her. Oh, yes, he felt her presence in ripples of power.

He left his bed and took a second quick shower to clean up. He put fresh clothes on, jeans and a black tee. Havily would be getting ready for work right about now. She and Marcus still inhabited the same room they'd taken over three months ago. Marcus had returned from self-exile on Mortal Earth at that time—but not just to rejoin the Warriors of the

Blood. Madame Endelle had appointed him High Administrator of Southwest Desert Two and given him a boatload of authority. He'd been making some kick-ass changes in how Endelle's administration dealt with her Territory High Administrators around the globe.

Darian Greaves, self-styled the Commander, had been in the process of turning High Administrators for the past fifteen years at the rate of several a year, each one aligning with his faction against Madame Endelle. If he could turn enough of them, Endelle and her warriors would lose this godawful war once and for all.

Marcus had put a stop to that. Not one High Administrator had quit in the past several months. Yeah, that was called progress.

As for Havily, she'd taken up darkening work part of the night alongside Endelle. Now, there was a shit-job if ever one had been created. In addition, Havily still made a Starbucks run to Mortal Earth for the Warriors of the Blood every morning. She'd meet up with most of them at dawn, bringing hot coffee and pastries and her warm smile. Jean-Pierre called her *soeurette,* which was French for "little sister." That's what Havily was to all of the Warriors of the Blood, a beloved younger sister.

Hell, he needed a drink. He left his bedroom suite and headed in the direction of the kitchen. He'd never been much of a drinker, but that had changed in the last several weeks. He'd developed a real taste for limoncello.

He crossed the long central hall of his villa, the front lawn to his right. After passing two sets of guest suites to his left, he traversed the large formal living room from which the back lawn was visible as a wide expanse. He'd built his beautiful home over two centuries ago.

He loved the place. But he'd give it all up, plus his entire fucking fortune, to have Parisa back safe and sound.

He crossed the foyer, then the smaller sitting room next to the dining room. The door to the kitchen was offset to the left so that the kitchen wasn't visible from either the foyer or any of the main south rooms.

He made a beeline across the kitchen to the fridge, opened the door, and grabbed the gallon jug of homemade limoncello. He took a glass off the folded linen on the soapstone counter. He always kept a glass handy.

Making his own limoncello had become part of his routine as well, one of the things that kept him sane. The recipe was simple: sugar, vodka, lemon zest and a lot of waiting.

He made a new batch every week so he'd never run out. The batches kept getting bigger. Lately, he'd needed more. A lot more. Shit. With this latest news, like hell he'd be able to sleep without being just a little drunk.

He took the jug to the dining table, but instead of sitting in a chair he moved to the far side closest to the adjacent sitting room, pulled two chairs at angles away from the table, hopped up, and planted his ass on the solid mahogany. He put a foot each on the angled chairs.

He started to drink.

He held the now cold glass in his hand. This was the other part of his routine. For a long time he couldn't understand why Kerrick liked his Maker's and Thorne guzzled Ketel One. Now he got it. Ordinarily, he preferred a fine Cabernet Sauvignon and his own label suited him just fine, but from the third week of Parisa's abduction, when it became clear she wouldn't be headed home anytime soon, he'd needed something a little stronger.

He brought the glass to his lips and took a sip. His tongue jerked with pleasure. While the tart lemon put sparks in his mouth, the drink began that long oh-so-necessary slide into sleep that only one-hundred-proof could bring.

It was the waiting that was killing him.

Waiting.

Fuck.

Though he'd finally gotten a serious lead, he still had to wait.

After his third glass, the numbing began . . . but so did the memories. He saw a woman, pregnant with his child, running through their olive grove in ancient Italy. She was laughing, holding her belly. She was five months' pregnant, showing nicely. He would walk through the Tuscan village, head high, his arm behind her back pulling her gown tight at the waist so that everyone could see what he had put in her, what he cherished. She would rail at him, shoving her fingers in his face and complaining about what a brute he was, how vulgar, how uncivilized. Then she would strut, thrusting her stomach forward as well. Ah, they were both proud. Married five months and five months with child.

Maria.

He smiled. Then another memory surfaced, the one that brought a searing pain to his heart, as though it were new and not thirteen centuries old.

He had died the night that tribesmen from the north had entered his farmhouse, bound him, and whipped his back into a thousand stripes while they raped his beloved wife, killed her, and stole the life of his son. *His son. His only son.*

That he knew his child was a boy was one of the first inklings he'd had that he possessed preternatural power. The strong sense of *knowing* had been on him from the moment of conception. Maria telling him a few weeks later that she was pregnant had been both a confirmation and a warning that his life was about to change.

The enemy had left Medichi to die, having thrust a sword deep into his stomach. He'd been bleeding out on the floor. But the sight of his wife calling softly to him, reaching out to him with the scarlet of her blood spreading over the white linen of her nightgown, had given birth to his ascended powers.

The human part of him died that night and the vampire was born. At first he didn't know what was happening to him. He ascended to Second Earth, appearing first at the Borderland outside of Rome and answering his call to ascension with a hand-blast. Thorne had come to him, majestically floating out of the air in a leather kilt and heavy battle sandals.

Thorne had been Medichi's Guardian of Ascension. He'd shared his suffering, eased his pain, shown him what he could do, made him a warrior that very night as together they battled death vampires. Greaves, even back then, had tried hard to make him dead. The bastard had failed.

After his ascension ceremony, Medichi asked permission of no one, but hunted down every one of his wife and son's murderers. He knew every face and watched with pleasure as each suffered, bled, and died. Vengeance had been born in him that night, war-like justice he'd meted out every night since, battling a new kind of enemy . . . death vampires.

The clatter of heels on the hardwood of his villa floors brought him back to the present.

Havily. Shit. He should have already disappeared into his bedroom and taken his limoncello with him. He tensed. He didn't want her to see him like this. He had a sudden impulse to hide the glass and the gallon jar. Then he relaxed. Who was he kidding? Both Havily and Marcus knew what he was doing. You can't hide that many lemons, that many bottles of vodka. He shifted on the table and dragged one of the chairs with his foot to bring it closer.

Marcus's *breh* appeared in the doorway and his heart thudded. At one time he'd had a little crush on Havily. Maybe all the warriors had—certainly Luken.

She looked lovely in her usual Ralph Lauren skirt and silk blouse. Her layered red hair floated around her shoulders. She wore leopard-print heels. His heart swelled with affection. "Morning, Hav. You're running a little late."

He watched a blush rise on her porcelain cheeks. She was very fair; a little embarrassment went a long way. "Well, you know, Marcus was with you boys last night and since he doesn't report to the office until the afternoon, he likes me to sleep in with him." Her blush deepened.

Medichi looked down. Black hairs darted at weird angles on his feet, especially on his big toes. He nodded but didn't meet her gaze. "You've been good for him."

"He's been good for me." Her voice was soft, low, compassionate.

Shit. He threw back the rest of the limoncello, almost choking. He huffed a sigh, shoved both chairs back with his feet, and slid off the table to stand in front of her. Suddenly he remembered he had some news. He told her about the death vamp's revelations, about Parisa and Burma.

"Can it be true? Will she be coming home soon?" Tears rushed to her eyes.

"I hope so," he said. Damn, his throat was tight.

He opened his arms wide. Havily walked into them then slid her arms around his back and squeezed hard. He felt her chest jump a few times. "Hey," he said, petting her back and trying not to mess up her hair. Havily was so damn stylish. "You're going to ruin your makeup if you keep crying."

Her chest jerked again, but he was sure it was a laugh this time. She didn't, however, release him.

His throat twisted into a knot. "Have I thanked you and Marcus for staying on at the villa?"

"Only every other day."

His turn to laugh.

After a few more seconds, she finally drew back and dabbed carefully beneath her eyes with the backs of her fingers. She glanced at the empty glass. "Still can't sleep?"

"Not without help."

She nodded. No judgment, thank God. She frowned, looked at the floor, wrapped her arms around her stomach.

His heart sank again. He felt the question in the air between them. He settled a hand on her shoulder, and she looked up at him. "Yes, I felt her again and I heard her call my name. So yes, she's still alive."

She released another heavy sigh. "Thank God. If only she could say more to you than just your name."

"That's all she ever could, you know, even three months ago. Her telepathic abilities just haven't emerged yet."

"I know, I know."

He nodded. "And now, I'm actually feeling sleepy."

With the heavy jug in one hand, his glass in the other, he returned to the fridge. He heard the familiar click of her heels as she followed behind. "How's the house coming?" he called from over his shoulder.

"Marcus had another big fight with the contractor. Imagine

that." Marcus ran a tight ship and his contractor didn't. Medichi felt an I'm-firing-his-ass coming soon.

Marcus and Havily were building a home at the foot of South Mountain. They wanted to be near Endelle's administrative offices, not far from Sky Harbor Airport on Mortal Earth. They were also building in the Pacific Northwest, but that was a getaway property and had nothing to do with their stay at his villa.

He put the limoncello away then washed out his glass. Yeah, time to get some sleep.

Havily stood on the other side of the dark soapstone island. "If you need anything, Antony—"

"I know. Just ask."

She smiled and her light green eyes sparkled. "You know where I'll be." Besides working with Endelle in the darkening, she also worked at administrative headquarters on special projects. It turned out that for all Havily's warmth of spirit, she had a temper to rival Endelle's; some of their fights had gotten so loud and so profane, they'd become legendary. But Havily really wasn't complaining. She'd never looked happier and somehow in all those blistering fights with the Supreme High Administrator of Second Earth, Havily had made peace with her new job and her new life.

She nodded, lifted her arm, and vanished.

Now that she was gone, Medichi planted his hands on the front of the sink and let his shoulders and head slump. Havily meant well. Christ, they all meant well, but the constant support and concern were fire on his nerves and he was getting sick of having to front.

Moving to the center cupboard, he grabbed a new glass, sixteen ounces this time. He drew the jug of limoncello from the fridge and poured it to the rim. How many was that? Three, four, five? It had to be bad if he'd started losing track.

Whatever.

He replaced the jug, drank off the top inch, then headed back to his bedroom.

For the past three months he'd slept maybe three, four hours at a stretch. He kept waking up to nightmares—seeing

Parisa but not being able to reach her; seeing her stretched out at his feet, dying, and being unable to save her.

As he lay in bed now reviewing how he might rescue her, he realized he'd reached the end of one of his ropes—he could no longer remain earthbound when he fought. He'd been going solo and battling death vampires in the air for months on his morning searches, but he still hadn't let any of the warriors see him mount his wings, or see the scars on his back. Only Marcus.

So, yeah, shit. After thirteen centuries he was going to have to reveal the truth to his brother warriors. And it would be tonight.

At midnight, Geneva time, Darian Greaves was in his penthouse, sitting up in bed, his HP on his lap as he read emails from Rith. With ambitions to take over two worlds, he kept his plans simple: He built armies of death vampires, and he turned High Administrators by appealing to their greed. When his army was big enough and when he "owned" a majority of Territories around the globe, he'd simply push Madame Endelle out of her office and get on with things.

Endelle, though quite powerful in her own right, had very little ambition and hardly sufficient executive prowess to stand against his persistence and dedication. Her values were too simple and her organizational skills too limited to be a real threat.

The light from a wall-mounted swing-arm lamp positioned above his lap cast a lovely half-moon glow on the shoulder of his most recent ladylove. When the bed was well occupied, he liked doing a little work between sessions.

He rubbed the soft shoulder. The marks he'd given her had already started to heal. The claw of his left hand was useful for so many things. He'd genetically altered his hand to create terror, but the applications during sex were just delightful. He loved how an idea made manifest could surprise him in terms of usefulness and innovation.

The woman whimpered when he dug a nail into the deepest wound. But he smelled her answering arousal. She enjoyed a little pain. He enjoyed delivering it. They were an excellent match.

He'd known for a long time that he wanted this particular woman in his bed and by his side. He just hadn't known exactly how she would come to him without creating problems in his Coming Order—she had belonged to one of his most loyal High Administrators. But this much he knew: All things come to him who waits. And so she had come to him because her husband had died . . . by the hand of a Warrior of the Blood . . . one of the few times he actually felt beholden to that group of hateful do-gooders.

He also believed that when life delivers lemons, you must make lemonade. In his experience of well over two thousand years, he'd made that particular philosophy his own. Yes, he was a positive thinker. Very evolved. He smiled to himself.

He'd been thinking positive thoughts about this woman for several decades. But how did he know that the day he'd turned High Administrator Eldon Crace into a death vampire by giving him dying blood, the idiot would fail to make use of his special symptom-diminishing antidote? The result had been somewhat unexpected: Crace had become a full-fledged monster with more power than was good for him, and Warrior Luken had killed him in his forge. That had been a black day.

Talk about lemons.

Greaves had sealed the forge permanently after disposing of Crace's body. That any of the Warriors of the Blood had found the means to fold directly into any part of his compound had enraged Greaves. If Crace hadn't already been dead, he would have killed him himself. Greaves had seen the security tapes of the event. He'd witnessed ascender Havily Morgan manacled to the wall and drained of blood, and he'd watched Warrior Marcus fold into the forge and attack Crace. He hadn't been surprised that Crace had dominated Warrior Marcus—the latter had just recovered from third-degree burns over most of his body. But how stupid could Crace have been not to have foreseen the arrival of another warrior?

Still, the violation of his compound by Warriors of the Blood had a silver lining that was truly magnificent: From the moment of Crace's death, there had been no impediment to his taking the man's widow into his bed. The exquisite Julianna now lay facedown beside him, the tips of her extremely long nails stroking the tender portion of his naked anatomy between his hip and the top of his thigh. As much as he was able, God help him, he loved her. She was avaricious, power-hungry, thought nothing of torturing anyone opposed to her schemes, and enjoyed both a dominant and submissive role in bed. In other words, she was his soul mate.

Right now, they had an equal number of wounds.

She stroked the lump on his groin just over the vein she'd tapped earlier.

He scrolled through the numerous Seers Fortress reports attached as documents to various emails. He found the usual: The Warriors of the Blood were gaining power through the ritual bonding of the *breh-hedden;* Warrior Marcus and his *breh,* Havily, were preventing High Administrators from defecting to Greaves's camp; Alison Wells, who was also Warrior Kerrick's *breh* and Endelle's personal assistant, was still slated to do some as-yet-unspecified glorious deed for Second Earth. How annoying.

The emails were sorted in order of importance by Rith Do'onwa, his most trusted and most submissive minion. As much as he could, he trusted Rith. The vampire had abducted Parisa—a feat of no small power—and had been keeping her concealed from Madame Endelle's forces all this time. The only fly in the ointment at present was that although Parisa had disappeared from the future streams for most of three months, she'd recently resurfaced as a threat to his Coming Order. She was a terrible conundrum.

His instinct was to kill her. Still, if he disposed of her outright, even through one of his minions whom he could later blame, her relationship to Warrior Medichi would invite Armageddon. The death of any of the women connected so closely to the Warriors of the Blood would ignite a frenzy of hunting and slaughtering. Greaves did not want to be caught in that sort of maelstrom if he could help it. The warriors would draw and quarter him at the very least for taking her life. As a man intent on ruling the world, he had learned to tread the waters of subvert-and-conquer very lightly.

His strategy with the Warriors of the Blood had been very simple over the centuries. He wanted to keep them exhausted but not overrun, not until he was ready to take over Second Earth. He didn't yet own COPASS and until he'd turned a majority of the members of that lawmaking committee, he wouldn't have enough pieces in place for the coup he was planning. But he was getting closer every day.

He shifted slightly against the pillows and felt the pull of dried blood against one of the wounds on his back. He rubbed back and forth; the ensuing rip of his skin sent a small slice of lightning into his groin. Delightful.

An email arrived all in caps.

Rith never wrote in caps.

THE CAPTIVE WILL ESCAPE. It was a message out of the Mumbai Seers Fortress, which had one of the highest accuracy rates of all the fortresses.

Lowercase followed. *Your orders, master?*

Greaves smiled. He adored Rith's manners. So many today had forgotten the proper use of titles of respect. *Master* was simply his favorite.

"What is it, darling?" Julianna murmured. "You're very tense." Her nails scraped along his hip, then his thigh, then the space between. She put terrible pressure on the lump. He hissed his approval. She giggled.

"Parisa is prophesied to escape. Rith wants to know what he should do. I believe he wants to kill her but I can't allow it. He could tighten security, of course. Maybe we should move her. Yes, I'm thinking we should move her." He hit REPLY and a new email opened up, the cursor pulsing at him. He started typing his orders with a bit of difficulty; the fingers of his left hand were permanently misshapen, albeit very slightly, from decades of shifting from claw to hand.

Julianna caught his wrist lightly. "My love," she said, leaning up on her elbows. His breath caught. The woman was exquisite. She had dark brown hair now hanging in masses around her shoulders, rumpled from lovemaking. Her eyes were an exquisite blue, like icy water, but it was the shape that pleased him so much, angled upward as they were from the corners, cat's eyes. "Why not let the winged mortal escape—after you forge a mind-link with her?" She smiled, that little devious Scarlett O'Hara smile of hers, the one that always warmed his heart.

"An intriguing notion. Go on."

"You know how worried you've been that the Warriors of the Blood might take the abduction personally, and act against you before you're ready. Why not make use of her?"

"So I could use her as a sort of spy."

"Well, you can't keep her, and you certainly can't slit her throat." She dug a nail deep between hip and thigh and drew blood. He hissed at the pain, but the resulting flow of endorphins made him wonderfully dizzy. He really did love this woman.

"I'll think on it," he murmured. He then sent an email to Rith to do nothing until he'd pondered the matter.

He set his HP aside and opened his left palm. He focused on the fingers and savored the burn as skin broke and disappeared, as bones expanded, as the claw took shape.

Julianna rolled on her back, the sheet catching just at hip level until she looked like a mermaid. Her cuts really did heal too fast.

She spread her arms wide, getting ready for him once more. Her breasts were large and perfect and unenhanced. They drifted to each side of her rib cage, the nipples already peaked. She smiled and sighed. "Hurt me," she whispered.

So he did.

At seven that evening, just after sunset, Medichi entered the Blood and Bite and froze. It was the smell that got to him first, full of lust, sex, and blood, everything he couldn't have, everything he'd been denied for the past three months because Parisa was gone.

The red velvet booths off to the right were covered in

varying degrees of mist, and would confuse the minds of all the mortal women present as well as most of the Militia Warriors. But his powers were advanced enough that he could see, hear, and smell everything. He used to enjoy the voyeurism. Now it was torture.

He knew what went on in the booths. He'd made use of them nearly every night from the time the owner, Sam Finch, had opened the joint too many decades ago to remember. The Warriors of the Blood always started out their night here, sharing drinks and bullshit, taking a beauty or two into one of the booths, getting a bit of respite before the death vamps started busting through the Borderlands.

He took a deep breath and ignored the onslaught of sensation as he turned in the direction of the bar. Now that he was here, he had another mission to accomplish, something he should have done a long time ago. Shit, was he really going to do this? After thirteen centuries, was he really going to tell the truth about why he never mounted his wings?

Jean-Pierre thumped his shoulder from behind. "*Allô,* Medichi. This is such good news about Burma. Have you heard from Central yet?"

Medichi turned to face the Frenchman. He still had a faint accent; he'd only been ascended a couple of centuries. Give him a few more decades, and his English would be perfect. "No. I spoke to Carla a couple of times this afternoon, but nothing yet. Jeannie's on deck right now. She's working with Colonel Seriffe. The grid over at Militia Warrior Headquarters isn't quite as powerful as Central's but it'll do in a pinch." Once night fell and the pretty-boys came out, Jeannie had to use Central's grid to track death vampire movements and keep Thorne apprised. Seriffe's less powerful grid would be searching Burma the rest of the night.

He had spent the day in and out of sleep, waiting without much expectation for Carla to call with news of Parisa. He had known from the first that the hunt would take days, not hours, but he had still been hoping for a miracle. When nothing came of the day's grid search and it was time to dress for battle, his nerves were shredded. Frankly, he needed the release of wielding his sword and battling an enemy he could actually get at. All this waiting was for shit.

Jean-Pierre clamped his shoulder, shook his head back and forth. "I'm so happy for you."

"*Merci, Jean.*"

"*Oui. Oui.*" The Frenchman nodded several times then finally just threw his arms around Medichi.

Jean-Pierre, at six-five, was the same height as Marcus. He had long wavy brown hair, on the light side. His hair tended to escape the *cadroen* and frame his face in loose curls, which the women loved. His eyes were greenish gray, the color of the ocean. He was probably the leanest of the warriors, but fucking strong. Women were known to swoon over the bastard, especially when he whispered soft French into willing ears.

The *cadroens* he used were strips of varying pastel brocade, hand-sewn to his specifications with combs, tied in a bow, an affectation he'd adopted at the French court and refused to give up. He had been an acquaintance—though not a lover—of Marie Antoinette. During those years, he had developed a serious and dangerous love for the political discussion of the day. In an act that had terrorized an enormous crowd, he'd dematerialized off the guillotine in 1793.

Non, he had not known of this power. *Oui,* he had made his way, just as Medichi had all those centuries earlier, to the European Borderland outside Rome, to begin his ascension process.

Of all the warriors, Jean-Pierre had been Medichi's biggest support during the last three months. When the music turned off, Medichi told him of tracking the death vamp to the Grand Canyon, Mortal Earth.

But when he finished the story, he added, "One more thing, *mon ami.* I'm telling everyone tonight."

Jean-Pierre frowned. "About your wings? Why you will not fly with any of us?"

Medichi nodded.

"*Mon dieu,* but I am glad of it. Will you fly in battle from this night on?"

"Yes. That's the idea, especially since we could get a call any time now from Central. When we head to Burma, I'll want to be ready to mount my wings."

"*Bon.*" He nodded several times.

Medichi turned around, took a deep breath, lowered his chin, and charted a course for the bar. Despite the six-deep bank of Militia Warriors, his height parted the crowd as if he had a ten-foot iron prow before him.

The brothers were there in full battle gear, Marcus included. Their uniform was meant for the hot desert temps: leather kilts, weapons harnesses with a leather strap down the back that allowed for wing release, heavy sandals, black shin guards, and silver-studded leather wrist guards. Thorne sat in his usual location at the top of the bar, with a hand on Luken's back. He ran the hand low to the waist, inspecting. "Jesus," Thorne muttered. "Not a single damn scar from those burns. A-fucking-mazing."

Luken grinned. Three months ago he'd been caught by an incendiary bomb while out fighting at the Superstitions. His wings had been burned off, but fortunately they'd regenerated and he'd been on flight duty ever since, like the rest of the brothers. Now the last of his scarring had apparently faded.

He headed toward the second duo, Kerrick and Marcus. The latter only fought two nights a week; the rest of the time he served as High Administrator of Southwest Desert Two. He'd taken a huge load off Endelle. Funny how that still hadn't improved her temper.

The two men had been enemies for the past two hundred years, but all that had been resolved. Now they were inseparable.

Marcus sat with his full attention fixed on Kerrick. Yeah, the two shared something in common—they'd both bonded with their *brehs*.

Marcus frowned at Kerrick. "What the hell did you do to your forehead?"

Kerrick rubbed above his right eyebrow and grimaced. "What, this?" Color crept up his neck. "Alison threw a shoe at me. She's not exactly been herself lately."

Marcus leaned back and laughed. "She's very pregnant these days. Whadya do? Tell her she looked *fat,* you dumbfuck? I'da thrown a shoe as well."

Kerrick sighed. "I know better than that. She was wincing and I asked if she was all right."

"Huh." Marcus frowned. "Maybe it was your tone. Sometimes they get mad because of *tone.*"

Kerrick just sighed again and rubbed the bump.

In other circumstances, Medichi could have appreciated the exchange—he'd been married once. But the sight of both men, happily bonded, their *brehs* safe, made his stomach loop into a very complicated figure-eight.

His gaze shifted to the right. There was Santiago, holding up a cocktail napkin to Zacharius. On it was a sketch of a dagger.

"Longer," Zach said. "I still think it should be longer."

Santiago chortled. "That is what all the women say."

Zach rolled his eyes. "You are so full of shit."

Medichi actually smiled at the joke. He couldn't even remember the last time that had happened, but then again he'd gotten good news today. He moved in and clapped each one on the shoulder. "How we doin'?" he asked. He didn't wait for an answer but jerked his chin at Sam. "Limoncello," he called out.

Sam nodded once, flung a clean white towel over his shoulder, gave a snap of his suspenders, and bent over to open the small fridge behind the counter.

Both warriors, still seated, looked up at Medichi.

"Hey," Zach cried, "Thorne told us your news. This is fucking great."

And that's all it took. The warriors rose off the bar stools, one huge-ass swarm of lethal warrior bodies, palms and fists pummeling him.

For some goddamn reason Medichi's eyes burned.

Marcus pushed his hair back. It had grown longer in the past three months, down to his shoulders now but still not long enough for the *cadroen.* "So, we sit tight until the grid at Central finds something we can investigate."

"Actually, we're using Seriffe's grid, the one at Militia headquarters. Jeannie's watching for blue-bastards, as usual."

Marcus sighed. Heavily. He shook his head. "We're getting our asses kicked," he muttered. As an administrator, he always had his eye on the larger problem: how to gain the upper hand over Greaves.

Medichi glanced past his friend and took the cold glass of limoncello that Sam held up. He drew the glass close, squeezed his eyes shut, and took a long drink.

His heart was thumping hard. The time had come to do what he should have done centuries ago.

When he opened his eyes, he looked straight at Thorne and said, "I need to see all of you at the Cave before we head out to the Borderlands tonight." His gaze skated to Marcus, willing him to understand what he intended to do. It didn't take Marcus more than a couple of seconds. He nodded and a faint smile touched his lips.

Thorne scowled at him. "What's going on?"

Medichi shifted his gaze back to him.

Thorne was one ruined warrior. In addition to the reddish, bloodshot look, he had dark circles beneath his eyes. It was like looking in a mirror, except Thorne had looked this way for decades now. And what the hell was his excuse except that his sister was stuck in the Creator's convent in Prescott Two and had been for over a century?

Of course, Thorne's avowed celibacy didn't help matters.

To be fair, Thorne was Endelle's second-in-command. That had to be one huge assfucking day and night. For all her power and her dedication to Second Society, Endelle was one volcano of a bitch, ready to spew on command. But she was the only thing holding their world together when Commander Darian Greaves was so close to tearing it apart.

As Thorne scowled up at him, Medichi knew he'd have to tell him something right now if he wanted him to agree to a meeting before the night's battling began. Thorne didn't like a disruption in his schedule.

Medichi drew a deep breath. "I need to show you my wings."

To reveal what has been hidden,
To offer to the light what has been long held in the dark,
These are the true acts of heroism.

—*Collected Proverbs,* Beatrice of Fourth

CHAPTER 4

"You need to show us your wings?" Thorne repeated. His hazel eyes looked blank. "What do you mean? Now? Tonight?"

The warriors, almost as a unit, froze and stared at Medichi.

"Yeah. Right now. At the Cave." He willed Thorne to say yes, to direct the warriors to the rec room.

"Shit" came out like a soft whistle from between Thorne's teeth. He glanced around. "Well, fuck. To the Cave, laddies."

Medichi didn't wait. He lifted his arm and folded. He touched down on the chipped black tile of the floor, then moved to stand near the pool table, his hands on his hips. He took deep breaths. Was he really going to do this?

Yeah. The time had come. The moment Central found anything in Burma, he'd fold to the location and do whatever it took to get to Parisa, including mounting his wings in front of God and all creation. So yeah, he needed to get this over with.

He felt the air move several times as seven big warrior bodies filled up the Cave. It was dark inside, a real hole in the wall in downtown Metro Phoenix Two.

Ratty brown leather couches, more like barges, lined two walls. A TV came on via motion detector whenever a warrior entered the space. It was turned to CNN—Marcus's request. He liked to keep on top of happenings on Mortal Earth.

The pool table had been recently replaced but already had a huge gouge out of one corner. The pocket was missing and had been replaced by a duct-taped black trash bag.

Medichi took the plunge. "I'm going to show you first, then you'll understand a few things." He stripped off his black tee. Damn, was he really going to do this? Parisa's arrival had changed everything. Every damn thing.

He met Marcus's gaze. Marcus dipped his chin once, his expression solemn, even hard. Marcus had seen the scars on his back the same day Medichi had met Parisa.

Medichi turned slowly until his back was to the men. He heard the soft, strained gasps. With his right hand he swept his long hair forward over his shoulder so that what he'd kept secret was a secret no longer.

He felt sick in his gut. He was showing them just how he'd failed his wife the night she'd died. His scars didn't represent what he'd suffered. His suffering had been nothing. No, the horrific silver stripes represented Maria's death.

For the first few seconds, a variety of profanities flowed, even Jean-Pierre's *Merde*. He gave them a good long minute to look.

It was Kerrick who spoke first. "We always wondered. What the fuck happened? Who did this to you?"

He turned back to face them, but his gaze found the floor and couldn't seem to move anywhere else. Guilt held him fast. He told the story in as few words as possible. A northern tribe descending on the countryside. Rapists. Murderers. He spoke of the whip, the laughter, the drunkenness, and finally his wife and unborn child. He talked of the sudden emergence of power that saved his life, but arrived too late to save his wife's.

When he was done, his brothers shifted through the room like rivulets of water seeking a place to drain. All except Thorne. He sat down on the floor and put his head in his hands.

For several minutes, no one said a word. They didn't look at him, either. Each expression was lost, haunted. Who among them hadn't suffered some tragedy or terrible loss or physical pain because of the nature of life or because of the war?

Finally, Santiago approached. He was too beautiful for words, this brother, with his thick, wavy black hair, dark eyes, and skin the color of a deep tan. He put his hand on Medichi's shoulder. He met his gaze straight-on. "I have felt your pain, *mi hermano,* but I have a scar that's worse than anything you have shown us tonight."

Shit.

Well, if that didn't make him feel worse.

The brother lifted his chin. "Do you remember a year ago that woman with the hair the color of a brilliant sunset and her eyes the precise shade of a violent sea?"

Medichi frowned. Sort of. He had a sudden fear that the woman had harmed Santiago permanently in the jewels. "Yes."

Santiago pounded his chest with his fist. His eyes looked wild, maddened. "She cut up my heart and bled me until I should have died. I tell you, the scar is deep, *hermano,* deep. I should have died that night."

Zacharius moved in close. "What the hell are you talking about? I don't remember a woman ever sticking you with a blade?"

"Who said anything about a weapon?" Santiago cried. "I begged her and begged her to go into the booths with me at the Blood and Bite. But she refused. I still bear the scar. What are Medichi's wounds when a woman has rejected such an invitation?" He swept a dramatic hand over his groin. "I ask you."

Everyone groaned, but Medichi laughed. Tears started to his eyes, but he laughed. "You are so full of shit."

"What?" he cried, his hands flung out in front of him. Then he slung his arm around Medichi's shoulders and hugged him. He even kissed him on the cheek. "I'm sorry about your wife and son," he whispered.

"Gracias, amigo."

Medichi laughed again. There were times when the brotherhood functioned just as it should and Santiago's absurdity had done what nothing else could have. The tension in the room thinned as the laughter flowed. Luken put Santiago in a headlock and slapped the top of his head a few times.

Thorne drew close and with his lips pressed tight together asked, "Did the scars affect your wings? I know you can fly. Are they damaged somehow? You don't owe us anything, Medichi. What you've shared tonight honors us."

Medichi met his gaze. The concern in Thorne's eyes almost undid him again. He shook his head. "It's nothing like that. My wings are fine. But it's time I started flying in battle. I've put it off way too long. When Jeannie calls with word about Parisa, I'll be in the air if I have to. I'm not holding back any longer. However, there is something I want you to know, and you'll understand better if I just show you."

"All right, then," Thorne said. "Let's see what you've got."

He turned his back to his brothers once more and focused. A few seconds later the apertures down his back wept and his wings began to release. The sensation was pure heaven, but as before, a few gasps and another stream of profanity hit the air.

"What the fuck," Zach cried. "You've got *royle* wings, just like Parisa. What the goddamn fuck?"

At eleven o'clock in the morning, Parisa sat in the garden waiting for Commander Greaves to visit her. He had never done so before. She sat on the teak bench beneath the tamarind tree, her nerves on fire and her heart beating a dull thud. Rith had sent her out here to wait an hour ahead of time, which didn't help her growing distress. What did he want with her, and why had he waited all this time to see her?

Rith's dark demeanor hadn't changed. He still watched her with a cruel light in his eye as though waiting for her to make a mistake so that he'd have an excuse to harm her.

She smoothed her hands over the cream silk dress she wore. For Greaves's visit, Rith had made sure she was well groomed, and that included her finest dress. Her makeup was flawless: The Burmese women loved to give her cat-eyes with heavy black eyeliner to bring out the amethyst color. Her dark brown hair had been sculpted into several loops down the back of her head. Talk about a gilded cage.

But whatever Rith was, Greaves was so much worse. In her opinion, he personified hypocrisy. He spoke and dressed like an aristocrat, but if even half the stories about him were true, he created death vampires of all those who served him. He might have the manners of a gentleman, but he had the soul of Lucifer and intended nothing but pain and suffering to the two worlds he meant to conquer.

A loud crash sounded from the direction of the house, like china shattering on the planked wooden floor. Parisa turned toward the porch of the large British Colonial. She saw movement just beyond the open doorway but couldn't make out what was happening. Figures grappled back and forth in the shadows. Grunting followed, and Rith cried out.

She rose from the teak bench as an unfamiliar woman appeared in the doorway. She wore loose light blue flannel pajama bottoms and a navy tank top. Her wavy chestnut hair hung to the sides of a beautiful face. She had large light blue eyes, almost silver in appearance, but wild looking. She was Caucasian, something Parisa had not seen in three months.

Parisa couldn't breathe. The woman caught sight of her and shifted in her direction. Parisa backed up until her legs hit the teak bench.

The woman raced toward her and knocked her into the bench. She fell on her, grabbing her shoulders. "Help me," she pleaded in English. "You have to help me. Get me out of here. Please, please."

When Parisa realized she wasn't being attacked, she held on to the woman's shoulders. "You're being held against your will?" It couldn't really be a surprise that another woman might be trapped in the same house, but Parisa hadn't seen or heard anyone else on the premises before. Where had she come from?

A shift of shadow near the porch drew Parisa's eye. Rith appeared in the doorway. She had never seen him look so angry, his chin low, his lips curved down. He pressed a cloth to his forehead, then looked at it. He tossed the cloth aside and moved swiftly in their direction, hips low, knees bent, hands splayed like claws.

"I—I can't help you," Parisa said. "I'm a captive as well."

"What?" The woman looked at Parisa's hair, her cream silk gown. "But you look so lovely. I thought this was your home."

"Oh, God, no." Parisa looked down at their joined arms. A tremor went through, a soft vibration, a *knowing*. She knew without understanding why that her future was connected to this woman. She stared into the silver-blue eyes. "I feel as though I know you."

"What are you doing to me?" The woman looked at their joined arms as well. "What is that vibration?"

Rith was almost on them. "What's your name?" Parisa asked.

"Fiona. Fiona Gaines. Of Boston from a long time ago. Who are you?"

"Parisa."

Fiona's eyes filled with tears. "Today would have been my daughter's birthday. I . . . I can't take being here anymore. Help me, Parisa. Please—"

Rith's strong pale hands caught Fiona's arms and pulled her away, a solid, heavy jerk. Because Parisa was unwilling to release the woman, she grabbed for her waist and fell forward onto Fiona, causing all three to tumble onto the lawn.

"Let go of her," Rith shouted.

Parisa refused. She wanted to help this woman, this fellow captive. Rith jerked and rolled in the direction of the house where the lawn slanted. Fiona rolled with him, which meant that Parisa's arms were quickly twisted as she got caught in the tumbling. She had no choice. She released Fiona. She cried out at the pain, not just of having her skin stretched and bruised but because of the separation from the unknown woman.

She sat up and watched the struggle. She rose to her feet ready to do battle as well but Rith caught her movement and lifted a hand in her direction. The gesture was way too familiar. Parisa had made use of her own palms earlier in her captivity and had been punished for it. There was nothing she could do, though. The next moment the hand-blast caught her in the chest. She flew backward into the bench once more and struck her head. Hard.

She slid to the ground on her side. Stars danced over her eyes. She blinked. More stars.

From the odd angle, she could still watch the struggle play out as Rith slapped Fiona several times until the woman fell limp into his arms. Vampires had a lot of physical power, even average-looking vampires like Rith.

He tossed her over his shoulder and carted her back into the house. Once she disappeared inside, Parisa had the strangest sensation that her life had just changed forever.

She sat up slowly to lean against the teak bench. Her head throbbed. Who was the woman? Why was Rith holding her captive—and were there other women hidden away somewhere inside the house?

She felt a vibration in the air and rose to her feet, an abrupt movement that caused her head to swim.

Greaves materialized in front of her. His brows rose as he looked her up and down. A frown appeared between his thick arched black brows.

She reached up and felt through her hair. Some of the elegant loops had come loose and now hung in an awkward mass down her back. She glanced at her gown and saw the grass stains where her knees must have slid over the ground. There was blood on the fabric as well, but she had no idea whether it was from her or Rith or Fiona.

Rith came running from the house. "My most humble apologies, master. We had an unfortunate accident just a moment ago. I will make the woman ready for you."

Greaves turned slightly toward him and inclined his head. "Yes, please do."

Rith swept to Parisa's side, hooked her beneath her arm, and dragged her on running feet from the garden. "How dare you involve yourself in that way?" he hissed, over and over.

A few minutes later, with her coiffure restored by two trembling Burmese servants, Parisa returned to the garden as ordered. She wore a new gown, a light green silk dress, tight at the waist and long at mid-calf, very conservative.

Reentering the garden, she saw Greaves from behind. He sat in a large teak chair, elbows planted on the wide arms. From her vantage, since the teacup was missing from the saucer, she presumed he was drinking his tea.

His bald head reflected the dancing shadows of the lacy tamarind leaves overhead. She rounded the table upon which the tea service sat and took up her place again on the teak bench.

He wore a charcoal-gray suit that bore a faint and oh-so-elegant pinstripe. His tie was lavender silk; a black onyx ring graced his right pinkie. He was handsome, though completely bald, and had the most innocent expression in his large, round brown eyes, a look akin to child-like wonder.

Whatever else this monster was, his appearance was tailored, crisp, clean. Yes, a very tidy monster. His sole imperfection was his left hand, which he held curled inward as though slightly crippled.

The elegant monster smiled, showing even white teeth.

Parisa sat with her hands held in a loose clasp over the fine green silk. Her fingers trembled but then why wouldn't they since her mind kept flashing on images of Fiona. Where was Rith keeping the woman?

She kept her expression calm, however, and measured her blinks. Only her elevated heart rate would give away the state of her emotions. Somehow she knew Greaves could detect each beat, track the rise in tempo, and even now smiled at her fear.

He had never paid her a visit before, so she couldn't imagine his reason for coming today. This couldn't be good.

He sipped the traditional local black tea enhanced with condensed milk. Parisa didn't care for the tea or much of the food. Her appetite still lagged despite the luxury of her captivity. She knew now why zoo animals often seemed so lethargic: Without her freedom, her spirit had shriveled.

"There is no need to fear me, Parisa." The monster's voice had a soothing quality, a gentle bubbling stream, a delight.

"I suppose not. I've been here three months and I've received excellent care."

"I have no doubt of that. Rith is one of my best servants. He always follows my orders to the letter—and where you are concerned, your care is of the upmost importance."

"But why have you brought me here, to Burma, Commander Greaves? I hope you've come to tell me your purpose. Better yet, to release me." Where was this boldness coming from?

He smiled. "I must say you smell of heaven."

She repressed a sigh. Was that the only answer he would give her? *You smell of heaven?* "I am bathed daily in fragrant oils." She knew enough to give a good report. Rith would hurt her otherwise. Given her misdemeanor earlier, she thought it likely a punishment already waited for her. Great.

Greaves nodded.

He settled the white teacup on its companion saucer, rising from his chair. Her heart rate took another step up, a quick fluttering that descended into heavy bass thumps. She lowered her gaze to the grass at her feet. She began counting blades.

He sat down beside her. He put a hand on her nape, a very controlling gesture. Rith must have pinned her hair in loops to give him access. For a moment, she wondered if he meant to take her blood.

"So beautiful," Greaves whispered. His left hand brushed over her left arm.

She tried not to breathe through her nose because, for all of Greaves's finery, he smelled strange. It was lemon furniture polish—or at least that was the closest she could come to approximating his scent. It wasn't entirely unpleasant, just odd.

She drew a shallow breath and tried to relax. Unfortunately, she felt his mind against hers. She could sense his desire to penetrate her head in what she had heard described as deep-mind engagement. But with each breath, she slammed her shields in place, one mental steel wall sliding down over another, working hard to keep him out.

He groaned. *Your shields are magnificent.*

She closed her eyes.

Let me in, he whispered through her brain. *Please, lovely Parisa. Let me in, or I shall have to hurt you.*

But she held fast.

The pain began as she felt him hammering against her shields, the sound like a sledgehammer striking against an enormous brass bell. Her teeth ached.

She didn't want this.

More pain. More pounding. Oh, God, slicing now.

Tears flowed. She couldn't have held them back if she'd wanted to. In some distant part of her mind she knew she was screaming.

Release your shields.

No. She might have to endure a captivity she didn't understand, she might have to do as she was told and follow Rith's schedule, she might have to fear that at any moment she could be killed. But by God she would keep her mind sacrosanct.

I need to be inside your head.

He eased his efforts, but it was only a respite.

Parisa sobbed at the sudden release from pain. Did he enjoy her suffering? She turned to look at him, his hand still a weight on the back of her neck. He dipped down toward her very suddenly and his lips were on hers, a soft, cool, dry touch.

Her thoughts slid strangely to Antony . . . and it happened. As though the mere thought of him was enough, her shields fell away, a kind of quick shimmering of leaves. She rose to her feet even though she couldn't quite see. She ran forward but collided with something hard. She fell . . . then . . . nothing.

Darian Greaves was absolutely fascinated with the woman lying at his feet. She was a mortal-with-wings. Incredible. He had read of her powers and now understood that she had the ability to voyeur, which was also astounding. To his knowledge only Endelle had the ability to make use of preternatural voyeurism.

But what intrigued him the most was that this woman was evidently the *breh* of Warrior Medichi. The mythical *breh-hedden* seemed to be happening to the Warriors of the Blood at light speed. It reeked of Upper Dimension involvement. Yes, at the very least the arrival of so many preternaturally powerful women, all in the space of a few short months and intended for the most powerful men on Second Earth, smelled of Third Earth involvement, perhaps even higher.

If he'd been suspicious of Endelle, he would have said he was the victim of her diabolical plotting, but She Who Would Live did not possess a complicated mind. He smiled. No, Madame Endelle had a warrior's mind. She would have performed much better at the head of an army than as Supreme High Administrator of Second Earth. Her inadequacies and failings had been a blessing to his ongoing efforts at world domination: candy from a baby. And if truth be known, up until Alison's ascension seven months ago—dear pregnant Alison—he'd been rather bored.

"Rith," he called out.

"Yes, master." Rith's voice was elegant, serene.

"I would like more tea, please." Somewhere in Parisa's stumblings the table had been overturned and the saucer broken.

Pity. The white Ironware was quite old.

"Shall I remove her?"

Parisa lay between his chair and the bench. A light rain had begun to fall, and he created a shield over his head and her body.

"No, that won't be necessary. I am not quite finished with her." He rounded her prone body to sit back down, stretching out his arms on the wide armrests. Parisa's back was to him. The green silk dress clung to her curves. She had a very small waist; the dip below her ribs looked like it would fit one of his feet.

He understood the real danger Parisa was to him even though she was oblivious and would be for a long time. The real danger was the silent warrior behind her. If it weren't for Medichi, Greaves would have killed her outright. But to do so now would put all his plans at risk.

Yes, Greaves felt the hand of a master in the sudden eruption of the *breh-hedden* among the Warriors of the Blood, a master not of Second Earth, but of an Upper Dimension, though he couldn't prove it. Like everyone else on Second, he had thought the mate-bonding ritual a thing out of ascension mythology, something written in fables to charm the feminine heart and to make men strong and lusty with their women.

But here it was, at his feet, real and dangerous. He felt the danger as a writhing fierce wind all around him. He still didn't know how to combat it, but today he'd made progress. He'd forged a voyeur's link with Parisa. Anytime she opened that link, he would be able to see and hear everything she saw and heard.

He smelled Rith before he came into view. The Oriental had an unusual body odor, like rust that somehow lived in the air and could be tasted on the tongue. Rith took a lot of Chinese herbs. Maybe some of them leaked through his pores.

Two of the females were with him. Greaves didn't like these women, but he couldn't say why. Rith had them completely under control, but there was a meanness to them he disapproved of. They were the kind of women who, if they caught mice in a trap, would cut their feet off before killing them. He disapproved of such traits in women. He liked their general submissiveness, but there was nothing gentle in any of them. He felt certain each would have made an excellent assassin.

The woman with the narrowest gaze righted the table then spread a fresh white linen over the top. The second woman set a tray down, a very pretty silver tray that held a Wedgwood set, an homage to the time of British rule in Burma on Mortal Earth over a hundred years ago.

He smiled as Rith prepared the sweet Burmese tea. Some traditions ought to be maintained just to remind everyone of the nature and necessity of dominance.

He dismissed Rith and his servants. Holding the cup and saucer in his hands, he sipped the aromatic sweetened tea, letting the creamy texture and bitter flavor roll around on his tongue.

He smiled. Yes, dominance was his favorite thing.

Savoring that dominance was another.

Okay, so he was a mere vampire and couldn't resist the temptation, but with Parisa unconscious, who would ever know?

He folded off his right shoe, sending it to rest next to the leg of his chair. He took a deep breath then settled his foot, encased in Bresciani, on that lovely deep curve of Parisa's waist. A sense of peace flowed within his chest. He left his foot in that position until he'd finished the last of the tea.

He had one small conundrum to resolve at this point. Given his suspicions of Upper Dimension involvement on behalf of Madame Endelle, should he strike now and attempt a takeover of Second Earth? Or should he wait?

He sipped his tea.

Problems, problems.

The next thing Parisa knew, she was on the grass, her cheek cool against the carefully cut blades. She faced the bench and the tree. Slowly, she rolled over onto her other side, trying to make sense of where she was and what had happened to her. She felt very dizzy.

Her view was obstructed by the legs of the small side table. Beyond it, she saw Rith's house. Pilings beneath the structure made the house seem to float on a lake—except that there was no water, only a strange-looking flat-headed cat that Rith called his fire cat. The animal stared at her. He was feral and alert. His fur was a beautiful gold and rust, maybe like fire. He had slightly webbed feet and preferred eating frogs to birds.

Why was she on her side on the grass?

Oh, yes. She sighed. She managed a small smile. Antony had kissed her. But how was that possible? Had she fallen asleep in the garden again? Had she been dreaming?

She rolled onto her back. She stared up through the feathery leaves of the tamarind tree. She wanted to go home. Why couldn't she go home?

She sat up. She felt certain she should remember something but couldn't. She rose to her feet and turned to look at the teak bench. She had been sitting there. She was sure of that. But how had she gotten several feet away? The chair set out for Commander Greaves was in position, as well as the side table meant to hold a tea service. She wondered when Greaves would arrive. She shuddered. He was a monster. He had the manners of a prince but he was a monster.

Or had he been here already?

She shuddered again. A vague memory arose—flashes of him sipping his tea then sitting beside her. So, yes, he had come and gone.

For no reason at all, her head began to hurt.

From the slatted blinds within his house, Rith stared at the woman now risen from her prone position on the lawn. He had hoped she would die, but he'd had no such good fortune.

The woman lived.

And Greaves had accomplished what he'd set out to accomplish—he'd forged a mind-link with her. He'd also told Rith that he was to allow the woman to leave.

Rith found it hard to blink. He had received more prophecies that the woman would escape, but as always he believed the Seers existed to help him shape the future, not simply to predict it.

He didn't know the method yet, but he knew this woman would be dead long before she had a chance to leave his home.

Death is but a journey.
Yet to return from the brink of the grave
Is a powerful call to service, to life, to love.

—*Collected Proverbs*, Beatrice of Fourth

CHAPTER 5

Medichi's phone buzzed. He was at the north end of the White Tanks. Jeannie had just done cleanup on five, *five,* fucking death vampires—and the night was young.

He slid his slim warrior phone from the pocket of his battle kilt. Tonight he was mounting his wings and learning to battle while in the air. It was only nine thirty, and this last squadron had about done him in. He'd flown for centuries, but not while battling, and right now muscles burned that he didn't even know he had.

He thumbed his phone. "Hey, Jeannie."

"Endelle patching through." The line went dead. Jeannie didn't even greet him, which meant the scorpion queen was in a mood.

"Medichi," Endelle snapped. "Get your fucking ass over to my office pronto."

"I'm alone at the White Tanks Borderland, Mortal Earth,

and I can feel the air cooling down. You know what that means. I'll be there as soon as I can."

"I mean *now,* asshole," she shouted into the phone. "Thorne's sending Santiago to take your place."

"I said—" He wasn't going to argue with her so he thumbed his phone. He might not have been thinking clearly, though, because in some part of his fatigued, stressed mind he realized he might have just hung up on the ruler of Second Earth.

Shiiiit.

But he had another problem right now. The air grew arctic, a sure sign a few pretty-boys were on the way, floating down through the dimensional Trough like Mary-fucking-Poppins.

His phone buzzed again. He ignored it. He wasn't leaving the Borderland until Santiago arrived, and he sure as hell wasn't letting Santiago arrive with death vampires already on the ground.

He held his sword at the ready but didn't mount his wings. He kept his gaze fixed on the night sky overhead. Hooray for preternatural night vision. And there they were, dim shapes at first, clearer as each second passed.

The air moved next to him. He turned, ready for a different kind of attack if necessary, but Santiago materialized, his eyes glittering, his sword held in exactly the same position as Medichi's, body crouched.

Medichi nodded.

Santiago smiled then looked up. "I am feeling a slight chill in the air. What about you, *hermano*?"

Medichi turned back to the sky. There were only four riding down the Trough. "You got this?"

"Is that an insult, *amigo*?"

Medichi laughed. "Fuck off." He lifted his arm and dematerialized, but not without catching sight of Santiago's middle finger as he vanished.

He arrived in the middle of Endelle's office to face a screaming woman.

"You hung up on me! You hung up on me! *You hung up on me?*"

She combined the last phrase with telepathy and split-resonance and it fucking hurt. He almost dropped to his knees. Holy shit. He felt like his brain was about to explode and only barely kept his balance.

He saw stars, then something passed in front of him, creating streams of air. He stepped back automatically, getting out of the way, until he bumped against the wall by the door. Shit, Endelle was in one wild state. She was in full-mount, her wings shifted color constantly like a kaleidoscope gone awry, and she left a trail of fireworks behind her in red, all in red, as she raced from one wall to the next. She wore some kind of dress made up of what must have been hundreds of peacock feathers trimmed around the "eye." What with the fireworks, the wind, and all the "eyes," she looked like a one-woman spectacle event.

Sure, he'd hung up on her, but she couldn't be that pissed about a hang-up. Maybe he needed to explain. "I wasn't about to leave Santiago with four death vampires on the ground while he was still in dematerialization mode. He could have been killed."

"I don't think she's upset about the hang-up, Warrior Medichi."

At these words, Endelle slowed her movements and actually stopped in front of her desk. She glared in the direction of the west wall.

Only then did Medichi realize he wasn't the only man in the room, if you could call what was there *a man.* His gaze followed Endelle's to the never-used fireplace on the west wall.

Owen Stannett.

Holy shit.

High Administrator of the Superstition Mountain Seers Fortress, manipulator of COPASS, law unto himself, lying bastard, enemy to Endelle.

Owen. Fucking. Stannett.

He had all but robbed Endelle of Seer prophecies, which

provided critical foreknowledge of the war. The Superstition Fortress was the most powerful in the word, probably because of its proximity to the five major dimensional access points on Second Earth. Every continent had at least one access point, but the North American continent had five, in the desert Southwest, all close to the Metro Phoenix area. A lot of power was focused in this part of the world.

Stannett was one of the main reasons Endelle and her administration were so fucking hamstrung in the fight against Greaves. The bastard had wined and dined COPASS to the point that he'd gotten several critical laws passed, one of which meant that Endelle could not cross the threshold of the Seers Fortress except by express invitation from its High Administrator. So guess who never got invited?

That Stannett had then constricted the flow of information came as no surprise, but every attempt to get the law repealed had failed. The committee insisted there needed to be a clear separation between the sanctity of Seer devotion and the activities of the State.

Naturally, *naturally,* Greaves had built his own powerful network throughout the world by securing the most talented Seers from those Territories aligned with him and settling them into the Fortresses at Mumbai, Johannesburg, and Bogotá.

Therein lay the difference between a dictatorship and a democracy. Greaves could do whatever the hell he wanted, but Endelle was bound not just by the laws of the land, but also by the ingrained rights of the local High Administrators to manage their Territories as each saw fit. Autonomy was a critical factor in creating a thriving world, both economically and politically. Every Seers Fortress had an allegiance first to its High Administrator and to the local needs of the people. Endelle could request information, but the High Administrators could respond in whatever way they felt was best for their people. So global Seer information for Endelle was much less reliable. Without her Superstition Fortress prophecies, she was up shit creek without a fucking paddle.

To say Medichi loathed Stannett was to say the sun was warm. *Loathed* was too small a word because in the beautiful way power plays trickled down and down and down, mortals and ascenders died every day as a result of the war, of the heinous depredations of Greaves's ever-increasing death vampire army, and of the lack of information Endelle needed to counter the enemy's Seer-based moves.

The question of the hour remained: What the hell was Owen Stannett doing in Endelle's office?

He was dressed in heavily embroidered white leather, complete with fringe, like a Las Vegas lounge entertainer. He had styled his dark brown hair with a lot of mousse into a lovely wave that rode the entire right side of his head. He met Medichi's gaze, unsmiling.

The next moment a shimmering in the air brought Medichi whirling in the direction of the latest arrival. He crouched, brought his sword to the ready, and waited.

Thorne.

Thank God.

Medichi could breathe again, but he said, "Look who's showed up, after how many decades of playing hide-the-Seer in the Superstitions."

Thorne dipped his chin to Medichi but shifted all his attention to the man by the fireplace. "Stannett." He offered a nod that was polite and challenging at the same time.

Stannett had the balls to make a slight bow, as though he were at the court of Queen fucking Victoria. "Warrior Thorne" eased from between the snake's smooth lips.

Medichi addressed Stannett and expressed his deepest convictions: "What the hell do you want, you motherfucking sonofabitch?"

Stannett spread his hands wide. "I come in peace this evening, Warrior Medichi. I need you to believe that."

He looked and sounded so sincere. Medichi hated that smug bastard's face. The night was young and had already been full of death vampires and battle and this asshole had the nerve to say he came in peace? Did he not comprehend his role in the fucking war? Or what his actions had cost the world?

Medichi's heavy arms jerked and twitched. He was just short enough on sleep and patience that he didn't exactly have the ability to suppress the impulse. He launched at Stannett ready to tear apart all that fine leather and anything else he could get at, preferably the vampire's slimy heart.

He didn't get far. Though Owen backed up against the fireplace, and actually looked frightened, Thorne had moved with preternatural speed and now stood between Medichi and his quarry, blocking him, protecting Stannett.

Medichi was powerful, one of the most physically powerful men on Second Earth. Even Thorne couldn't match him muscle for muscle. But then Thorne didn't need to. He had one hand on Medichi's chest and was pushing him backward, not by might, but by wave after wave of modified hand-blast energy. Jesus H. Christ, Medichi couldn't imagine the level of power required to control a hand-blast like this. It didn't exactly hurt, but the pulses shoved him backward one step at a time.

"You're not helping," Thorne said. "You're. Not. Helping." He repeated it until Medichi calmed the hell down.

Medichi was breathing hard, one breath after another. He saw red as he glared at Owen.

Thorne got into Medichi's face. "You calm now, buddy? If I take my hand away, you gonna stand right there and be good for me? Look at me."

Medichi finally shifted his gaze away from Owen and blinked at Thorne. "Sure," he said.

Thorne wasn't buying. "You want to try that again?"

"If you let me at him, I can make him talk," Medichi said quietly. Every muscle in his body was jumping.

"Stannett will fold out of here before you can touch him, you know that." He sounded so reasonable. "And you won't be able to follow him to the fortress. He can block a trace just like Rith. Would you use your head? Just for one little minute?"

Medichi wasn't insulted—not when Thorne was right. From the second he'd realized he'd been staring at a time-delayed hologram of Parisa, that Rith had abducted his woman essentially right from under his nose, Medichi had lost a good portion of his rational mind. He was more beast than man, the darkest parts of his ascended vampire nature in the fore.

Why wouldn't he be? Parisa had been gone from him for three months and guilt was like a gut-eating worm in his soul. Sure, Jeannie might get a fix on her at any time now, but it didn't change what had happened.

Thorne cupped the back of his neck and held his gaze in a hard stare. "Stannett has critical information about the war straight from his most powerful Seer. All right? If you pull another stunt like this one, I'll have to take you out of here, but the bottom line is that Stannett requested your presence."

Medichi frowned. "He did?"

"Yeah. So, how about you pull it together."

"Yes, Warrior Medichi," Stannett said. "I have news that concerns you as well as the woman, the mortal-with-wings."

Medichi grew very still as these words settled into his brain. All the previous jumping and twitching melted away along with his urge to pound his fist into Stannett's pretty face.

"We good now?" Thorne asked. He commanded the Warriors of the Blood for a reason. He was damn powerful. Then Thorne smiled, a little off to the side of his mouth. "Yeah, I want to kill him, too, but we can't do it just yet. Not if he knows anything that will help us keep Greaves from taking over Second Earth."

Something inside Medichi finally let go. His next breath came from way down deep, and his shoulders settled down. Shit, they'd been tightened into a pair of bowling balls.

He glanced at the High Administrator of the Superstition Seers Fortress. "Sorry, Stannett. Lost my head."

Endelle decided to enter the conversation. "Why don't you just tell Medichi what you told me."

Stannett drew in a deep breath. "One of my Seers witnessed something in the future streams about the mortal-with-wings, the woman Parisa Lovejoy, the one with the amethyst eyes. Is this the one you are missing?"

"Yes," Medichi barked at the same time as Endelle.

"For three months now, Stannett," Endelle said. "You'd know that if you didn't spend all your time in that Seers Fortress of yours with your balls in one hand and your dick in the other."

Stannett's left brow rose and he appeared to swallow, bile maybe, or maybe his rage. Endelle could be hard to take.

"Maybe this was a mistake," he said, his right arm rising in the air, the universal signal that he intended to dematerialize.

"Now, now, Stannett, come off your high horse," Endelle said. "We're here and we're listening. But what I really want to know is why you've broken your silence after all these years. That's not like you, which means there's something else going on, something you may or may not want to tell us. In fact, I think it chaps your hide to even be standing here in my office."

A dozen thoughts streamed over his face, quiet messages of frustration, anger, maybe a sense of being torn. Finally, he smiled, that oily false smile of his. He lowered his arm then waved the hand as though the visit were casual. "We need to be better friends than this, Endelle. I've always thought so."

"Hard to be friends with a python."

For some reason, Stannett laughed. Medichi had the impression that Endelle could hurl a thousand insults at him and it wouldn't matter. He'd made up his mind about something.

He settled an elbow on the mantel of the fireplace, which drew his leather jacket open. Medichi scowled. He wore a red leather vest cut low to reveal a lot of black curly chest hair. He was a strange man, affected, weird. Just looking at him made Medichi uneasy.

"Spit it out, Owen," Endelle said.

"Very well. I shall speak plainly. The future streams have revealed an impending battle, a very big battle."

A wind suddenly flew around the room and struck Medichi in the back before moving on. What the hell? His gaze landed on Endelle. Her arms were held aloft and power streamed from her but in no particular direction, just a wind that flowed around the room. It hit him again. Damn. So much power. Yeah, she was a little upset.

"What do you mean, a big battle." Endelle scowled and punched at the air with two fists. "Like army-to-army?"

"That's exactly what I mean, except—" He broke off. He looked serious.

The flow of wind hit Medichi again.

Endelle's nostrils flared. "Except *what,* Stannett? Would you spit it out, for Christ's sake. We're not children here."

"The prophecy is all tied up with the mortal-with-wings and the possibility of her death. Apparently if she dies you lose big-time, and Greaves gains everything."

"In what fucking way can this woman, a mortal, not even ascended, be critical to the outcome of a war?" Endelle's thick black hair was writhing around her shoulders. Medichi had seen her temper a dozen different times, but he'd never seen her hair display her rage before. That was considered a Third Earth ability.

Stannett looked grim, his mouth a tight line. "The future streams rarely reveal the *why* of anything. You know that, Endelle. What I can tell you is that more than one of my Seers has recently predicted a major battle, as well as the failure of your administration, if the woman dies."

Medichi couldn't let this go. "And what kind of accuracy rate does the Superstition Fortress have anyway, you motherless piece of shit? And why should we believe anything you have to say. You haven't helped us in years. Why now? Why would you give a good goddamn fuck now?" He couldn't bear the thought of *his woman* dead while the man stood there like he was reading an article on how to make head-cheese.

Endelle turned to face Medichi. She shook her head at him and mouthed a couple of curse words then sent him another blast of wind, this one with grit attached. He breathed the wrong way and drew some of that grit into his lungs. He bent over and hacked like he'd swallowed half a dozen fur balls. Okay, he got the point: He wasn't helping.

"My warrior makes a lot of sense, Stannett. Accuracy is always a problem with Seers, the future being as unpredictable as earthquakes."

"My prime Seer has a ninety-three percent accuracy rate."

Silence hit the room. Endelle froze like she was a figure at a wax museum. She wasn't even breathing.

Holy shit. Medichi looked at Stannett from his hinged position. He coughed again.

Time resumed. Endelle's eyes bulged. "That's not possible."

"It is with this one." His gaze skated to Thorne, held for the space of two long seconds, then shifted back to Endelle. What the hell did he mean by staring at Thorne?

Endelle took a step toward Stannett. "Tell me this, Owen. Why haven't you come forward before this? I know you're an ambitious man, but did it ever occur to you that I might be a better ally than no ally at all?"

For all Stannett's frivolous clothes, hair, and even his affected manners, his face suddenly looked made of steel and his gray eyes glinted. "I will never be beholden to anyone, Endelle. That's how I got this gig. Lots of politicking, bending over at the waist for centuries, taking it deep so that one day I could stand here and say, today, it pleases me to let you have this choice bit of information but that's all you're going to get from me."

She narrowed her eyes. "Fine, Liberace, unless you have any more 'choice bits' to share, I guess we're done here."

Medichi ran his gaze over Stannett. All that embroidered white leather and fringe. Jesus H. Christ. Had the man no pride?

Medichi had hated Stannett from the first time he'd laid eyes on him nine centuries ago, when the bastard had ascended. In very monk-like fashion, he'd worn black robes and a solemn demeanor—except he'd styled and pomaded his hair, even back then.

Stannett licked his lips.

"Oh, for fuck's sake, just say it," Endelle cried.

His gaze shifted to Medichi. "Just save the woman, at all

costs. And . . . well, make sure she uses her wings to good effect."

"You mean her *royle* wings," Endelle stated.

Everyone knew about Parisa's *royle* wings, and now they knew that Medichi's were the same. They both had wings that promised in some mystical way to bring peace to the land.

Stannett nodded. "Yes. Precisely." He lifted his arm and before any of them could press for more information, he was gone.

Medichi didn't wait. He closed his eyes and felt the man's trace, the line of power that followed after him. He focused on the stream of red and black, Stannett's unique signature, and dematerialized in pursuit.

But he hit some kind of metaphysical wall and woke up in Endelle's office on his back staring up at Thorne and Endelle. Shit, how long had he been out? "What happened?" he asked.

Endelle made a disgusted wet sound in her throat and turned away from him.

Thorne offered him a hand. "What made you think you could trace after Stannett? He's almost as powerful as Greaves."

Medichi took the proffered hand. He saw stars as he gained his feet. He took deep breaths. Oh, shit. The future streams had predicted not just Parisa's death but dire consequences for Second Earth if she died. He had to find her, but what more could he do? It was all up to either Central's grid, or right now the grid at Militia HQ. Would they find her in time?

Endelle stared out the window that overlooked the east desert, which stretched for miles. The Superstition Seers Fortress lay some sixty miles in the same direction, to the place also known as Thunder God Mountain. "What a poser," she muttered. "Although, I did like some of that embroidery, especially the yellow flowers."

As Medichi recovered from his ill-advised pursuit, his

mind settled into a loop: *Battle coming, must find Parisa, battle, Parisa.* "I have to find Parisa," he said. Had he spoken the words aloud?

Thorne clapped his hand on Medichi's shoulder. "We've got the grid burning juice at Militia HQ. Hang tough. We'll find her. We'll bring her home."

Medichi met Thorne's red-rimmed eyes and saw reflected what Medichi felt, panic laced with despair. Shit, what more could they do to find her? What if Parisa was killed before he could get to her?

Thorne squeezed. "The best thing you can do is get back to the White Tanks. Burma's too big a place for any of us to hunt mile by mile for a shielded anomaly. Head over to the Borderland and take care of business. This is what we can do right now. This is what we can control. Okay?"

"Yeah." Fighting would be best. He'd go mad if he had to sit around for hours with nothing to do but wait for some inexplicable blip.

"One more thing, keep a lid on this Seer information for now, until Endelle and I and maybe Colonel Seriffe can work out a strategy, okay?"

"You don't want the brothers knowing?"

"Not yet." Thorne scowled. "Got it?"

Medichi didn't exactly agree with the decision but yeah, right now his job was focused more on the keep-Parisa-safe part of the model rather than oh-God-Armageddon-is-coming.

Okay. One fucking problem at a time. Right now that meant he needed to work to keep death vampires from reaching Mortal Earth.

He folded back to the White Tanks.

The hour was nine at night in Burma, which meant seven thirty in the morning in Phoenix. Almost time for Antony.

Parisa had been opening her voyeur's window every fifteen minutes, but she focused her efforts on just his bedroom. If she voyeured Antony himself, she was afraid she'd find him battling death vampires—and she really didn't want those images in her head. She'd made the mistake only once during the early part of her captivity. Once had been enough.

The Burmese slaves were outside her room. Every once in a while she'd hear a cough or a shifting on a mat.

She pushed the covers back and rubbed her arms. Her nerves had taken on a life of their own and seemed to climb up her arms, then back down, then up and down. She had been on edge all day, ever since Greaves's visit. Something wasn't right, and Rith still followed her with cold eyes. She shuddered thinking about it.

Her thoughts once more turned to Fiona, as they often had throughout the day. Fiona had begged for her help—but what could Parisa do when she was just as much a prisoner in Rith's home as Fiona was?

She rubbed her arms again trying to soothe her fiery nerves.

Yeah, what could she do?

Fiona rarely fought the bindings, but tonight she couldn't help it. She didn't care how many times the female assistant, the one with the cruel black eyes, slapped her and hit her. She didn't want to give her blood one more time. She didn't want to die again. She didn't want to come back from the dead again.

She fought until she felt a sharp prick deep into the muscle of her upper arm. She turned to her left and watched the young male assistant depress the plunger on a syringe. She blinked up at him. He was the one new to the job, the one who perspired into his surgical mask. She'd heard him vomiting more than once. Good.

Except . . . she heard their words now as from a great distance, and though she tried to swing her arms away from their grappling hands, she couldn't. She felt her arms strapped down hard to the table. She heard the evil woman laugh like a monster, chortling deep and long. She felt the prick on the inside of her right elbow, then the left side.

They would drain her from the right, then start refilling

her from the left. Her eyes closed. She felt so sleepy. Maybe this was a good thing, a good way to die. She even smiled.

The next thing she knew she stood in a strange place and it was night, although there seemed to be light coming from somewhere. She looked around. She didn't know where she was. She wore the usual, a tank top and pajama bottoms, nothing else, not even shoes, never shoes. How could a slave escape without shoes?

A man sat on a bench, a rather smallish man with gray hair. He cooed low in his throat and tossed sunflower seeds to a group of birds clustered around his feet. Pigeons. Black ones, white ones, brown ones, and every mix between. She wrinkled her nose. She'd never cared for pigeons. They nested in every crook and corner of every city in the world.

"You must go back, Fiona."

The man spoke. He lifted his eyes to her. They were ancient eyes, not lined exactly but surely he had seen a lot of life, much more than her 125 years.

"I'm going home this time," she said. How surprised she was by the strength in her voice, the determination. "Today is my daughter's birthday. She would have been one hundred and seven. Yes, I know. She was mortal and would be long since buried in the earth, but don't you see"—she felt herself smile—"there is nothing for me here. And I'm tired, so very tired. Yes, I want to go home."

He tilted his head. His lips were compressed and grim. "We each have a job to do, Fiona. Yours is to live, and I can promise you that something extraordinary awaits you if you'll but try."

Her gaze fell to the pigeons. She shook her head. "Do you know what I've endured?"

"No, because I've never had to suffer as you're suffering. I've had my own trials, of course. Every human, ascended or otherwise, has trials to endure, some worse than others. But I beseech you to hold on just a little longer. You must live. Think of the young pregnant woman who came in three days ago."

"She will lose her baby," Fiona said. Her voice sounded

flat. "The baby never survives the mother's first death and resurrection."

He nodded. "I understand that's how it must be."

"Then why should I return?"

"There is a chance she and the baby will survive if you return."

She shook her head. "No, I've lost the will to go back." She felt a tremor flow through her, a deep ache in the center of her chest. She pressed a fist between her breasts. She could hardly breathe. "It's begun. They're using the defibrillator now."

The man rose to his feet. He wasn't very tall, maybe five foot seven to her five-ten. She tried to take a step back but couldn't move. She glanced down and laughed. She didn't have any feet. She must be just in spirit form right now. How strange. Maybe she was having one of those near-death experiences.

Another tremor slammed through her. She cried out. She was in pain now. Terrible pain.

The man moved quickly and stood beside her. He held her arm and looked deeply into her eyes. "I am begging you with all my heart to go back, Fiona, to live just one more time. Please. It is imperative. You must live. You must try. Do it for the young pregnant woman. She and the others will not survive without your presence. You know what you mean to them. You know how many you kept alive."

"But they all died anyway throughout the years. I'm the only one who's lived this long."

"You can stop the death and resurrection process, Fiona, but only if you live. Live, Fiona. Live." His words seemed fainter, his presence less distinct.

She took a deep breath and another. A third tremor seized her. The pain felt infinite. She doubled over. She recalled the young woman's eyes, the latest of Rith's acquisitions, her fear, her hand pressed to her swollen belly. Could she save her?

Will you try? She couldn't see the man anymore, or the pigeons. She could only hear his voice, and even then it was as though he'd spoken inside her head.

Fiona's stubbornness sank into the well of her usual guilt. She had to try. She could do nothing less.

When the fourth shock pummeled her heart, she began to claw her way back from death.

When the walls have fallen down,
Open your voice and let your cries be heard.
Heaven will answer the faint of heart.

—*Collected Proverbs,* Beatrice of Fourth

CHAPTER 6

Parisa sat up in bed. Something was wrong, so very wrong.

Help me.

Fiona. She could hear her. The woman was in trouble somewhere in this horrible house.

Parisa couldn't leave her room or the women would wake. They would tell Rith, and he would hurt her. She rarely traveled voyeuristically through the rooms, searching, but she did so now. She had to find Fiona.

She opened her voyeur's window and traveled into the hall. The women were lined up in a row on the floor, all asleep, each head aimed in the direction of her doorway. Better to hear her if she awoke.

She moved her window past them until she came to Rith's office. She paused outside the doorway to listen. She heard a soft rasping sound. She moved her window into place and saw Rith in the corner, his back to the doorway. His right elbow was moving rhythmically, his head bowed, his body tense. At first she thought *sex,* but then he lifted something into the air that glinted in the lamplight of the room.

A blade. He'd been sharpening a blade. He tested the chiseled edge with his thumb and smiled.

She backed her window out of the room and realized she was breathing hard, her heart pounding in her chest. Was he coming for her? She had no way of knowing except that her instincts were screaming.

Whatever. Right now she needed to find Fiona.

She moved past the doorway to the end of the hall. She hadn't been beyond this doorway in life and for some reason, she couldn't move past doors like this. She couldn't explore a place she had never been.

So she focused instead on Fiona. Having seen her, having been with her in the garden, there was a good possibility she'd be able to find Fiona through the special window.

She closed her eyes and concentrated. She relaxed her mind and focused on the beautiful woman with the chestnut hair and silver-blue eyes.

The window opened again, but in a completely unknown space. She seemed to be at the far end of a long stone hallway lit by three large overhead round globes. Parisa moved slowly down the hall and panned left and right. Women of all nationalities were held in the cells, all curled in the fetal position, all asleep. There were six in all, but a seventh bed was empty.

The space expanded to include a large glass-enclosed area, maybe fourteen feet by fourteen, large enough to hold a table upon which a woman was strapped down, several carts of what looked like medical equipment flanking the stone wall, and a man and a woman both in medical scrubs standing nearby.

Her heart pounded again as she brought her window closer and closer to the room. She became focused on the woman on the table, whose hair was a lovely flowing chestnut. Fiona . . . who stared up at the ceiling, her eyes glassy, her skin terribly white. She looked . . . dead.

No, no, no.

Beside the bed were bags of . . . blood. Fiona's blood.

A faint alarm went off. The technician standing to the right of the bed, a man, held the familiar paddles of a defibrillator. Another sweep of the room and Parisa saw that a bag of blood was now flowing into Fiona's arm, apparently to replenish what had been taken from her. The technician to the left of the bed capped off the drained blood. They were quiet as they worked.

Two more technicians, also wearing scrubs, arrived by an adjoining hallway. They loaded up Fiona's blood into two separate large Igloo containers. Within a minute they were gone.

Talk about an efficient process.

She panned back to Fiona. The remaining two technicians, a man and a woman, performed basic CPR and occasionally jolted Fiona's bared white chest with the defibrillator. There was such an air of boredom surrounding the woman that for her it must have been the same-old, same-old. The man was sweating. Not so indifferent.

The woman took a loaded syringe and stuck the needle into a connector to the IV. She waited, glanced at the man with the paddles. She nodded once. Fiona got hit again, hard, her body bouncing on the table.

She had to be dead. Her lips were blue.

Then her chest rose and fell. Parisa could hear a groan. Fiona's eyes rolled in her head.

The woman still looked bored. The man put the paddles back onto the machine.

The woman struck Fiona a few times across the cheek and yelled at her.

Fiona's eyes opened, rolled a little more. The woman held a cup to her mouth, the contents of which were red. Fiona tried to fight it and the liquid, very thick, rolled down her chin and onto her bare breasts.

"No," Fiona whispered. "Please, no."

The woman slapped her a few more times. The man grabbed her arms and pinned her. They forced her mouth open and succeeded pouring the liquid . . . had to be blood . . .

down her throat. Fiona coughed and sputtered. They released her.

But the blood was magical. Color returned in a swift wave over Fiona's body, and within seconds she was the picture of health. A few seconds more and she writhed on the bed and moaned. The woman laughed at her but released the restraints.

Fiona pressed her arm deep between her thighs and turned on her side as she worked her arm back and forth. A few seconds more and she cried out. What had they given her?

Oh. God.

If Parisa understood what had happened, Fiona had just orgasmed, hard. What kind of blood was that?

A few minutes later, the techs gathered up all the medical equipment, turned the lights out, and left her on the table. Parisa drew close to the woman and looked down into her face. The soft light from the hallway lamps revealed dull eyes and no tears.

Parisa waited with Fiona. To leave seemed cruel. She couldn't converse with her, reach her, or comfort her, but she understood her despair so she stayed.

"I can feel someone there," Fiona whispered. "I don't know how, but I can."

Parisa jumped, and her window flickered. She brought it quickly back in focus.

"I must have startled you. I'm not sure who you are or why you're watching me, perhaps you're the woman in the garden. Your name is Parisa, right? I felt your power when we clasped arms. If this is you, please help me. My name is Fiona Gaines and I was taken from Boston in 1902. I was one of the first that Rith experimented on. I'm a D and R slave: death and resurrection. Although, Rith usually calls us blood donors. So clever. Please find me and take me out of here. I'm begging you. Please." Her eyes closed. "I don't know if I can do this again. Please." She released a heavy sigh. Not long after, she fell asleep.

Parisa waited for a few minutes then explored the space a little more. Opposite the large glass-enclosed room was a staircase that probably led up to Rith's home. She was sure of it when the door at the top of the stairs opened and Rith appeared. He looked down into the room. He waited for a moment, then, apparently satisfied with what he saw, he closed the door.

.   Parisa in turn closed her preternatural window. Fully back in her room, she stared at the wall opposite her bed. The familiar statue of Buddha greeted her. She had come to love the gentle, peaceful expression on the man's face. Rith had told her that the statue was from Mandalay and very old, over a hundred years now, and made of brass. This Buddha was lean, peaceful, intelligent looking. She always felt calmer when she looked at him.

What would Buddha do?

The thought made her laugh. Still, inherent in the absurd question was something she needed to know.

Yes, what would Buddha do?

If Buddha had just witnessed what Parisa had seen through her voyeur's window, what would he do?

The next question made perfect sense: *What would Parisa do?*

She kept staring at the statue and thinking of Fiona. She could draw only one conclusion about what she had just witnessed, and the thoughts that now ripped through her mind made her sick. She put a hand to her mouth and took a few deep breaths.

Rith had somehow perfected the process of killing these women—in order to harvest dying blood—then bringing them back to life to do it all over again. She did the math. One hundred and twenty-five years. Fiona had given dying blood for 125 years. She'd been kept prisoner, in this house, for over a century, held captive by Rith.

Parisa tried to conceive of an incarceration that long. She had only been held prisoner for three months, and already she saw the signs of her captivity: her lack of appetite, a hateful sense of powerlessness, and a steady diminishing of her will.

That Fiona, after 125 years, had attempted an escape meant something.

Parisa's heart rate rose. New thoughts began to flow through her mind—of her *royle* wings, of her preternatural voyeurism, of her emerging powers. Yes, Rith was powerful, but so was she. So it was possible that her sense of helplessness in this situation was an illusion. No one held a knife to her throat, just the threat of one.

Still, if she started down this road, she needed to admit one thing to herself, here and now: She could die. She had felt Rith's inexplicable rage toward her. She could sense his desire to harm her, and given his belief that slavery was a perfect fit for the female mind and soul, there was no reason to believe he wouldn't kill her. If only for defying him.

The world began to look different to her. Even the mahogany floor gleamed a little brighter, and the moon pouring through the slatted blinds laid brilliant stripes on the wall.

She put her hand between her breasts. She could feel her heart beating out a strong cadence, tougher than before, more purposeful, more hopeful, *resolved*.

Something had happened to her while watching Fiona's terrible ordeal, some internal change she had not planned— but oh, how she welcomed what she felt. Above all, if she could help Fiona, then she would do whatever she had to do . . . tonight.

She pushed back the tightly secured top sheet then slid her legs over the edge of the bed until she could feel the cool polished wood beneath her bare feet. She looked down and wiggled her toes. Then she flexed her back muscles. Time to fly.

Somewhere among all the events of the day, change had come to Parisa. From this moment forward, her life would be different, whether she lived as an ascended vampire or as a winged mortal.

But where she lived no longer seemed important.

On the other hand, what she did seemed like everything.

She listened for the sounds of the servants. The women

were quiet on their mats, hopefully asleep. One of them was snoring, a good sign.

She stood up, slid her nightgown off her shoulders, and let it fall to the floor. For what she was about to do, she needed her back unencumbered. And yes, for what she was about to do, she would be perfectly naked since she couldn't risk moving around the room or opening armoire doors to find a haltered dress to wear. Any of those noises would awaken the servants, which would be a disaster. She understood their loyalty quite well. If they even discovered she was out of bed, she'd be in for it.

She kept very still as she cleared her mind and began to focus. She opened her voyeur's window, thought one powerful thought about Antony, and found him at the Cave with the battle-weary Warriors of the Blood. A quick pan around the room told her they were all there, all except Marcus, who probably had the night off. Jean-Pierre sat next to Antony on an enormous brown leather couch against the back wall.

Antony was staring at the floor, and he looked really mad.

Jean-Pierre said, "So we are waiting now to hear from Jeannie for news from Burma." Jeannie's name sounded soft and beautiful on Jean-Pierre's French tongue.

"Yep." Antony flicked the hilt of the knife on his chest. He'd been battling, she could see that, but to her surprise he wore a kilt and a weapons harness, which meant he'd revealed his scarred-up back to his warrior brothers. Wow. What on earth had shifted in the past few hours to have wrought such a huge change in the warrior?

But the question was, could she communicate with him telepathically? After months of trying and failing, could she do it now?

She smiled. Yes, things had changed within her.

Antony, she sent, hard and forceful.

She watched him sit up. *Parisa?* he returned. He scowled and looked around.

I'm here. Outside Mandalay. I'm flying through Rith's double dome of mist and you'd better be here. Now repeat what I just said. Say it to Jean-Pierre who's sitting next to you.

He turned to Jean-Pierre. "I've just heard from Parisa." He tapped his head. "She's flying through two domes of mist, she's near Mandalay, and I'd better get my ass over there."

Jean-Pierre's eyes went wide.

Telepathically, Antony sent, *When are you doing this?*

In about two minutes.

Shit. I'm coming.

"Let's rumble," he said aloud, jumping to his feet.

Medichi looked at his warrior brothers. They'd battled all night and everyone was exhausted. Havily had come and gone with some coffee and pastries so they'd tanked up, but still. Were they up for this?

"Parisa's escaping . . . now. She just told me, in my head."

All movement ceased. Bodies rose slowly off stools and leather couches.

"Where?" Zacharius cried. "Where is she?"

"Mandalay, Burma. Second Earth. Shit. What do I do?" But as soon as the words left his mouth, he whipped his card-like warrior phone from his pocket and thumbed Central.

"Central," Jeannie's voice came on the line. "How can I serve?"

"Jeannie, I've just heard from Parisa. She's in Mandalay."

"Holy shit." He heard tapping. "I'm moving the grid as we speak. There we go. There we go. Give me a minute, probably less."

"Hurry, Jeannie. We're in trouble."

He focused on Parisa and sent, *You've got to narrow this down for us if you can. Which side of the city?*

Just past the outskirts at the southern end.

"Southern end," he said into the phone. To Parisa, he sent, *Are you on Second Earth?* He wanted to be sure.

Yes. But Antony, there's something you must know. Rith keeps other women here, as blood slaves. I saw how he did it. He causes their deaths while he harvests their blood, then he brings them back to life. One of the women, Fiona, was abducted from Boston. She's been here since 1886. Can you get her out as well? All of them?

Oh, God. Blood slaves. So they existed. Now it all started making sense, how Greaves was able to turn so many High Administrators as well as members of COPASS. He must be using these women to provide dying blood. There had been rumors for years. Now there was proof.

But as much as he wanted to, he couldn't make these unknown women his priority. He knew nothing about Rith's security setup, or the layout of the building, nothing. And right now, Parisa was his primary concern.

I'll talk it over with Thorne. But we're going to take this one step at a time. Let's get you out of there first.

Right. Right.

God, had it really happened? And how had Parisa been able to speak into his head? What had changed? What had happened to make the impossible possible? But then who cared? *I'm on my way.*

To Jeannie, he said, "Listen, Parisa spoke of being beneath two domes of mist. I know her signature doesn't show up on the international grid, but Rith's might. He's a powerful SOB. Maybe that will show up on the grid as something unusual. Do you have Mandalay in front of you?"

"Yes. Scanning the southern sector now. Come on. Come on."

To his brothers, he said, "And which of you is coming with?"

As one, they drew into a half circle around him, Jean-Pierre beside him. Words weren't necessary. His chest took their joint support and loyalty as a heavy-fisted blow. Shit, his eyes burned. He glanced at Thorne. No one could go anywhere without his permission.

All the warriors turned toward him. Thorne's mouth was a thin grim line, but he nodded and said, "We all go."

Medichi lifted his chin. "We'll materialize nearby and I can't tell you what to expect. I don't know if we'll face death vampires or what."

"Fuck, yeah!" Luken cried. "Bring 'em on!"

"Jeannie," he pleaded into the phone.

"I think I've found it. It's enormous—it's like the time Kerrick went to that medical complex and a huge part of the parking lot was held in some kind of misted disguise. I thought only Greaves had this kind of power. No wonder Rith was able to take her. And did you say a double dome of mist? Holy crap."

Medichi ignored this speech, one of the longest he'd ever heard Jeannie make. He addressed the only important element. "You've got seven to fold."

He glanced at them all, overwhelmed by the support the brotherhood gave him. Jean-Pierre nodded. Luken put a fist against his chest. Zacharius and Santiago, almost as one, took their daggers from their weapons harnesses and held them aloft. Kerrick smiled, that knowing look that only a warrior caught in the *breh-hedden* could possibly offer, a look full of sympathy and hope. Thorne's jaw worked. "Let's go get your woman."

Jeannie gave a cry. "I've got the coordinates. But there's one powerful signature there. Has to be Rith. You boys ready?"

"Shit, yes, Jeannie."

We're on our way, Parisa.

I'm outta here, she sent.

Medichi took a deep breath. "Fold us now, Jeannie."

The vibration began.

Parisa slipped past the three servants outside her room, moving on tiptoes until she was outside on the back lawn of the garden. A gentle rain descended through the air, which meant beyond the domes a real storm could be pounding the land. Oh, shit. Then again, she didn't really care. The time had come. Rith had it in for her and Fiona needed someone to get her out of her blood-slavery prison.

Her heart beat like a jackhammer, and serious vibrations rocked her chest. She panted and almost couldn't catch her breath. It occurred to her that if she didn't calm down she'd never be able to mount her wings—and *up* was the only way out of this prison.

She'd been testing the interior dome of mist for weeks now, rippling her hand as she flew. There was nothing about it that felt impenetrable. She just hoped the second dome was as forgiving.

From what she had experienced with mist, however, its purpose wasn't so much physical as a mind-bending disguise.

Besides, even if she struck a brick wall traveling at top flying speed, she just didn't care. She'd made her decision. She was leaving her captivity now.

She closed her eyes and focused on the apertures of her back. She blocked everything else out. She felt the weeping begin, the release of fluid that would allow the feathers and superstructure to emerge. She smiled.

She voyeured Medichi and her heart leaped. He stood on the bank of a rice paddy, the Warriors of the Blood flanking him on either side. A storm raged and as lightning flashed, lighting up the night sky, he suddenly looked like a god, so tall, muscular, his expression fierce.

Antony? she sent in that new forceful way.

Parisa, are you ready? We're here, all the brothers. We're waiting for you. I can see the dome of mist. Are you safe?

Yes. I'll be flying straight out the top, but you'd better come get me. I'm not wearing anything.

She closed the window and shut her mind down.

"What are you doing, Parisa?" Rith's voice spoke calmly from the doorway.

"I'm ready to fly."

"In the nude? This is repulsive behavior. Besides, it's raining. Put some clothes on first." His English really was perfect.

"Sure," she said. She enjoyed speaking the lie. She closed her eyes and willed her wings to come with a single thought.

Out they flew straight from her back, into full-mount in an easy motion she had never known before. Hells, yeah! *She had changed.*

She launched and flew straight for the top. She heard growling behind her, and a quick glance showed her that Rith had stripped off his shirt and was even now mounting his wings.

Oh, God.

She smashed through the interior dome of mist. Rain struck her face and dragged at her wings, but she beat them frantically. As she headed toward the second dome, she kept feeling a hand grabbing for her feet.

She plowed through the second barrier and the storm hit her full in the face. Rain and wind caught her wings, sending her spinning. She worked to remember what Havily had taught her. She stretched one wing out, brought in the other and leveled, but the wind caught her again and sent her into a second spin. At the same time, the rain pounded her.

Once she righted herself, she saw Rith heading straight for her.

She began to tumble again back toward the dome of mist. But before she had gotten far, she saw that it wasn't Rith at all, but Medichi who flew toward her, his wings huge, rain beating on him, his face more determined than she'd ever seen him. She concentrated and pulled one wing in briefly then fluffed them both. The tumbling stopped and she righted herself even though she pitched back and forth in the wind. She shivered.

The next moment Medichi was next to her and took hold of her hand. He became a tremendous anchor. Even though she pitched about wildly, she knew he would hold her steady.

He didn't say anything. He just started pulling her into the wind very gently, then down slowly toward the earth.

"Bring your wings into close-mount if you can," he shouted above the noise of the storm. "That's it. Yes, keep doing that." She struggled to bring her wings in and not flip over or start to roll to one side or the other. She was soaked head-to-toe, feather-to-feather.

She kept her gaze fixed on him, nothing else. He was so powerful and manipulated his wings with centuries of experience as though each sudden shift of wind, each onslaught of rain were but a bump. The adjustments he made were brisk, small, and kept him floating in the air without the smallest sign of distress.

She, on the other hand, felt like she was in a washing machine on the agitation cycle.

Lightning flashed through the sky above. She gasped and almost lost her equilibrium again—but this time for a different reason. Antony's cream-colored wings were streaked through with reds and oranges, blues and greens, as though lit on fire. The colors moved, flying from feather to feather in a pattern of ever-changing flames. Strands of his hair had come loose from the ritual *cadroen* and flew about his face. He looked like Zeus half standing and half floating in the air, his hand extended to her.

The closer she drew her wings to her body, the more she started to lose altitude, but he held her aloft. "Now the rest of the way and I'll catch you."

She had to trust him but she gave a cry as she drew her wings in to close-mount position and started to fall. Then he caught her very gently around the full circumference of her wings, shifting to cradle her in his arms. His concentration was fierce as he battled the monsoon. He headed toward the earth, diving closer and closer to the ground, toward the rest of the Warriors of the Blood, all in black leather kilts and harnesses.

Closer. Closer. When his feet touched the ground, she closed her eyes and sighed. Tears dribbled from her rain-soaked face.

She watched as Medichi brought his wings into his back, awkwardly at times because of the weather.

Her nakedness was covered by her wings as he set her on the ground. "You have to draw your wings in before we can fold out of here."

She glanced at all the warriors. "I . . . I'm not wearing anything." Then she laughed. Who cared? She was outside the prison she had endured for three months, and she was still alive. Antony was holding her in his arms. What else mattered?

"You'll be okay," he said.

She nodded and smiled. Rain ran down his face. She touched his cheek just to make sure he was real. He turned into her hand and kissed the tips of her fingers. She felt him sigh.

When he set her on her feet and she begun unfurling her wings, he lowered himself to his knees, still facing her, and put his arms around her in order to shield her chest and support her against the wind and rain. In the glow of each bolt of lightning, the scars of his back were visible, a sheet of silvery lines and ridges.

She put her hands on his back, splaying her fingers. She closed her eyes and with the wind whipping her wings around began what turned out to be a painfully slow process of bringing her wings into her back.

The warriors didn't pay attention to her. They moved to form a protective circle all around her, facing outward, swords drawn in case the enemy attacked.

At long last, her wings finally retracted. But as the powerful ripples that formed her wings from nothing began to settle into her muscles, Rith appeared at the top of the dome, his wings barely moving. He retreated into the mist when he saw Antony and the other warriors.

"Do I take the bastard?" Santiago cried.

Thorne grunted. "No. We're here to get Parisa home safe. That's all that matters right now."

As Medichi rose and encircled her in his arms, lightning set his face aglow. A long roll of thunder powered over the land.

She looked up into his face as he petted her cheek.

Jean-Pierre shouted into his phone. "We have her, Jeannie. Bring us home. To the front lawn of Medichi's villa."

Parisa closed her eyes.

The villa. She had dreamed of Antony's home for weeks.

The vibration began, followed by the long, swift glide through nether-space.

The moment Medichi felt the front patio of his villa beneath his heavy battle sandals, he didn't wait to speak with any of the warriors materializing around him. His woman was completely nude, soaked, and shivering.

"It's daytime here," she murmured through chattering teeth.

"Yes, it is," he said.

"Of course."

He moved to the entrance, shoved the massive door aside, and once in the foyer slammed it shut behind him. He took long brisk steps as he carried her down the hall to his bedroom.

He took her straight to the shower, fearing she was cold. He flipped on the row of lights above the broad mirror but turned the dimmer down low. With her still clutched in his arms, he shifted her to one arm with her feet dangling off the floor. She didn't protest.

He turned the water on and set all eight heads to flowing. Only then did he dare set her on her feet, draw her face away from his chest, and look at her.

She tilted her head back. "Antony," she whispered. She was soaked and trembling. "We have to go back for them."

He smiled because it wasn't what he expected her to say. He expected her to rail against her captivity, maybe even to thank him for showing up. Instead, she was concerned about the fate of other women.

He nodded. "Thorne and I discussed it while we waited for you outside the domes. Jeannie's doing a satellite feed to see if Rith brought any death vampires in. If not, the warriors are headed back."

"Oh, good. Good." Her teeth chattered.

She needed to get warm. Maybe it was shock, or maybe she was just chilled. Maybe both. Didn't matter.

He still had on his leather battle flight gear. He thought about folding it off, but he didn't want to scare her by having a suddenly naked man in the shower with her.

"How's the temp?" he asked as she held out her hand to the water.

"Good."

Only then did he turn her so that her back could feel the spray. She nodded and put her hands palms-up behind her.

She wiggled her fingers. "Oh, that feels good." She took a step into the spray.

He smiled and stepped away . . . about three inches. He knew she needed space, probably wanted space, but he couldn't seem to make himself move. He just stood there, his back and kilt getting hit by the spray.

She just looked at him, her amethyst eyes dark in the low-lit room. She moved back another inch and tilted her head so that the water flowed down her hair. She closed her eyes. She looked . . . dreamy.

He made a big mistake but couldn't seem to help himself. He took a long journey down her neck, down her chest, and came to a full stop at her breasts. He had forgotten just how, well, stacked she was. And his eyes bulged.

Her breasts were drawn into tight peaks. Kissable peaks. Suckable peaks.

Oh, shit. In his urgency to make her safe, to get her the hell out of Burma, he'd forgotten about this part of the arrangement, the mind-numbing need he had to possess her body.

His gaze fell farther and his lips tingled as he watched rivulets of water circle, run into, then fall away from the most beautiful navel in the world. A shallow lake formed at the base of her belly button; he wanted his tongue right there, sucking the water into his mouth.

His gaze wandered a little more, down and down, landing on the nest of her hair and staying there.

Only then did he realize the steamy room had filled with a delicate tangerine scent. Only then did he remember what his presence did to her. Only then did he nearly double over in agony as a sudden fierce erection fought with his kilt and the snug briefs he wore under it.

Jesus H. Christ.

First love,
Oh, the thrill
But savor what may not last.
Yes, savor.

—**Collected Proverbs**, Beatrice of Fourth

CHAPTER 7

Parisa was right where she wanted to be, more than any place in the entire world . . . in two worlds.

She smiled and let the warm water heat up her chilled skin. She took a deep breath and there it was, the one thing she could not experience when she voyeured Antony: his sage scent. The strong masculine smell pierced her brain and sent shivers over her entire body.

Her knees buckled and she would have fallen but he was suddenly there and caught her. He still wore his black leather kilt and battle sandals in the shower, but her hands landed on his bare chest. "Are you all right?"

She nodded. Sort of. He was pressed up against her. She could feel him, all of him. His erection was a hard line up past her belly button. His height and long legs put her at a disadvantage unless she wore heels, stilettos maybe. She'd always felt gangly at five-eleven but his height made her feel petite. "My knees sort of gave out." She couldn't tell him why because suddenly her cheeks were on fire.

He had been her fantasy for well over a year now, from the moment she had first voyeured him. She had thought of him as belonging to her, even all those times she'd watched him take women into the red velvet booths at that naughty club, the Blood and Bite. She understood the needs of a man and she felt his need right now.

The only question was, what was she going to do about it?

Three months ago, she had been prepared to leave him behind—the world of ascension had been too brutal for her. She had intended to refuse ascension and return to her quiet, solitary library life.

But three months in captivity, added to her discovery of what Fiona Gaines had endured since the late 1800s, had shifted something inside her.

She couldn't go back to Mortal Earth, not now, not ever. It wasn't so much that she believed she belonged on Second Earth; rather, she had a job to do, and she could only do it if she chose this world here and now. Maybe choosing ascension would mean an eternity with Antony, maybe it wouldn't. But right now she wasn't choosing Antony, she was choosing a sense of duty and purpose.

But how did this man, this *fantasy of maleness,* fit into her change of heart? She just didn't know. The thought of being with him in a real sense, not a fantasy, frightened her—and not because he was powerful. What frightened her was how vulnerable she felt when she was with him, as though the real power he had over her was that he could hold her heart in his hand and crush it, something she had not allowed from anyone since her fiancé had walked out on her. She had kept her heart close and safe in the same way she'd kept her friends at a distance.

She had learned from an early age to live a life of independence.

But now she was here, in Antony's shower, with his arms wrapped around her holding her up. From the moment she had first seen him, she'd wanted to kiss him, to press her lips to his beautiful mouth, to see what it would be like to be connected in that very simple way to this powerful warrior.

He looked down at her now, his arms tense behind her back, his nostrils flaring, but he seemed frozen. Perhaps he sensed her reticence, or maybe he was just being considerate after all she'd been through.

So she moved. She slid her arm up and around his neck, his thick, muscled warrior neck. His hair was trapped in the *cadroen*. She leaned up on tiptoes. She drew very close to his face. He searched her eyes.

"So beautiful" came as a soft murmur, a gentle waterfall from his lips.

She pressed her mouth to his, just so, not hard, not gentle, a first meeting, an invitation, a decision.

He trembled. She felt it all down his body, in every place he was connected to her.

He moaned and his body moved serpent-like, a fluid motion of sensation. His arms traveled around her even more, gathering her close. She drifted her mouth from side to side, and his lips parted. She kept drifting until she took his breath into her body and all that sage traveled into her lungs.

His scent rose inside up and up, then penetrated her brain. She weaved on her feet.

One of his arms left her back, and he shut off the water. "Will you come to my bed?"

The decision was already made. She couldn't deny the man who had saved her life, who had saved her sanity during a period of incarceration, who smelled of heaven and earth blended into one.

She nodded.

He backed out of the shower, still holding her close. Was he afraid she would vanish from his arms? But then why wouldn't he be? She had done that already when Rith took her from his villa. He had told her of his fears. He had told her during those wicked moments of self-pleasure when he knew she was close but couldn't hear her.

Antony, she sent now.

He grabbed a towel and wrapped it around her, never losing eye contact or physical connection. *I hear you.*

Can you hear all my words now? Can you hear every thought I send? Tell me in a way that I can understand.

He smiled, and the tenderness in his eyes and in the curve of his lips made something deep within her chest begin to burn with life. "I can hear every thought you send, Parisa."

She sent, *Every damn fucking horrible thought?* She dared him to hear her and to repeat her words.

The curve became a smile, a grin, a promise of the future. "Yes. Every damn fucking horrible thought. But Parisa, what happened? How did you suddenly find your telepathic voice? It seemed like a miracle. But how?"

She threw her arms around his neck and held him close. "I don't want to talk about it, not yet. Oh, Antony, you came for me. You came for me."

"Of course I did." The towel fell to the floor as he enveloped her in his powerful arms and pulled her against him.

She almost couldn't breathe, but she didn't care. She had been breathing and alone for the past three months. Let him suffocate her with his nearness, with his embrace, with his musky sage scent.

She turned her face into him. Leaning up on tiptoes, she licked his skin right below his ear. He tasted like something she should eat. She bit and nibbled and he held her tight. He lifted her off her feet and waggled her legs in the air. He turned her in a circle.

"There is something I must know," he said. He set her down and looked into her eyes. All the sudden joy had left his face.

"No," she said, understanding the question before he spoke the words. "He did not touch me. No one touched me. I am unharmed in that way." Because she saw the doubt in his eyes, she added, "Rith did not violate me, nor did any of his people."

"You were never harmed," he stated.

He stared into her eyes. She knew she could withhold nothing from him. That would be an unforgivable cruelty in her opinion.

"Tell me what your eyes are saying," he said. "Speak the words."

"Rith *disciplined* me into obedience. He invaded my mind when I displeased him. It hurt. Badly. I learned very quickly to do as I was told and to follow the schedule. Rith was very big on schedules."

His jaw worked until it became a tremor. He began to shake until he had to release her. His hands formed fists and he lifted his head and released a cry to the ceiling. He cried out again and again. The cries became howls until the mirror shattered and fell straight down onto the black marble sink.

Only then, as the glass fell, did the anguish seem to expel from his body.

She moved toward him. His eyes were glazed, sunken, his cheeks gaunt. He needed time to heal as much as she did.

She put her hands on his chest. She rubbed his skin and let her fingers drift over the fine black hair between his pecs, something she had wanted to do for so long. She bent her head and began to kiss the round, fierce strength of his muscles. She licked and kissed and stroked. She lowered her cheek and rubbed her face against his chest. His hands rested lightly on her shoulders.

His body grew stiff and unyielding. "I failed you," he said. His voice had a dead quality. He had retreated someplace very dark.

She dipped lower and ran her tongue over his nipple. Then she bit him. Hard.

He pulled back and cried out. A heavy scowl rode his face, pulling down. "What was that for?"

"Apparently, you think you need to be punished for not being all-powerful. So I punished you."

A half laugh broke from his throat, but he shook his head. "You don't know what it was like."

"And you don't know what it was like for me. I survived without going mad because I could turn to you day or night and see you, voyeur you. And every night when I went to bed, we'd make love even though we couldn't touch. I'm alive, my mind is functioning, because of you."

"If I hadn't been lax that day . . . I allowed you to wander too far away from me. I had my back to you while I talked to Thorne. I was foolish. If it had been anyone other than Rith, you could have been raped, or worse."

His eyes grew distant once more. Instinctively, she knew that he wasn't just thinking about her and his failure to keep her safe on his property. But wherever he had gone pissed her off. She had no intention of letting his memories affect this moment, or her gratitude, or her desire.

She stepped back from him. Using both hands, she cupped her breasts and rubbed her thumbs in slow circles over her nipples.

He blinked and frowned. "What are you doing?"

"You know what I'm doing. But you didn't get to watch me. I was the voyeur. I saw your long fingers work your cock but you couldn't see me. I want you to watch this time. I want you to see what I did to myself. It's only fair."

He drew in a long deep breath. His gaze fell to her breasts and her thumbs. A heavy wave of sage rolled over her; she had to step back to keep her balance. She smiled.

"Tangerine," he murmured.

"I know that's what you smell, Antony, when I'm near. You suck the tangerines, because that's what I would taste like in your mouth, that's why you plunge your tongue inside while you come. Tell me I'm right."

"Yes." He blinked several times. "Don't do this. We should talk, figure everything else out. This . . . this can't be wise."

She moved one of her hands slowly down her belly and used a finger to rim her belly button. "I want your tongue here."

He groaned. Good.

She moved her hand lower, descending, now sifting her fingers through her dark triangle of hair. She spread her legs and another groan flowed from him.

He tracked the movement, breathing hard. The smell of sage was so thick in the air that she could taste it on her tongue.

She leaned forward just a little, slid her finger lower, and dipped it into the core of her body. "This is what I did,

Antony. I pretended this was you, sometimes your cock, sometimes your finger, sometimes your mouth." She closed her eyes and moaned.

When she heard a growl, she opened her eyes, but he hadn't moved. She spread her legs a little more and kept working her finger in and out. She was enjoying the sensation—but what turned her on more was the look that slowly reworked his face. His eyes darkened. His nostrils flared as he sucked in air hard. His fangs emerged.

Oh, God, his fangs. Her neck throbbed with need in direct response to the muscles of her core. She licked her lips.

Pleasure now flowed through her and intensified. She was so wet. "Antony," she whispered. Her gaze skated over his broad shoulders, the sculpted muscles of his pecs, his abs, the lines leading to his groin, the heavy strength of his thighs. She was breathing so hard just looking at him. But when a growl filled the space between them, an orgasm swept over her with such force that she staggered as she cried out.

He moved to her in a blur, caught her, dragged her against him. He kissed her hard, thrusting his tongue deep into her mouth. His hips drew back and she watched the kilt and briefs disappear, folded somewhere. He was suddenly naked. Just what she wanted.

She couldn't look anywhere but at the size of his cock, at the veins thick and doing what they did best. She still couldn't breathe. He picked her up. With a wave of his hand, all the glass shards drifted to the far corner of the sink, a sound like rain. He drew a towel from the rack by the shower and set it down. He planted her bottom on the towel then pushed her legs apart and moved his hips between.

She settled her hands on his shoulders. Her mind had turned to mush. "Do it, Antony," she whispered. "I need you." Damn, she felt ready to cry for no reason, but she had wanted this for such a long time.

He held his cock in his hand and breathed hard, his chest expanding with each breath. Her hips rocked. She reached down and touched him. He groaned and flinched.

"Shit," he murmured.

He was holding back. She thought she understood why but she didn't care. Right now, he belonged to her. She didn't care what happened afterward.

She scooted to the edge of the counter, using his shoulder to keep her balance. Sliding her legs around his hips, she rocked her pelvis forward, took his cock in her hand, and guided him to her opening. She made little grunts between pants and cries. "Do it," she cried.

He shuddered and began to press into her. He moaned as inch by inch he made his way into her body. He was so damn big and she hadn't been used in a long time but it was wonderful.

"You feel so good," she cried.

"I don't want to hurt you but . . . aw, hell." He grabbed her buttocks with one hand and shoved into her . . . hard.

She cried out. Maybe it hurt a little; she couldn't tell.

"God, you're so wet."

"What else would I be?"

His mouth landed on her neck, and he began to suck at her skin. She started maneuvering his lips. She knew what she wanted, where she wanted his mouth. She bent her neck sideways, and when his lips landed over her vein she cried out.

His hips surged forward then pulled back. Her body shed fluid. He glided, stroked, pushed and pulled. Heaven.

His tongue rasped over her vein now, long smooth glides. "Is this what you want?"

"Yes. Yes." She panted, she moaned, she thrust her hips into his as he surged forward. "Take my vein." The words were a hushed command from between dry lips. "Oh, God. Please, please."

"Parisa" tumbled from his mouth. "I want to stop, but I can't. I feel I should give you time, but I can't. God help me." Her neck was wet as he struck. The flash of pain went straight to her core and tightened her as pleasure followed and began to build.

Her cries now filled the steamy bathroom. His hips thrust as he began to draw her blood into his mouth. He groaned low and deep in his throat, a rumbling sound that could have been a growl, the sound of a beast taking what was his.

The smell of him rose and thickened in her nostrils. The orgasm rolled down on her hard and she screamed and cried out. He continued to pump, fast now, grunting. His body moved in a slow wave as he released her vein, his shoulders arching back as his hips moved forward. He shouted as he released into her, his cock thrusting and solid.

Another orgasm caught her, her core tightening around him again. It sent a shudder through his body and he groaned again as he bent forward and captured her in his arms. He drew her against him, thrusting over and over until sated.

She leaned her head on his shoulder, stroking his back, the scars a soft ripple beneath the pads of her fingers. She touched her neck with her hand where his fangs had entered her. "There's so little blood," she whispered.

"When the fangs retreat, they leave a chemical that seals the wound. Did I hurt you?"

She drew back and met his gaze. She ran a finger over his lips, the one that had been inside her. He sucked the finger into his mouth and licked in a swirl of sensation. *You even taste of tangerine,* he sent.

Oh, Antony. That was . . . amazing. You're . . . amazing.

He released her finger with a sudden pop then smiled. He pushed her damp hair away from her face. "What am I going to do with you?"

She smiled back, but her heart ached. "I don't know." She was suddenly filled with the knowledge that difficult things separated them. Though he could enter her and please her, though he could release into her, life had delivered terrible blows through the years, through the centuries. How were they to bridge the divide?

He was still connected, a large heavy presence in the center of her body. He felt so good. Her legs were still wrapped around his hips possessively, locked at the ankles. She didn't want to release him. She feared letting him go. Once the connection was broken, where would they be really?

She knew the past haunted him and that Rith's ability to

steal her right off Antony's property when he was just a dozen yards away had undermined his confidence. Even so, she knew, *she knew,* that wasn't the whole story.

And her story? Oh, God. She didn't want to feel like this.

She leaned forward and once more rested her head on his shoulder. Her eyes burned. She stroked the *cadroen,* the warrior clasp that bound his hair, then let her fingers drift again to his scarred back. What had happened to mar the perfection of his skin? Had he deserved to be cut and whipped? Of course not. His character was fixed. He was a man of honor. No way he had done anything to earn all those lashes.

But where could any of this go?

She thought Antony should know how uncertain she felt, yet she didn't want to say it aloud. So instead she unlocked her ankles, drew back, and gave a slight push on his shoulders. He looked at her and frowned slightly. He withdrew his heavy shaft from the core of her, and she barely withheld a gasp. How cold she felt suddenly. And empty. And alone.

But wasn't that always the way for her?

He smiled, albeit crookedly, and lifted her off the counter. He carried her back into the shower, flipped the lever, and started up all eight heads once more. "Let's get you cleaned up."

She looked up at him. Damn, he was tall. And muscular. And gorgeous. His expression was so tender, so understanding that her eyes burned all over again.

"Don't worry," he said. "This doesn't mean we have to get married or anything."

Great. Just great. He was going to keep being a nice guy. Great.

Medichi was so screwed. One hundred percent fucked . . . up.

As he poured shampoo into his hands and began to lather up his palms, as Parisa turned her back and he settled his hands into her hair, his heart swelled to about the size of Rhode Island. Jesus, why did he feel so much for this woman?

It was the damn *breh-hedden,* working his body like a mad scientist who knew every button that needed to be pushed in order to set his libido on fire. The shampoo usually had an edgy smell but he really couldn't tell because all his nose, sinuses, and brain registered was the delicious scent of tangerines. She was a bowl of fruit he wanted to devour.

He worked his fingers into her scalp and she moaned, her body going liquid again. He tried to keep his distance because his cock was responding to her scent and he was already hard again. Shit, if she saw him like this after he had just filled her full to overflowing, she'd probably land a fist against his mouth.

"Antony, what are you thinking about? I can't smell the shampoo anymore, just all this sage you keep shedding like a spice factory."

He laughed. "Well, you'd better get used to it. Let's get you rinsed off. Close your eyes." He guided her into the stream nearest her and worked her hair to get all the bubbles out.

She turned into him, and her gaze fell to his erection. Part of him felt an urge to cover himself for her sake, but the other part was proud of what he was. His hips rolled in her direction. "I would apologize, but . . ."

She looked up into his face and her lips parted. Her eyes flared. Whatever this was, it worked both ways. He had expected Parisa to be shy with him: Her general demeanor was restrained. Apparently, he'd been mistaken.

She gave a squeak and a cry as she flung herself at him. Before he could protest, or think, or do anything else, he had her up against the shower wall, plunging into her, and she was raking her fingernails over his shoulders and writhing.

He didn't last long but it didn't seem to matter since she was screaming at the ceiling as he came.

Afterward, he took her to bed. She slept cuddled against his side, his arm around her. He wasn't ready for sleep. The master bedroom was huge, with a den on one side; the other overlooked the back lawn. The shutters were open slightly so that he could see beds blooming with purple lantana and a vine covered with lavender flowers. Yellow verbena punctuated the beds. The occasional hibiscus added its stature.

The landscape maintenance company would be on his property all day tomorrow with several crews. Rith had made his way onto the property months ago with the cleaning crew, which had allowed him to abduct Parisa right from under his nose. Maybe he should take Parisa somewhere else until the gardeners were gone. Yet his property was vast, including an olive grove, several acres of vineyard, and a formal Italian garden with many hidden alcoves. How could he be sure the crew all left? He needed better security, someone to monitor the comings and goings of the service workers and winery personnel. He'd been so busy trying to get Parisa back that he hadn't thought all that much about what would be required to keep her safe once she got here.

Shit.

He couldn't trust anyone or anything, and Rith would sure as hell make an attempt to get Parisa back.

When she moved against him and an unhappy sound left her lips, he glanced at her. Her eyes were still closed, and he wondered if she was reacting in her sleep to his sudden tension. He took a deep breath and forced himself to relax. His gaze rested on her and his heart in turn swelled then constricted. What kind of miracle had happened that had made her extraction possible? How had she suddenly been able to communicate with him, at such a distance, telepathically? How had she even stayed alive?

He released a heavy sigh, weighted with three months of tortured searching. She was here. She was safe. She was home. Tears touched his eyes.

He resisted the impulse to draw her closer, to hold her tighter still, to see if he could press her into his skin so that he would never part from her again. She felt so right against him . . . but how did she feel about being here?

Earlier she had pushed him away and he had felt her distance, her profound withdrawal from him. She hadn't said a word and he hadn't asked, but he'd understood her without needing to ask the question: It was too soon to be this close, this intimate.

He was in trouble in more ways than one, and he suspected she was as well.

His warrior phone buzzed. He slid the card off the marble surface of the nightstand where it always rested, rubbed the front, and murmured, "Medichi."

"Thorne wants to patch in."

"Thanks, Carla." He spoke as low as he could, but Parisa stirred beside him. She lifted up on an elbow, and he ran a hand over her damp hair. "Sorry," he murmured. "Thorne."

She nodded.

"You there, Medichi?" Thorne barked.

"Give."

"We went back. Thought you should know, the whole place was cleared out. But shit, all that equipment was still lit up like they'd just drained someone."

"That's what Parisa said."

"The rumors were right. That place was a death and resurrection facility. We found bags of blood, tubing, defibrillators, a modern-day torture chamber."

Medichi closed his eyes. Something inside his chest gave way. "Was there any kind of data? A computer? Anything?" His voice sounded almost as gravelly as Thorne's.

"Not a damn thing. There wasn't even a trace. There were vehicles parked out back. A van or two. We suspect Rith drove off with his slaves, then probably folded the whole lot to another secure location. Tell me you're not surprised the place was empty."

"No. Rith is one clever motherfucker."

"Sorry, Medichi."

"Thanks for going back."

He heard a faint rumbling that might have been a *you're welcome,* but he couldn't be sure. The line went dead. Thorne wasn't exactly a talkative man.

He pressed the card-like phone to his chest.

"What happened?" Parisa asked.

He looked down at her and hugged her. "The warriors went back to Mandalay but everyone was gone. I'm sorry."

He felt her sigh, but for a long moment she didn't say anything. Finally, he asked, "You okay?"

"I want to see Endelle."

"Sure," he said, but he felt uneasy. "Tomorrow. Maybe give you some time to settle in?" Of all the things Parisa might want right now, so soon after leaving Burma, he hadn't expected a request to see the Supreme High Administrator of Second Earth.

"No," she said, her fingers playing with his chest hairs in the center of his sternum. "No, I really think I want to see her today, right away. There are some things I need to get settled."

He didn't like the sound of that. "Okay. If that's what you want."

"That's what I want."

He nodded several times, but he could feel that he was frowning. He wanted to argue with her but how could he?

He released a sigh. "I'll set it up."

He called Central and had Carla patch him through to Her Supremeness. She agreed to see Parisa in an hour but barked, "Make sure she has some clothes on this time." Her laughter rang in his head as he swiped the phone. Endelle shared Parisa's preternatural voyeuristic talent; either she'd witnessed Parisa's rescue or Thorne had shared the details with her when he reported in. Either way, Endelle had the worst sense of humor, not to mention timing.

Parisa rose. "All set?"

"Yes. One hour." She reached a half-sitting position on her knees, which unfortunately put her quite magnificent breasts at eye level. His body responded with one giant leap.

Her eyes widened. "All that sage," she murmured.

He licked his lips. He reached for her but she rolled off the bed, landing on her feet. She jerked the black top sheet to her, wrapped herself up good and tight, then waggled a finger at him. "I want to. I do. But we don't have time. I need to get dressed."

He nodded in rapid-fire motion. "Of course." But the sheet she'd taken had left him completely uncovered and he now stood at full-mast. So he folded his hands behind his head and smiled "Sorry. Can't really help this."

She covered her eyes and started walking mummy-fashion in the direction of the doors. "Are my clothes still in the other bedroom? All my toiletries?" The last week she'd been in his house, Havily had taken her shopping. There was practically a full wardrobe in the guest room waiting for her.

He wished he'd had the foresight to move everything to his room, but all his thoughts had been focused on bringing her home. "Yes, everything's as you left it." He sat up and drew the comforter over his lap. "I'm decent now," he said, but he was smiling. Was *decent* the right word when all he could think about was what the hell he was supposed to do with a raging hard-on?

She lowered her hand and looked back at him. She gasped. "What is it?"

"You . . . you look so beautiful like that, with your hair over your shoulders. Antony, you're so beautiful." Her gaze drifted down his chest, and he flexed his pecs for her. This time she moaned softly.

When he growled low in his throat and started to throw the cover back, she gave a little yip then scurried out of his bedroom. He flopped back onto the bed. So this was how it was going to be. All she had to do was compliment him, give him a look or two, and he was ready to grab her and throw her on her back.

Jesus H. Christ.

The greatest reward
Comes to the heart capable of love.

—*Collected Proverbs*, Beatrice of Fourth

CHAPTER 8

Jean-Pierre returned from Burma to the Cave in Metro Phoenix Two with the rest of the brothers. He said good-bye to one warrior after another. When only Kerrick remained, he yawned and said he was headed to his home in Sedona for the remainder of the day to sleep. That was a lie.

He did fold the distance to the front yard of his home and stood for a moment beneath the fragrant Arizona sycamores, but not for long. He wasn't sure exactly what had gotten into him, but he felt a pressing need to return to Rith's home, if only for a few minutes more.

He folded back to the tamarind tree in Burma, drawing his sword into his hand from his Sedona weapons locker. The double dome of mist still covered the property. He turned in a slow circle, making sure that he was alone.

He stretched his preternatural hearing but except for the sound of frogs, nothing came back to him. He made his way into the house, again listening carefully and watching every shadow in case a death vampire, or Rith himself, might choose to return to what they all now knew to be a death and resurrection facility.

As he crossed the living room, the mahogany floor creaked beneath his feet.

He checked every room, one by one, hunting for the smell that had stuck to him when he'd come back with the rest of the Warriors of the Blood. It was the scent like a bakery or a French patisserie, like fresh-baked buttery bread or perhaps croissants.

But all he smelled here was garlic and turmeric.

He sighed as he made his way down the hall. He reached a second shorter hall that led to the basement stairs. He opened the door to the stairwell and once more listened for the sounds of the enemy.

He heard nothing.

Crouching, he descended, one quiet foot after another. He sniffed the air and, *oui,* as before, he could smell the bakery aroma.

At the bottom of the stairs, he looked right, then left, then right again. No one was there.

He lifted his nose into the air, closed his eyes, and just breathed. He took several long slow inhales through his nose, scenting the air like an animal. He felt *un peu* dizzy.

The largest room was opposite the stairs and still held several pieces of medical equipment: a cart with wheels, two stands for hanging bags of blood or fluids, even the hated defibrillator.

Mon dieu, the horror of what these women endured. Medichi had told the warriors that one of them, Fiona, had been taken from Boston in the late nineteenth century. He put a fist to his chest. How had she survived such trauma to her heart all these terrible decades? He did not understand the spirit of such a woman, how she had lived only to be killed and brought back to life over and over.

A shimmering in the air appeared not far from him. Shit. He should not have come. He held his sword in a firm grip as he shifted to face his new enemy—but it was only Thorne.

"What the fuck are you doing here?" Thorne cried. He scowled at Jean-Pierre. "And I sure as hell don't remember you asking for permission to come back here. Now you have two questions to answer."

Jean-Pierre had nothing to tell him. "I am not certain why I came," he said. "I was distressed and felt compelled to return. Perhaps we missed something."

Thorne looked around and shook his head. "I had the same damn feeling. Endelle wanted me to come back and have one more look, but goddammit, Jean-Pierre, you should have checked with me first."

"Would you have let me come?"

"No," Thorne barked. He barked a lot these days.

Jean-Pierre merely smiled and shrugged.

Thorne did as well. It was so much like their *chef,* their boss, their leader. He had a quick temper, but his rage disappeared as fast as lightning.

"Well, now that you're here we can have a look around together."

Jean-Pierre took his time. He went into every cell, and with each successive room his spirit grew heavier. His anger grew and grew. He raged that such horrible things had been done to innocent women.

When he reached the last cell, the aroma of bread—no, more like croissants—permeated the room, but he did not know why. There was a vent above, but that was true of all the cells. Had someone baked something recently? If so, then why did not every room smell like this one?

All that he knew was he wanted to linger, to stay close to the aroma.

"What is it?" Thorne asked.

Jean-Pierre turned and looked at him. Thorne stood in the doorway, his hands on his hips. He scowled as always, his hazel eyes red and so very sad. He carried a terrible load. Jean-Pierre had no intention of adding to his concerns. *"Rien,"* he responded. "I have found nothing."

And that was the truth. Nothing except an aroma of croissants that made no sense in this dungeon of terrors.

* * *

Parisa had just slid into a clean bra and underwear when a knock sounded on the door, but it sounded faint, not like Medichi. "Who is it?"

"Havily. Can I come in?"

Something inside Parisa's chest warmed up, as if someone had just turned up the heat beneath a pot. "Just a minute." She searched for and found a black silk robe in her closet. She shrugged into it as she crossed the room. Opening the door, she smiled.

Cradled in one arm, Havily carried a huge vase full of at least two dozen white roses. "You're home," she cried. She opened her free arm.

Parisa burst into tears and fell into that welcoming embrace. Havily held her close and sniffed as well.

"You'll spoil your beautiful makeup." Havily always looked like she'd stepped out of the pages of *Vogue*. She wore Ralph Lauren, and her red layered hair floated around her shoulders.

"I missed you, girlfriend. I've had no one to fly with." She sighed as she released Parisa. Moving into the room, she expanded on her theme. "Alison doesn't have her wings yet and besides that she's *really* pregnant now and *feeling* it. But even if she did have her wings, Kerrick would throw a hissy-fit."

Parisa laughed and closed the door behind her. It was very difficult to picture a Warrior of the Blood throwing anything that could resemble a hissy-fit. He might throw a tornado of rage, but a hissy-fit?

"How are you and Marcus doing?"

Havily looked around the room and headed to the table by the window. She settled the vase there. Then she looked back at Parisa. "Are you even staying in this room?"

Parisa felt her cheeks warm up. "I'm not sure . . . no. I guess not." She shook her head. "As long as I'm here I'll be at the end of the hall." She pointed in the direction of Medichi's bedroom.

Havily's chest rose and fell with a sigh. "I thought that might be the case. I'm glad. Parisa, he's really suffered. Did you know he started drinking limoncello?"

She nodded. "I saw him once or twice." Her gaze fell away from Havily, and her mind grew a little fuzzy. "I found I couldn't voyeur him as much as I wanted to, not because I was unable but because it just hurt so much to see him and not be able to communicate with him. We kind of fell into this routine that I would voyeur him when I was ready for bed and he was through fighting for the night."

She didn't realize Havily had crossed the room until she felt an arm around her shoulders. Then Havily drew her into a big hug and held her for a very long time.

Finally she drew back. "There's one thing I really need to know. Were you hurt? Did Rith *hurt* you?" Her voice sounded scraped and raw.

Parisa knew what was on everyone's mind. "I wasn't raped. I thought I would be. I thought it would be the first order of business. I guess that's what a woman will always think when she falls into the hands of a bad man. But I wasn't. I don't know why. The truth is, I don't know why either Greaves or Rith allowed me to live."

Havily shook her head slowly. "I don't have answers for any of that. We . . . I didn't think you'd be coming back. There were so many attempts on your life as it was." Then a smile suffused Havily's lovely face.

"What?" Parisa asked.

"I'm just so damn glad you're home." Once more her eyes filled with tears, and once more Parisa was gathered up into a welcoming embrace. But when she drew back this time, Parisa said, "I'm going to see Endelle. That's where I'm headed once I get dressed."

"She said you were coming to see her. That's why I thought I'd come by first. I figured if you could see Endelle, you could tolerate a visit from me."

Parisa laughed. "I'm going to ascend, Hav. I wasn't going to, not before I was . . . taken. But now I have to find them. I have to search for them. I think I'll be able to find them because I met one of them, a woman named Fiona. She said she'd been a D and R slave for over a hundred years."

"D and R?"

"Death and resurrection. That's what they call it because they're drained of their blood, filled with donated blood, then brought back to life."

Havily's eyes grew pinched. "Oh, God. So it's true."

Parisa nodded but didn't match the tears in Havily's eyes. What good were tears? She needed to get busy, to prepare herself, and to find the women. "I have to get ready now but I'll see you soon?"

"Of course. I have to change clothes and head to the palace myself. I work with Endelle four hours a night in the darkening."

Parisa nodded. Darkening work was critical for the war effort, and only Madame Endelle and Havily had darkening capability. It meant they could split-self; the second self would travel through a region of nether-space called the darkening and hunt for Greaves. The work was difficult and tedious, but when they found him he always had death vampires ready to fold to Metro Phoenix Two. The more death vampires Havily and Endelle blocked, the fewer the Warriors of the Blood had to battle every night.

Havily blew her a kiss then lifted an arm and vanished.

Parisa took a step back. She'd forgotten how often everyone did that. For the past three months, no one had dematerialized in front of her, not even Rith.

She moved to the closet and shifted hangers to look through the wardrobe. Half the clothes still had price tags on them. Shopping with Havily seemed like a hundred years ago.

She paused for a moment and dropped her chin. Wow. She was home—sort of. She was back in Medichi's villa, but she had another home on Mortal Earth in Peoria, a neighbor of Phoenix. That home would have been vacant for almost four months now, from the time that Marcus and Havily had first materialized into her courtyard to visit her and protect

her. Her wings had been in full-mount and she'd been naked. Not long after, Crace had come to kill her.

For just a moment as she pulled a cornflower-blue silk top
off the hanger, all the reasons she had decided back then not
to ascend flowed through her. She'd only spent a few days on
Second Earth before Rith had kidnapped her, and those days
had been nothing short of a nightmare. That experience had
been the primary reason she had planned on refusing her
ascension.

At least Crace was dead by Warrior Luken's hand, thank
God, but everything had led her to the conclusion that she
wasn't built for war.

Then Rith had enthralled her just beyond the whitewashed building that housed the olive press.

She gave herself a strong shake and slipped the blouse
over her head. But she was here now, her thinking and therefore her life altered dramatically, and she was about to face
the most powerful ascender on the planet, a woman who had
venom for blood.

She straightened her spine and found a black silk pencil
skirt. She didn't want to face Madame Endelle in something
casual. Not when she intended to make at least one serious
demand of a woman who never gave ground to anyone without a fight.

War changed people.

Endelle looked down at the survivor, otherwise known as
Parisa Lovejoy. She had lovely eyes—not lavender, not rose,
that place in between. Amethyst.

Parisa had been taken from the villa three months ago a
naive, frightened, overwhelmed young woman. She returned
with a fire in her eye that had nothing to do with the warrior
at her back.

Endelle glanced at Medichi. His jawline had turned to
stone.

Huh. This couple had been arguing.

Arguing among the *breh*-couples seemed to be an epi-
demic these days. Alison had thrown a Jimmy Choo sandal

at Kerrick and left him with a goose egg for a few hours until his normal preternatural healing kicked in. Havily had been screeching into her iPhone at Marcus most of the day, something about how she needed to be trained with swords, knives, *and* guns. Marcus was dragging his heels. Leave it to a man to want to protect his woman but not give her the tools to protect herself when the dumbfuck wasn't around.

And now it looked like the latest duo slammed with the *breh-hedden* had already been at each other's throats, metaphorically and physically, because, wow, Parisa had one bite mark on her neck. Jesus H. Christ.

The woman's complexion was flushed, too. She'd gotten good and well fucked. She really shouldn't be complaining, but here she was all fired up.

"So what is it you want, Parisa?" Endelle asked. Funny how when someone else had a rock in her shoe, she could be relaxed and gracious.

Parisa lifted her chin. "I want to ascend right now. No ceremony, just give me a pair of fangs so I can get on with what I have to do next."

Endelle worked at not smiling, but it was tough. So their little librarian had made up her mind and the rest of them could go fuck themselves. She liked the spirit. Hell, she even approved. Ascension wasn't for sissies. And before her captivity, Parisa had been a little too much on the feminine-sniveling side to please Endelle. But here she was showing some balls.

Yeah, Endelle approved. "And what is it you have to do next that's got your thong hiked up around your waist?"

"I have to go back for them."

"Back to Burma?"

Parisa clamped her lips shut. She even breathed dragon-like through her nose a couple of times. Then she marched in Endelle's direction, her arms spread about a foot apart, her hands straight out in front of her as though she meant to shake both of Endelle's hands at once. That or she was trying out a Frankenstein impersonation. Endelle was pretty sure neither was what she intended.

She was a bit surprised, however, when Parisa drew close

enough to stand right in front of her and one extended hand landed on either side of her face. Parisa pushed back Endelle's yellow headband of cockatiel feathers. The amethyst eyes closed and Endelle felt a hard push against her mind. She really didn't think the librarian could hurt her, so she released her shields.

And she really shouldn't have done that. The images flew like knives at first. She had to remind herself to relax and let them flow. Holy fuck the mortal-with-wings had power.

Endelle relaxed and the shared memories slowed down. *Start over,* Endelle sent.

Parisa took a quick breath and the images ceased. Then they renewed, beginning with a young woman in light blue flannel pajama bottoms and a dark blue tank top racing across a green lawn, begging for Parisa's help. Tangling with that bastard Rith followed. Later, Parisa woke up with the woman's name on her lips, *Fiona.*

That's when the nightmare started. Endelle felt her stomach squeeze up in slow stages, hardening into a knot. She watched the whole show, the glass cells in a stone-like dungeon in which all the women lived, then the focus on the woman Fiona who was strapped down on a table, dead, really dead. Eyes glazed, blue lips, white complexion. But the techs brought her back, draining a bag of blood into her and using the defibrillator.

Finally, Fiona took a renewing breath, blood was forced down her lips, and . . . holy shit, was that an orgasm?

When the woman lay alone in her cell, the images stopped.

Parisa drew back. She met Endelle's gaze but tears now tracked down her cheeks. Endelle didn't hesitate, not even a split second. She grabbed Parisa and hauled her into her arms. She let Parisa cry and didn't think less of her for it. The whole time she stared at Medichi over the young woman's head.

Even Endelle's eyes leaked a little, and her tears plopped onto Parisa's head. "I didn't know," Parisa whispered. "I was there for three months and I didn't know. I didn't know." The same words flowed over and over.

She'd heard rumors for decades that Greaves was experimenting with women, turning them into blood slaves, but she'd never believed it was possible. She thought about the small dose of blood the woman, Fiona, had been forced to drink. Without a doubt, Greaves must have been sharing his blood with the donors, not just keeping them alive but helping to bring them back to life. With the increase in preternatural powers, an ascender's blood gained restorative properties as well.

When Parisa was no longer trembling or weeping, she pulled away from Endelle. Parisa met her gaze fully once more, but her eyes were red-rimmed and her nose swollen and dripping. Endelle folded a tissue into her hand from the desk behind her and handed it to the young woman.

Parisa thanked her then blew her nose. "The warriors went back for the women but all that was left was some of the medical equipment."

Medichi moved in close. "There's no sign where they went. Not even a trace to follow. He probably moved them to a nearby location by van then folded them elsewhere."

"Makes sense. That's what I would do." She looked down at Parisa and slid her finger under Parisa's chin. "How do you propose to do what my warriors couldn't? How do you intend to find them?"

She sniffed and blew her nose. "I can voyeur them. Well, not all of them, just Fiona, the woman with the dark blue tank top."

"Then what?"

"I don't have everything figured out but we have to do something. Now that I've seen the horror they endure, I won't stop until we have all of them safely here."

"And that's why you're pushing for the ascension ceremony?"

"Yes. Of course."

Endelle nodded. She glanced at Medichi, but the stone of his jaw was still in place. "What do you think?"

His gaze fell to Parisa, and he shifted his jaw around a couple of times. "I can appreciate and certainly approve of the use of her voyeur skills to locate Fiona, to try to contact her, but she's talking about making the run herself. That's all she's been talking about for the last hour. I think it would be foolish."

"Why?" Endelle asked. She was baiting him because sometimes it was just plain fun to watch one of her warriors go apeshit.

"Why?" he thundered.

Ah, there it was.

His face turned a dark, angry red. She particularly loved how Parisa shifted to glare at him. She even planted her hands on her hips.

"Yes, Warrior Medichi, why?" Even Parisa's voice had grown stronger in the last three months.

He began to pace. He moved crazy-fast. She was only surprised steam didn't flow behind him. "I've just gotten her back," he cried. He flung an arm in Parisa's direction. "Do you know what the last three months have been like for me?" He froze in mid-step.

"Shit," he cried. He pulled his *cadroen* from his hair and threw it at the plate-glass window. It was a good throw and ordinarily would have done some damage, but she'd put in bulletproof glass after the last time she'd lost her temper. It was on the top floor, for Christ's sake, and even with the glass company hiring the preternaturally gifted who could levitate, the whole process had taken a week—and it was summer in Phoenix. So, yeah, bulletproof glass.

His *cadroen,* made of leather and rhinoceros tusk, plopped onto the closest zebra skin. He stared at it. "It's too soon to be talking about this. I'm too raw."

He turned back to Parisa. He drew close and caught her on the inside of her elbow. "I know I'm behaving like a mad-man but I don't want to fail you again, can you understand that? And the thought of you being anywhere near Rith—" He closed his eyes and drew in a long, loud breath through his nose. "Well, the whole thing makes me nuts."

"Yeah. I'm getting that. But maybe we'd better come to an understanding right now." Parisa faced him dead-on.

Endelle had a perfect view of her profile. What was with these *brehs*? Dammit, they were all so beautiful. But then maybe that was the least these men deserved for the way they had to put their lives on the line every night.

"You're not responsible for me anymore, Antony. I'm making the decision to ascend. I spent the last three months in a really weird kind of captivity but I also learned a lot about this world. Rith had a library, and one of the books I read was *Treatise on Ascension,* by Philippe Reynard. Do you know the one?"

Medichi nodded. "A little pompous but he's got most of the facts right."

"According to Reynard, one of the tenets of this world is service, and that is one thing I happen to agree with. I know I've been given some strange gifts but I want to serve with them, to do my part. And it's more than that. The whole time I was under Rith's domination, do you know what I hated most?"

He shook his head. His eyes slid around uneasily, like he wasn't sure he was going to appreciate what she said next. Endelle braced herself for another fit.

"What I hated the most was that I was incapable of just leaving—he had enough physical power over me that I couldn't escape. And I was never once confined with locks or ropes or chains or anything. The doors were always open so that fresh air blew through the house. The domes of mist were so easily penetrated, as you very well know, but I didn't have the skill to just leave.

"If I'd had some of your abilities, your flight skills for instance, I could have flown through the mist, gone somewhere, done something. If I'd had some battle skills, I could have used one of the many sharp knives he kept in the kitchen and made good use of it. Maybe it wouldn't have mattered because he has a great deal of preternatural ability, but at least I could have tried. I couldn't even try, Antony."

Endelle knew her mouth was agape. Parisa had made a compelling case, and Endelle agreed with her. But what caught her attention was how she called Medichi by his first name, as though she'd been doing it all her life. For some reason that bugged the shit out of her.

She crossed her arms over her chest and said, "Just so you know, O winged creature of Peoria, I do get a say in what you do and don't do once you ascend."

At that, Parisa turned toward her, amethyst eyes wide. "Would you forbid me to arm myself or to go after the D and R slaves?"

Endelle got totally sidetracked. "D and R?"

"Death and resurrection. Perfect epithet. That's what Fiona called it. The women died then were resurrected with defibrillators."

"Jesus." Endelle felt ill all over again. She moved back to her desk and leaned her hips on the edge. The fur she wore itched and she scratched her arms down both sides. "Shit, I think I'm allergic to this fur."

"What is it?" Parisa and Medichi asked in unison, both noses wrinkling.

"Coatimundi. We have 'em here in Arizona. I'll have to talk to my taxidermist."

"Taxidermist?" Medichi asked. "You mean *furrier*?"

She slid her thumb under the edge of the vest and scratched. "No, I mean taxidermist. You don't think an actual furrier would touch this shit, do you?" She blew air from her cheeks. "Okay, let's take this one fucking thing at a time. Parisa, we'll get you ascended, but you'll have to have a ceremony with witnesses. COPASS has rules about that now. And because you've had a Guardian of Ascension, your boyfriend here"—she jerked her thumb in Medichi's direction—"I'll have to perform the ceremony myself." She looked past them and shouted, "Alison."

A few seconds later, the blond beauty, *breh* of Warrior Kerrick, appeared in the doorway. She had dark circles under still-lovely blue eyes rimmed with gold, but she gritted her teeth, her hand pressed to her way-too-big-belly for being seven months with child.

"Maybe you've got twins in the oven," Endelle said, scowling at her stomach.

Alison crossed the threshold but didn't close the door. "The doctor only found one heartbeat at four months. She would have found two if there'd been two. Believe me, she worked my stomach over every which way. This baby is just really active, and frankly I blame Kerrick. He's too power- ful. I should never have bonded with him." She wasn't even smiling when she said it.

Alison had gotten knocked up right away and now she was a trifle irritable. Aw, too bad.

Again, Endelle worked hard at not laughing. "Okay, what- ever. Listen up. Parisa is ascending. Set up a ceremony at the palace for tonight at five. We'll have a sit-down dinner before the warriors head out. Got it?"

"Got it," she muttered as she turned away. The door closed behind her. Shit, she didn't even say hello to Parisa. The pregnancy had really gotten the better of this usually calm, we-are-the-world therapist.

Medichi frowned and said quietly, "What's going on?"

Endelle shrugged. "Hell if I know. She's been real bitchy for the last few weeks and no, I don't know why. I've never been pregnant. Don't want to be. At least she'll get her figure back. That's one excellent benefit to ascension." She glanced at Parisa then scowled at her. "I hope you're using protection."

The woman had the good grace to blush scarlet. Then her eyes got very round, as though she'd just thought of it. Ter- rific. Medichi stared at the ceiling, studying the inset spot- lights. "All right, get out of my office. I'll see you both here tonight at five."

"Thank you, Madame Endelle."

"Whatever, ascendiate, just use your head. One grumpy pregnant woman around here is about all I can stand." She started to round her desk, thinking she'd better check her emails, then decided to offer Medichi a little advice. "And Warrior, for God's sake, go buy some condoms." She turned back thinking she might expand on the theme, but the cou- ple were already gone.

"Idiots," she murmured.

She rounded her desk to sit in her big comfy executive

chair. She leaned against the Appaloosa horsehide she had draped over the back.

Shit. Death and resurrection slaves.

Great. Just fucking great.

Didn't she have enough to worry about with Stannett's prophecy about an upcoming battle to end all battles?

But when all was said and done, that Greaves had developed a medical system by which he could harvest dying blood on a regular basis was some kind of sick-ass genius. So, yeah, D&R slavery made complete sense. How would so many High Administrators and COPASS members ever agree to become addicted to dying blood without the promise of an easy supply that didn't involve killing someone through a personal use of fangs? Bunch of pansy-ass, goddamn fucking hypocrites. She hated Greaves for a lot of reasons, but she swore she hated these hypocrites more—the ones who would take dying blood because they didn't have to be involved in either the slaughter or the slavery required for the harvest.

Shit.

Condoms.

What a rookie mistake.

Medichi stood in the foyer of his villa and didn't look at Parisa. He shoved a hand through his hair then pulled his fingers out and looked at them. He'd left his *cadroen* in Endelle's office. He rolled his eyes. Whatever. He pushed his hair over his shoulders to hang down his back.

He glanced at Parisa. Her color hadn't diminished very much. Her cheeks were still bright pink and she was staring at the dark plank flooring.

"Maybe I should go back to the guest room," she said.

He drew in a breath that sounded like someone was strangling an animal. "No" came out half growl, half hiss.

She looked up at him and took a step back. She put a hand to her chest. "Antony."

He squeezed his eyes shut then turned away from her. "Sorry. Just the *breh-hedden* rearing its ugly head. I . . . I have these instincts that just keep getting stronger. You know, like I want to lock you in my bedroom and never let you out of there—for more than one reason." He stiffened at what he'd just said.

He whirled back to her. "Parisa, I'm so sorry. I didn't mean . . . and I would never do that to you." He stopped.

A ghostly white shade had completely replaced the previous flush of her complexion. Her gaze fell back to the floor, this time skating from side to side. "I know you wouldn't. This is an adjustment for both of us. I've come back here and I want to ascend but"—she lifted her eyes to him—"I don't know where I belong, even where I should live. You and I are dating, I guess. I told Havily that I'd be sharing your room but we really shouldn't be doing that, should we? I mean, I can't just move in with you. I don't know anything about you. I know I trust you. Of course I trust you."

She frowned then pressed on. "I have to get through the ceremony first, and then I want training. I know Kerrick trained Alison. I guess I should do something like that. I don't know." She put her hand to her forehead and turned away from him.

Medichi stood very still, afraid that if he took a single step right or left, she'd leave him, she'd choose to live someplace other than beneath his roof, and he couldn't have that. She'd suffered terribly, but so had he. How could he explain to her that the *breh-hedden* had been its own prison, that he hadn't been his own man for the past three months, that worrying about her had consumed his mind, his heart, his every waking action? He'd had only one thought in all that time, to get her back whatever it took. Now she was back and he felt her slipping away from him.

He was trying to be reasonable, to find his rational thoughts, but fear rode his skin like a current of electricity. Even his jaw felt tight and hinged shut. He knew she needed space. She should have space. But if she didn't share his bedroom, sleep in his bed, let him feel the weight of her next to him, her hands reaching for him at night, her body pressed against him . . . yeah, he thought he would go mad.

"I have no right to ask," he said, his voice somehow managing to push past the tightness of his jaw. "But would you please stay, at least for the next few days. Please." He swallowed. A rock had lodged itself in his throat. "Don't go."

She looked up at him and blinked. Her turn to stiffen. Her lovely eyes widened. She didn't seem to be capable of breath. "I don't want to go," she whispered. "But . . ."

"Please." It was a war of whispers.

She moved toward him slowly. She searched his eyes once more, then put her hand on his cheek. He loved that she was tall. In heels she didn't have far to go to reach him. Her palm was cool against his skin. Tears glimmered in her eyes. "I . . . I forgot for a moment what this has been like for you but I've remembered. I wouldn't be so cruel as to walk out now.

"I saw you every night, remember? I mean every morning. I mean it was night for me and morning for you. You would tell me every night what you'd done to look for me, where you'd gone. You gave me hope and that hope kept me sane. I saw how you suffered. I saw you lose weight. I watched the circles under your eyes darken and deepen. I didn't even think that was possible for an ascended vampire, but a lack of sleep will do it, won't it?"

He nodded. He lifted a hand and slid it over hers. He pressed gently.

"We'll give this some time," she said. "I won't leave your home, not now, not yet. We'll take this one step at a time. I can feel your distress and I can see your need. I won't go."

"You'll share my bed?"

"I'll share your bed." She paused. "For a few days, maybe a week. Okay? Until we get everything figured out."

He moaned and dragged her into his arms. He held her close. She wiggled against him, straining. At first he thought she wanted him to release her, but when he gave her a little room she threw her arms around his neck and held on.

Christ. This was too much emotion for people who knew so little about each other. He closed his eyes. He could feel her heart beating in her throat, dull heavy thuds. His neck was getting wet. What a mess. Goddamn the *breh-hedden*.

The one taken suffers the most,
But do not forget the warrior left in the breach.

—Collected Proverbs, Beatrice of Fourth

CHAPTER 9

That evening, Parisa stood in the center of the rotunda floor, Havily behind her and to her left, Antony back and to her right. The rest of the Warriors of the Blood were ranged another ten feet behind her, standing tall and straight, sentinels of Second Earth. Each, like Antony, wore a black leather tunic and a brass breastplate with a silver sword emblazoned down the front, point down, with a green laurel wreath around the hilt.

Endelle's palace was a collection of white marble rotundas, hanging off the west face of the McDowell Mountains as though suspended in the air. Most of the rotundas had open walls and large terraces with a stone balustrade serving as the only separation from hundreds of feet of airspace.

She had spent the day sleeping, something she'd desperately needed. Antony had kept his distance, giving her some space by stretching out on the couch in the den of his bedroom suite. She had told him it was okay if he shared the bed with her, but he'd only lifted a brow, pulled a pillow off the bed, and headed for the couch. He'd been right, of course. If they'd shared a bed, how much sleeping would they have actually done?

So here she was, somewhat rested and ready to ascend, at last, to Second Earth.

She stood in front of Endelle listening to the careful words she read from a large ceremonial book that she held open in both hands. It detailed the terms of ascension: the necessity of service, the nature of which would be dictated by the Supreme High Administrator; the careful standards of Second Society; and the vows to abstain from committing the most heinous act of partaking of dying blood.

Was she really going to do this? Was she really leaving her old world on Mortal Earth behind?

She watched Endelle's lips move but she really couldn't hear her. Her fingers shook so badly, she had to ball her hands into fists. She hadn't thought she would be nervous, but somewhere between committing her life in service to Madame Endelle and the promise not to drink someone to death, the reality that she was ascending suddenly got to her.

"Ascendiate," Endelle cried, her voice a hard bite.

Parisa's hearing cleared. "Yes, Madame Endelle?" Just above the neckline of Endelle's black ceremonial robes, Parisa could see a line of leopard fur. The Supreme High Administrator had a predilection for animal skins and hides, for bird feathers, and even on occasion for the skins of reptiles. Havily called her fashion-challenged . . . to say the least.

Endelle rolled her eyes. "Do you agree to serve Second Earth with a mind and heart dedicated to service?"

Parisa nodded. "I do."

"Do you agree to abide by the laws of Second Earth, especially as they apply to the limitations of involvement with Mortal Earth?"

"I do."

"And do you solemnly pledge your loyalty to me, as Supreme High Administrator of Second Earth?"

"I do."

"Then I proclaim to this gathered assembly, who stand as witnesses to your ascension, that you are hereby granted ascender status. Come forth and allow me to imbue you with all the blessings of the vampire nature." She folded the ceremonial book away.

Parisa couldn't make her feet move. She felt dizzy and strange as she stared at Madame Endelle's outstretched hands. Was she really going to do this? She had forgotten that part of the ceremony would involve the acceptance of near-immortality and vampire fangs for the taking of human blood and the releasing of potent chemicals.

Oh. God.

"Parisa, don't flake out on me now," Endelle cried. "Get your ass over here."

Endelle's sharp tone and irreverent words knocked some of the fear out of Parisa. She moved forward, although unsteadily in her four-inch heels. When she stood in front of Endelle, the disparity in height set Parisa at eye level with the leopard fur.

With warm hands Endelle touched Parisa's cheeks oh-so-lightly. A tingling began to build between her hands and Parisa's jaw. She looked up into Endelle's eyes, but they were closed.

Dizziness once more assailed her.

Endelle's eyes popped open. "What the hell is with you women? You're as bad as Alison was during her ascension. Goddammit, release your fucking shields!"

Parisa gasped. She closed her eyes this time, dove inside her mind, and let loose what she perceived to be those shields. Even Greaves had marveled at her shields, calling them magnificent.

"Finally," Endelle snapped.

Power flowed, a torrent through Parisa's body, of warmth and light, of a tremendous sensation of well-being. Her upper gums began to tingle at the base of each incisor. At the same time, she felt tendrils touching her mind, trying to reach within. She knew that sensation, and it had nothing to do with the ruler of Second Earth.

"Something's happening," she whispered.

"You're getting your fangs, just relax, vampire."

"No, it's not that."

Rith. She knew it was Rith. She recognized his touch, although this one was a gentler version of all that she'd experienced while under his control.

An image of him, his Asian features, his broad forehead and wide nose, his black hair, flowed through her mind.

She closed her eyes and focused on him. Oh, how she wanted him dead. She had never thought she would say that about anyone, but Rith's heinous blood-slavery operation had changed that. What if she could reach the monster and be rid of him permanently?

His smiling face taunted her. Without thinking, she thought the thought, and the vibration began. The next moment she was drifting, flying, moving.

Oh, God, she was folding!

And somewhere in her consciousness, she knew she was folding straight to Rith. Somehow, the vampire had tricked her.

Medichi had remained as close to Parisa during the ceremony as he could manage without doing anything improper. The palace had open walls through many of the connected rotundas, and it wasn't so long ago that Greaves had organized an attack here following Alison's ascension ceremony. He had a right to be nervous despite the state-of-the-art security system Endelle had in place. It couldn't guard against every preternatural contingency.

Like this one.

He had watched Parisa weave on her feet more than once during the ceremony. But just as Endelle had empowered her with ascended life and with her vampire fangs, she disappeared. How? Why? Worse, was she in danger?

He rushed forward and met Endelle's surprised gaze.

Her Supremeness blinked and said, "Well, that's never happened before."

No shit.

Parisa had dematerialized. She had folded for the first time, but where had she gone?

As far as Medichi knew, she hadn't manifested that power yet or she would have left her captivity long before this. Had the ceremony brought on a new power? Probably.

He didn't wait for permission or direction. With a thought, he folded off the cape and breastplate that would hinder him if he had to do battle. He closed his eyes and found her trace, which was made up of beautiful amethyst trails of light. The color was not a surprise.

He followed the elegant pathway, his hand itching as he traveled through nether-space, ready to fold his sword into his hand the moment his feet touched solid ground.

He materialized and at the same moment swept his sword into his waiting fist. Rith stood eight feet away, both hands on Parisa's arms, his expression intense, forceful. He was working hard, his concentration focused. Whatever he was trying to do, it was taking every ounce of his energy and his awareness. Her body shimmered with energy. She was battling to keep him from folding her with him. If he succeeded, he'd lose her again, because Rith could block his trace.

"Hell the fuck no!" he shouted. He raced toward her, his preternatural speed shrinking time to a nanosecond. He slid his left arm around her waist, pulled her back into him, then swept the sword through the air at the level of Rith's waiting neck.

He'd expected to strike bone and decapitate the bastard so that when he sliced through air, and got caught in the momentum, he ended up whirling Parisa in a circle.

Rith had escaped. Folded. Damn that vampire was fast.

He glanced around, a layer of sweat blooming over his skin, adrenaline singing through his veins, heart pounding. Was another enemy waiting? A death vampire maybe? A dozen? A hundred?

What the hell was this place? It looked like an underground cavern. But some of it was man-made—at least two of the walls were almost flat and the floor was a smooth, polished surface.

He turned in another circle, his sword outstretched. Parisa was limp around his arm. What had Rith done to her? Like he didn't know. He'd forced his way into her mind trying to break her resistance to his will.

He swung her toward him, flipping her in his arm and gathering her close, his sword still flexing in his right hand. She whimpered against his chest.

He thought the thought, the vibration began, and he was back at the palace right next to Endelle.

"What the fuck happened?" Endelle asked.

He turned to look at her, his gaze shifting about. He was in full warrior mode. Even his sword was still in his hand, something hard to do while dematerializing. Given the dangerous nature of his identified sword, he folded the weapon back to his weapons locker in his villa.

"Rith," he stated. "Almost had him, but he moved too damn fast. Can you block both our traces? We don't want that fucker showing up here."

"Shit, yeah," Endelle said. She closed her eyes, put her hand on Medichi. He felt her power, a smooth warm flow through him, through Parisa, and back into nether-space.

Medichi felt their pathways slam shut. At last he could take a breath.

Parisa moved in his arms then started hitting him and screaming. What the hell had that bastard done to her?

"Hey, hey, hey," he whispered against her ear. But she couldn't seem to hear him.

"Let me go," she cried. "You fucking bastard!"

He released her. She flew out of his arms, backward. That she wore heels and didn't stumble seemed like some kind of miracle. She lowered her knees into a crouch, dropping her shoulders at the same time. She glared at him. She blinked. She glared some more.

"Where is he? I'll kill him. I swear to God I'll kill him."

Her cheeks were flushed bright red and her hands clenched into white-knuckled fists.

The Warriors of the Blood drew closer to her. Only then did Medichi realize each was armed with a sword, each expression wild, ready to protect her.

Medichi crossed to her and stood in front of her. He held his hands out at his sides, intent on keeping her from moving too far away from him. She hadn't quite returned to herself, and the palace had many open terraces that dropped away to hundreds of feet below.

"Parisa," he said, trying for a firm voice.

She met his gaze, squinting. "Antony?"

"Yes. I'm right here."

"Rith. I saw Rith."

"I know. I followed you. I brought you back."

"It was some kind of cave. Then I looked into his eyes and I thought, *Not again*. He tried to fold me away, but I fought him."

"Yes, you did."

"But you followed after me? How did you know where to find me?"

"It's called a trace. When someone dematerializes, they leave a trace of light to their next landing point."

"Right." She nodded. "That's the reason that Thorne thinks Rith first moved the D and R slaves by vehicle—because if he'd folded them straight from his Mandalay home, he could have been followed."

"Exactly."

She shook her head several times back and forth.

Endelle drew close. "Are you telling me that Rith, who has a shitload of power, tried to fold you with him and you fought him off?"

"Yes. I did."

"But how could you do that when he folded you out of here, out of the palace?"

Medichi drew close to Parisa. The whole thing had rattled him. The same old questions surfaced: Could he keep her safe? Alive? Sweet Jesus.

Parisa shook her head. "He didn't fold me out of the palace. I folded to him. You had just completed the fang-face thing and his image took shape in my mind. I think he planted the image. He tricked me into leaving the palace. I had this moment of wanting him dead so badly that I thought the thought and suddenly I was flying through nether-space."

"Then the fold was all yours," Endelle said. "Well, shiiiit! That's fucking beautiful. Well done, ascender."

Leave it to Endelle to find the silver lining in a second kidnapping attempt.

Medichi tried to take Parisa's arm but she jerked it away. "Don't touch me." She looked wild-eyed as she met his gaze. "I'm just too upset. It's not personal, Antony. I . . . goddammit, I want to hit something, I'm so mad."

"All right," he said. "All right. You've convinced me, or maybe Rith has."

"Convinced you of what?"

"I need to train you to do battle: swords, knives, guns, hand-to-hand, whatever you fucking need."

At that she finally grew still and the tension eased out of her. She drew a deep breath. "Good."

Havily's voice rose to the rafters. "There, you see, Marcus! They're not even bonded and he can see reason. Why can't you?"

Medichi turned to stare at the elegant redhead. Her hands were on her hips as she glared at her *breh*. Marcus glared back.

"They have an entirely different situation," Marcus said, his brow low on his forehead, his nostrils flaring. "And I'm not discussing it. That subject is closed."

"You want to know what else is closed?" Havily lowered her chin, and there was nothing sugary or sweet about her attitude.

Marcus growled low, his eyes glittering.

"Don't even think it, Warrior. When I say closed, I mean *closed*." Split-resonance. *Nice*.

But again Marcus growled, and his lids fell to half-mast. Medichi foresaw trouble back at the villa. Havily was damn serious, and Marcus's testosterone had just leaped off the charts in a really unfortunate direction.

Medichi understood something about Marcus in this moment: The whole situation was arousing as hell to him. Yeah, Medichi so got that. The minute Parisa opposed him, about anything, it awoke some kind of bizarre sexual dominance instinct that sent electricity into his groin.

"Somebody get a hose." Endelle laughed, then her gaze shifted to Parisa. "As for you, ascender, let me check your fangs. You disappeared before I could see if everything worked."

"I'm not lowering my shields," she cried. "Because if that freak tries to invade my mind once more, I don't know what I'll do."

"Chill, ascender. You won't need to lower your shields. Now c'mon, because the caterer's telling me our dinner is ready."

Parisa returned to the cradle of Endelle's hands.

"All right, open your mouth."

Parisa obeyed.

"Now lower your fangs. It's not rocket science, just think the thought."

Parisa closed her eyes and relaxed her shoulders.

Medichi watched her tense suddenly and then he saw them emerge, sharp, pointed, and erotic. This meant one thing—his woman could take his blood.

A shiver ran through his body so profound, he actually took a step back to balance himself.

Parisa's head swiveled in Endelle's grasp. "What's with the sage?" she cried. She sounded a little funny because of the fangs. She put a hand to her lips then closed her eyes once more.

Slowly she opened her eyes again, then her mouth, and touched her teeth. She had drawn her fangs back into her gums. "Well, that was really weird." But she looked over at Medichi again and must have realized his present conundrum. "Oh. My. God."

"Yeah," he said, but his voice had dropped about an octave. His eyelids felt heavy. The wave of tangerine that hit him forced him to take another step back.

"Your fangs are working all right," Endelle said. "But I think we're going to need another hose. Jesus H. Christ." She made a disgusted sound at the back of her throat. "Okay, you're officially ascended. Let's eat."

She stepped away from Parisa and headed to her right, to the adjoining rotunda, her stilettos clacking across the marble floor. Her robe disappeared at the same time, revealing a leopard-skin dress. The warriors followed her. Trailing behind, Marcus and Havily argued in whispers.

"Babe, be reasonable," Marcus said. "You're protected because of the bond. Parisa will be, too, once she completes the *breh-hedden*."

"Bullshit," Havily whispered back. She quickened her pace and disappeared into the dining room.

"Babe," Marcus whined, following after.

The ceremony rotunda was now empty.

Medichi kept backing up and Parisa followed after him, her gaze locked to his, her mind all but reading his. He backed up until he hit a wall and both he and Parisa were invisible to the other guests.

"I want a taste . . . now," she whispered.

Medichi groaned and God help him, he was going to give it to her. Talk about playing with fire. She put her hands on his shoulders and rose up on tiptoes, her gaze pinned to his throat. With her heels she didn't have that far to go, even though he was six-seven.

But he stopped her.

"Why not?" she asked, a squeak in her voice.

She stared at the vein in his neck, which throbbed heavily now. He wanted her to have it but he leaned down next to her ear and said, "If you take my vein I won't be able to control what I do and I don't think you want anyone finding us in here *like that*."

He drew back. She blinked up at him. "Wrist?" she asked. Dear God, she licked her lips again, and the tips of her fangs showed.

"You'd better do it quick and when I say stop, you'd better stop."

"Okay." Could her voice sound any more seductive? And she was shedding tangerine like she was an orchard.

He offered his wrist. She took it in both hands, then licked a line over the collection of veins that showed blue. She looked up at him. "I used to watch you when you would take women into the booths at the Blood and Bite."

"I know," he growled. "You told me." He should have been shocked. She was a good little librarian. Okay, maybe not so good, but it wasn't helping the problem his erection was having with his tunic. He was making one fine tent out of it. Once more he leaned close to her ear.

"Lick it a few more times. Because you're a vampire now, the veins will rise to the surface just right." She obeyed him. Her tongue was small and wet, very feminine. He became a thin glass window that would shatter with the slightest pressure. "Yeah," he murmured. He kissed her earlobe. "Now go ahead, do what feels natural."

She did.

Her fangs struck and he hissed. The sharp sting, the knowledge that she had pierced him, that she could pierce him in other places, sent pleasure streaking up his arm and spreading like fire down his chest and into his groin. Then she started to suck, her head bobbing over his wrist. He groaned. He was so close to coming and she wasn't even taking blood from his neck, for Christ's sake.

She whimpered as he stroked her hair, her cheek, her chin. *Antony,* she sent, her voice plaintive through his mind. *I can taste sage as though your scent flavors even your blood.*

He wanted her to take it all, to drink him empty, to take the last fucking drop. The *breh-hedden* roared through him as if his life force was her food.

The scent of tangerines rose into the air around him until he was mindless. *Antony, I don't think I can stop. And I want you. I want you between my thighs . . . now.*

He didn't want to stop, either, but the voice that had been seductive had turned deep and guttural, more animal than woman. Dammit, he should have waited until they were back at the villa. He tried to speak, then thought—*Why not let her have a few more swallows?* He put his palm on her neck, riding the sucking bobs of her head, then moved in close and ground his erection against her hip. She made mewling sounds now and sucked harder. Dammit. For a terrible moment, he actually considered turning her into the wall and penetrating her. He knew she'd welcome him.

With a will that came from the simple knowledge that a room full of people waited for them, he used his free hand and slid a finger into her mouth. As soon as he broke the suction of her lips, she withdrew her fangs and took a deep breath.

His wrist was reddened from the sucking. He smiled. He'd wear it as a badge tonight. He wished it was possible to create a scar so that he'd always have a reminder of this moment. It was the rare scar that stuck, though, in the ascended world.

He held her close.

"I feel dizzy."

"Sharing blood like this will do it."

"All I could think about was how much I needed the rest of your body. How much I want you inside me."

"I know. We'll do that later."

She shifted against him to look up at him. "But not much later."

"No. Not much later because right now I'm in pain."

Her smile cast the world in a beautiful glow. He leaned down and kissed her on the mouth, the taste of his blood lingering on her lips. He pulled back.

"Welcome home, Parisa."

Thorne sat on Endelle's right, always on her right, her right-hand man, her second-in-command, Thorne the Reliable, Thorne who sipped gazpacho from his spoon but couldn't look at any of his warrior brothers.

Stannett's recent fucking revelation ate at him.

The large soup spoon trembled in his hand and he set it

down. Thank God there was so much noise at the table.
Right now Endelle was yelling at Santiago, clear across the
enormous round expanse of white linen, telling him that his
latest blade design was more a short sword than a dagger. He
was arguing back. To Santiago's right, Havily listened with
feigned interest. He doubted she cared about the subject at
all. She probably just wanted an excuse to turn a cold shoulder to Marcus.

So the *breh-hedden* didn't result in automatic relationship-
bliss. But then what the hell did?

He was done with his soup. Hell, he hated these kinds of
functions, wearing his dress uniform, his cape flipped back
over his shoulder. At least they'd removed the ceremonial
brass breastplates, which now sat in a row against the rotunda wall looking like disembodied chests. Next to the
breastplates, the wall opened up to one of the several palace
terraces.

Luken leaned close. "You think Parisa's okay?"

Thorne glanced at the dark-haired beauty. She had such
an interesting face, a slightly pointed chin, full lips, and
those amethyst eyes. Her cheeks were flushed, the kind of
flush that came from taking blood. Medichi had flashed
his wrist when he returned from the rotunda with Parisa
hugging his arm. The *breh-hedden* really was riding this
pair.

He had to look away. Sex, or at least the promise of it,
shimmered in the air between them. He could almost see the
glow of expectation. If Parisa seemed a little remote, what
of it? She'd been through hell for three months. She had a
right to look remote.

But Medichi had that look, like he knew he'd be taking
his woman to bed soon. It made Thorne want things he
wouldn't be able to have for another twelve-hours-plus. Once
a day, he went to be with his woman in the Creator's Convent. Once a goddamn day and no one knew. His sister was
the excuse but yeah, he went to see his woman.

He picked up his wineglass and downed the remainder of
the sangria. He then lifted it in the air and waggled it at the

waiter. He wanted maybe two more to help him calm the hell down.

Stannett and his damn prophesy about an upcoming battle.

After waging war against death vampires all night, and bringing Parisa safely home from Burma, he'd spent the rest of the morning with Colonel Seriffe. With Endelle's permission, he'd shared the prophecy with the head of the Militia Warriors. If Greaves intended an attack, the Militia Warriors would have to be involved. But the whole thing was fast becoming a nightmare. The Militia served both to keep the peace in regular ascended society and as backup against death vampire squads. But it was not a large force—maybe four thousand strong in the Metro Phoenix area.

Stannett's Superstition Mountain Seers Fortress had once been the world's most effective predictor of future events—it was the primary reason that until the twentieth century, Endelle had been able to control Greaves's intrusions into Second Society. But under Stannett's command, information from the fortress had dwindled to, as Endelle liked to put it, *a frog's stream of piss.*

Stannett had a lot of talented Seers, so either he didn't know how to make use of them, or he had plans of his own. Thorne knew the bastard well. He suspected the latter.

Endelle was frustrated to the point of madness but her hands were tied, as they often were, by the Committee to Oversee the Process of Ascension to Second Earth. COPASS. Yeah, the acronym suited this body of assholes. They'd backed Stannett when he denied Endelle admittance to his facility. If she even asked for information from the future streams, he'd shrug, smile, and apologize that his Seers, for inexplicable reasons, simply lacked the expertise and power. All lies, but who could prove it? He was no longer required to let anyone audit or even see his organization.

"You okay?" Luken whispered.

Both of Thorne's hands were shaking. "Sure," he said, glancing briefly at Luken. "Too much Ketel One, but I'm cutting back." It was both a lie and the truth. He was trying to cut back, yes, but that was only an excuse. In fact he knew something Endelle didn't: The Seer whom Stannett had re-ferred to—the source of the ominous prophecy—wasn't at the Superstition Seers Fortress. She was at the Creator's Convent. Thorne knew her well, really well. So, yeah, Stan-nett had spoken the truth about her abilities.

Where the hell was the waiter with his sangria?

He'd had more than one conversation with Endelle since Stannett's revelation, but she hadn't been all that helpful. Her latest suggestion was, *Would you please take a fucking chill-pill? It's probably just some Seer shit.*

But it wasn't.

Christ. A major battle coming and he couldn't talk about it to Endelle, because he'd vowed never to reveal the Seer's identity to Her Supremeness. Endelle was obliged by CO-PASS law to send any talented Seer to the Superstition For-tress, and that place had to be a hellhole right now. It certainly wasn't a bastion of freedom.

That Stannett played a double game by making frequent visits to the Creator's Convent, and not telling Endelle, had made Thorne's life close to unbearable. The Seer was his woman and had been his woman for the past hundred years.

Christ, what a fucking mess.

More sangria would really help about now and he almost barked at the waiter when he finally refilled his glass.

Endelle was still arguing with Santiago about his dagger. The Latin warrior stood behind his chair with his latest de-sign in his right hand, its hilt encrusted with three rubies—always rubies for Santiago. He showed her some moves. Most of the brothers were watching. Santiago loved to put on a show, and thank God for it because the tremors had moved up Thorne's arms.

They were all here, every damn one of them, all eight now because Marcus had returned, battling two nights a week. He loved them all. He needed them all. If he lost even one of his men, how would they survive as a unit, not to mention win this goddamn war?

* * *

Time, even this hour-long dinner, had given Parisa a little perspective. Her gaze kept flipping to the bruise on Antony's wrist. He'd had thirteen centuries to get used to taking blood and she hadn't. Not that she'd hesitated. She'd fantasized about it dozens of times, from the first moment she'd voyeured Antony, watching him enthrall mortal women at the Blood and Bite, gaping as he took their blood at wrist and neck—and once, shockingly, at a woman's ankle.

Desire streaked through her at the memories. At the same time another part of her brain recoiled: *You can't really be a vampire. This has to be a dream. Maybe a nightmare.*

Had she really sucked on his wrist and swallowed his blood?

Vampire. She kept rubbing her tongue over her incisors. More than once she thought the thought just so she could feel her fangs emerge, then disappear. The whole thing was so unreal.

She glanced at Antony. "Will you be battling tonight?" What a strange question to ask, and yet it was the right one. Antony was a warrior and fought death vampires every night of his life.

He leaned close and put an arm around her shoulders. "No," he said quietly. "Thorne wants me to stick close to you, at least until we can figure out a safer arrangement."

She shivered, and he laid a hand over hers. She knew he meant to offer comfort, but a terrible feeling of being contained came over her—boxed in, controlled. She pushed his hand away.

"What is it?" he asked.

She shook her head. "Not here."

"Okay." His arm slid away.

She let her gaze skip from warrior to warrior, then to Havily who was still ignoring Marcus, and finally to Endelle, now standing beside her throne-like dining chair and holding Santiago's dagger in her hand. She tossed it back and forth, feeling the weight. Where was Alison? Oh, yeah . . . baby troubles.

Parisa felt confused. She had left her prison but right now

she felt as though she'd locked herself into another one. A different kind of prison, with different rules of service and war. But still a prison.

She stood up as the caterers were arriving with bowls full of flan. The sight of the egg-custard dessert, so different from Burma and rice and turmeric, made her gag.

"I need to leave," she stated. She felt light-headed. "The food was lovely, Madame Endelle, but I have to go."

No one was listening to her. Santiago had just said something suggestive about the dagger and Endelle was chortling, her head thrown back.

Her chair scraped on the marble as she pushed it back. Her linen slid to the floor. She was turning away from Jean-Pierre, who had risen to his feet as well. She knew Antony was at her back.

"What is wrong, *cherie*?" Jean-Pierre's hand was on her arm.

Parisa stared at it. Rith always had his hands on her arms, controlling her, enthralling her. She shook his hand off. She backed away.

Antony slid in front of her. "Leave her alone," he said to Jean-Pierre, too loudly.

"She is not well. Look at her."

"Don't fucking touch her, Jean-Pierre."

Parisa backed away from the sudden anger. The table had become a tableau of frozen movement. Everyone stared at Jean-Pierre and Antony, then slowly each gaze turned to her.

Only then did Antony leave his bull-like stance with Jean-Pierre and meet her gaze. He frowned. "What is it?"

"I want to go home. Now."

"That's fine. Are you all right?"

She shook her head. "Just please take me home."

He nodded. He walked toward her, a hand outstretched. Rith used to do that. He would stretch his hands out, first one then the other. *Look at me,* he would command. She would meet his gaze and be lost.

"Don't touch me."

Antony lifted both hands in surrender but kept coming.

She kept moving backward. She stepped past the boundary of the wall. In some part of her mind she knew she was now on the terrace, and it was bounded by a low balustrade, nothing more.

But Antony kept advancing on her.

"I can't take you home if you don't stop moving. I have to touch you to fold you back to the villa. Do you understand?"

She nodded. Some part of her understood. Sort of.

He stopped suddenly but she kept moving backward. A breeze, hot and full of rich desert scents, blew over her. The stone railing stopped her progress, hitting her low at the top of her thighs. She blinked, glanced over the edge, then jumped back in Antony's direction. "Oh, God."

Suddenly Endelle was there. "What the fuck is the matter with you?" She scowled. "This is ascension, chickie. Get used to it quick."

Warrior Kerrick drew up beside her. "She needs Alison. I'll get her on the phone."

"No, don't," Parisa cried. She reached a hand toward Kerrick, who paused with his BlackBerry halfway to his ear. "I don't want Alison. I don't need her. I just—" She couldn't finish the sentence. She took a deep breath, and her gaze fell to the bruise she'd put on Antony's wrist. Her mind was an ocean that flowed first to one continent then back to the other.

She felt dizzy again and weak. So weak. She put a hand on Antony's arm. "Please take me to your home. Now. Please."

To sweep someone through nether-space was always one of the great pleasures of my ascended vampire life, second only to the giving and taking of blood.

—From *Memoirs,* Beatrice of Fourth

CHAPTER 10

Medichi didn't wait for permission. He didn't even glance anywhere but at her face. He slid his arms around Parisa and thought the thought. The next moment he stood holding her in the foyer of his villa.

But he didn't know what to do with her except release her.

She took several steps away, leaving him with a cold weight in the center of his heart. He'd been foolish. He knew that now. He had somehow thought that just being together would make for a quick transition into ascended life. He'd become convinced of it when he'd seen her amazing recuperative powers. When she'd taken his blood, he'd believed himself home free.

Foolish, indeed.

He gave her space. He even turned away from her to take a couple of steps to the central table of the foyer, the one that held an intricate and tall arrangement of white magnolias. The table was made of thick wood and, despite his size, he didn't hesitate to turn and lean his hips against it. Almost everything in his villa was warrior-sized. He crossed his arms over his chest and waited.

"You're angry with me," she said, her eyes haunted.

"I'm angry with myself. I've been very stupid about this, about you. I've been thinking with my dick and that's about it."

At that, a smile tugged at the edges of her lips.

"Glad I amuse you," he said.

"Your turn of phrase amuses me."

She was a librarian. She would notice things like that. He felt his lips curve, then he sighed. "I want to do right by you here, Parisa. Tell me what you need from me. I'm not without a lot of experience."

"Thirteen centuries' worth," she murmured.

"Yeah. And a few decades."

She nodded. "Precisely. I've had a total of three decades of living and none of them here, none of them in this dimension."

An hour or so ago he'd felt like a thin sheet of glass. That's what he saw in Parisa now, only for her it wasn't sexual as it had been for him. He thought he understood her better in this moment than he had all along.

He lifted off the edge of the table and moved a few feet away. The foyer was a large space, meant for mingling during large parties, the serving of cocktails, even dancing if anyone wanted to. There hadn't been a dance here in over a hundred years. That's how bad the war had gotten, the seemingly inexhaustible war.

He sat down on the floor as if he were sitting at a campfire, crossing his ankles then settling his forearms on his widespread knees. The ceremonial black tunic hung low and kept necessary things private. The cape and brass breastplate were back at the palace. Whatever.

She seemed surprised as she looked down at him. "What are you doing?"

He shrugged. "Giving you time and space and all my attention. No one is here to force you to do anything. Endelle might bluster and try to bully you, but common sense always wins with her in the end. Still, I think since Alison's ascension she's grown more capable of listening to reason. Not much more, but *more*. As for me, if I'm too possessive right now, I can't take the full blame for that. Your scent clogs all my logic and most of my sensitivity."

She released a deep sigh, so he knew he'd done the right thing for her. Space. Funny, it was the last thing he needed.

"So what happened?" he asked.

"What do you mean?"

He glanced at his loosely clasped hands then met her gaze straight-on. Shit, he was going to ask the hard question, the one he'd never been able to answer. "I never knew what happened the day that Rith took you. Do you think you could talk about it? Tell me? Tell me how I screwed up?"

Her arms fell away from her chest. "How you screwed up?" The question didn't seem to make sense to her.

"I was your guardian. I let some preternaturally powerful asshole drag you off and I didn't even notice, not for half a minute."

She took a step toward him. "So you really didn't see me disappear?"

Talking about it brought the memory sweeping back in a slow flood of horror. He told her what it had been like for him, how he'd been talking on his phone to Thorne while he kept track of her from his peripheral vision, and that only after a while had he realized that she was standing too still—not even the breeze moving through the grove touched the hem of her sundress.

He talked for a ridiculously long time about the day of her abduction, how the warriors had all gathered at the villa, how the grounds had been searched and every building turned upside down to make sure she wasn't somewhere on the property. He talked about his sleeplessness. He talked about the limoncello.

He'd meant to get her talking, and now he couldn't stop the flow of his own words if his life depended on it.

By then she was kneeling beside him, her fingertips

touching the circles beneath his eyes. He met her eyes, wet with tears. She leaned close and kissed him on the lips.

He held very still. He wanted to drag her into his arms but he was probably always going to feel like that. He had enough sense to know that this wasn't the time for his male aggression to be at the fore. He sighed and kept his hands clasped tightly together.

She sat as he sat, with her ankles crossed and drawn close, her knees spread. She slipped off her shoes and set them next to her. Her white flowered dress draped in folds over the empty cradle of her lap. She put a hand on his knee and drew a deep breath.

Then she began to talk.

"The house was lovely. Rith's house. It was made entirely of mahogany. It was a replica of an old British Colonial house. You didn't see it, did you?"

He shook his head. "Only you flying through the dome of mist." Her hand was warm on his bare knee. "The rest of the warriors saw the house, but not me. Maybe you and I should go back, look around."

She shook her head. "Maybe, but not yet."

He wanted to ask her a dozen questions. They piled up on his tongue and tried to break through his front teeth but he held them back.

Her nails scraped gently at his skin. She probably wasn't aware she was doing it. "The same day that he brought me to his house, he pierced my mind until I was screaming. When I first arrived, I didn't know what I was doing in that beautiful home or even who he was. He told me I wouldn't be hurt if I did as I was told, and that Greaves had asked him to house me for a week or so. Yes, he said a week or so. *What then?* I had thought. What would happen after a week?

"He left me sitting on a bench beneath a tamarind tree. It was the most beautiful garden. No one has ever had such a lovely prison, but it was like being punished by having an endless number of cotton balls thrown at you. They might not hurt, but after awhile the craziness sets in, the despair.

"So I sat under that tree. I waited for hours, not knowing

what to do. Finally, I went in search of him. I found three female Burmese servants who only glanced at me. I tried to speak with them, to ask them what I was supposed to do and where Rith had gone. None of them would respond.

"I eventually found him in his study. He didn't even seem angry when he saw me. But he took me into a back bedroom and he must have enthralled me again because when I woke up or came to consciousness, I was bound to a very comfortable recliner, like a La-Z-Boy.

"Then he entered my head. It was like whirling knives. I screamed and screamed until I was hoarse.

"When he withdrew, he spoke five words: *You do as I say.* That's all he said to me during that first day. The lesson, however, was complete.

"Looking back, life was simple after that. When I didn't do something exactly the way he wanted it done, he put his hands on my arms, then shot his mind into mine. The pain was brutal. But it always started with the hands. That's . . . that's why I recoiled when you reached out to me like you did earlier, at the palace. I wanted you to understand."

He nodded, taking deep breaths. The thought of Rith going mind-diving sent his protective instincts skyrocketing. But this wasn't about him, or his reactions to what she was saying. This was about *her.* "So what happened at the dinner to put you back there, back in your prison?"

She shook her head and released another sigh. "The whole situation suddenly felt the same to me as being in Rith's home. Go here, sit there, do this, obey. Nothing else is important."

"Endelle, then. You know she can be a pain in the ass."

"It's not that. Did it ever occur to you that you're all living in the same kind of prison? This is a beautiful villa, but Antony, you've been a warrior for thirteen hundred years and it appears to be without end. You don't do anything except make war."

"But I *choose* to serve Endelle."

"Do you?"

Her expression was so earnest that he was taken aback.

He thought for a long moment. "Life isn't simple, Parisa. Not as an immortal, not as a vampire, not for anyone. There are worse things than what I endure as a warrior or what you've endured as a captive."

He was afraid his words would be offensive to her, but she nodded. She leaned forward and stroked a hand along his back so that her fingers rippled over his scars. "Fiona has suffered more than I ever did," she murmured. "Like I said, I had three months of being struck by cotton balls and all the while she was a D and R slave."

He nodded. She didn't seem quite so distressed.

"Thank you for not coddling me," she said. "I don't want to be coddled. I know I'm not strong like you, but I'm trying. I want to be stronger, Antony, I really do. I want to be of use, but I also know it's going to take some time for me to adjust to everything." She slid her hand over his shoulder and down his arm, all the way down. He shivered.

She turned his wrist to face her. "This freaked me out at dinner. This is what set me off."

He leaned forward. "Damn, I'm so sorry but I thought you enjoyed it. In fact—"

"I did," she cried. "I loved . . . taking your blood." Color flooded her cheeks. Was she going to start weeping? "I don't know if I can explain it but it just became so real while I was sitting next to you that I'd entered the world of the vampire. I guess I felt claustrophobic."

At that he smiled. "In a building with ceilings fifty feet high, you felt claustrophobic?"

She squeezed his arm. "Yeah. I did." Then she laughed, a long trill that warmed his heart. Afterward, she leaned forward and rested her head on his forearm.

He shifted slightly and stroked her lovely dark brown hair. It wasn't fine but coarse. He'd pulled her onto his lap at the Ambassadors Festival, the night Havily had been abducted by Crace. He'd held her close then. She'd gone through so much during that time without being ascended yet. Then she'd lived for three months as a prisoner. Now she was here, ascended, bearing fangs, confused, distressed.

"I can really see how this must feel like just another prison to you."

She released a heavy sigh. "Yes, it does, but thank you for understanding or trying to."

"I do understand and you're right, I sometimes feel like a prisoner of this war."

"So what do we do?" She remained leaning on his knee.

He kept stroking her hair. He wanted to hold her, to kiss her, but he also didn't want to disturb this time with her. "Well, I start training you to do battle, and after that, let's bring Fiona home. I think that's our first duty, Fiona and the rest of the D and R slaves."

She lifted her head and looked up at him as though seeing him for the first time. "It is that simple, isn't it. We take one step and then another—"

"—and we try not to let the horror catch up with us."

"That's it exactly. Yes, I felt exactly like that. I was sitting there and then I realized, *Now I'm a vampire.* It turned me upside down."

He smiled because he'd just realized something himself. "You turned me upside down. I was going along splendidly, behaving myself, except at the Blood and Bite, of course, and the next thing I knew I was smelling tangerines in my villa. Just out of a shower, still dripping, and there you were. The most beautiful woman in the world standing in my kitchen."

She smiled. "The most beautiful in the world?"

"Yeah." His voice had dropped an octave again.

She met his gaze, and something flickered in those amethyst depths. "You dropped your towel."

He nodded and shrugged. "I dropped my fucking towel. Have I apologized for that?"

"There was never a need for an apology, Antony." Her voice had gotten very low as well. "I had never seen anything so beautiful. I thought I was looking at a god."

He leaned close and dragged his lips across the line of her cheekbone. "Do you know what I remember about that day?"

"No, what?"

"I remember that you put your hand to your neck and stroked your skin, right about here." He used the knuckle of his forefinger to touch her throat. "Do you remember?"

She nodded. "Uh-huh. I do. My vein was throbbing." She drew back. "Right here, pulsing like it was waiting for you."

He leaned a little closer lowering his knee so that she was forced to move into him. "Is your vein waiting again?"

He could smell a thick wave of tangerine rise from her body, flowing around him, drifting heavily into his nostrils, his sinuses, his brain. There wasn't a lot of room to maneuver, sitting the way they were, but he balanced on his hip, slid an arm around her back, and held her in place as he dragged his fangs across her throat.

Here, he sent directly to her mind.

"Oh, God, yes," she murmured. He felt her fingers now on his throat. As he drew back, her lips parted and he saw her fangs. Oh, shit, he was so in the wrong position to have his cock start demanding attention.

He rose up on his knees and caught her around the waist with his hands. He drew her close and kissed her. "Will you come to bed with me?"

She nodded, "Uh-huh." Her lips were still parted, the tips of her fangs calling to him.

He whispered, "My vein throbs for you as well."

Parisa rose to her feet, Antony with her. She dipped down to pick up her shoes. He slid an arm around her shoulders and guided her into the adjacent formal living room, then down the long, long hallway to his master suite. The house smelled sweetly of his rich sage mixed with leather and the musk of his skin.

He didn't say anything.

The trouble with walking such a great distance was that her mind had time to fill up with images again, but not ones that involved Antony's throat or her newly created fangs.

Her thoughts started moving around, gnawing on problems

she couldn't solve right now, fretting over just how hard it would be to learn to do battle or to protect herself, worrying about . . . pregnancy.

She stopped in her tracks and turned to him. "Condoms?" she asked, her cheeks warming.

He nodded, then he smiled. "Come on. We'll be okay." He urged her forward with a tug on her arm but she still couldn't move.

The trouble was—and this was so wrong,—she didn't want him to use a condom. She wanted to feel him just the way he was, all of him, inside her.

"We don't get diseases," he said, "of any kind, in case you were wondering. No herpes or HIV."

She hadn't been wondering, but, "Good to know. That means me as well now." Huh. Yes, there were definite advantages to ascension. She started walking again.

They reached the doors to his bedroom, a beautifully carved double set that had to be at least twelve feet high. He had his hand on the knob when she touched his wrist. "I had my period three days ago."

She looked up at him, knowing full well that her cheeks were now flaming. Would he take the hint?

But his eyelids dropped a good half inch and a soft growl sounded deep in his throat. "You sure that's what you want?"

The only thing she was sure of right now was that she just was about to die of embarrassment. She barely knew Antony. They'd only had sex once not counting mutual self-pleasure for three months, and here she was discussing contraceptive methods. And here she was saying she didn't want a bit of latex to interfere with her pleasure. Oh, God.

She put her hands on her cheeks and squeezed her eyes shut. Okay, maybe she was being childish. She drew back her shoulders and met his gaze. "I want to have sex with you, we're fairly safe right now, and I don't want you to wear a condom." There, she'd been brave and said exactly what she wanted.

He threw the door open, caught her up in his arms, and carried her to the bed, pausing only to kick the door shut. He tossed her on her back at the foot of the bed. Her legs dangled over the edge.

"Now," he said, dipping down low and planting a hand onto the mattress on either side of her head. "Tell me how you want this. You've been through hell. Let's see if we can make your life a little better."

She writhed under his gaze, his dark brown eyes glittering in the dim light. The sun was on the wane, but the shutters drawn almost three-quarters created a twilight in his bedroom.

She smiled up at him and slid her hand along the side of his cheekbones. His face was almost sculpted, the bones strong and pronounced. He was so beautiful. She hadn't been kidding when she said he looked like a god.

"First," she said, wondering how she'd gone from completely embarrassed to ready to tell him exactly what she wanted and in what order, "I want your clothes off. I want to look at you."

He smiled then grinned. He pushed away from the bed, drew up to his full height, waved a hand, and that was it, clothes gone.

Oh, yeah . . . ascension. She sat up and pushed at his abdomen. "Move back," she commanded. "I want to see you."

His smile remained. He stepped away from her and moved in a slow circle, his hands spread wide. Her gaze traveled up and down over a hard warrior body. Shivers moved along her shoulders and back, over her legs. He was lean, muscled, with broad shoulders angling to narrow hips and long powerful thighs. He was covered in fine black hair that made the tip of her tongue tingle as certain thoughts drifted through her head.

When he returned to facing her, she dropped her gaze to his cock and to his heavy, rippled sac. Pubic hair covered a good amount of his groin. He was partially thick so that he hung long, broad, and just off to the right . . . as though with a touch or two, he would spring up, making all sorts of promises.

She had seen him stroke himself through her voyeur's

window. But she wanted to see him do it now in front of her.

"Touch yourself," she whispered. She still sat on the bed, her feet flat on the floor, her white, flowered dress fanned around her hips.

He smiled, a small crooked smile, and his eyes looked knowing and very dark. He drew close, maybe a foot and a half away. His hand wrapped around his thick stalk and in a slow languorous movement rubbed himself from stem to stern and back.

"Closer." Again she spoke in a whisper.

He moved to stand just inches away.

She put her fingers on his hand as he pumped. Then she leaned close and kissed the back of his hand. He stopped all movement and, groaning softly, let his hand fall away. Now she was kissing what she had wanted to kiss from the beginning.

She drew back and stared at the beautiful, broad head. She ran her thumb over the tip. He was wet. She leaned forward and licked the tip, the aperture where good things came from. Then she took the head in her mouth and sucked. He almost filled her.

"Oh, my God," he whispered. As he groaned the room filled with sage. Shivers poured over her shoulders, tightening her breasts and working like fingers down her abdomen and lower.

She planted her hands on his hips and moved in, taking as much of him in her mouth as she could until he hit the back of her throat. With her fingers, she played up and down with what remained outside. When she cupped him low, he hissed and pulled himself out of her mouth.

She looked up at him and smiled.

"It feels too damn good."

She nodded.

His eyes swam with fire. His fists were clenched at his sides. "What would you like to do next?"

The question felt like chocolate mousse after an already rich meal, decadent, unholy, way-too-much, and yet perfect.

She smiled again. A ripple of possibilities sped through her mind. As she picked one idea up and set it aside, then another and another, she stroked his thighs, carefully avoiding his raging erection.

Choices. Choices.

She looked up at him, way up. "Take your *cadroen* off. I want to feel your hair, all of it. I've been craving my hands in it more than I can say."

He lifted his arms, swelling the muscles of his chest and upper arms. Her heart sped up. He *was* a god and right now he was hers as he released the *cadroen* and let his hair spread over his shoulders, down his arms, and down his chest.

She rose to her feet. "Now sit down so I can do this right."

They traded places as he sat down. She turned into him and moved between his spread legs. He was a banquet, oh such a feast, but first—his warrior hair.

She drifted her fingers from the top of his head all the way down past his shoulders and over his chest. She lifted her hands and thrust her fingers into his hair just below his temples.

She had wanted this from the first time she had voyeured him after a shower. She couldn't explain how his hair made her feel, but it was as though something essential lived there, a reflection of who he was, certainly of his warrior status.

She took a large portion and wrapped it around her hand. Then she loosed her grip and the strands eased, separated, and flowed over her fingers. He had very fine hair, so different from her own. She grabbed another thick portion, pushed her fingers through, and dragged downward until she hit a snag. She withdrew. She kept tugging, stroking, playing until he groaned and his lips found her in a surprising kiss. She hadn't realized how close she was.

She opened her mouth to gasp and his tongue filled her. "Oh," she murmured, leaning against him.

She suckled his tongue and his arms glided around her back, his erection still firm and hard against her abdomen. His hips rocked, and she felt that sturdy length glide up her abdomen. He kept thrusting his tongue and gliding his cock as he pushed the fabric of her dress around.

She drew back. Her lips felt swollen. "I want my dress off."

He put a hand to her shoulder and folded the dress off. She had a glimpse of the white and splashy flowers appearing on a chair near the blinds.

She smiled. "That's a great trick."

His hands were on her shoulders and he pushed away from her. He growled as his gaze drifted over the rest of her clothes, red lace underwire bra, red lace panties, no stockings.

"I'm smelling sage, lots of it," she whispered.

He made a sound like a grunt and grabbed her around the waist. He rose to his feet and lifted her to kneel on the bed. This put her breasts, in a most fortuitous happenstance, right at mouth level. She giggled. He scooped each breast out of her bra to rest in large mounds on the underwires. She drew back just out of reach of his mouth.

He looked up at her, uncertain, but she shook her head. "I didn't say you could do that." But her look dared him and begged him at the same time.

He put his hands on her back and never lost eye-contact. His brown eyes were black in the twilight. He pushed on her back, forcing her toward him, his lips parted, his tongue drifting over his bottom lip.

Oh, God.

She resisted. She put her hands on his shoulders. She stared at him and pushed back, but he was stronger and kept pulling her toward him. Her nipples grew peaked, giving the lie to her resistance.

His tongue was so close. The well of her body tightened. She cried out, gave way. He pulled her in tight and took her left breast in his mouth, as much as he could. His movements were rapid and harsh, just what she wanted, as he sucked, pulled, licked, and worked her into a frenzy.

In this position, his thick cock found the inside of her left thigh. She pressed her legs together so that his cock could stroke the tight space between. He was way too low to penetrate, but the feel of his mouth on her breast brought deep moans from her throat.

Antony, she sent, straight to his mind. *I need more. Now.* Yes, her telepathy had improved.

She had meant for him to penetrate her hard and fast because she was so ready for him.

Instead he released her breast and, in a quick movement, grabbed her both high and low, behind her shoulders and across her bottom, then laid her out once more on the bed. He dragged her hips to the end so that her legs hung off the side, then he sank to his knees on the floor.

She leaned up, intending to protest, but he pushed her back. "You've had your way," he said, holding her chest down with one hand while the other ripped her lace panties off. "Now I'm going to do what I want to do."

She might have protested but then he put his mouth against her lower lips and French-kissed her.

Oh. Dear. God.

He was a big man, and so was his tongue. He glided over her and she cried out. He kissed her labia then poked and prodded every fold of her with the tip of his tongue until she was gasping and panting.

"Hold on," he whispered.

"Hold on for what?" She looked down at him and he looked up. He smiled but it was a wicked smile, full of purpose and design and, oh, God, his fangs emerged.

He bent low once more. Nestling his face against her lower lips, he drew back then struck.

Oh, shit, he'd used a fang. Just one. She felt a warmth right there. The pleasure started, a tingling at first, then like rivulets of electricity and pleasure mingled. Potions. That's right. His fangs could release chemicals. She whimpered and her eyes rolled back in her head.

He slid a finger deep inside, then two.

Her upper body felt frozen as the sensation glided over her. She flung her legs wide as though trying to escape it, which of course only made things worse, or *better,* since he groaned and his groan clutched something deep in her chest.

Tangerine, he whispered through her mind.

He stroked her with his fingers. He laid his tongue flat against her and just rolled over her, the barest pulse of movement, but with the potion working it felt as if a dozen tongues were flicking over all that sensitive flesh. His fingers moved faster and then she cried out because it was like nothing she had ever felt before. If this was ascension, oh, God, give her more and more and more.

The orgasm struck, a bolt of lightning that traveled through her in a pulse of pleasure. She was bucking off the bed, but he kept her pinned now with an arm across her hips as she rode the orgasm. He kept moving his tongue, helping her along, sustaining the roll of ecstasy. Only as she stopped straining against his arm, only as her body settled down, did he pause, his fingers quiet, his tongue not touching her.

Even so, little jolts of orgasm struck her over and over.

Finally, when she lay quiet on the bed, he asked, "Ready for another?"

"Another what?" Her heart skipped a few beats. "There's more?"

Without asking for permission or giving her a chance to catch her breath, he thrust his fingers into her again and again, hard and fast. He laid his tongue against her once more, pressed into her, then rippled over her flesh. Another orgasm chased the last one, streaking through her until she was screaming and screaming. A full minute passed before her hips grew quiet. She couldn't stop the panting, though, and her heart raced.

His deep throaty laugh blew between her thighs. She heard the smugness, the delight, the thrill, and she knew he wasn't done.

Oh, dear God.

He worked her three more times.

Three more times.

Three more outrageous screams at the ceiling, more orgasms that were no doubt blinding her for life. The pleasure was so intense that tears streaked from her eyes and rolled into her hair.

She lay panting, *again,* a hand pressed to her forehead. "I don't think I can take much more."

"Parisa," he said, his voice almost singsong.

Her hand fell away and she lifted her head and met his gaze. Such teasing, laughing eyes, so happy, so very wicked.

He rose up from his kneeling position as though moving in slow motion. He pushed his hair back with his hands and laced his hands behind his neck.

Her mind had turned to mush but her gaze had sharpened. He knew exactly what he was doing as his pecs and arms swelled and his abdomen tightened. Male beauty personified.

She took her time looking. Despite all the orgasms he'd given her, hunger drove her all over again. As she took in the wonderful size of him, the beauty of his crown, the veins bulging and filling what needed to be filled, the heavy sac, she heard a growl and realized that her throat had formed the sound, a predatory and extremely possessive sound—a vampire sound.

He lowered his arm slowly to hold his sac in one hand and show her one long stroke of his cock with the other.

"You want to finish this, vampire?" he asked.

She met his gaze and for a moment time stopped. Never in her life had she felt more of a sense of belonging than she did at this moment. *Vampire.* She rolled the word around in her mind and something clicked into place. Maybe there was a reason why she'd felt so separated from those around her. Maybe she'd never really belonged on Mortal Earth.

But she belonged here, in Antony's bed. Of that one thing, she was certain. She belonged in this warrior's bed.

She opened her arms and he glided between her legs as he stretched out on top of her. She was wet but he was big, and it took a few strong, wonderful pushes to make his way inside. As he did, she felt full—as though he wasn't just connecting sexually but working his way into her heart as well . . . and she let him, whatever that might mean for the next few hours, days, or years.

He filled her and for some reason she felt whole. Yes, that's how she felt in this moment with Antony's body on top of hers, the weight of him pressing into her flesh, her muscles, her bones, she felt whole, as though the healing had begun. After everything she'd gone through, what a surprise that sex with him would make her feel like this.

He looked into her eyes then kissed her, and she tasted all that she was on his lips. He began to move, to thrust, to draw back and push in. She slung an arm around his neck and kissed him back. She drove her tongue into his mouth and he groaned.

This wouldn't take long. She was already tightening around him, and the potion he'd put into her was still acting like an aphrodisiac to all her sensitive lower flesh. She writhed beneath him, seeking contact in a dozen different places at once, which made all his groans deepen. She bucked beneath the pressure of each thrust until she was meeting him, slamming into him, dragging her internal muscles over the impossible length and girth of him.

He sped up. She gripped his back, sank her nails.

"Parisa, Parisa," he whispered between groans.

She could hear her voice, almost a high keening sound. The pleasure was intense and building, swelling, rising. She felt the orgasm coming, an enormous wave; when it descended it crashed over her, pushing Antony up as she thrust her hips into him.

He gave a shout, moved impossibly fast within her, pumping hard and with another shout spent himself. The jerks of his thick cock brought yet another climax, pushing her again to the heights. His eyes were wild as he met her gaze.

Antony breathed through her mind as it had every night for three months. A smile took his lips.

I'm here, he whispered and her tears began to fall once more as she sank into the mattress.

He collapsed on her, which forced a sigh out of her throat.

She held him close, her arms wrapped around his neck and all his warrior hair. His breathing was labored. So was hers. She closed her eyes and just let herself rest and breathe with the minutes that began to pass one after the other.

Maybe she didn't know a lot about what her life should be, but yes, she belonged here, at least for now.

After what seemed like an eternity, her eyes opened. She looked up at the beautiful dark wood coffer beams that formed a three-dimensional chessboard on the ceiling.

As her gaze grew more focused, she saw that words, in what looked like Italian, were burned in a beautiful flowing script along each beam, crossed and crisscrossed, one line running into the next. She followed each line and realized that at one point, the lines began to repeat, probably three times in all from one end of the long room to the next.

"Antony," she whispered, her voice hoarse, her throat raw from making so much noise.

"Yes," he mumbled against her neck.

"What is that writing on the coffer beams?"

He turned his head slightly and looked at her. He put his fingers to her lips and a heavy, deep sigh left his body. "A poem my wife wrote."

"You were married?" Of course he would have been married. He'd lived for centuries.

He nodded. "A long, long time ago, before I ascended."

She felt the sudden stiffness in his body and wasn't surprised when he eased out of her and rolled onto his back, his gaze also drifting to the beams. She could feel the pain of those few words as though he'd spoken it aloud. She didn't want to ask. She didn't want to know, not the meaning of the words, not why he ascended without his wife, but she had opened the subject, unwittingly.

She turned on her side toward him. She felt his seed and her wetness begin to spill out of her. "Hey, magical one, can you get me a few tissues or a washcloth?"

He smiled then laughed. He folded what she needed into his hand but instead of giving it to her, he rolled toward her and murmured, "Spread your legs."

Still on her side, she lifted her left leg. He very gently covered the well of her, then cupped her. She lowered her leg, pinning his hand and the tissues in place. Because he faced her, he leaned toward her and kissed her. "Thank you for not asking."

She kissed him back. "Thank you for making love to me. It was exactly what I needed. Now I feel like I'm home."

That made him smile.

CHAPTER 11

The next morning, Parisa stood on a semicircle of pavers in front of the villa, the place where Havily had taught her to fly. Now she was trying to learn something new, but what Antony wanted her to do had her stomach tied up in knots.

Jean-Pierre and Havily stood a good distance away, maybe twenty feet or so, giving her space as if they, too, sensed her struggle. Jean-Pierre had agreed to help with the training, and Havily, against Marcus's wishes, had insisted on being part of the lesson. Havily held a sword in her hand.

"The only way you can do this," Antony said gently, "is if you lower your mental shields."

She shook her head. Her gaze seemed permanently fixed to his black tee just below the ribbing around the neck. She couldn't seem to look at him; nor could she explain why. "I don't think I can do this," she whispered. "I know I asked you to help me so that I could learn really fast, but I'm kind of stuck here."

Only then did she lift her gaze to his. A slight furrow marred his brow. He lifted a hand and touched her cheek lightly. "I've never seen you this . . . frightened."

"I am frightened, aren't I?"

"Why? Because you're afraid Rith will find you again?"

She shook her head. "No, that's not it. I have no doubt that Rith has sufficient power to track me, but he can't make me fold to him again. What happened at the palace caught me by surprise. I felt drawn, so I folded. But believe me, Rith won't be able to do that a second time."

"Well, if that's not what's bothering you, then what is?"

The light went on. "Letting someone, *anyone,* inside my head. I just have the worst feeling." And suddenly, the memory returned to her, so fast that she listed sideways. Antony's hand caught her and kept her from stumbling. "Greaves came to me. I remember now. Oh, God. He sat in that large teak chair across from me. He drank tea from a white teacup. I was sitting on the bench beneath the tamarind tree, the one I told you about. Remember?"

"Of course I remember. What happened?"

"He drank his tea and he watched me as though trying to figure out how to take my mind, how to bypass my shields. Then he came to sit by me, but that's all I remember. Later, I woke up on the grass." She put a hand to her forehead and rubbed back and forth slowly. "Antony, I think he might have gotten inside my head. That's why I'm so uncomfortable right now. At least, I think that's it."

"Well, I'm not Greaves," he said. "Do you trust me?"

She met his gaze again. "Yes. Of course I do. With my life."

"Can you focus on that?"

She took another deep breath and closed her eyes. He put his palms back on her cheeks, where they'd been for the last several minutes.

She tried. She really tried. But she just couldn't let her shields down.

"Are you sure you trust me?"

"Yes, of course."

"Maybe not as much as you think."

She glanced up at him again, her eyes flying open. "That's not true."

"There is a current thought that suggests our mental shields reflect our life in some way. Maybe you need to ask yourself why your shields are like steel."

Parisa had to admit it made some sense. She met Antony's gaze again, but this time she smiled. "Do all preternatural powers have some basis in neuroses?"

At that he laughed. "You'd have to ask Alison. She's the psychologist, but it's an interesting theory. A more accurate word, I think, might be personality. You have something of an analytical mind. Your tendency to shield like a citizen of the third dimension and not Second Earth might have something to do with that."

She sighed and focused not on her fear or her disinclination to lower her shields or whatever the hell this was, but instead on the woman who had come running out of Rith's house begging for her help. She couldn't be of use to Fiona if she didn't learn some battle skills. She had to be ready to defend herself, even in a limited way. As soon as Central got a fix on Fiona's location, the warriors would need her voyeur skills on-site, and she would be there.

Maybe it was remembering Fiona's desperation or her terrible death and resurrection, but she took Antony's hands and placed them on her cheeks. "Let's just do this," she said, her jaw tight. And without debating the damn subject one more second, she let her shields fall, like gravity tugging apples straight down.

Antony's battle memories didn't rush at her. Instead, they came in a long slow glide. When the first image hit, of standing beneath a starlit sky at the Superstition Mountains, of Jean-Pierre beside him, of three death vampires in the air and four on the ground, she breathed in each passing frame like a sweet breeze.

She lived the battle with him and felt the strength of his emotional web, the pure adrenaline of a Warrior of the Blood, of his simple intention of making all the horrible monsters in front of him very dead. She felt all his expertise of having wielded a sword and a dagger for thirteen centuries. She experienced exactly how his body reacted while facing the enemy, the flexing of all the powerful muscles of his arms, back, shoulders, thighs, and calves; how he performed impossible feats of speed, of dematerialization, of whirling, of levitation, of strength. How he worked in tandem with Jean-Pierre, always marking the brother warrior's location to keep both of them safe and battling at peak performance. She saw the ground in front of him run red. She saw bodies and severed parts and feathers and wings scattered across the desert, a painting on a macabre canvas worthy of the worst of horror films.

She drew in deep breaths as though she were running a race, inhaling along with him in the memory, sucking in air.

Within the memory, she felt Antony fold a cloth from the villa, a stack that he kept next to his weapons locker, and with it he wiped down his sword as well as his dagger. She felt him call Jeannie and heard the woman's matter-of-fact voice repeating his commands to remove the battle debris. She closed her eyes with him, saw the flash behind her closed eyelids, opened her eyes, *his eyes,* and marveled at the clean earth.

The memory ended, almost too abruptly. Antony began to withdraw from her mind, which felt like a long pull of taffy until the stretch thinned, then broke. She stepped back and bobbed her head. "That was so strange."

When he didn't say anything, she looked up at him. His lips were parted, swollen. "I liked being in there," he murmured, his voice like tumbling into a deep well.

She drew in a soft breath as sage surrounded her, pelted her, touched her in deep private places.

"I'd like to be there again." He moved closer, less than an inch away.

She shivered and felt her body respond to this very sensual invitation, but she had other concerns on her mind. "Hold that thought, Warrior."

"Right, right."

She understood. He couldn't exactly control all that was happening to him because of the *breh-hedden*.

She took a small step back and met his gaze. She even put her hand on his chest as though holding him back.

"Are you all right?" he asked. Just like that the sage receded.

"I'm not sure. It was amazing. I experienced what you felt while battling, and I'm not even upset about what I saw."

"But you're distressed. I can feel it."

She blinked a few times. How could she tell him that what bothered her had to do not with the battle images but with how close he was standing to her, that he had already expressed how much he'd like to be inside her head again.

It occurred to her in a swift flash that her life had never been about *again,* but more like *never-again.* For whatever reason, a collage of her own memories shot in front of her eyes, of being a child and later a teenager, the number of times she'd been taken out of school, right in the middle of class, and moved across country. In her entire life, she'd never been in a situation where she could develop long-term friendships, except at work. Even then she kept her personal life separate.

Later, when she'd fallen in love, she was convinced her college sweetheart, Jason, was the one; whatever her life had been before, love had found her and she would build a new life with him. Then he'd walked out that last night. He'd called her inaccessible, which had made no sense to her. She had opened her heart to him and he'd left. So, yeah, *never again.*

But why was she thinking of this now?

"Parisa, what is it?" He frowned now, heavily.

She shook her head. She didn't know what to say to him. "I'm not sure."

"Did I hurt you?" he asked.

"I'm fine," she said. "I . . . it's just it was such a strange experience." She couldn't tell him the truth: that sharing his memory like that had left her frightened of something she couldn't explain. She just didn't want to be that close . . . to anyone.

So she ordered her mind and walked away from him, swinging her arms about and focusing on the feel of the memory. In other words, she changed the subject. "Even when I walk, I'm feeling your muscles in my arms and legs. It's extraordinary, Antony. Do you think I could try wielding a sword now? And I'd like to practice throwing a dagger as well."

Medichi stared at Parisa, at *his woman.* He had never felt as far from her as he did now. For him the sharing of his battle memories had been sexy as hell, and he wanted more. In fact he wanted it so much he could taste it, but was it him or just the horrible demand of the *breh-hedden*?

It hardly mattered. Parisa had shut him down. She'd closed up her mind and shut him down.

On the other hand, maybe it was for the best. What was he to her, anyway, but her Guardian of Ascension, the warrior assigned to keep her safe? Yes, he was her *breh,* just as she was his. But wasn't that all just destiny bullshit?

Parisa would be wise to keep her distance, shore up her defenses, turn him down. This was war. One long horrible war.

Fine. Then he'd teach her to make war.

He had several swords in his weapons locker. Only one was identified, which meant the rest would be perfectly safe for Parisa to handle. Identified swords were deadly weapons designed specifically for battling death vampires. If anyone but the swords owner touched the hilt or cross-guard, it would result in death.

The only exception was Alison, who had endured a one-on-one battle with Warrior Leto, a former Warrior of the Blood. Alison had brought *his* sword into her hand and somehow, through power he had never seen before on Second Earth, recalibrated the identification before the grip touched her palm.

He wasn't taking the chance that Parisa had that power. She was clearly a preternaturally exceptional ascender, but yeah, he wasn't taking chances.

For practice, therefore, he brought two unidentified swords and a dagger into his hands.

The swords were warrior-big and because Parisa had much smaller hands than even most Militia Warriors, the sword seemed disproportionate.

But the moment he gave it to her, she fell easily into the rhythm of his battle moves. She stepped away from him and went through a series of thrusts and blocks. He shook his head and smiled. Sometimes the vampire abilities aston- ished him, even after living on Second Earth for over thir- teen hundred years. To receive his memories as she had and make use of them like this was simply amazing.

Jean-Pierre stood on the lawn beside Havily, but at a dis- creet distance from Medichi and Parisa. The newly created ascender was determined to become a warrior as quickly as possible. She had asked her Guardian of Ascension there- fore to give her some of his memories, mind-to-mind, and by the way Parisa now swung her sword in large perfect arcs, the experiment was quite successful.

Havily ground her teeth. "Do you see how simple this could be?" She held the practice sword in her right hand, the tip aimed at the dirt.

He turned to her and smiled. "I take it Marcus does not know you are here?"

She snorted. "He would skin me alive."

"So, you did not tell him. Instead, you asked me to ac- company you, but your *breh* does not know?"

She had the good grace to blush.

He continued, "*Soeurette,* your man will not wish me to show you how to throw the dagger or hold a sword. He does not approve."

She sighed. "I don't care anymore, Jean-Pierre. I must learn how to fight. He can't be with me every minute of the day, and we're at war."

"Yes, but—" He looked at her. Insight pierced his skull. "*Cherie, non, non, non!* Tell me you do not expect me to share memories with you? If I entered your mind, a most intimate act, then *oui,* he would kill me, a blade straight through my heart. I would not like that."

The lovely redhead lifted her chin, fire rolling from her eyes. "I must learn to defend myself. You saw what happened to Parisa. Rith found a way to trick her to folding out of the palace. *Out of the palace.*"

"But I am not the one you need to convince."

"He will not listen to reason and I'm desperate."

Merde. What was he supposed to do? Marcus was his friend now. All had been forgiven. The past was as if it had never been, and for that the Warriors of the Blood had Havily to thank.

She had brought Marcus back into the fold three months ago. She had allowed the *breh-hedden* to take her for a magnificent ride and then she had ridden the beast to its knees. She would always be *soeurette* to the Warriors of the Blood.

But this? He could not do it, not to his brother, so he lifted a brow to her. She lifted her chin in response.

He chuckled. There was so much to like about Havily. Even her name was a delight for his hopeless French accent. "He would be very angry with me, *cherie.* I cannot do it."

She drew a deep breath that swelled her chest. She held that breath for a moment then let it fly out as though carrying her irritation with it. "Marcus has no say in this. We may be bonded but I am not the dirt beneath his shoes."

Jean-Pierre grinned. "The dirt beneath his shoes? That is very good. I will tell him you said that."

A shout of triumph drew his attention back to Parisa. While Jean-Pierre had stood arguing with Havily, Antony had folded a target to the front yard. The dagger now rested not far from the bull's-eye.

"See," Havily cried, gesturing with a toss of her arm in the direction of the target. "And now, I politely request that you download your battle memories straight into my brain because this sword feels ridiculous in my hands. I might as well be holding a log."

He shook his head. "I am willing to teach you the skills

of the sword but I tell you again, Marcus would put a blade through my heart if he knew I had entered your mind so . . . intimately."

Havily rolled her eyes and groaned. She gestured with a slice of her left hand toward Medichi and Parisa. "But that is what I need to be doing right now. Look at her. It's as though she's been wielding a sword for centuries."

His gaze slid to Parisa. It was true. He had seen Kerrick give his memories to Alison all those months ago, and the result had been the same—quite magnificent. It would seem that because both Parisa and Alison were powerful, and could receive the memories from one mind to the next, they could learn the battling skills in the flutter of an eyelash.

He sighed. He wished he could oblige Havily, but he could not.

"Well," Havily said. "I can see you intend to be as stubborn as my *breh,* so I guess I'll just have to find Luken. He'll do it for me. He'd do anything for me."

Jean-Pierre gasped. "You would not wound him so," he cried. Luken had been in love with Havily since he'd served as her Guardian of Ascension over a century ago. "To invite such intimacy when you know that his heart calls to you—"

Havily met his gaze. "I was the one trapped in a forge with a madman draining the blood out of me. I know why Parisa has insisted on being trained to fight. Neither you, nor Marcus, nor Antony, knows what it's like to feel so powerless."

"But were you not drugged? How could you have fought such a man anyway?"

Havily glared at him. "I have thought about this a lot, Jean-Pierre. There was a split second when Crace grabbed me during the Ambassadors Festival that I could have fought him. Instead I froze, and he carried me away. I didn't even think to struggle in his arms. Maybe if I'd had a few skills, even how to handle a dagger, I could have folded a blade into my hand, sliced his arm, and escaped. I don't know. But I didn't even have the option. That's what I want here, enough skill to have a chance if another death vampire attacks me.

You warriors are so physically big, so powerful, you can't imagine anything else."

He stared into her intense light green eyes. He had not considered how impotent she must have felt. He could not imagine what she had endured in Crace's terrible forge.

After a long moment, he nodded. Finally, he withdrew his Epic phone from the pocket of his jeans. He held a finger up to Havily. "I have an idea but you must be quiet. Will you be silent for a moment?"

She nodded.

He made the call. *"Allo,* Marcus? I hope I do not disturb you."

Havily gasped but she was true to her promise. She pressed her lips together in a punishing line and remained silent.

"I'm in the middle of a staff meeting," Marcus said. "Can this wait?"

The warriors always took one another's calls, day or night, meetings or no meetings. Jean-Pierre continued to stare at Havily. He once more took in the set of her chin. His resolution strengthened.

"In five seconds, *mon ami,* I'll be linking my mind with Havily's and sharing my battle experiences. It must be done." He said nothing more but ended the call and returned the phone to his pocket. He counted backward. *"Cinq, quatre, trois, deux . . ."*

The air shimmered beside him and a second later Marcus went chest-to-chest with him. "The fuck you will," he shouted. His brows were little more than slashes above his light brown eyes, but right now they seemed to sink into his eyes. His face turned the color of a beet, the rich hue of rage.

Jean-Pierre stepped away from Marcus with a wave of his hand in Havily's direction. "You must settle this with your *breh.* She has threatened to ask Luken to help her, which is something I believe we must avoid for Luken's sake. But after listening to her, I believe you to be in the wrong."

The moment Marcus turned in Havily's direction and began chastising her about Luken, Jean-Pierre crossed the lawn to join Medichi and Parisa, who both stood with eyes wide as the shouting began.

Jean-Pierre gestured to the door. "Perhaps we should go into the villa?"

He held the door wide for them. Parisa walked swiftly before the men. Within seconds the door was shut upon the war that now raged on the front lawn of Antony's home.

Parisa didn't understand why the warriors were so resistant to training the women connected to them. Maybe she could never understand, not being male. Antony hadn't exactly been eager, to say the least, but Marcus was particularly adamant. Was it because they had completed the ritual, the *breh-hedden*?

She glanced at Antony. He frowned at the door. The words of the argument were indistinct, but the highs and lows, the sharpness of tone, slid easily through the thick wood.

Antony gestured with an arm in the direction of the kitchen. "Coffee?"

"Oui," Jean-Pierre said. He nodded a couple of times.

Jean-Pierre was not as tall as Antony; none of the warriors was. He stood shoulder-to-shoulder with Marcus and was just a little shorter than Kerrick. He had the most interesting lips of any man Parisa had ever seen: a full lower lip and the upper in two points that would have been pouty on a woman. He looked . . . sensual. His eyes were gray-green and in turns thoughtful and amused. She'd always had the impression that he was the kind of man who would probably make his lover mad as fire with a joke at just the wrong time for the sole purpose of getting a rise out of her.

He extended his hand as well to the doorway, an Old World gesture. She led the way. Coffee sounded good. Her mind still fluttered like a flock of birds. She had wanted to continue the training, but nothing could be done until Marcus and Havily had settled their differences.

Downloading the battle memories had been fantastic. Even now, as she walked through the sitting room, she matched the roll of Antony's walk if not the length of his stride. She knew what it was to move, to run, to fly in his skin; which muscles flexed and how they reshaped every movement when he thrust or sliced with his sword.

Taking a lesson in swordplay afterward had been like talking in shorthand. She simply *knew* how to wield the long thirty-inch blade.

Another lesson in daggers would be next. She couldn't wait.

Antony made coffee with a French press, which of course Jean-Pierre had given him years ago. The warriors seemed to speak in shorthand as well. She sat at the island and sipped her coffee from a heavy white mug, the kind that reminded her of old-fashioned diners.

The men also held mugs and stood facing each other between the island and the refrigerator. She sat on a stool opposite, her elbows propped up on the dark soapstone. She squirmed on the stool. She was feeling muscles she was pretty unfamiliar with, small ones on the insides of her thighs, muscles low on either side of her back. Her calves and triceps burned. Her mind may have known how to do battle, but the rarely used muscles were starting to fire up—and not in a good way.

"Why is Marcus so distressed about teaching Havily?" Parisa asked.

Antony slid his glance to her. "It's hard to explain. I didn't want to at first, either. In fact, I have to say that my first instinct, a crippling one, was to lock you up in my bedroom and never let you out."

Parisa knew what he meant, but other images flashed through her mind and brought warmth to her cheeks.

He frowned slightly then his nostrils flared. His eyes widened. She shifted her gaze quickly to the light brown coffee in her mug. She liked cream, lots of cream in her coffee. Her cheeks were now flaming. She took a hurried sip and came up choking.

"Are you all right, *cherie*?" Jean-Pierre asked.

Choking was an excellent excuse for her red face. She

coughed happily and bobbed her head several times. "Fine. I'm fine."

But when a cloud of sage suddenly swept over her, she didn't dare look at Antony. Instead she swiveled completely on the stool so that her back was to the men. She coughed a few more times then tried to take deep breaths.

She glanced down at her breasts. Her bra and T-shirt were too thin. Her nipples were drawn into stiff peaks. There were so many ways that this experience, this *breh-hedden,* had become something of a torture.

She slipped off the stool and meandered toward the door. Maybe she could walk it off. Maybe if she moved around, she'd stop feeling so much.

"Parisa," Antony called to her, a question in his voice.

"Mmm?" she responded, sliding the mug up to her lips and taking a sip. Her forearms in that position covered her nipples. If this was the way it was going to be, she was so getting a different wardrobe. The size of her breasts had always been something of a struggle. It wasn't like either of the men in this room would fail to notice her arousal.

Oh, God. She was about to die of embarrassment.

"Do you think you're ready to voyeur Fiona? Jean-Pierre has suggested, rightly so, that we should think about moving fast on this."

"I agree. Yes, let's do it." With her mind turned to more important things, she lowered her arms and walked toward them. Two pairs of eyes dropped to her chest and she gave a little squeak. Ooooh, shit.

Jean-Pierre turned politely away but Antony's lips parted and he couldn't seem to tear his gaze away from her breasts.

"Well, let me see," she said, drawing her cup once more toward her lips. "Where would be the best place to do this? Also, I'd like to touch your mind and see if you can see the vision as well. Endelle can."

But Antony leaned in her direction as though he could move through the island. *I'd like to touch something else,* he sent.

Antony, she chided. *Jean-Pierre is right here.
He's looking out the window.*

Stop it with the sage. Her lips trembled.

Let me see you again and I will.

She was shocked and yet he was serious. She lowered her arms, and his lids fell to half-mast. He drew his mug to his lips and sucked a stream of coffee into his mouth with a hiss that made her thighs tremble. She knew, *she knew,* that if Jean-Pierre hadn't been in the same room, Antony would be all over her.

She had slept in his bed all night.

She had awakened to his big warrior body spooning her.

She had turned into him and stroked what was already hard and ready between them. The lovemaking had been brisk. She'd risen to her orgasm within a handful of minutes. Her body was like dry kindling to his lit match.

She knew one thing—she wasn't wearing a snug T-shirt around him anymore. In fact . . . "Will you both excuse me for a minute? I'll be right back."

She met Antony's surprised gaze but shook her head at him. She didn't want him following. She set her mug on the counter then hurried into the adjoining parlor, breathing a sigh of relief: Neither man could see her from this point on. She needed a different shirt and she needed it now. She also needed some distance from the sage-machine in the kitchen.

She passed into the foyer and realized she couldn't hear Marcus and Havily arguing. Good. Maybe Havily would join her in Antony's lessons. Marcus would have to return to work, but maybe Jean-Pierre could spar with her.

She passed into the formal living room and glanced out the front windows, but couldn't see them from that vantage.

She moved down the long central hall, aiming for Antony's bedroom, but when she reached the hub of the guest room suites, opposite the library, she heard Havily moan, a distant sound from behind the closed door of their bedroom. She should have kept going but for some reason she stopped in her tracks. The voyeur in her raised its ugly head and she took several steps in the direction of what used to be her guest room on the right and what was still Marcus and Havily's room on the left.

Rhythmic thumping met her ears and she put her fingers to her lips. She shouldn't be doing this, but she was caught by the sounds of their lovemaking. The squabble was over. She wondered if Marcus felt a need to stake his claim all over again.

Probably.

When the moans turned to cries, when she could hear Havily calling out Marcus's name, she woke up to the improper nature of what she was doing. She retraced her steps to the central hall then ran the rest of the distance to Antony's bedroom.

She went inside and closed the door behind her. A second suite of guest rooms separated Antony's vast master suite from Marcus and Havily's rooms so she couldn't hear them anymore. She took several deep breaths, forcing her body to calm the hell down.

She pushed away from the wall and moved into the bathroom suite, which contained two enormous closets. She just hoped she had something suitable to wear that would allow her a little modesty.

Jean-Pierre had felt trapped in the kitchen. Even though Medichi was the third warrior to be struck by the *breh-hedden,* the varied ways the obnoxious ritual affected the lives of the men involved was getting on his nerves. *Mon Dieu,* Parisa's nipples had been ripe as plums, ready to be plucked, and Medichi stared at her like he was most willing to do the plucking.

All Jean-Pierre had been able to do was get out of the way. He was surprised, however, when Parisa left the kitchen. Surprised even more when Medichi did not follow.

Of course, that left Medichi bent over the island, his elbows holding up his head. He'd dragged the *cadroen* from his hair, which hung in thick straight walls on either side of his face. Jean-Pierre could not see any part of his face, but he understood his suffering. The *breh-hedden* was nothing less than torture.

Jean-Pierre remained by the window overlooking the

front lawn. Marcus and Havily were no longer there. He was not certain where they had gone. Right now, he did not know what to do so he crossed his arms over his chest and stared out at the front landscaping.

"Sorry about that," Medichi said at last.

Jean-Pierre shrugged. "It must be very difficult."

"Oui," Medichi responded.

Jean-Pierre glanced at him. *"Oui?"*

"Oui." Medichi's smile broadened, then dimmed. "Hey, I've been around you a long time. I know a little French. And I am sorry."

The sounds of quick footsteps could be heard in the foyer. A moment later Parisa, now wearing a long, loose blouse, appeared in the doorway. She cast each man a quick smile. Though her shoulders looked tight, she said, "I'd like to be in the library when I first voyeur Fiona. Will you both come with me?"

Rith seethed. An unusual state for him.

Even though the Seers had predicted Parisa's escape, he had not meant for her to leave; he had meant for her to die. But just when he'd folded to her bedroom to get the job done, he'd found the bed empty. After a quick search through the house, he'd discovered her nude in the backyard. Disgusting. He still couldn't believe she had escaped. He still couldn't believe she'd cared so little for modesty that she'd flown into the air with nothing on.

Worse, of course, now Greaves had a link with the woman, a very intimate mind-link. Rith despised her for it.

He was in France now. He had several emergency transfer locations. This one was just outside Toulouse Two, in the south of the country. The blood donors were situated quite nicely in three bedrooms at the end of the hall. Drugged, of course. The necessity of moving them had created a great deal of anxiety and more chatter than he could tolerate.

He sat very still in front of his desk, in his Herman Miller Embody Chair, his feet flat on the floor, his shoulders relaxed, and his spine perfectly aligned. His computer was in front of him.

He'd developed a program to track the predictions from the Seers Fortresses of the highest-performing groups, Mumbai, Johannesburg, and Bogotá. The program ran constantly. He could watch it stream; anytime two or three Fortresses delivered the same prediction, the various reports were automatically shuffled into a separate document.

But the information that came through was always the same—Greaves would make use of the newly forged mindlink to his advantage.

He couldn't let that happen. Not if he could help it. But he was nothing if not a great believer in acting on Seer information.

From the time he had learned of Parisa Lovejoy, the mortalwith-wings, he had wanted to capture her for the Commander. Greaves would have use of her, and he would do anything for his master. There had just never been a hint from the Seers about a possible mind-link. If he'd known, he would never have abducted her.

He stared at the streaming reports and found the movement comforting. When it came to an end, he started from the beginning just to watch the documents flit by.

He trembled, a long shudder down his body. He had a very simple problem. He needed to get Parisa back. Well, the truth was that he needed her dead, but clearly that meant first he needed to kidnap her again.

He took a deep breath, but another shudder traveled the length of him. He was not a sexual man; he did not have that capacity because of a certain unfortunate event several hundred years ago. But he believed his desire to have Parisa back came very close to that sort of base need and drive. He craved to have her once more under his control.

He had almost succeeded during the woman's ascension ceremony. He'd teased her mind with an image of himself, and she'd folded to him. He shook his head. So very close.

What a coup that would have been . . . except for the fact

that he didn't have permission from Greaves to go after Parisa again. He was playing with fire.

What no one knew was that because Rith also had limited voyeur ability, he was able to find Parisa anytime he wished to. He had but to open what he called his little window, think of her, and there she was. Right now, she was seated in the library of Warrior Medichi's villa. He listened for a few minutes and realized she was attempting to voyeur Fiona. What a coincidence, but not a surprise.

Unfortunately, he couldn't share this information with Greaves—for the simple reason that Greaves didn't know he had the ability to voyeur. Indeed, he'd only been able to voyeur two people so far, one of them being Parisa. The other was Greaves himself.

What a tightrope he walked.

The phone on his desk rang, a soft chime. He answered it quickly. "Yes, master."

Greaves's deep, pleasant voice filled the space. "Good evening, Rith. I hope your day has fared well. How are the donors doing?" He was always polite. Just hearing from his master made Rith smile.

He put the phone on speaker then shifted slightly to his right. He had a bank of monitors, with cameras fixed on each slave, just as he'd had in the Burma location. All the donors were asleep. "The sedative is working quite well. All shipments should proceed as usual."

"Excellent, but then I would expect nothing less of you. I just checked my messages and discovered that you had called. I trust nothing is amiss."

Rith took a deep breath then plunged into the delicate issue. "I called to request permission to secure the captive again." He held his breath. He had little hope of having the request accepted—he knew Greaves was working his own plan—but he had to try. He had to.

Silence returned to him, not pressing, which was good, but silence nonetheless.

Finally, Greaves said, "You have need of this captive?"

Rith nodded, then became aware he hadn't spoken aloud. "Yes, I do."

"I realize that for you to place your request was no small thing, but I am sorry. I am waiting only for Parisa to open her voyeur window to begin utilizing the link. Though I am disappointed with the limitations of this link, I have great hopes of entrapping a warrior or two."

"Yes, of course, master."

"I will promise, however, to contact you the moment I have information of use to you where the blood donors are concerned. I also wish to thank you for how well you kept Parisa perfectly groomed, healthy, and compliant. I commend you, Rith."

His heart softened, like pudding in his chest. "Thank you, master."

"As for Madame Endelle and our blood donors, no doubt she's been informed of our little operation and will want to disband it. I do expect the Warriors of the Blood to attempt to locate and assault your facility, and I suspect that they will try to do so through Parisa. With that in mind, I want you to choose among the death vampires at the Phoenix Estrella Complex, twenty of the very best, and bring them to your home in Toulouse. Then I want you to prepare to evacuate the facility upon my command. Do you understand?"

Rith was always surprised that anyone would interest themselves in his blood donors. The women involved had no particular value. Why would the warriors waste such critical time and energy on such a useless mission? But then he often found the actions of the warriors to be incomprehensible. Why, for instance, had they come as an entire unit to Parisa's aid?

"I have no doubt they will attempt a rescue," Greaves said. "Yes, yes, I already know your opinion. And I concur. Such a waste of military expertise on behalf of partially ascended mortal women—I am as incredulous as I'm sure you are. But we can use their absurd sense of chivalry to our advantage."

Rith smiled. "Yes, master."

True friendship bridges every terrible abyss.

—*Collected Proverbs,* Beatrice of Fourth

CHAPTER 12

Jean-Pierre thought the library was a sensible choice for Parisa. She was going to voyeur the woman Fiona, the death and resurrection slave, and since Parisa was a librarian by trade, she might feel more comfortable surrounded by books.

It had to be difficult for the dark-haired beauty to attempt contact with a woman she had met in such terrible circumstances. Who would want to be reminded of a captivity such as Parisa endured? But here she was, settling herself in the chair by the farthest wall, ready to do what she must.

Medichi had to be very proud of his woman. She was learning to battle with sword and dagger, and she was intent on rescuing those she had left behind. *Oui,* Medichi should be very proud.

Parisa now wore a loose white blouse that was gathered low on her hips.

Jean-Pierre remained in the doorway to give the young woman some space. He crossed his arms over his chest and smiled. She had been humiliated by the earlier evidence of her *interest* in Medichi. The two of them were so clearly in the first throes of love, embarrassed and excited by turns. It was a beautiful thing to behold—especially to see Medichi caught, because he never allowed himself to love. To chase women at the Blood and Bite, *bien sûr,* but never to love. Seeing him now with Parisa, so kind and attentive, his eyes shining with affection, with desire, *oui,* very beautiful.

He wondered, though, what the *breh-hedden* might mean for the rest of the Warriors of the Blood. Three already had been caught by the fever—Kerrick, Marcus, and now Medichi. Was this portentous? Was there a chance he would fall next into Cupid's lovely web?

A shudder went through him. He had been a lover of women his entire life, and every decade or so he enjoyed a deeper entanglement, an emotional one, but always the women were unable to handle the warrior's life and commitments. But the women who had come to his three brothers were so very powerful. Could it be different if such a woman came to him? A world at war in this way was a horrible thing. He saw how Parisa suffered, how she was struggling to grow, to meet her challenges. Could he bear to see a woman he loved suffering in all these ways? He thought not.

He glanced around the room, looking for distraction. Medichi's library was very tall, with bookshelves all the way to the fifteen-foot ceiling. He had been collecting since the printing press was invented. Most of the books were leather-bound. Jean-Pierre liked the fragrance in the room. Leather had a strong presence, a perfect binding for fragile pages and black print, very male and very female at the same time.

A tapestry hunting scene served as a valance over tall windows overlooking the front lawn. Wooden blinds kept the light at a minimum.

Medichi drew a chair close to Parisa's. He was not convinced that he was needed, but Endelle had assigned him to assist both Medichi and Parisa as they shaped their plan to locate and extract the slaves.

As Parisa leaned back into the chair, her dark brown hair

disappeared into the chocolate color of the leather. She took deep breaths. He tried to imagine what this must be like for her, so new to ascension, so recently freed from her captivity, so overwhelmed by the *breh-hedden*. He admired her courage and God help her but she would need courage to be bonded with a warrior, to live as his *breh* to whatever degree they chose to accept the *breh-hedden* into their lives. He wished her well, he wished her joy and every happiness but he did not think she understood yet just how hard life would be mated to a Warrior of the Blood.

He repressed a sigh.

"I see Fiona," Parisa said.

So soon. Jean-Pierre was very impressed. Parisa had a soft voice, in the lower registers, very pretty, like velvet. Her cheeks bore a flush of excitement.

"Where is she?" Medichi asked. "Can you see her environment at all?"

"She's walking outside, alone. There is a high wooden fence and beyond that, tall trees, but not the tamarind trees of Burma."

"Try communicating with her telepathically."

At that, Parisa opened her eyes and stared at Medichi. "Do you think I can?"

He smiled, so reassuring. He was gentle with her. Parisa did not need a heavy hand. Medichi was exactly the right man for her.

Parisa once more closed her eyes. A frown of concentration formed between her brows.

Jean-Pierre's nostrils flared and he looked behind him. Was someone baking? He smelled croissants . . . again . . . rich buttery croissants, like the ones he had smelled in Rith's house.

He heard footsteps and Havily appeared. Her eyes glittered and her lips looked bruised. He turned away so that she would not see his smile. She had been well kissed and perhaps more.

"What's going on?" she asked quietly as she drew up next to him.

"Parisa can see Fiona now," he whispered. "She is trying to communicate telepathically." He leaned closer. "Were you in the kitchen baking?" The words seemed absurd, but he didn't understand what he was smelling.

"No, but I brought scones home from my Starbucks run."

He nodded. "So, I must know—are you to learn to battle with Parisa now?"

She nodded and appeared just a little pleased with her-self. "Yes, I am," she stated, keeping her voice low. "After work, Marcus will do the download and I'll start training with you boys and Parisa tomorrow."

"*Très bien.*"

"You approve?"

"*Bien sûr.* I think it wise." But he frowned. If he had a *breh,* would he speak so easily on a subject that meant his woman might attempt to engage a powerful death vampire in combat? A shiver went through him. Mercifully, he did not have to worry about such a thing.

He did, however, feel uneasy. The aroma of the croissants made him hungry . . . for many things. How very strange.

Fiona stood very still. She glanced around her. No one else was in the garden, but she always felt as though several pairs of eyes were on her. From the moment the woman in the Burma garden, Parisa, had escaped, Rith had doubled, maybe tripled his surveillance of his blood slaves.

Right now, however, she swore she heard a voice whis-pering inside her head: *Fiona, can you hear me?*

Again, she looked around then put her feet in motion. She wore sandals and her usual pajama ensemble. The fab-rics were soft but she so craved something else, anything else, to wear, like the jeans so many of the newer arrivals wore. Jeans and a blouse and underwear. How lovely that would be.

Fiona, this is Parisa, can you hear me? Don't be afraid. This is telepathy and I'm not very good at it yet so if you hear me just say something aloud. A simple yes will do. Re-member, I can see you. I'm a preternatural voyeur.

Fiona walked because she was afraid if she stopped and turned around to hunt for the source of the voice, Rith would jump out of the bushes and frighten her back into the house. But she didn't think it would do any harm to say a single word aloud. How could that be interpreted as something dangerous?

"Yes."

A faint girlish squealing sounded through her head and she almost covered her ears. It wasn't loud, but it had startled her. So she said aloud, "If you really do exist, and I'm not just making up voices in my head, no more squealing, please."

Oh. Oh, I'm so sorry, Fiona, but because I'm voyeuring you I can both see and hear what's going on and I heard you. But just to make sure we're communicating, say yes three times in a row.

Well, if she was going mad, this was not a hard phrase to repeat. "Yes, yes, yes."

I heard it and I saw your lips move. Fiona, listen to me, I am doing all that I can to locate you and I'm not alone in my efforts. The Warriors of the Blood are helping me. We're all working to locate you. After I escaped from Rith's house, Warrior Thorne and his men returned for you but Rith had already moved you to another location. We think it was done first by van or some sort of automobile then by dematerialization. Are we right?

If this was her mind circling down the drain of insanity, she was certainly speaking to herself in remarkably lucid terms. "Yes," she said aloud. "You have it exactly right. He put us in a vehicle, a Hummer, I think, but only for fifteen minutes or so. Then we were dematerialized here."

Where are you? If we can pinpoint your location, I think we can come and get you, but we have to know which part of the world you're in now.

It was at this point that Fiona's heart began to thrum, to beat so hard in her chest that she could hardly breathe. Could it be this simple, after all these years?

Tears rushed to her eyes. She kept walking. She had almost died for good during the last blood-drain. If it hadn't been for James, that strange elderly man who sat on a bench and fed sunflower seeds to a flock of pigeons, she wouldn't be here right now. He'd pressed her forward, into the future. He'd put courage in her heart when she had been depleted. He had said she had reason to hope. She hadn't exactly believed him, but now she did.

Aloud, she said, "I've heard people speaking French."

Another squeal, which caused her to put her hands over her ears.

Oh, I can see that I hurt your mind again. I'm so sorry, but even a language narrows the search.

This time, Fiona smiled. "I'll find out as quickly as I can."

She saw movement from the corner of her eye. One of the Burmese servants had been tracking her movements and listening.

"I have to go now."

"Who you talk to? You go crazy? Come. Rith want you back in your room. Enough walking."

Don't worry, Fiona. I heard her and I can find you anytime. I'll be back for you.

"Don't fail me."

"What you mean, fail you? You go crazy. You been here too long. Not normal."

"Yes," she said. "Crazy." She then made a face and gave a little cry, which caused the woman to draw back.

"I tell Rith what you do. He no like."

You do that, Fiona thought. Then the next time Parisa struck up a mental conversation, the women would ignore her. It wouldn't be the first time one of the D&R slaves had ended up babbling endlessly to herself, but it was usually the beginning of the end. It usually ended in the woman's death at her next blood-drain.

Parisa leaned forward in her chair. She was thrilled at what she had just experienced, but for some reason her head ached fiercely.

Medichi touched her arm. She looked at him, at the concern

in his dark brown eyes. "I'm okay. I have the worst head-ache, but I don't know why."

"This is all very new for you."

She sat up very straight and held her head immobile. Jean-Pierre and Havily stood near the doorway. Both frowned at her.

"Are you all right?" Havily asked. "You're very pale. Antony, look how pale she is."

"I see it."

Parisa heard them talking, but the throb in her head worsened. She could still see Fiona. She trailed after her in voyeur fashion, but the pain intensified so much that she finally shut down her voyeur window.

A moment later the pressure in her head eased, but tears tracked down her cheeks. "That hurt so much and I'd had such success."

"It's okay. It's okay," Antony said, his fingers stroking her forearm lightly. "This was your first try. I take it you communicated with Fiona? You squealed a couple of times."

She glanced at Antony, who had slid from his chair and was now on his knees and leaning over her. He wiped at her cheeks. "I spoke into her head and even though she wasn't able to answer back, telepathically I mean, she responded to my questions aloud and I could hear her. It was just as all of you said—Rith removed the slaves in a vehicle, a Hummer actually. He drove for about fifteen minutes then demateri-alized the group somewhere."

"As a group?" Jean-Pierre asked. "That would be a shit-load of power."

Parisa smiled. *Shitload* sounded like *sheetload*. She loved his accent.

"What else can you tell us?" Antony said.

Parisa tried to recall the conversation word for word and began relating it as best she could. She ended with, "One of the women who worked in the Burma house as a servant was tending to Fiona, ordering her around. She kept asking Fiona if she was going crazy, probably because Fiona was talking out loud."

"I'm wondering," Havily mused. "You said Fiona was walking in a garden. Was it daylight?"

"Yes. Yes it was. Oh, that's significant, because it's still daylight here."

"What about the shadows? Were they long or nonexistent?"

"Very long—as in it was almost evening."

"That's excellent. Now, what of the gardens. What kind of plants did you see?"

"Lavender. I saw lots of lavender. Juniper, I think. The garden had rocks, herbs maybe, I'm not sure."

Once Parisa had answered all pertinent questions, Antony called Carla at Central.

Parisa could hear her squeals, sounds that echoed her own earlier cries of excitement. By the time Antony got off the phone, he was smiling. Carla felt certain, given all the information they'd been able to provide, that they might be looking at the Mediterranean region. If her hunch was correct, she would have a fix on the location of the death and resurrection slaves within the next few hours.

Was it possible?

Antony, however, frowned.

"What's wrong?" she asked.

"Well, now we need to get Thorne's approval to go after them. I'll want at least some of the Warriors of the Blood with me."

"Is there a chance he won't let them go?" Thorne always had the final word.

Antony nodded. "Yes."

"What about the Militia Warriors? Could we take some of them instead?"

He shook his head. "I wouldn't want to chance it. Death vampires can easily overpower a Militia Warrior. It takes a minimum of four Militia Warriors to take down one death vampire."

Parisa blinked several times. The profound difficulty of the war came into much sharper focus for her. "I know I must have heard that statistic before but until just this moment I didn't get it. No wonder Greaves has an advantage. He's creating death vampires left and right."

"And supplying them with the necessary dying blood."

She felt ill. If she hadn't been sitting down, she would have fallen back into her chair.

Of one thing she was certain: Somehow Thorne had to give them enough Warriors of the Blood to bring Fiona and the blood slaves home.

Greaves repressed his fury. Rith was not at fault for what had just happened, or rather for what *hadn't* happened, when he made use of his voyeur-link to Parisa.

As soon as the voyeur session had ended, he had folded to Rith's home in the south of France. He wanted to see for himself what Parisa had voyeured, and here he was.

He walked in the Toulouse garden, Rith beside him. The visual part of the voyeur had worked perfectly. He would never mistake this place for anything other than the setting in which the preternatural event had occurred. But another part had failed, some imperfection in the link.

"Parisa appears to have a connection with the woman, Fiona. Were you aware of it?" Greaves spoke in his usual tone, but Rith's stare had gone blank.

"I was not aware of a special connection, but I believe I might know when it occurred. Do you recall that when you first met Parisa in Mandalay, her dress bore grass stains and her hair was askew?"

Greaves nodded. He slowed his steps to watch Rith carefully as he spoke.

"For some reason, the blood slave Fiona had succeeded in escaping. She approached Parisa, begging for assistance. When I tried to draw her away, Parisa got caught in the ensuing struggle."

"I see. And there was physical connection, touch involved?"

"Yes."

Greaves nodded again. "One small correction, though, my dear Rith. We call them *donors*, not slaves. There will be no acknowledged *slaves* in the Coming Order. Please make use of the correct term."

Rith bowed. He seemed genuinely distressed. "Of course, master. Forgive me." When he rose back up and met Greaves's gaze once more, Rith continued, "But please help me to understand exactly what has happened. Are you saying that Parisa voyeured our blood *donor* in this garden? Here in Toulouse? And you say they spoke? Are we undone already in this facility? I hesitate to move everyone since I am draining a female even as we speak."

Greaves narrowed his eyes. Rith had not been himself since the gifted mortal escaped his Mandalay home. That was clear to him now. Something about Parisa's escape disturbed Rith. Greaves wished he had known. He didn't like waves, even small ones, in his extensive organization. If he'd known that Rith would be knocked out of stride by losing control of the mortal-with-wings, he would never have agreed to Julianna's plan in the first place.

However, as upsetting as Rith's disquiet was, Greaves had a greater reason to be disappointed in his mind-link scheme. Though the plan had seemed clever at the time, a serious flaw in the usefulness of the link had emerged— Greaves had been able to *see* the entire exchange but not to *hear* it. He had vision through the link, but not hearing.

He didn't know why it had failed, only that it had, probably because the woman was more powerful than even he understood. In addition, he could only make use of the link when the woman opened it. He had truly believed that successfully engaging the voyeur capacity of the infamous mortal-with-wings would have afforded him more access. But it hadn't. He struggled even now to calm his temper.

He did not normally give himself to profane speech, but in that moment he had succumbed.

When Parisa had made contact with Fiona, Greaves had felt the mind-link vibrate within his head. He had opened the link and flowed along the preternatural highway until he could see all that Parisa saw through her voyeur's window. He had experienced a tremendous flush of excitement because the applications of the link with the woman, now ascended, seemed endless in scope.

The moment he recognized the blood donor walking in the garden, he had breathed a sigh of pure exhilaration. That is, until he saw the woman look around and he noticed that though her lips were moving, no sound was coming forth, which meant that though Parisa was speaking telepathically to the woman, he'd been unable to capture the conversation, either side. What good were pictures without words in such a situation?

When the Burmese servant had arrived to take Fiona back to her cell, he had cut off Parisa's voyeur window with a prolonged punishing slash of his mind. Yes. He'd been angry. He still was. He could not believe that with his vast array of preternatural power, he was somehow deaf in his voyeur-link with Parisa. Yet so it seemed.

Still, he controlled his temper.

"We are in no immediate danger, but you can always leave a donor behind if you're forced to vacate quickly. The women are meant to serve the greater good. Please don't get squeamish about this."

Rith shook his head. "Not squeamish. Orderly. I merely prefer to keep the shipments as regular as possible."

At that, Greaves smiled.

"Do I amuse you, master?"

"You please me. You always have an eye to efficiency, and your indifference to the lives of the donors is very uplifting."

Rith nodded. "I know how to sustain the correct priorities. I have learned well from you."

Greaves recalled the garden from Parisa's voyeur perspective. He put himself in her shoes, especially since she was so well connected to the Warriors of the Blood. It would be just a matter of time, probably less than twenty-four hours, before the Toulouse location was discovered. "I take it you have an escape plan in place?"

"Of course, master. Across the seas this time I think but I will not allow the slaves, that is, *donors,* outside anymore. Shall I take them at once? It would be no hardship."

Greaves pondered the situation. "No, I think not. I want to make use of the voyeur-link again, to see if I can improve its function. I'll let you know what the opposition plans to do. I have no doubt a rescue attempt will occur. So make your plans, be sure to secure at least twenty death vampires as previously discussed, and keep me informed. And now I must return to Geneva." He did not wait for further conversation, or to hear Rith's final obsequious salutation. He lifted his hand and was gone.

"You think I like saying no?" Thorne's voice thundered through the Cave.

It was now nine in the morning and all the Warriors of the Blood were present, except Marcus. He'd served his two nights a week battling; the rest of the week he performed the difficult office of High Administrator of Desert Southwest Two.

Parisa took a step backward, forgetting that Medichi stood right behind her. Thorne had been thundering for a few minutes now, pacing the length of the room, glowering. Yes, the warrior glowered.

Antony's large hands landed on her arms and steadied her. He leaned close and whispered against her ear, "You okay?"

She nodded, her head brushing his chin and cheek. A lovely rush of sage distracted her for a moment until Thorne reached the end of the room, headed back, and met her gaze.

"You don't understand what you're asking," he cried. "I've got five critical Borderlands to protect here in Metro Phoenix Two, every goddamn night. And you want to take them all with you on this mission? Right now the warriors need to be resting and sleeping, not out in some other part of the world doing battle. And if the grid does pick up another anomaly after nightfall, how am I supposed to keep death vamps from riding down the Trough and feasting on mortals without warriors guarding the access points? Answer me that."

Parisa couldn't. She knew the Trough was the space between

dimensions, and that most of the death vampires weren't powerful enough to just fold through. They had to ride through the Troughs in order to get to Mortal Earth.

"I don't know, Warrior Thorne," she said. "I don't have an answer. I just know that I can't leave those women there."

"At least they're alive," he barked, now standing in front of her. His skin was flushed, and the whites of his eyes were bloodshot. "But every time a death vamp reaches Mortal Earth unimpeded, through the Trough, women die. Some men, too, but mostly women are the targets. What do you think I should do?"

Parisa made a quick decision. She moved into Thorne and touched a cheek with each hand.

He stepped away from her. "What are you doing?"

"Let me show you."

He shook his head, but he didn't move when she lifted her hands to his face again. His gaze flickered with something like panic but he held still. She closed her eyes and let the memories of Fiona's death and resurrection flow.

His whole body jerked. He gasped at first, clearly resistant, then lowered his shields. It was like feeling a dam give way, her mind flowing into his as the images rocketed through. The only part of the memory she withheld was what had happened to Fiona after she drank the small glass of blood. At that moment, she removed her hands from his face.

Thorne stumbled back a few steps, his eyes squeezed shut. "Shit, shit, shit." He repeated the word about a dozen more times. He ended up leaning his hips against the pool table. He stared at the black tile floor and shook his head.

He looked even more wrecked than before, so she crossed to him then put a hand on his arm. "Now do you understand? I was only held there for three months and not as a blood slave. Fiona said she was taken from Boston in 1886."

"Jesus. She's been a blood slave that long? Even before the days of the defibrillator?"

"She almost didn't make it back this last time, and I feel compelled to get her out of there. I think she's reached her limit. Also, though I can't explain it, I feel a connection to her."

He blew air from his cheeks and slid his fingers into his hair, dislodging several strands from the *cadroen*. For just a moment, his messy hair made him look younger. He turned beseeching eyes to her. "Can you go tomorrow, right after dawn? That way we could all go. The Borderlands will be quiet by then."

Antony drew close as well. "We've considered waiting, but once Carla or Jeannie has a lock on the site we have to move fast. It could be any time now. Given the vegetation, the length of the shadows, there's a good chance we're looking at the Mediterranean. It's still a big area to cover for the grid but we want to be ready to go at the drop of a hat."

Thorne sighed. "You've really got it narrowed down then."

"Yes," Antony said.

Thorne looked up at him. Everyone looked up at Antony. He was two inches taller than Thorne. "Fine. You're right. You have to go. Take three warriors with you but if I know anything, this smells like a fucking trap." Thorne's lips curved in a crooked smile.

"I know."

"You fucking call me if you end up facing a regiment."

For a reason Parisa couldn't explain, Antony smiled. Must have been a warrior thing because she hadn't heard anything funny *at all*. Antony added, "I know how you hate missing a party."

Thorne nodded but his lips flattened to a more familiar grim line. He grabbed Antony's arm and squeezed, his knuckles whitening. "Call me if you need me." He stared into the warrior's eyes for a long, determined moment then dropped his hand and turned into the room. "Who the fuck is going with them?"

All the warriors volunteered. Thorne nodded again, and this time he smiled. "All right, then. All right." Parisa glanced up at him. His voice sounded like it had gone through a shredder.

"I am going," Jean-Pierre said. He stood by the bar, shaking a martini. "I will not be left behind on this one."

"Done." Again Thorne barked.

Both Zacharius and Santiago stepped forward and together gave a shout like a battle cry.

Thorne grinned. "So the two of you want to go?"

The warriors gave another shout.

"Fine," Thorne barked. "Fine." He drew close to Antony
and poked him several times in the chest. "Just make sure
you bring them home safe and sound. Got it?"

"Yes, *jefe*."

Thorne shook his head and ended the conversation suc-
cinctly. "Fuck."

Half an hour later, Medichi had Parisa back at the villa, in
his bedroom. He lifted a female weapons harness, made of
black leather and silver buckles, over Parisa's shoulders. The
openings at the sides would be closed with a number of small
buckles, a different configuration than for the male warriors,
especially since the size of Parisa's breasts added a new level
of adjustment. In that sense, the harness was a clever work of
art. Endelle said she'd designed it herself since a man just
didn't understand the numerous problems associated with
trying to fit a single type of garment to the various sizes and
shapes of female breasts.

"This is heavier than I thought," Parisa said as she pulled
the harness down to her waist.

"It's meant to offer protection from moderate dagger
thrusts. A sword will cut through it, of course." He'd already
told her that a good sword would cut through bone. He didn't
intend to tell her again.

He fought the panic that swirled at the base of his gut.
Yeah, he was nauseated. He didn't worry for himself, but
Parisa had only had about three seconds of training to his
thirteen centuries. She wasn't fit for battle, but then hopefully
this wouldn't become one. Hopefully, Carla would come up
with the coordinates, they'd slip inside the facility, take the
slaves, and leave.

Right. And hell wasn't hot.

"You don't have to go," he whispered. He shouldn't have
said it but he couldn't hold back. He felt her stiffen beneath

his fingers as he continued to make the various buckle adjustments.

"The hell I don't," she responded.

At her tone, he drew back and looked at her. He met her gaze and saw the hard light in her eyes, dimming the pretty amethyst to something like raging purple. He nodded. He knew that look. He'd seen it, oh, about a hundred thousand times when he'd looked in the mirror getting ready for another night of battling.

He'd never thought of his librarian as a warrior, but shit, right now as she started easing one of the buckles into position just below her breasts, she looked like one. A librarian hard-ass. Who'd've thought?

Of course it was easier to have these thoughts than the other ones. Like how untried she was, or that with every minute he spent with her he was sinking into the bond that kept drawing them together, or that his heart ached now when he looked at her.

So . . . shit.

Whatever.

He went back to buckling. He folded the appropriate dagger into his hand, a short blade meant for the slot beneath her breasts. He handed it to her and let her work it in and out of the sheath several times until she said it felt right to her. It was a slick, flat, stainless-steel knife and could do some good in a battle.

When he was happy with the way the front looked, he turned her around. The harness made a T-formation from the shoulders to the lowest part of the waist, to allow for wing-mount. He wasn't expecting that they'd have to fly but they were, as always, preparing for every contingency. Her back therefore stared at him and he couldn't help what he did next. He put his hands on the exposed skin and stroked in a long glide straight down.

Antony, she sent. Even within his mind, she sounded surprised but not displeased.

She shivered under his touch and a swell of tangerine rolled over him. He closed his eyes and did it again. Another shiver, another wave. Jesus. He moved in close, fitting his body against hers, folding his arms around her, gathering her in tight.

She didn't resist and her breaths were high in her chest. She tilted her head to fit into the scoop between his neck and his shoulder. He ground his hips, letting her feel what she'd just done to him.

Her arm swept up and caught his face. She leaned into his cheek and caressed him. *Antony* came as another sweet drift through his mind. She was getting better at telepathy all the time. He worked his arms tighter around her. He rolled his hips forward. She pushed her hips back. He groaned. *I could take you right now.*

I'd let you.

He groaned again, but it ended in a sound between a grunt and a sigh. He turned her in his arms. She caught his mouth and before he could think, her small feminine tongue was between his lips pushing. Hard.

His back bowed and he realized he was about fifteen seconds away from coming. Maybe a quickie . . .

His phone buzzed.

Shit.

She eased back but even as she did, he caught sight of her lips, swollen and red. Her eyes danced with fire.

He kept an arm around her waist as he slid his phone from his pocket. "Give." His voice sounded hoarse.

"Hey, Medichi. Jeannie here. Good news. We've found it, that heavy dome of mist again. Double dome, I guess."

"Where?"

"Just like you said. The Mediterranean. South of France. Outside of Toulouse Two."

He took a deep breath because suddenly he couldn't breathe. "Great. Thanks. I'll gather the troops. Maybe five minutes."

"I'll be ready."

Jeannie always was. She'd served a long time at Central. In the old days—and that was only a century or so ago—she'd held mind-links with the Warriors of the Blood, taking and receiving messages. It was an exhausting job, and the modern inventions of the phone, then the grid, saved so much time and energy. She always worked a twelve-hour shift, serving alongside the Warriors of the Blood. There were others, Carla, for instance, but for the men, Jeannie was *the one*.

He thumbed his phone and slid it into his pocket. Funny how a brief conversation could take the edge off even the most profound erection.

"So it's happening?" she asked.

"Hell, yes."

Parisa moved away from him and all that beautiful tangerine scent faded. Her gaze fell to the floor, and he could feel her sudden anxiety like a whiff of smoke in the air.

"You'll be all right," he said, his voice firm. "Just stay at my back. Don't try to wage war if it comes to that. Use the dagger if you get up close enough but only if you can do serious damage."

She drew a breath. "Because an adversary can take the weapon away and use it against me."

"Exactly."

She lifted her gaze to him. "I'm not ready, am I?"

He wouldn't lie to her. "No. Not by half. But it doesn't matter, does it?"

She shook her head. "No. Not at all. I'm going on this mission no matter what. I wanted to have some skills but I know it'll take years to be a capable warrior. That isn't what this is about."

He nodded. "I know. Just remember, you've got a good throwing arm. You're one of the best I've ever seen. Use it if you think you can make a difference. That's what these weapons are for."

She drew in a deep breath and held her arms out. "Is everything in place?"

His gaze unfortunately fell to her chest, emphasized by all the leather and buckles. "Oh, yeah."

She rolled her eyes. "Okay, Mr. Subtle. Let's just get this show on the road."

He chuckled. He put a hand on her shoulder and without telling her what he intended, folded her back to the Cave.

When she arrived, she yelled, "Hey! Give a girl a warning. I'm so not used to that." She shook herself like a dog coming out of the water then patted her arms.

"Sorry. But you seem so comfortable in our world. I keep forgetting."

Sometimes you need to smash your enemy into the ground,
Or at least try.

—Braulio, former leader of the Warriors of the Blood, 3334 BC

CHAPTER 13

Parisa might have argued with Antony but they weren't alone. Zach stood near the pool table, his thick curly hair drawn away from his face, tucked away in the *cadroen* but flared over his back as though the clasp couldn't contain it all. His eyes were his best feature, cornflower blue, thickly fringed with black lashes. There wouldn't be a woman in the world not jealous of those lashes. His lips were full, his nose curved, even sexy. He was the usual warrior height, which Havily had once told her was six-five. None of the warriors was shorter than that.

Jean-Pierre looked unsettled, his eyes floating back and forth. He hooked a thumb in the waistband of his kilt and scowled then shifted on his feet. Something was bugging him, but she didn't know him well enough to either guess at the problem or ask about it.

Santiago crossed from the brown leather sofa on the right and moved to stand in front of her. He took hold of her hand.

"It is my pleasure to serve you, Parisa." He bowed over her hand and placed a kiss on her fingers.

She felt Antony move in tighter to her back. She could feel a growl rumble through his chest.

Santiago looked up from his bent position and grinned. What a tease. He drew back abruptly when the growl left Antony's throat. She glanced over her shoulder and stared at him. "You're going to start that now?"

He offered her one as well, a warning. She turned a little more, still holding his gaze, and thought for just a moment that he was not just a man but a vampire as well. His deepest instincts had shifted when he ascended: She had to keep reminding herself that she was ascended now, that she had entered the world of the vampire, and that she was no longer on Mortal Earth.

She patted his cheek. "Okay, down, Fido."

She had meant it as a joke, but Antony grabbed her hand and where Santiago had kissed her fingers he licked a long slow line. She gasped. She understood his intention but all she could feel was the softness of his tongue.

Her body gripped low and tight. Antony slung an arm around her waist and kissed her hard on the mouth. She knew he was marking her, claiming her, and part of her wanted to protest this absurd caveman behavior but her body was one complete betrayal of thought.

Tangerine, he whispered through her mind.

Sage, she responded.

Jean-Pierre cleared his throat. "I do not mean to disrespect this *petite* love-fest, but we need to be going, *non*?"

Antony released her, his dark eyes flashing. "Yes." But he turned to Santiago first. "Don't ever do that again."

Santiago shook his head. *"Madre de Dios,"* he cried, both hands tossed in the air. "I keep forgetting the *brehhedden* has command of you in this way. *Lo siento.*"

"Apology accepted." He took in a deep breath and let it out. "Jeannie has the location in the south of France. We all know the drill. We have no way of knowing whether the enemy has troops in position, but we're going in armed as though the place will be crawling with death vamps. I'll keep Parisa at my back. When we touch down, she's going to try to contact Fiona and we'll go from there. Everyone ready?"

Three nods. Four, including Parisa.

"Let's go."

The words seemed so inadequate given what they were about to do.

Parisa looked up at Antony. He slid his arm around her shoulders. "You ready for a fold?" he asked.

He remembered.

She smiled and nodded.

He lifted his arm. She felt the vibration first, then a soft swish through time and space as though she were floating, a kind of metaphysical blink. She arrived outside a very familiar dome of mist, probably a double dome, in a grassy countryside. For a moment, she recoiled at the familiarity of the mist and a shudder passed through her chest. Could she do this? Could she return to the monster's lair?

She drew a deep breath, however, and ordered her nerves to calm down. It was her idea to come on the mission. She had no intention of losing heart now just because of a little mist.

The warriors each turned in a full circle and folded their swords into their hands. Fists pumped weapons, fingers adjusted grips. She had held a sword with the full advantage of Antony's memories, and she knew how complete a warrior could feel with his sword in hand. She wished for one now, but she knew it was ridiculous to think she could square off with a death vampire no matter how vivid the memories.

Santiago took point. He slipped quickly through the mist, disappearing, then returned with equal speed. Without a word, he waved the warriors forward and whispered, "Two layers."

Antony put his arm around her and kept glancing over both shoulders. It seemed ironic to her that once inside the double dome, he relaxed a little and let his arm drop away. Given the circumstances, she was probably in more danger inside the domes than out.

The warriors remained grouped at what proved to be the far end of a garden and the back door of a small stone farmhouse. Chickens pecked in the gravel yard and a wooden table sat outside the door. The place looked empty.

"No one's here," she whispered.

None of the warriors spoke. Each faced the house, waiting.

Antony whispered, "Go ahead, Parisa, see if you can contact Fiona."

With his arm around her, she relaxed enough to open the voyeur window. She thought Fiona's name and came suddenly into a small whitewashed room. The woman's beautiful chestnut hair was fanned out on a pillow. Her arm hung off the side of the bed, her hand limp. She was asleep in what was afternoon in France? Something wasn't right.

Fiona, she sent, a sharp word through Fiona's mind. *We're here.*

The hand twitched and at almost the same moment, a violent headache struck Parisa's mind, just like the one she'd experienced in Antony's library. Voyeuring had never been this way, ever. Had her ascension to Second Earth caused an unexpected problem? She stumbled backward and would have fallen, but Antony caught her.

"Are you all right?"

"Headache again. Give me a minute. I can see Fiona. I still have the window open. She appears to be asleep on her bed." The pain sliced through her like a knife. Tears rained down her face. She wanted it to stop. She held her hands over her lips to keep from crying out. She took deep breaths, one after the other. Only after an excruciating half minute did the sensation finally ease, then disappear.

"Oh, God," she murmured.

"What is the matter, *cherie*?" Jean-Pierre asked, frowning.

"Headache," she said wiping at her face and smoothing her damp hands on her soft flight pants. "It's been happening lately when I voyeur. I'm okay now. Let me try again."

Once more she opened the voyeur window. Again, she called to Fiona in sharp telepathic tones then finally shouted,

Wake up. Fiona, we're here. Wake up. Each time the hand would pop up and down. Once her foot moved.

"I think she's drugged," Parisa said. "She can only move her hand and her foot."

Zach glanced back at her, his curly black hair moving like a cloud over his back. "Then let's go. Let's see if they have anything planned for us."

The warriors moved as a quick organized unit, knees bent, swords held at safe angles away from one another.

A sudden shimmering covered the entire back of the house, in front of the wooden table. The next moment, an array of death vampires, sixteen strong, appeared.

Parisa stopped in her tracks. Antony turned to her. "Stay put, but watch for Rith. Don't look him in the eye if he comes to you."

She nodded. Her vision grew blurry in the wake of a burst of adrenaline that pounded her heart. The warriors spread out, preparing for battle at a ratio of four-to-one, which she knew from conversations with both Havily and Alison was fairly SOP for the warriors. They fought hand-to-hand with death vampires every night.

What were sixteen more?

Another shimmering, however, brought eight more into sight, and more than one of the warriors muttered, "Shit."

Antony took a step back toward her but the battle was just suddenly on. Death vampires moved like the warriors did, with preternatural speed.

Parisa drew her dagger out of the harness. In the distance, she heard Rith cry out, "I want the woman alive." He sounded so certain he would prevail.

Rith. She'd heard his voice but where was he? Safe, no doubt, near the house.

Something cold settled within her chest, her heart turning to flint.

Rith.

Her gaze sought him and found him in the doorway that led into the house. He watched her.

The next moment he was beside her. She didn't hesitate but slashed at his arm. She struck home. He cried out, recoiled, and took a step back. Antony turned, ready to use his sword, but at the exact same moment Rith folded away.

The war in front of her hurt her virgin eyes. She had never seen the warriors engaged in battle like this. Each had six to contend with and several of the death vampires, in full wing-mount, had launched into the air.

The moment that happened, the warriors fell back in her direction. Before she understood the intent, she was surrounded by them in a wide circle. Because she was theirs to protect, none of the warriors mounted his wings.

She held her dagger aloft in warning, but all movement became a blur of speed. Through the batting of wings and swipe of swords, death vampires fell. She kept turning in that broad circle in case her blade was needed.

Zacharius leaped into the air, spun in a circle. He took an arm and part of a wing and sent a death vampire spiraling out of control. He came back to earth, met steel with steel, lunged, and another death vampire fell backward screaming.

The screams were all around her as swords slashed and clanged.

She turned. Jean-Pierre withdrew one of two daggers from his weapons harness with his left hand as he battled in lightning speed with two death vamps. He threw the dagger at the same time, a powerful throw in an upward motion that pierced the abdomen of a flying death vamp up through the fleshy part below the sternum.

The death vampire flew backward, his wings flapping slowly. He lost control, sliding into a roll that aimed his body toward the earth. He was soon flat on his back in a messy tangle of wings. He wasn't breathing.

Santiago had only two death vamps left and he fought both with a single sword that moved in a whir of motion from one to the next. She began to understand how it was that only eight Warriors of the Blood were holding back the tide of war.

She grew calm and as the death count mounted, she shifted her attention to her voyeur window. She gasped. Fiona was sitting up in bed. "Parisa?"

I'm here, she sent. *Do you know where you are in the farmhouse? The warriors are battling death vamps at the back of the house on the stone drive.*

"Come straight through . . ." Her speech was slurred. ". . . then take the hallway to your left. Go to the end. The door on the left is mine."

Jean-Pierre was free. Parisa called to him. "I have her. I know where she is."

Jean-Pierre moved back to her, his sword held at the ready and off to his right side. "We will fold." She nodded.

With his left arm he held her firmly and folded her directly to the door, away from the carnage. When she touched down, she moved just as Fiona had told her, to the hall, then headed down to the end.

Jean-Pierre was right at her back. "Do not open the door, *cherie.*"

She waited for him, her hand on the latch.

He moved in front of her but kept his sword out of her way. The identified swords could be deadly. He gave the door a hard shove.

Rith was there, in the far corner, as though waiting for her. He had Fiona in his arms. He smiled and disappeared.

"Can you trace to them?" Parisa shouted, desperate.

Jean-Pierre had the same idea because he moved in their direction then vanished but was immediately back, stunned. "*Merde.* The bastard blocked his own pathway. How in the name of heaven did he do that?"

Parisa turned around. "Maybe there are survivors in the other rooms."

Jean-Pierre moved swiftly past her into the hall, his sword again ready for action. He crossed the hall and pushed the door open. Parisa looked within. Empty.

She glanced down the hall. Santiago, spattered with blood, his brows in a tight furrow, looked at her and nodded.

He also shoved doors open. "There's no one here." He hit another. He stood and stared. Oh, God, she could tell by the way he froze that something was in there.

Parisa felt weak as she watched the warrior pale. He lowered his sword and moved on slow feet into the room. His lips worked. He was saying something.

Parisa didn't want to know what he had found but she followed him anyway. She had to. No more holding back or hiding from the truth of what this new world was all about.

She felt Jean-Pierre at her back. "*Non, cherie.* This must be very bad."

"I know," she responded. She kept walking. She reached the doorway and saw the familiar machinery hooked up to a woman with coloring similar to the Burmese women. Her eyes were open. Blood had pooled onto the floor from open tubing still connected to her arm. Her lips were blue, her pallor, despite her dark skin, the color of ivory silk.

Santiago knelt beside the bed, his knees in the blood. He took the woman's hand. He put the lifeless fingers first to his lips then to his forehead.

Parisa once again felt that flinty sensation in her chest. She drew close to Santiago and put her hand on his shoulder. He clutched at her hand, and this time when his lips met her fingers there was nothing flirtatious or teasing in the touch. His cheeks were wet. "Who would do this?"

The question was rhetorical.

The answer simple.

Greaves.

Greaves was the author of it all, the supreme creator, the monster.

Jean-Pierre heard Medichi's voice. He turned and made way for the warrior.

As Medichi moved in, Jean-Pierre returned to the hall. Zach stared into the room. "Jesus. Would you look at this."

Jean-Pierre glanced at him. They were all feeling it, the shock of what was being done to these women.

He did not want to stay close to the murder scene. His

feet turned back down the hall, down to the small room at the end, where he had witnessed that bastard Rith holding the woman Fiona, one hand over her mouth, one around her waist. The woman's eyes had seemed not quite focused. Parisa had called it . . . drugs.

He stood in the doorway. The window was boarded up, the room dim like twilight. There was a strange scent in the space, though, like a Parisian *boulangerie,* where bread was made. They were in France. Perhaps that explained the aroma. He moved toward the bed, his brow pinched in a hard frown. He reached down to the linens and drew the top one to his face.

Oui, the scent was there. He breathed it in. Such a delicate aroma, like a very fine croissant, buttery, like bread but better.

He took another breath and another. He had his eyes closed.

"Jean-Pierre?" Zach called to him.

He turned but couldn't quite see the warrior. He lifted the cloth to his nose and closed his eyes again. In the distance, he heard Zach call for Medichi.

What did the warriors know of good French baking?

He kept breathing, deeper and deeper. He widened his nostrils. He opened his lungs. The aroma dove into his brain and made circles, a hundred circles, a thousand. The scent became a whirlwind and swept through his body, changing him into something he had never been before.

Animal.

He ripped the linens from the bed, bundled them into his arms, and squeezed them against his chest. He picked up the scent and drank it into his body, into every cell. Blood from the battle came away but it didn't matter. He pressed once more. All that mattered was this scent and bringing it into himself, into his body, into his soul.

He left the linens on the bed. He hunted the scent through the room, but only the bed held it. He opened the old armoire but there was nothing inside. Still, a whiff of croissant rose to his nostrils. He dropped to his knees and smelled every corner of the bottom of the armoire. Nothing, yet the scent was stronger.

He pressed his chest to the floor.

The scent was coming from the bottom and from the left. He crawled on his knees and sniffed like a dog all the way to the back. The scent grew stronger and stronger.

He reached with long fingers and found what he hunted. It was cool on the tips of his fingers. Metal, perhaps.

He pulled it out from under the armoire. It looked like a locket, but his vision was not clear. He pressed it to his nose and smelled the heavenly bouquet. His heart ached deep in his chest, like a wound that had just opened up and would never again be healed.

He put the piece of jewelry into his pocket and turned back to the bed. There was nothing more of the scent to be found. The chamber was sterile, not lived in, at least not very long.

Everything in his life that had come before seemed so very small in this moment. All that mattered now was finding the woman, Fiona, the one who had a scent like a French *boulangerie*. He returned to the place where he had seen Rith disappear with the woman. He found the trace. He pushed against it. He tried to fold himself after the trace again, but landed back in the small bedroom over and over.

He began to pace in a circle, a lion trapped in a cage. He punched the air and cried out. He roared. He punched and punched. Again he folded into the trace. Again, the block pushed him back into the room. Over and over he punched the air.

He roared and shouted.

He heard voices calling to him but could not make sense of them. Was it her? Was she speaking? Summoning him? What was being done to her? Was she being hurt? Raped? Killed?

He could not bear the thoughts, and the part of him that was man disappeared. His arms stiffened straight to his sides. His fists clenched tight, his back bowed. His fangs emerged. He roared at the ceiling and could not seem to stop.

Hands pressed on him now, held him in place.

He felt a vibration and still he roared through nether-space, flying through time and darkness and hunger.

His feet touched down and he fell into an abyss as deep as hell.

Medichi stared down at Jean-Pierre. He drew his phone from his pocket and swiped his thumb across the front.

"Jeannie here. How may I serve?"

"I need you to get Alison for me. We have a problem at the Cave."

"One of the warriors hurt?"

"Not exactly. Let's just say I think Jean-Pierre needs Alison's help. We're not really sure what happened."

"I'll send her."

He thumbed his phone then returned it to his pocket. He didn't know what he was looking at. Jean-Pierre had passed out. His behavior at the farmhouse near Toulouse Two had stunned him. Zach as well. Parisa and Santiago had been with the blood slave and hadn't seen the worst of it but they'd heard the roaring.

The sound had been like a hurricane, like great winds had poured through the house. He still didn't know what had happened.

Zach said he thought it was the *breh-hedden* stretching its claws out once more, but Medichi hadn't experienced anything like this, and he sure as hell hadn't passed out. Jean-Pierre was still out, lying on one of the ratty brown leather couches on his side, his body completely quiet, unmoving. Not even his eyelids moved.

Parisa slid her arm around his. "Will he be all right?"

"I don't know what's wrong with him."

"Do you think Rith caused this? Affected his mind?"

"I don't know. He seemed crazed but I don't know why. He kept partially dematerializing then bouncing back like he'd hit some wall he couldn't penetrate."

She squeezed his arm. "I think I understand. He was trying to reach Fiona."

Medichi looked down at her. "So you think it's the *breh-hedden,* too? You think this woman, Fiona, is *the one*?"

She released a heavy sigh. "I don't know. Maybe. Oh, God, probably."

A faint movement of air sent Medichi whirling around. At the same moment, he stepped away from Parisa and folded his sword into his hand, ready for who the hell knew what.

But Alison materialized and his shoulders slumped. He folded the sword away.

She didn't seem distressed as she looked at him. By now, after seven months of living with a Warrior of the Blood, she knew the score. She understood the ever-present danger in which they all lived. She was very pregnant.

She nodded. "What happened?"

"We're not sure." He explained the sequence of events and Jean-Pierre's strange behavior.

Alison just stared at him. "Didn't Kerrick go through something similar at the Blood and Bite? I mean, before we got together? Didn't he end up here at the Cave with all you boys around him?"

Medichi felt himself pale. "I had almost forgotten how crazed he was. So, you think this is the *breh-hedden*?"

She glanced down at Jean-Pierre. "What would you have done if the first time the *breh-hedden* struck, you found that the woman you needed to be with, to protect, had been abducted by a madman?"

He thought back to that moment of seeing Parisa for the first time in the kitchen of his villa, of having caught her tangerine scent, of having been driven toward her in a hypersexual way. He recalled the complete loss of rationality, of reasoning. He'd turned into some kind of Neanderthal caveman who had to have his woman.

Marcus had done him the profound favor of punching him on the jaw and bringing him back to his senses.

All so primal and to a large degree humiliating.

What man enjoyed being so out of control?

Alison dropped to her knees beside the couch. Jean-Pierre's battle gear was still blood-spattered but she'd seen it before. He'd once asked her how she bore it and she'd said simply, *When I see the blood, I know that other lives, innocent lives, have been spared, so I'm grateful.*

Alison was a pragmatic, soothing presence.

She put her hand on Jean-Pierre's head, a light touch. She didn't stroke his forehead or pet him, just settled her hand on him. He'd experienced that touch more than once, and he knew that right now healing waves were passing through Jean-Pierre's mind.

After a minute, the warrior began to move. His eyelids fluttered, his fingers shifted, even his left knee drew forward.

A few seconds more and his eyes opened. He leaned up on his elbow.

Alison sat back on her heels, her hand falling away. "How do you feel, *mon ami*?"

He glanced down at his chest. "Was I wounded?"

She shook her head. "Do you remember what happened?"

He glanced up at Medichi then Parisa. "Where is Zach? Santiago?"

"Thorne sent them home to get some sleep," Medichi said.

Jean-Pierre sat up, a deep furrow between his brows. He pushed a fist into the couch beside his hips and started to lift himself up, then fell against the back cushion. "*Mon Dieu,* my head feels as though it will explode. What happened? My throat, it hurts."

"So you don't remember the farmhouse."

He stared straight ahead, his lips parted, the furrow growing deeper. "The farmhouse. Toulouse." The city name rolled elegantly off his Frenchman's tongue. "*Oui,* I remember some things. Battling. I saw Rith. And I saw . . ." He gave a sudden harsh cry and bent forward, his elbows on his knees, his long fingers pulling his hair out of the *cadroen.* He started rocking back and forth. "He has her. He has the woman. He has Fiona. *Mon Dieu, mon Dieu.*"

Alison put her arm around his shoulders. "Yes, Rith has Fiona. That's right. You've remembered correctly."

He rocked and rocked.

Medichi heard a strangled sound beside him. Parisa held the tips of her fingers to her lips. Tears ran down her face.

He put his arm around her and drew her close against him. Despite his bloody shirt and harness, she buried her face against him.

Medichi stood very still, offering what comfort he could but for some reason, watching Jean-Pierre rock back and forth took him on a hard, swift journey thirteen centuries back. He had rocked just like that, except that he'd held his dying wife in his arms. He spoke the words that shot through his mind. "Jean-Pierre, she's not dead."

Everyone looked at him. Even Jean-Pierre ceased rocking and stared. Medichi said it again: "She's not dead. Fiona is not dead."

"How can you know?"

He released Parisa and looked at her. "Will you find her for Jean-Pierre? That will give him some peace."

She nodded but winced. She took a deep breath. He remembered her headaches.

"I see her. She's in a long room with five other women. There were seven in Burma and one just died in Toulouse. How I hate this man." Her voice quavered as she added, "All of them are on cots even though the sun is shining through the windows."

"Are you certain she lives?"

Parisa nodded. "I can see her chest rising and falling." She suddenly clutched her head. "I'm sorry. I have to close this." The moment she did, she gave a little cry. "Oh, God that hurt."

"It doesn't now?" Medichi asked.

"No. I don't know what's happened. The voyeur never hurt before, not even a twinge. But now it's like knives in my head." She took a few more deep breaths then shifted her gaze to Jean-Pierre. "She is alive, Jean-Pierre. I've seen her."

He put his head in his hands, his elbows still on his knees. "What has happened to me? Why do I feel as though a rock sits in my chest? Why do I care so much about this woman I do not know?" He grew very still.

Medichi could barely breathe. How long would it take before Jean-Pierre figured it out?

Not long. *"Non! C'est impossible. Pas moi. Pas le breh-hedden.* I love women. All women. I cannot devote myself to one, not now. *Jamais!* Fuck."

Medichi bit his lower lip hard. He understood the frustration. Completely.

But it was Parisa who started laughing. She laughed so hard that more tears ran down her cheeks.

Jean-Pierre's fury expanded. "You laugh at me?" he cried.

She nodded then laughed some more. *"Oui. Non.* Oh, Jean-Pierre, all of us have felt what you're experiencing right now."

She cast an arm in Medichi's direction. "Do you think I wanted this? To be enslaved by the *breh-hedden*? To be dragged into this war in this violent way? No, but here I am." She wiped her cheeks and the laughter fled her as suddenly as it had come. "Fiona has lived for over a hundred years as a blood slave and if you are being brought into her life—to protect her, to love her, to care for her . . . I think it's the very least she deserves."

A shared meal
A glass of wine
A sweet dessert
And you

—Collected Poems, Beatrice of Fourth

CHAPTER 14

Parisa stood in the shower, savoring the hot, hot, hot water beating on her neck and shoulders. she had hidden herself away in the guest room so that she could be alone for a little while.

A sad light had passed through Antony's eyes, but he hadn't argued. He'd simply kissed her on the forehead, said he would take a shower as well, then prepare a light repast. Yep, he'd really said *light repast*. The warriors often slipped into speech patterns that belonged to prior centuries, even earlier languages.

So she was showering in the guest room. She felt like a wrung-out towel.

Poor Jean-Pierre.

Poor Fiona, who must have known, even drugged, that she had been close to a rescue.

Instead, Rith had used her as bait. All the other blood slaves had already been moved to another location. Except the one who had died. The only consolation was that twenty-four death vampires were now well and truly dead.

She planted her hands on the wall of the shower stall, the tile cool beneath her fingers. She stretched her neck. That felt a little better.

She had seen the small clock in the foyer, the one that sat next to the magnolia centerpiece. It had been not quite noon.

She did have one satisfaction. She had cut Rith. Funny how she had always thought of herself as a nonviolent person, but right now all she wanted to do was hurt that horrible man.

Exhaustion suddenly dragged at her body.

Though it was only noon, and she'd had a good night's sleep, it was all too much—her recent escape from Burma, having entered into an extremely intimate relationship with a man she barely knew, ascending to Second Earth, the presence of fangs in her mouth, learning to battle by having Antony's memories downloaded directly into her mind, dematerializing, battling alongside the Warriors of the Blood, for God's sake, and watching the *breh-hedden* overtake yet another warrior. And not to mention the headaches that now accompanied her voyeur window.

But underneath everything was a fear that Antony would one day want more from her than she could give. Her heart had been broken once just a few months before her wedding. After that, she'd lost interest in pursuing a relationship of any kind. She had a very specific drive toward Antony, a very powerful *need,* but beyond that she preferred to keep thinking in terms of *her* life, not *theirs*.

She felt caught in a maelstrom and yes, she had chosen to ascend and yes, she had worked to try to rescue Fiona and the other D&R slaves, but it was all too much.

Oh, whatever.

She shut off the water and dragged the towel from the nearby rack. She caught the towel under her arm, bent her head sideways and squeezed the excess water from her hair. She was just a little pissed off at how hard life was right now so she dried her body as though punishing her skin, then did the same thing to her hair. She made little huffy cries of protest but to what? Fate? Life? God? Or the rough towel work?

Why was life always so damn hard? Even when she was a child, things hadn't been easy. Her parents had moved her around so much that she'd never had any real friends. Early on she'd learned that life could be cruel. She thought she'd made peace with it, but right now she was just mad all over again.

She stomped around the bathroom a few times, punching at the air . . . until the smell of sautéed *something*—onions, maybe mushrooms, definitely Italian sausage—floated through a vent. Her stomach rumbled.

And just like that all her angst fled. If Antony was also cooking pasta, she thought she would die and go to heaven.

And there it was, the truth about existence as she saw it, that yes life was difficult but there were always pleasures, many pleasures to balance the hardships.

The smell of sautéing vegetables and meat, especially since it didn't smell of Burmese ginger and turmeric, was one of those pleasures.

She brushed the tangles out of her wet hair then fluffed it a little with her fingers. She put lip gloss on then peered at herself in the mirror. With everything she'd been through in the past forty-eight hours, she was certain she'd look hollow-eyed, her nose swollen from crying, her eyes red. But that was so not the case.

She sucked in a breath.

She had ascension skin and health. She actually looked *good*. Well, damn.

She heard a rap on the bedroom door. She hugged the towel around her body then laughed at herself. Antony had seen her naked . . . more than once. Still, she felt embarrassed. "Yes?"

"The pasta is almost ready," he said. "Shall I put it in the warmer?"

"I'll be there in two minutes. Promise."

"Good. Okay. See you in two."

She hurried into a black lace thong, a pair of jeans, a black lace bra, and a loose purple T-shirt. Well, it was loose everywhere except across her chest.

She left the odd sense of security she'd had during this time in the guest room, and raced for the kitchen. The aroma made her mouth water. But when she did the little zigzag through the dining room to the doorway of the kitchen, what stopped her wasn't the candlelight on the island, or the sparkling glasses of dark red wine, or the sight of steaming pasta being gently coaxed into a white bowl from an oversized sauté pan. All that was amazing, but what brought her to a full halt was Antony standing shirtless, his chest beautifully on display, his button-down jeans loose below his belly button, and his hair hanging damp almost to his navel.

Oh. Dear. God.

She could almost forget entirely about her empty, growling stomach at the sight of so much exotic masculine beauty. He looked up at her with the sauté pan still at an angle and the last bit of pasta tumbling onto the plate and he smiled, that smile of his loaded with teeth and confidence. His eyes glittered in the candlelight.

"See something you like?"

Yes. God. Yes.

Medichi nearly dropped the sauté pan at the wave of tangerine that suddenly hit him. He did take a step back to steady himself. Yeah, *his woman* liked what she saw.

He settled the pan and large spoon in the oversized sink, picked up both bowls of pasta, and moved around the island. She came forward at the same time and took the seat on the right.

She didn't meet his gaze but leaned over her plate. Holding her damp hair back, she closed her eyes and took a deep breath. "Heaven," she whispered.

He looked at her, at the delicate fingers on her hair, at the profile that seemed carved from ivory, at that which had become most precious in these few short months. His heart swelled when it shouldn't have.

She was here.

She was safe.

She was right. This was heaven.

Spearing a slice of sausage, she sank in her teeth and moaned.

Okay, *that* reminded him of a different kind of meal. He faced forward, grabbed his own fork and spoon, and began spearing and twirling. The moment he did, his hunger roared at him. One thing battling required was a solid, heavy intake of calories.

He avoided speaking to her because he knew what would happen. He'd get lost in her voice, or the color of her eyes, or her scent, and he'd start nuzzling her neck. Besides, the way she had launched into her pasta told him she was just as starved.

"I'm sorry," she said. "I'm being rude. I'm slaughtering this meal and not saying one word to you."

He glanced at her, smiled, then gestured with his fork to her bowl. "Eat. We both need it."

She nodded, smiled in return, and reapplied her efforts. When the contents of her bowl were about half demolished, she said, "You know, I've been thinking about how to locate the women."

He put his hand on her arm and said, "You don't have to do this right now. We just got back from a tough situation. You can take a break, breathe. It's important."

She huffed a sigh and twirled her pasta slowly around her spoon. "How about just a couple of points and then I'll let it drop, okay?"

"Okay, but just a couple."

"Good. Okay." She nodded. "First, have you already contacted Carla?"

"Yes, before I started cooking. She's opened up the grid in France even though Rith could have taken the slaves anywhere. But she had to start somewhere."

"Good. That's point one. The grid is already in place and searching. I was concerned about that." She shifted slightly and met his gaze. "You know how the earth rotates on its axis?"

He laughed. "Yep, twenty-four hours a day."

"Yeah. If I voyeur Fiona and can find a window near her, we can help pinpoint her location by a sunrise or sunset. Yes?"

He stared at her. "You realize, Parisa, that you've just cut the hunt time down by anywhere from one hour to twelve."

Parisa smiled. "That's what I thought. I think we have work to do."

"What about the headaches?"

"Guess I'm going to have to suck it up, but I also thought if I can just swing in, take a snapshot, and get out, maybe the headaches won't be so bad. In fact, I want to give it a try right now."

"Why don't you wait until you're done eating?"

But she'd already set her fork down. She'd already opened the window.

She blinked. "Well, that was easy. And no headache."

"Good. What did you see?"

"She's asleep on a cot in a long room with several other cots. There was a bank of windows, and it's full light outside."

"No window coverings?"

"None. Just a lot of deep blue sky." She smiled. "I could open my window every half hour and check the sky. That would be a good start, right?"

Medichi whipped his phone out of the pocket of his jeans and thumbed.

"Carla here, how can I serve?"

"We've had a little brainstorm." He explained their new plan.

"Wow. I should have thought of that. Tell Parisa we just cut the search area by *a lot*."

Medichi laughed. "I will."

He thumbed his phone and relayed Carla's part of the conversation. Once more, he gestured with his fork to Parisa's bowl. "Now eat. And no more discussion."

She grinned at him over a lump of sausage. When she'd taken another sip of wine, she said, "You're a wonderful cook and this is just heaven. Fresh basil?"

He nodded. "I grow it in the herb garden." He gestured to the west wall. "I have a garden back there."

She held her wineglass by the stem and swirled. "You're a renaissance man."

He shrugged. "I like to cook. We had good food on our farm in Italy all those years ago. We had a vineyard and an olive grove as well, like I do here. I'm thinking about having a wood-fire oven put in."

She glanced around the space. "Where?"

He waved a hand to his left. "I'd like to take out this entire bank of cupboards and counter and start over. I want to push this wall out, add French doors that will open onto the garden. I made the mistake of planting the garden out there, where the only access is going through the foyer doors to the back terrace. It's not that far but it's not convenient either. Besides, I'd like to have a view of the White Tanks from this room."

She nodded and sighed. "Sounds like a good plan." Her shoulders looked a little slumped. Well, a good meal, red wine, and trauma would do that to a body.

He shifted his gaze away from her. She needed to get some rest, he could see that. He felt uneasy because he was torn down the middle. The *breh-hedden* wasn't just a sexual entity but demanded that he think of his woman in all respects, one of them being that she needed her rest. But the other half of him was a long drive of need that he'd been keeping a lid on, oh, hell, from the last time she'd left his bed.

Dammit.

He pushed his empty bowl away and planted his elbows on the soapstone. "You probably could use some rest right now," he suggested, still not looking at her. He cleared his throat. "If you want to sleep in the guest room, I really would understand."

He waited, but she didn't say anything.

* * *

Parisa tried to interpret this suggestion, but her mind had switched from alertness to one big mud slide of lethargy. The meal, as wonderful as it was, had acted on her like a sedative.

She released a heavy sigh and put her wineglass back on the soapstone. "I can't believe how tired I am."

He glanced at her, his gaze open, speculative, wary.

She frowned a little. "Are you mad at me?"

His eyebrows shot up. "No. Never."

She smiled at that. "Never? You'll never be mad at me, ever?"

"Well, not right now." He smiled as well.

"Do you want me to sleep in the guest room?"

"Honest?"

"Yeah. Honest."

"Hell, no."

At that she laughed. "Why did you suggest it then?"

He looked away almost like he was embarrassed. But by what?

She put her hand on his forearm—and the moment she touched him a soft buzzing sensation, a delicate vibration, ran through her hand. She stared at her hand and his skin, at the fine black hair. Her fingers drifted over his arm, savoring the muscle beneath and the texture of the hairs above.

He was so masculine, every bit of him, every line of him, and the hardened feel of his warrior muscles started waking her up but this time in an entirely different way.

She lifted her gaze to his and caught the roll of his scent, sage and all his wonderful maleness. She started sliding off the stool without even realizing she was moving, until she stood with her hips against the side of his. With her hand she started low at his waist and climbed, beneath his long hair, feeling both the gentle dips and swells of the scar tissue on his back as well as the larger, harder mounds of muscle.

He flinched and she pressed the tips of her fingers into the scars. "This is part of you," she whispered. She pushed his long hair away from his back. He had tensed up, maybe uncertain, maybe ashamed. She leaned over his back and began to kiss and lick the stripes he bore.

He shuddered and leaned forward.

She slid her hand off his forearm then moved to stand behind him. She split his long black hair into two parts and pushed each part over the closest shoulder. She looked at his back in the soft candlelight. His wing-locks were visible as well as his scars. She drew close then took a deep breath.

Your skin smells of sage and something very male, she sent. *It makes me . . . hungry.*

He groaned and aloud, said, "Tangerine."

She drew back. "Do you have any?"

"Any what?"

"Tangerines."

At that, he shifted toward her, turning so that he could meet her gaze. His lips were swollen with need, his eyes dark. He nodded. He started to rise but she pushed him down with her hand. "Tell me where they are. I'll get them."

"I put the last batch in the fridge, the drawer on the bottom."

She rounded the island, opened the refrigerator door, and found them. The cool air flowed over her skin, tightening her nipples. As she drew one of the tangerines out, she blushed at the very wicked idea that had taken hold of her.

She closed the door then turned toward Antony. He stared at her unblinking, his chin low. His palms were now flat on the soapstone. He looked ready to spring at her, land on her, take her to the floor.

She set the tangerines on the island. She pulled off her shirt but kept her bra on. With a knife she split one of the tangerines in half then pierced the fruit with the sharp tip again and again, grinding the blade into the wedges, tearing up all the connecting fibers, until the half tangerine was a wet, pulpy mess.

She set the tangerine on the counter, put her knife in the sink, and rinsed and dried her fingers. Very slowly, while watching Antony's face darken, she lifted each of her breasts out of her bra so that she was supported by the underwires.

She didn't want to think of exactly how this looked—but she knew Antony. He was loving this.

She lifted the tangerine and held it low to the tip of her breast and slowly brought the juicy center to float over her peaked nipple. Tangerine juice dribbled down her abdomen.

She watched him, his gaze flooding with heat and something like pain. His arms fell wide. His chest rose and fell. Damn, he would hyperventilate if she didn't do something.

"You stay right there," she said.

He nodded, one deep low nod. She moved around the island, the tangerine still rotating, his gaze fixed to the sight. When he breathed, he now made a sound like a train engine.

As she drew around the second corner, he shifted on his stool. "I have to stand up. You understand."

She glanced at his jeans. He was at a bad angle. She nodded.

His hips flexed.

"Lose the jeans," she commanded.

His gaze flickered over her chest from one extended breast to the next. He folded off his pants.

Yes, he'd gone commando.

And he was a rigid line of pleasure waiting to happen. He wept from the tip. His breathing was still harsh, chugging along.

As she drew close, she lifted the tangerine from her breast and put it against his mouth. He groaned loud and long, leaning toward her but sucking hard at the fruit. The sight brought a strange rush of tears to her eyes. She reached low and touched his cock, stroking him very lightly just at the smooth round head.

Antony, she sent softly into his mind, *did I tell you how much it meant to see you each night, to watch you pleasure yourself? To take tangerines into your mouth? It helped me to know you were real and you were there, that I wasn't alone. You kept me sane.*

He drew the tangerine from his lips. His breathing eased. His hips flexed and he pushed his cock farther through the grip of her hand. "This is better."

"Yes. Oh, yes."

He caught a tear as it rolled down her cheek, then sucked the drop from his finger. He moved into her, his cock folding up to fit against her abdomen. He slid his arms around her back trapping her arms low, then he kissed her, a tangerine-flavored kiss that knocked her senses flat.

He pushed his tongue into her mouth and made her pulse throb with each thrust. Her arms drifted around his waist. She clung to his skin, pulling and kneading, even the ribbed scar tissue.

He left her mouth and kissed down her neck. When he licked over her vein pleasure shot through the well of her body, anticipating a hard strike of fangs. But he didn't linger there. He moved lower, bending over and angling his head so that he could reach what she had offered by the refrigerator.

His tongue licked down her chest and moved to the tangerine nipple. He groaned all over again as he drew the tip into his mouth and began to suckle.

Her body tightened very low and began to pull inward with each suck of his mouth and lips. Her breathing transformed into soft pants, one after the other, until she was dizzy. She settled her hands on the top of his soft hair.

Her hips bucked at the sensation between her fingers, the pull of his mouth on her breast, and the responsive tugs between her legs.

"Antony," she cried out. Frustration had her now. She needed more from him.

He drew back. His lips were red and swollen from suckling her, his eyes wild.

"Help me, Antony." She slung an arm around his neck and kissed him.

He picked her up in his arms and cradled her against his chest. She pressed her face into his neck. She felt her fangs emerge and began to lick his throat. He moved her into the hallway that led in the direction of the pool and the guest-house, but not very far. She thought maybe he meant to have her in the pool.

Instead he turned up the narrow spiraled staircase, holding her at a careful angle so that she didn't scrape anything. He was almost too big for the space himself, but he managed it.

"The bed in the turret room is at a perfect height for what I want to do to you."

She hissed and shivered. A low chuckle rippled from his throat. "I'm going to do you, Parisa. I'm going to do you over and over right against this bed. And you'll be screaming."

Her hips bucked against him. She needed to get her pants off. She needed him inside her.

In the turret he put his hand against her pants and folded them off. Cool air flowed over her skin.

He slid his fingers down the sides of her thong and she heard the lace ripping as he pulled it apart. But, oh, God, the sensation of him *doing things to her* made her ache deep inside her body.

He moved her backward step by step until the back of her legs hit the bed. He pushed her onto her back and followed. Her feet just touched the floor. He spread her legs wide and eased down onto her.

She hissed again and wriggled her hips.

"So anxious for me," he whispered against her neck. He licked her throat, and her vein throbbed.

"Yes, yes, yes," she whispered. She wanted him to strike.

Instead he rose up a little and began to push inside. She closed her eyes and breathed, savoring every inch of him as he pushed, drew back, pushed a little more, fitting himself carefully inside her.

"Is this what you wanted?"

"Yes . . . but faster."

He chuckled again, very low. He kissed her eyelids. "I'd ask you to open your eyes and look at me, but I have something different in mind."

Of course then she had to open her eyes. She looked at him. "What?"

"Open your voyeur's window."

"Why?"

He just smiled. A certain thought occurred to her, and a flush flowed up her face. Yes, she was embarrassed.

He leaned close. "You want to do it," he whispered into her ear. Shivers chased over her neck and down her arms. "I know you do."

"I do, but it's so . . . naughty."

"I want you to get as close as you can and watch me push into you. I want you to see. Believe me, if I could do it, I would. I'd love to watch this."

Parisa couldn't believe she was about to do this. Yes, she had voyeured Antony when he pleasured himself but somehow this felt different.

And yet . . .

She opened the window. The pain hit hard, but this time she pushed back at it until it seemed to fall out of her head. Then she raised her shields hard. She took a deep breath, but the pain didn't return.

"You okay?" he asked. "I forgot about the headaches."

She smiled. "I think it was a shield problem. I'm okay now."

He nodded. "Good." Then he pushed into her in a long silken glide. She was tight but very wet and she gasped before she could say, "You sure you want me to do this?"

"Only if you describe it to me."

At that, she brought the window in close to Antony from behind. What a glorious sight, better than a mirror. Watching his buttocks flex over her at the same time she could feel what he was doing inside her doubled the sensation.

She clenched.

"Yeah, that's what I wanted," he whispered against her cheek. "What do you see?"

"You. Your backside rippling over me as you push inside."

He groaned. "Get in closer. Really close." He pulled out of her almost to her entrance, then hovered.

She panned the window around his buttocks to the side—and there it was. His cock, long, thick, and hard. "I can see the length of you. Antony, so beautiful." Her mouth was dry.

Oh, yeah, she was panting. He started to push inside and she gave a cry.

"Faster," she whispered. "I'm so close and all I've done is look at you, but oh, God . . . so big, so beautiful."

He groaned, pushing harder and faster. She kept the window positioned at his hips; he maintained just enough distance that she could watch his cock go in and come out, over and over.

"You're like a piston, Antony." She couldn't really breathe very well. He was big and he was hitting her cervix and suddenly she was just full of pleasure and screaming. The window closed but a rush of ecstasy drove through her, tightening and releasing, drawing him out.

He bowed backward and gave a shout, then another.

He spilled his seed but didn't slow. Another orgasm caught her hard, really hard. Pleasure spiraled up through her body then down, streaking up her labia and clitoris. She rocked against him and still he kept pumping into her.

She drew back and looked at him. His eyes were rolled back in his head. "More," he whispered. "Oh, God there's more." He cried out and as he ejaculated again, she was swept up into the stratosphere, pleasure like lightning moving over her entire body while she clenched and tightened around his driving cock.

Finally, her body quieted, and Antony was able to slow his movements. He lowered himself onto her, released a sigh, and relaxed. She surrounded his shoulders with her arms.

"I haven't felt this way in a long, long time," he said.

"How long?"

His body stiffened, then he forced himself to relax. "Not since my wife. I haven't allowed this kind of closeness since my wife."

She held him tighter. "And for me, not since my fiancé. He kind of broke my heart. We were planning our wedding, I'd just bought the invitations, and he announced he couldn't marry me. He thought I was inaccessible."

"I'd offer to break his neck but I'm too glad you're not with him anymore."

She laughed. Funny, that was the first time she'd ever thought of Jason without hurting. She sighed and slid her arms around him even harder. Only her fingertips met in the middle. All his powerful warrior muscles got in the way. Ah, too bad.

She giggled.

He sighed.

"You know what the bad thing is?" she asked.

He lifted to look at her. "What?"

"That your bedroom is so far away. I'd love to curl up next to you right now and take a nap."

But a slow smile spread over his face. The vibration began.

The next minute she was lying in exactly the same position, with him still inside her, but stretched out on his bed. She'd totally forgotten he could do that.

"Hey," she cried. "I told you to give a girl a warning."

But he only laughed and nuzzled her neck. "Couldn't help myself."

She chuckled. "What a world," she said. "Right this moment, I'm glad I'm here."

"Me, too."

No greater gifts exists on Second Earth,
Then that which comes from the vein.

—*Collected Proverbs,* Beatrice of Fourth

CHAPTER 15

Greaves made several attempts to break back through the shield that surrounded his voyeur-link with Parisa. He sat in his Geneva office contemplating the most recent occurrence.

He'd caught a strange glimpse of naked bodies, a breast, a very large breast, the scars on Warrior Medichi's back; then he'd felt Parisa's mind push at him, hard. He hadn't been prepared, otherwise he could have prevented it, but she actually pushed him out of her head and slammed impenetrable shields in place.

The level of her power had surprised him. He questioned his wisdom in letting her escape from the Burma house.

He had only himself to blame. At the time, he'd thought Julianna's suggestion rather brilliant but now, given that the newly created ascender had more power than ever, he realized his error.

But this most recent event which involved the loss of twenty-four death vampires to the attack by the Warriors of the Blood on the Toulouse farmhouse, really elevated his blood pressure. On the other hand, because he'd had the foresight to order Rith to import a proper amount of death vampires, Rith been able to fold all the blood donors out of Toulouse and secure them in a new facility. In that sense, the smooth running of his emerging empire was kept firmly in place.

There was that silver lining again.

As for what he meant to do next, well, those decisions were presently dancing in the air. Rith's most recent, Seer-based emails had changed his view of the future, especially where the mortal-with-wings was concerned.

The emails had been both encouraging and alarming. The most powerful Seers Fortresses had predicted a major decisive battle, which he would win. On the surface, this sounded like good news, but Greaves was not a neophyte in any sense of the word. He might have been exhilarated by the prophecy, *a millennium ago*. But he had lived too long as a vampire not to know how changeable the future really was. His only real difficulty right now was determining exactly what he should do with this information.

But it was the other set of emails that concerned him most, that had the power to send little shivers down his neck and spine.

Though Greaves knew, by Rith's account, that Parisa had *royle* wings, he hadn't given the circumstance much thought or even interest. The supposed magical nature of *royle* wings had, over the millennia, slid into the category of vampire mythology, nothing more.

Legend held that such wings had the power to create peace. According to Philippe Reynard's definitive work on the history of ascension, the actual translation for *royle* from the ancient language was "benevolent wind." Greaves could recall that as a little boy, when he'd been in the care of his mother, she'd told him stories about the first vampire, Luchianne, her *royle* wings, and how she had the power to create a vast wind that could calm an entire army's fighting rage.

It was absurd, of course. Yet because he'd heard the story

at his mother's knee, somehow the fable had intense meaning for him. He was a man more of instincts than analysis, and in this situation, he *felt* the critical nature of all the emails that had begun flowing his direction concerning the emergence of Parisa's *royle* wings, more than he had about a possible forthcoming decisive battle.

So, the larger question for him had become what to do about Parisa Lovejoy. The smaller question—should he orchestrate a battle—he had already turned over to his generals in his Estrella Complex in Metro Phoenix Two. They had been ecstatic to learn he actually wanted two full divisions assembled in northern Arizona, as surreptitiously as possible—yes, that had been a little joke. Setting up supply lines alone for thirty thousand soldiers would be a work of monumental proportion.

Even now, General Leto was importing death vampires from all over the globe, provided by his allied High Administrators. He did take a moment to smile, even to fantasize about such a battle. The truth was simple: He could take Endelle's forces in a heartbeat if it came down to a numbers game. And he was a smart enough vampire to work the numbers.

But there was that other pesky, nagging truth that often wars weren't won by the numbers. So many other factors could alter an obvious outcome. One had only to follow both amateur and professional Mortal Earth sports to know this was true, that occasionally the team with all the right numbers could lose a championship to a phenomenon known as 'heart.' Absurd but true.

So he was preparing, and in his preparations he was cautious. What else would a vampire over two thousand years old be?

Rith arrived with the usual empty medical blood bag, plastic tubing, and sterile needle. Time to feed the blood donors.

He rose from his chair and removed his suit coat. He pinched the shoulders and brought the sleeves together to effect a careful fold. He paid a fortune for his suits, tailored as they were by Hugo Boss on Mortal Earth. He had fittings four times a year.

He removed the French cuff link from the right sleeve of his silk shirt, an amethyst color this time in honor of his continued pursuit of the mortal-with-wings. Though she was now ascended, for him Parisa Lovejoy would always be the mortal-with-wings. She had been an anomaly as great as either Alison Wells or Havily Morgan.

Three powerful women had arrived to serve as *brehs* for the Warriors of the Blood.

He sighed as he set the amethyst link on his desk.

He moved to the large plate-glass window of the building he owned, a stone structure that resembled work from the mid-1800s but of course with electricity and running water. The basement, blasted out of the earth, held his famous Round Table, the seat of his Coming Order. Greaves did value modern times, enormously, but there were occasions when his soul longed for the earlier days of stone and earth, of fire, and of hundreds of servants to carry out the menial tasks of slaughtering and preparing food, and scrubbing laundry on the banks of a river.

Now he had to hire his help and pay decent wages.

As he began rolling up his right sleeve, he looked out over Geneva Two. Its population was a mere hundred thousand, a fraction the size of Mortal Earth's city. He had chosen his site well, at almost the tip of the Petite Lac, that part of Lake Geneva that seemed almost like a lake unto itself. The view from his penthouse was really exquisite, especially at night with the black expanse of the water surrounded on both sides by the twinkle of modern lights.

With his right sleeve rolled up past his elbow, he turned and made his way to the black leather sofa. Rith already had the necessary equipment set up.

He sat down, and Rith used the tourniquet to bring his vein forward. With the precision of decades, Rith drove in the needle and the blood started to flow. He donated once a week; his blood formed the basis of the cocktail that brought his female donors back from oblivion and had them ready to serve in another month's time.

He glanced at Rith, at the broad forehead and relatively unattractive features. Rith didn't partake of dying blood, though many believed he did. He could have used a little beautification. But the man was staunchly opposed.

He watched the bag fill. "Have you ever tasted my blood?"

Rith glanced at him, giving him his infamous blank expression. "No, master. Never."

Darian flared his nostrils. He breathed in the perfume of the man's skin. Most of the time he could smell a lie, but not today. Or at least not on Rith.

"Have you read the latest emails about the Mumbai and Bogotá predictions?"

"Yes, of course. You flagged them."

Rith's fingers actually trembled. As well they should.

"What are we to do?"

Rith pulled the needle out and pressed a square of gauze against the wound. He taped the gauze in place. "I have begun the process of mobilizing my army. As for the mortal-with-wings, I wish to know your opinion. What do you think we should do about her?"

"I think we should find her and kill her, of course. She is too dangerous for the Coming Order."

Darian smiled then chuckled. "I adore how you speak of killing her the same way you would speak about creating a floral arrangement. *We should put the roses in first, then the lilies.*" He chuckled again. Rith eased him. He always had. In some ways, Rith was an extension of his own careful, ordered, sociopathic mind.

"She is dangerous, master. Very dangerous. Only an hour ago, another report came, from Johannesburg this time, as they used to when Alison was in her ascension process, that Parisa will change the course of the war."

"Alison was supposed to have that kind of effect, but she has accomplished nothing of significance. If anything, Havily Morgan has wrought more damage since she brought

Warrior Marcus back from Mortal Earth to serve as High Administrator of Desert Southwest Two." A faint shudder went through him. Marcus had indeed stalled Greaves's efforts to turn High Administrators. "I give you permission to do what I see in your heart you wish to do anyway." He watched Rith carefully. "Good God, Rith, are you actually smiling?"

"Yes, master." Rith placed the blood in a special pack then settled it in a cradle within an Igloo container. He had a runner outside ready to transport the blood to a lab that created the cocktail for the various blood donor facilities. It pleased Greaves to think that a drop or two of his blood ensured that his donors remained alive and healthy so that they could keep producing.

In that way, he was a true sustainer of life.

Which made him chuckle again.

With all his equipment packed up, Rith turned and headed to the door. Greaves rolled his shirtsleeve down and rose to his feet. "It is a lovely thing to see you so happy, Rith."

"Yes, master."

Rith actually bowed. Greaves was in favor of the gesture, but it was an antiquated European cultural tradition that was considered passé.

With a dismissive wave of his hand, he bid his servant good-bye.

Parisa dreamed of peaches rolling around in her mind.

They moved around, crashing into one another and pummeling the inside of her head. All that movement *hurt*. Finally she jerked awake and put her hand to her forehead.

Oh, thank God she had only dreamed the pain.

She glanced at the clock. She had been checking her voyeur window every half hour. She must be on Fiona time since she'd only drifted off for about fifteen minutes.

Once more, she opened her voyeur's window. Still daylight. She shut it down fast. Good, still no headache.

Antony was right next to her, his warm body pressed close to her side, his back to her. She shifted to look at all the silvery scars and his long warrior hair. She wanted to touch him but didn't want to wake him. He'd been through so much in the past three months.

She stared up at the ceiling, at the coffer beams and the words in Italian burned into the wood. Antony had said it was a poem his wife had written. She hoped one day he would share the translation with her.

Her thoughts turned back to her dream. So what had she been dreaming?

Oh, yeah. Peaches. How weird to think of a sweet round fuzzy fruit banging around in her head and causing such pain.

She flung an arm over her head and took a few deep breaths, grateful the dream hadn't been real.

How comfortable this was, feeling the movement of Antony's regular deep breaths rising and falling against her side.

She was naked.

He was as well.

He'd made love to her—she smiled—in the turret room so that he could create just the right angle. He'd enabled her to see that beautiful part of him thrusting between her legs and disappearing. Tears welled up in her eyes just thinking about it. She hadn't taken a lover since her fiancé; she didn't believe in promiscuity. She never had. Yet here she was, bedding a man she hardly knew.

She released a sigh. What was she doing, anyway? What was she thinking to have become so instantly involved with Antony?

At the very least, she should give herself time and space to make sense of this new world, to discover where she fit within Endelle's administration. She should get her own apartment—only how was she supposed to be safe when it was clear Rith was still after her?

Endelle had continued to sustain the dome of mist over the villa, a constant protection for her. And when crews came to work in the vineyard or the olive grove or anywhere else on the property, the plan was that she would either stay at Endelle's administrative headquarters or have Carla or Jeannie fold her directly to the palace. Whatever.

Her thoughts shifted to Fiona, as they often did. Because she'd seen the woman several times now, both in person and through her voyeur window, she felt a connection to her and certainly a powerful drive to release her from the terrible slavery that held her prisoner. She recalled touching her for the first time, holding her arms and feeling the peculiar vibration flow between them.

Though her own captivity had been relatively gentle, she knew what it was not to be free, to be held to a strict schedule, to never be allowed to leave a narrow, tightly governed space.

Peaches.

Peaches.

Greaves was sometimes called *the little peach*.

She sat up suddenly, which caused Antony to jerk awake. He leaped from bed and before she knew it, he had his sword in hand, his very nude body hunched in an aggressive position. He turned slowly in a circle examining every corner of the room. "What is it?" he cried.

She glanced at him and covered her mouth. She was trying not to laugh. "I'm sooo sorry, Antony. I had a nightmare." That was partially the truth.

His sword vanished first, then he slumped forward onto the bed and groaned. "Thank God." He looked up at her, his eyes bloodshot, weary. "Thank God." He shifted to stretch himself out on the bed next to her, propping himself up on his forearms. "Are you all right? What kind of bad dream?"

She settled down beside him, her head on her pillow. She dragged the sheet up over her breasts and under her arms. She put her hand on his bicep, one of her favorite places, her thumb stroking back and forth. "I think I know what happened, why I had headaches during the recent voyeurs, even though I'd never had them before."

He rubbed his eyes. "Why?"

"Greaves."

He looked back at her and scowled. "What do you mean, Greaves?"

Then the memory came forth, of being on the teak bench that last day, of Greaves coming to her and sitting down next to her, of doing battle against his mind, of his intention to break through her shields. She again shared all this with Antony. But only in this moment, maybe because of the peaches-like-bowling balls dream, did she remember what else he had done. "He kissed me."

"He did what?" he barked.

"He kissed me. I'm only now just remembering. The moment his lips touched mine, I thought of you and my shields just fell flat. Then I must have passed out because I woke up on the grass, on my face, without being able to remember anything. But, I'm telling you, Greaves got through, he broke through my shields, and he's been in my mind. Antony, I think he's been causing the pain when I open my voyeur window. He's linked to me somehow. That's how he knew we were coming for the D and R slaves. That's why Rith met us in Toulouse with all those death vampires and all the slaves but Fiona gone. Greaves warned him."

Antony stared at her for a long hard moment, his eyes darkening in stages. His chin dipped low. His shoulders hunched.

She didn't at first understand what was happening to him.

A growl emerged, a sound that told her his ascended vampire nature was in the fore and his rational brain had taken a hike. "I'll kill him. I'll fucking kill him."

She thumped him on the shoulder. "Antony, stop! Don't go all Neanderthal on me. This is good news because now I know what's going on. We can use it to our advantage."

He looked away from her, rolled onto his back, then took several very deep breaths. "It's the *breh-hedden*. In all my ascended life I have not experienced anything like this. For a moment, the only thing I wanted was to find Greaves and tear him limb from limb."

"Yeah, I got that."

He released a deep sigh then shifted to meet her gaze. He

put a hand on her shoulder and said, "So you think Greaves has some kind of link with you. A mind-link to your voyeur window."

When he said it like that, she suddenly felt cold, sick, clammy. The thought of such a monster having control of her turned her stomach. "Yes," she said. "I believe he does. Is there any way I can get rid of it?"

"The person establishing the link has to break it. At least, that's the way it's usually done."

"Oh, God, I just remembered. He saw us. When I voyeured, you know, *us,* in the turret room, he saw us."

At that Antony drew his hand into a fist. He muttered a string of obscenities, which seemed quite appropriate. "You think he saw the whole damn thing?" He was shouting now.

Parisa thought it through. "Wait. Maybe not. When I first opened the window, the pain began and I pushed it away. Mentally. I remember thinking that I so didn't want to have pain right then, so I gave it a hard push and then I felt nothing. I felt like I normally did."

He met her gaze and nodded. "You may have pushed him out. Jesus, what power."

She leaned into him and bumped her forehead against his shoulder. "Oh, God, I hope so. I think so." She bumped her head a few more times, which seemed kind of silly but it comforted her. "You know, if my life gets any weirder, I don't know what I'm going to do."

He slipped his arm around her and pulled her up next to him, holding her close. "Get some rest. Later maybe we can experiment. But if this is true, then it would explain why we had a greeting party in Toulouse."

She rolled into him and snuggled close. She slung a leg over his legs and an arm over his stomach.

"How did you figure out it was Greaves?"

"I dreamed of peaches rolling around in my head, crashing into one another. Then I remembered that Greaves was sometimes called *the little peach.* On some level, I must have known, but it was only through my dream that the knowledge was able to break through to my conscious mind."

"Wow," he muttered.

"Yeah."

She wasn't sleepy. Not even a little. Her mind worked over the dream, over Greaves's mind-link. Because she couldn't sleep and because she was nestled against Antony, she opened her voyeur's window. Instead of focusing on Fiona this time, however, she chose a more innocuous object: the White Tank Mountains just beyond the villa. She panned her window back and forth. She wanted to see if and when the pain would come.

After a few more seconds, there it was, a flash of pain, but smaller this time, *thank you God*.

She shifted her attention to the pain, but it retreated. She relaxed and watched the pain until it faded to nothing. She remained very still within her own mind. She needed to understand, she wanted to understand, exactly what was going on.

She took slow, even breaths and waited. She panned to the north side of the villa property, in the direction of Antony's olive grove. She began moving the window through the grove as though searching, but the whole time she kept her attention focused on the point where the pain had receded.

She moved to one end of the grove and back. She crossed a dirt lane and moved into the vineyard.

She waited.

After what felt like five minutes, she felt a twinge within her mind—then a distinct *absence,* much like what she'd felt when she'd pushed Greaves out of her mind in the turret room.

So she was right. Greaves was there. She also thought it was very telling that the level of pain the mind-link usually induced had diminished. If all her suppositions were correct, no doubt Greaves was working his end of the equation as well.

She repeated the process two more times. Each time, the experience was the same.

So it was all true. Greaves had formed a link with her. She knew that telepathic links could be forged between powerful ascenders—Endelle had one with Thorne, her second-in-command. When she needed him, all she had to do was think about him and send a command. He could respond mind-to-mind.

This was similar. But was it telepathic, or was it related strictly to her voyeur's window?

Only one way to find out. She closed her eyes and, without opening her window, focused all her mental attention on Greaves. *Are you there, Commander?* she sent.

She waited.

Nothing returned to her. Nothing. Not a flash of pain, not even a twinge.

She made the attempt several times.

Nothing.

If all her musings were correct, then Greaves had apparently formed a link with her voyeurism but not with her telepathy.

A flush started at her forehead and climbed down her face, her neck, her chest, and over her arms. She felt hot and cold at the same time. Her palms were clammy.

Antony's breathing was now deep and even. The warrior needed a nap.

Slowly, she pulled away from him. She slid off the bed and padded her way to the bathroom. The toilet had its own little room. She grabbed a towel, went inside, and closed the door. She was completely naked so she wrapped the oversized black bath towel around her body and sat down on the lid.

She leaned over and, with her elbows on her thighs, she put her head in her hands. Sweat now dripped down her neck and from beneath her breasts.

She couldn't breathe very well so she worked at that for a long time until she knew she wouldn't hyperventilate. She wasn't sure exactly what was wrong with her but of all the things she had experienced in the past three-plus months, the thought that Greaves had a link to her made her nauseous. She felt controlled and put in yet another box. She hated these boxes. She hated that she was living in Antony's villa again, with another dome of mist over the property, she hated that she'd spent the last few months in Rith's residence living like some kind of mystical bird that had to be coddled and caged, and she really hated that anyone had access to her mind like this.

But what distressed her most of all was that she was sharing Antony's bed as though they'd been lovers for years. Where was her choice in any of this? She hadn't exactly *chosen* Antony. He'd simply shown up in her voyeur's window about the same time she'd mounted her wings for the first time.

Her previous life, the one she'd lived as a librarian on Mortal Earth, had been a life of her *choosing*. No one had forced it on her. No one had come along insisting that she shelve books to assist the war effort. No, she'd become a librarian by choice.

Now she was locked into some kind of übersexual relationship with Antony and as pleasurable as it was, *what was it really?* Well, if she'd understood everything that had been going on since she'd first been brought to the villa, her entire relationship with Antony was because of the *breh-hedden,* something she didn't understand, but which had also locked her down and helped force her into this box.

Right now, she felt no different, well maybe a little different, than when she'd lived in Rith's house in Burma, like a jewel that was owned by someone else and needed constant guarding and polishing and tending.

Her thoughts weren't entirely fair, maybe not as rational as she wanted them to be, but something about Greaves having possession of her mind had sunk her, put cement in her spirit and taken her to the bottom of the lake. Maybe she needed to cry. She worked at it, and squeezed out a couple of tears but she just wasn't in the mood to give vent to her feelings through her tear ducts.

No, that wasn't what she needed.

She needed the link broken, but how? Maybe Endelle

could do it. Everyone kept mentioning how much power she had.

Then again, Endelle certainly couldn't change the fact that she was sequestered in this villa, unable to even walk about on the grounds without Antony glued to her side.

And now she had a voyeur-link with a monster.

When she left the bathroom, she'd come to at least one decision. She intended to move into one of the guest rooms. Not the original one she'd used—it was across from Marcus and Havily's room—but one closer to Antony.

With the towel still wrapped around her, she padded through the bathroom. She was surprised to see Antony sitting up in bed, his arms folded across his bare chest, his long hair hanging around his shoulders. He was looking in the direction of the den, through to the windows that opened onto the front lawn. She knew he could hear her, but he didn't turn in her direction. He just stared across the room.

She rounded the bed and stood a few feet away facing him. His gaze was still fixed in the same direction. She waited.

"You were in the bathroom awhile."

"I was thinking. And I thought you were asleep."

"I was. I woke up to an empty bed and I panicked. Then I realized you were probably in the bathroom. I got up and checked. I could hear you breathe and sigh. Your thoughts were very loud, I just couldn't read them."

He sort of smiled, a half smile.

"I've had a lot to digest."

"So have I." His frown deepened. "I think we should complete the *breh-hedden*."

Somehow it was the last thing she'd expected him to say. She even moved back a full step. "Why?" she asked. Okay, so she'd almost shouted the question.

Maybe it was the tone of her voice, which she admitted did sound incredulous, even to her, but his brows shot up and his arms unhinged but they didn't come apart all the way. He looked wound up, braced for anything, tight.

He heaved a sigh. "Because if we complete the *breh-hedden*, which involves moving into each other's minds at certain times, then I'm guessing that no one can form this kind of voyeur-link with you ever again. Certainly not without my knowledge."

"You want to complete the *breh-hedden* so you can have charge of my mind?"

"No," he said, shaking his head. He pushed a hand through his hair on the left side until it hung away from his face. "Not have charge, never that. But maybe I could protect you better."

"Lots of maybes." She sat down on the edge of the bed, the very edge, as in she took up three inches of mattress at the most.

Her head wagged back and forth and her gaze fell to the dark planked floor. The villa was beautiful and the wood gleamed, another lovely prison. "I don't want to complete the *breh-hedden,* and I don't want you to move into my head . . . ever." She turned to him. "I'm not even sure that I want you, really want you. I feel trapped, Antony. This . . . this *thing* grabbed hold of both of us and chained us. That's why we're here. Then Madame Endelle assigned you as my Guardian. Well the *guard* part of that word feels about right."

He looked appalled, his eyes wide, his brows raised, his lips parted. His cheeks had a drawn look, liked he'd sucked in the shock of her words and couldn't let it back out.

"Jesus," he murmured. "I guess you have been thinking."

"Yeah."

"You know, I've just realized how inaccessible you are."

She stood up and stared at him. "I can't believe you just said that." Thoughts of Jason and the way he'd broken up with her shot through her mind. He'd used that word to describe her as well, but this wasn't fair at all.

"But it's true, isn't it? At least be honest with yourself about what it is you're doing right now, about all the things you just said to me. You just said, *I'm not even sure I want you.*"

"That's not what I meant. I meant this *breh* thing has charge of us both right now. Maybe you don't even want me."

He blinked, a strange slow movement. "Maybe the fuck I don't."

She was breathing hard, and panic began to rise. What was she doing? Was she breaking up with him? Had she been cruel? By the look on his face the answer had to be yes.

She felt an urge to apologize, but when she opened her mouth what came out was, "I want to move into one of the guest rooms."

"Fine. Take any one you want. It doesn't matter to me."

She felt the bitterness in each word. Fine. This was for the best. She needed space. She'd been needing space for three long months.

She gathered up some of her clothes and left the room.

How fucking strange.

Medichi stared at the closed door, the carved wood panels that comprised a thick private partition between his room and the rest of the villa.

His arms hung loose at his sides now, like they had nowhere of importance to be. Less than an hour ago, one of his arms had held his woman tight, now he had no woman, just this pit in his chest that had taken the place of his lungs.

Parisa wasn't completely off base. She had posed at least one rational question. How could either of them know what was real or what was just some bullshit preternatural creation of the *breh-hedden*?

There was just one problem.

He pulled her pillow up to his nose and smelled. Tangerine. The whole time she'd been talking and arguing and looking edible with just a black towel around her luscious body, the whole time she'd been yelling, he'd been hard as a rock and ready for her. Goddamn *breh-hedden*.

On the other hand, he took a deep breath and admitted the other truth, the one that lurked in the back of his head: He was just a little bit relieved that she wasn't here, wasn't beside him, wasn't reminding him of his new duty as a Guardian of Ascension, as her *breh*.

Fuck. Him. Because he almost smiled.

Relief flowed through him like a dam had just given way.

He was free.

Shit. He was free and he loved it, bastard that he was. He shouldn't be feeling this way. He cared about Parisa. He really did. Or maybe it was just that he felt he should care about her.

But time peeled away in a great rush and as had happened a thousand times since his ascension so many centuries ago, the image of his wife in his arms, bleeding her life away, beat the shit out of him.

He understood then what haunted him about Parisa, about how protective he felt toward her, about how the *brehhedden* had fucked him over. He'd lived a relatively secure life in his Italian world. His family had owned a small country house for over a century and had worked their vineyards and olive groves for multiple centuries before that.

So when the enemy came, he'd been unprepared. He wasn't responsible in the sense that he had failed to do a soldier's duty. He'd failed because he was a man, not a soldier, and overtaken by superior numbers and weaponry.

But now he was a warrior, seasoned and powerful, and he'd already lost Parisa once while under his protection.

She had been returned to him and in the overwhelming aftermath, the pure heady relief of having her under his roof once more, he'd been unable to stay away from her. He'd needed her in his bed, needed to bury himself inside her, to feel that she was truly alive and safe in his care.

In his care.

She didn't want to be in his care.

She wanted to be as free of the *breh-hedden* as he did. She wanted her freedom. He wanted to be free of the guilt of keeping her safe when he knew damn well that was an impossible task. He'd already failed once. He would again.

So . . . shit.

He could train her, though. He could continue to layer skill upon self-defense skill. He could help her with flying, with the dagger and sword. He could teach her more about her shields and how to withstand Rith's attempts to enthrall her.

Yes, he could do that.

But would it be enough?

This was a world at war.

Nothing would ever be enough until Greaves was dead and buried and his emerging empire crushed.

But how the hell would that ever happen?

The first path seduces by promise,
The second appeals to pride,
But the worthy path demands surrender.

—*Collected Proverbs,* Beatrice of Fourth

CHAPTER 16

When Parisa left Antony's bedroom, she made her way to her original guest room because it was familiar, most of her clothes were still there, and she was really upset.

She got dressed in jeans and a cherry-red silk tank top as her mind spun in circle after circle trying to make sense of the stupid *breh-hedden,* and the hunky man naked in bed at the end of the villa, and how her body kept crying out for him.

She was reeling and she knew it. She also knew something else. If she didn't let this out, she'd go crazy. But who could she talk to? Right now, it couldn't be Antony. The truth was, the whole time he'd been sitting up in bed, he'd shed his sage like a spice grinder; leaving his room had been a supreme act of will.

Her thoughts turned to Havily. Yes, Havily.

She left the guest room and headed to the leather-and-book haven to make her phone call.

Havily, bless her, said she'd be at the villa in five minutes and she'd bring coffee.

While Parisa waited, she opened her voyeur window, thought of Fiona, and made a swift check of the room. The windows were still really light. She closed the window and as before with just a sneak-peek, no pain. Well, at least that was something.

She made her way to the foyer, barefoot, and waited. A few minutes later, there she was, the red-headed beauty, and Parisa's first ascended girlfriend.

The relief she felt was surprising but if anyone might know what she was going through, it was Havily. Three months ago, Havily had walked through her own private *breh-hedden* heaven-and-hell combo.

With a mug of coffee in hand, Havily suggested a walk through the formal garden. It was still hot for September, but Parisa didn't care. It was just great to be with a friend, to be outdoors, to be chatting about the weather, about the flowers, about nothing important.

Parisa walked on as many of the grassy portions of the garden as she could find. Sometimes she had to step onto gravel, but mostly she found lawn to cross.

Havily asked to hear her version of what happened at the Toulouse farmhouse. Parisa told her from beginning to end.

"To have come so close to rescuing Fiona, to have seen her, and to have watched Rith drag her away, you must be really upset."

"I am. Jean-Pierre almost had him but Rith blocked the trace."

Havily whistled. "That is a lot of power. As far as I know, none of the Warriors of the Blood can block a trace." She was quiet for a moment then asked, "How did Jean-Pierre take it? I mean none of the warriors likes to fail . . . at anything."

Parisa glanced at her, uncertain what she should say. "I'm not sure if I should tell you, but I have a feeling Marcus will know by the end of the day anyway."

Havily stopped her with a gentle hand pressed to the inside of her elbow. "What happened?"

Parisa shook her head. "It was the *breh-hedden*."

"What?" Havily cried. "You mean, Jean-Pierre?"

Parisa nodded. She let her friend figure the rest out.

Havily gasped. "Fiona? The blood slave?"

"Exactly. Do you remember when I was first voyeuring Fiona in the library? You were there and you were standing next to Jean-Pierre."

"Yes. Oh, now I remember. He asked if someone was baking something."

Parisa nodded. "He said he smelled croissants."

Havily bit her lip. "Croissants?" She chuckled. "Oh, I know it isn't funny. The *breh-hedden* has its truly horrible moments, but these scents are ridiculous and so . . ." She waved her hand in the air.

Erotic. That's what Parisa thought but she didn't want to say it aloud. She knew by the faint flush on Havily's usually creamy cheeks that her thoughts had taken a similar turn. Parisa knew that Marcus, for Havily, smelled of fennel, which Parisa couldn't imagine being in the least seductive. But then until she'd caught Medichi's sage scent, never would she have thought to experience such terrible *need* from a spice reminiscent of poultry and Thanksgiving, for God's sake.

"Wow," Havily murmured. "So, the *breh-hedden* strikes again. Do you realize that makes four warriors? *Four!*"

Parisa shook her head. She let Havily move into the next garden room beneath an arch bearing a vine covered with lavender flowers that were a unique shape, sort of curled in on themselves.

The next room bore white flowers on varying shrubs and smaller plants: roses, white lantana, even star jasmine that climbed a half dozen trellises at evenly spaced intervals.

"Jean-Pierre must be going mad by now," Havily whispered, as though speaking aloud would somehow wound the absent warrior.

"I hadn't thought of that. I've had my own troubles this afternoon."

"Uh-oh. I recognize that tone of voice. So, what happened, girlfriend?"

"What do you mean, what happened?" Parisa knew her voice sounded strange, even shrill. She had never been good at lying.

"Come on. Talk to me. It doesn't take advanced preternatural power to get a phone call from you and not know something was going on. Besides, you kind of have *break-up* written all over you, and I so get that."

"You do?"

Havily laughed. "What did you think? That the *breh-hedden* hit me and I opened my arms wide and that was it? I fought it tooth-and-nail for a good long while."

"I think I hurt Antony."

Havily smiled.

"What? Why are you smiling?"

"Oh, it's not what you think. I just love that you call him Antony. No one does, you know, except me. Alison has started doing it as well, but that's it. Endelle calls him 'asshole' like she does all the warriors. Otherwise, he's been Medichi, I think since the day he ascended. Of course, I don't know for sure. I've only been here a century."

"Wow. A century. You've seen a lot, then." She took another sip. Coffee always cooled down too quickly. She preferred it so searing hot that she had to sip to keep from burning her tongue.

"I don't intend to guilt you by saying this, but I have loved seeing Antony with you. Marcus said he's never even had a girlfriend in all this time, all these centuries."

At that, Parisa stopped. "What do you mean? As in *never*?"

"As in never. As in, he's been shut down since he ascended. Oh, he gets laid plenty. All the Warriors of the Blood do. That's what that wretched club is for, the one in south Phoenix."

"The Blood and Bite."

Havily shuddered.

Parisa didn't look at her. She didn't want to admit that she'd voyeured the club lots and lots of times, and spied on

Antony when he made love to other women. She felt her cheeks heat up. She wasn't exactly proud of this part of her, that she was by nature something of a voyeur. Although, to be fair, she never voyeured the other warriors, just Antony.

"I need to ask you something," Parisa said.

"Anything."

"If the *breh-hedden* didn't exist, do you think you'd still be drawn to Marcus, still be in love with him, or have you ever thought this could just be one enormous lie?"

Havily put both hands around her mug and sipped. Her gaze flitted around then finally landed on Parisa. "You're very analytical, aren't you?"

"Yes, I think I am."

Havily lifted her brows. "Truth? I've asked myself the same question many times, but in the end I went with my instincts. I started out loathing Marcus because he had deserted the Warriors of the Blood two centuries ago, but the more I was with him, the more I understood the whys of what he had done and I truly came to respect and value the honorable man I know him to be. I don't think the *breh-hedden* can overcome things like poor character, cowardice, embedded personality traits we can't respect.

"Your difficulty may lie elsewhere because if I've understood your voyeur gifts as you've explained them to me, you've known Antony for well over a year now. And as you probably already know, he's a fine man, a good man, and he has a great heart."

Parisa had to look away from the sincerity in Havily's eyes. She took refuge in bringing her mug back up to her lips. Oh, her friend was way too right about that. Antony was a good man.

"In fact," Havily continued, warming to her theme, "I wonder if something else is bothering you, something that has nothing at all to do with Antony."

Yes, her friend was way too perceptive. She opened her mouth to speak, even to argue but one word slid through her mind and created way too much pain. *Inaccessible.*

She squirmed. She even tossed the remaining inch of her

now cool coffee into a bed of ferns and trailing white lantana.

Inaccessible.

"It's all too much," she said. The explanation sounded weak, but it was all she had.

"I know I'm going to sound just like Alison and all her psycho-speak, but here goes—you have every right to these feelings. Look at what you've been through. Hopefully, Antony will give you the time you need to sort everything out. The *breh-hedden* isn't exactly fair. It's like this massive hand at your back pushing you into things you're sure you should stay well out of."

"So what do you suggest?"

"You won't like it."

"Try me."

"Enjoy the sex and let life happen."

Parisa laughed. "Are you kidding me?"

Havily shrugged. "Well you have to admit it's kind of amazing, isn't it? I mean, these warriors are, well, *big,* and if you recall I was there when Medichi dropped his towel. He reminded me of Marcus. Oh, I sound just like Endelle and now I've made you blush." She laughed again.

When Parisa was quiet, Havily nudged her with her elbow. "So how is it with him?"

Parisa drew in a breath. "Amazing. The connection—"

"I know. It's instantaneous. Have you been in his mind yet?" She sounded terribly eager.

Parisa met her gaze. She didn't want to tell her that that was the last place she wanted to be—and she certainly didn't want Antony in her own head—but the look that overcame Havily's face was something medicine should study. She looked in turns euphoric and *hungry.*

"No, I haven't been in Antony's mind. I'm not sure I think it's a good idea. And if it's all right with you, I need to change the subject."

Havily sighed. "Well, believe me, I do understand what you're going through."

"Thanks for coming, Hav. This really helped."

"Good. I've missed you, you know."

Parisa nodded. This was such a strange sensation. Havily really was her friend, had been her friend from the beginning. She'd never really had friends on Mortal Earth. She enjoyed the women she worked with but friendship was something she'd known so little of and really didn't quite know how to embrace.

Havily reached into the pocket of her cream-colored tailored slacks. She withdrew her phone and glanced at the screen. "Oh, Lord, it's Endelle. I have to get back. I kind of snuck out. She probably just figured out I was missing. I'm on a very short leash these days."

"Well, you know it's not like she's going to fire you or anything."

At that, Havily burst out laughing. "It's sooo true." She chuckled a couple of times, then said, "Well, I'd better be going. Please, call me anytime."

"Thanks. I will." And she meant it.

Havily lifted a hand in the air and vanished.

Parisa stared at the empty space. She was moving in the direction of the house when the air shimmered. She smiled. What had Havily forgotten to tell her? Something more about what it was to make love to a warrior?

But it wasn't Havily.

A second more and Rith smiled at her, that easy blank smile of his that sent shards of fear slicing through her chest. She couldn't breathe.

"Rith," she murmured. Her heart banged out a few beats and threatened to give up completely.

He moved toward her, slow steps, his arms outstretched, always outstretched. She felt that lazy sensation in her mind, like sluggish pond water. She blinked. She felt so sleepy.

No. *No. No!*

She closed her eyes, set an image in her mind, a simple location, a very familiar place, and thought the thought. She felt the vibration.

Fear held her immobile—or maybe it was the sensation of flying through nether-space without someone else to serve as a tether, something she'd only done once before. The journey ended with her bare feet on hard planked wood in Antony's bedroom, her mug still in her hand.

She glanced at Antony, who stood in front of the shattered mirror in the bathroom, his brush poised halfway down his hair as he stared back at her. He wore jeans and, once again, no shirt. She felt the air move near her and whirled around. Rith had followed her, traced after her.

She pointed at him and cried out, "Rith!"

From her peripheral vision in the direction of the bathroom she saw a flash of steel then Antony moved with preternatural speed as he streaked by her and blurred into the bedroom. His sword cut through empty air in exactly the same space the monster had inhabited a split second before.

He turned back to her, his eyes wide.

It had all happened so fast. "Did you see him?" she cried. "You saw him, right? Rith? Right?"

He nodded, his mouth agape. He looked at the floor as though trying to make sense of what had just happened. He shook his head. "Shit!" He vanished but popped back into the bedroom. He did this a couple of times.

"Shit! This is what happened to Jean-Pierre in the Toulouse farmhouse. How the fuck does Rith block a trace like that?" He was breathing hard. He looked confused.

He glanced at his sword and folded it away.

He moved toward her. "Are you all right?"

"Yes, I think so." Then her mind reviewed the last half minute of her life, in particular that very bizarre moment of watching Rith move toward her then make a simple decision to escape. "I folded again," she said. "I thought the thought and I folded."

"Where were you?"

"In the Italian garden, in the room with the lantana and ferns and the ficus trees. I was standing barefoot on the lawn. Havily had just folded back to Endelle's office." She looked down at her feet. "See. I'm still barefoot." Which of course made no sense in terms of what she had just done, but somehow it made it more real for her.

He stood in front of her now, his lips parted, his eyes wide. He kept searching her face. She wasn't sure what he meant by it. "You dematerialized again," he stated.

She nodded.

"Of course you did. Shit, Parisa, we need to practice that, too." He reached out and touched her arm almost as though he didn't believe she was real. "I love that you're so fucking powerful."

Parisa looked away from him. His hand slid down her arm. He caught her hand. She didn't let go. "Hey, you okay?" he asked.

"I got away from him but it feels like I just got lucky. That's all." She squeezed his hand. "He got through a dome of mist that Endelle, *Endelle*, created. He knew where I was and he waited until Havily was gone to try to abduct me again. He almost had me again." Her chest felt tight but there were no tears. No more tears. She needed to figure this out. "How is that even possible?"

"I don't know," Antony said.

She drew her hand out of his and wrapped her arms around her stomach. "How am I supposed to stay secure or even stay alive if that bastard can get in here like this?" She paced in a circle. He didn't try to stop her.

"We need to talk this over with Endelle," he said. "I think we're in real trouble here. We need a plan of attack. For whatever reason, Rith is determined to get you back."

No shit.

Half an hour later, Parisa stood at the railing of Madame Endelle's favorite garden at White Lake, the place Her Supremeness had elected to take the meeting. The garden had been modeled on the Butchart Gardens on Vancouver Island, Mortal Earth, which Havily had suggested she visit many decades prior. It was hard to imagine such a difficult woman being inspired by anything, but the sunken garden had done just that.

"I love this pit," Endelle said. "How deep do you think it is, five hundred feet? Has to be more than that." Both her hands gripped the iron railing that overlooked what amounted to paradise. Thousands of flowers, trees, and shrubs filled every bed. In the center, just like at Butchart, a small hill rose, a sort of earthen castle, a playground to climb, savor, and be enjoyed by children.

Parisa wondered if there would ever come a time when she would stand anywhere near Madame Endelle and not want to either cringe beneath her hard gaze, or scream at her. She was the hardest woman she had ever known. The warriors both feared and loved her. And she was tall, taller even than Antony when she wore her stilettos. And she always wore stilettos.

She sported cowhide today. Not fine leather, but actual hide in squares of brown and white, alternating like a checkerboard. The skirt was short and stiff, bristly. Parisa never knew what to make of the woman's fashion choices.

She resisted the urge to pet the hide.

The strange piece was offset with a soft brown suede vest, cut deep so that four inches of cleavage showed. She had muscular arms. Had she not been Supreme High Administrator of Second Earth, Parisa thought Endelle could have served as a Warrior of the Blood.

Looking up at the formidable woman, Parisa asked, "Have there ever been any female Warriors of the Blood?"

Endelle's brows rose. "What do you think?"

"I suppose not, but what about Luchianne? She was the first vampire. Was she warrior status? I'm told you knew her."

Endelle shrugged. "I've never thought about it, I suppose. I knew the woman nine thousand years ago." She squinted her ancient lined eyes as she looked into the past. "She wasn't as tall as me but she bested Alison. Maybe six foot two. She came out of Sumer, or at least that region. Marcus came out of Sumer as well but he was born millennia after Luchianne's ascension to the Upper Dimension. So what the hell did you want, Parisa? I take it you didn't demand an audience just to discuss ascension history?" Endelle always sounded, even in conversation, just this side of angry.

Parisa told her about Rith.

Endelle glanced at Antony. "You didn't kill the bastard?"

Antony explained about the trace block that Rith had employed at both the Toulouse farmhouse and now his own villa.

She glanced at Parisa and scowled. "Shit. He folded through my mist. And he folded straight to you. Shit." Her scowl deepened as she continued to stare at Parisa. She also nodded several times. "So let me understand you, vampire. So far, you've escaped Rith by cutting him with your dagger while in France and today by dematerializing?"

"Yes."

"Both times you got lucky."

"I would have to agree with you."

Endelle grimaced and cocked her head. She wore a headband that bore an assortment of brown feathers angled into the air, pheasant maybe. If they'd been arranged to stand straight up, Parisa thought the headpiece came shockingly close to images of Native American culture.

Her Supremeness continued, "How the hell were you able to dematerialize when you've only been ascended about half a minute? I mean, I could do that when I ascended, but then I'm, well, *me*."

Parisa shrugged. "How the hell did I have wings on Mortal Earth?"

At that, Endelle laughed. "You know, your speech patterns have changed. You used to be rather stiff in the ass. You're loosening up. I think that's a good thing. Medichi good in bed? Is that why you seem so different? Does he satisfy you? He should. He's hung like a horse."

Parisa's mouth opened and stayed that way. Her cheeks flamed.

"Endelle, for Christ's sake," Antony cried.

Endelle rolled her eyes. "Creator, save me from prudes." She turned around and leaned against the railing. She cast her gaze up and up. "I love the White Tanks. They just do it for me. The contour of the entire mountain range is goddamn breathtaking."

Parisa slid her gaze up Endelle's profile. She really was a great beauty even though it was hidden most of the time behind her sailor's mouth. She had lovely olive skin and features reminiscent of an Arabian princess. She should have been draped in lovely silks instead of cowhide and feathers.

Parisa gave herself a shake. She was here for a reason. Focus. "I don't know what to do. If Rith can get onto the villa grounds then he'll find a way to enthrall me again."

Endelle nodded. "Is Medichi still training you? Are you flying much?"

"We were going to do that after we talked to you." Her thoughts whipped to Fiona, and she turned to Antony abruptly. "What time is it?"

Antony drew his phone from the pocket of his jeans. "It's been half an hour."

"What the hell," Endelle cried. "Do you have someplace better to be? Am I fucking boring you?"

Parisa couldn't help it. She laughed. "I'm sorry but you're so funny."

That wasn't the right thing to say. The pheasant-like feathers lifted straight up. Parisa added quickly, "I've been voyeuring Fiona, quick snapshots, to see the sky in the window above her bed." She explained about the search grid.

The feathers eased down and Endelle's brows rose. "Well, damn, ascender, you've got a brain in that pretty head of yours. Not half bad." She narrowed her gaze and appeared to be thinking. After a moment, she said, "Okay, keep up with the weapons training. The more you know about how to use your dagger, the better." She looked past Parisa to Antony. "I think we should set up some Militia Warriors to serve as guards around the property as well. Rith isn't a fighter, so he'll be less likely to try to take Parisa if there are warriors everywhere. When I get back to the office, I'll give Seriffe a shout. Also, why don't you set up a telepathic link with Parisa? That way she can reach you instantly."

Parisa put a hand to her chest and stared once more into the sunken garden—anywhere but at Antony or Endelle. Paths meandered from one to the other, crisscrossing. Tourists walked to and fro.

A teenager, wearing baggy pants, stripped off his T-shirt and mounted his wings. He flew in the lumbering pattern of youth all the way to the top of the hill. A voice came over the loudspeaker. "There is no mounting of wings in the garden. Retract immediately or we're sending security in."

The teenager, now standing next to a teen girl, lifted his hand in a one-fingered salute, but he drew his wings in then put his arms around the girl. Parisa smiled. At least some things hadn't changed on Second Earth. It all seemed so *normal*. There was that word again . . . *normal*. There was nothing normal about a vampire trying to abduct her . . . again.

She looked back at Antony. He frowned at her and she could probably guess at his thoughts since they'd so recently had a fight about this very thing, about how he thought they should get closer as in complete the *breh-hedden* and how she didn't. Yes, it might make it safer but she didn't want to be that close to Antony, or anyone, much less share what amounted to a Vulcan mind meld.

"So do you think this is a good idea?" she asked. "A telepathic link?"

He smiled but it was crooked and maybe just a little bitter. "Yep. It means that we could communicate telepathically over long distances."

"We do that anyway," she said. "I called to you from Burma, remember?"

"This is different, a solid connection, a link. No one else could break it or interfere. With ordinary telepathy, someone could cut off our conversation. That wouldn't be possible with a mind-link."

"What the hell is the problem, ascender Lovejoy?" Endelle cried. "Why are you resisting this? You need a fucking link to Warrior Medichi. EOS. It's also like GPS. He'll know your location without needing you to send a mental image and don't frown at me. Just do it. Damn, I'm so sick of the whining. Do you want to live or not? Huh? Answer me that, because it's a goddamn simple question."

One thing about Endelle, she could boil an issue down in

two or three sentences. Did she want to live? Yes. Did she want a mind-link with Antony? No. It meant intimacy and it felt like she was being forced into yet another box.

"Fine," she muttered. "But I'm not happy about this."

Endelle snorted again. "Who the hell cares if you're 'happy' or not?" She made air quotes.

"There's something else," Parisa said. "And it might even interfere with a telepathic link."

Endelle met her gaze. "I can't even begin to imagine what would interfere with a mind-link."

"A voyeur-link."

Endelle moved her head back and forth slowly. "What the hell is a voyeur-link?"

"I think Greaves created a link with me when I was in Burma." She told her about Greaves's visit, about the kiss, about dropping her shields, and waking up on the grass. "The thing is, whenever I opened my voyeur window from that moment on, I would experience pain, sharp pain. Lately it's gotten better, and now after a few seconds it disappears but I suspect that's because Greaves is trying to be discreet."

Endelle was nodding. "Which would explain why there were so many death vamps waiting at the Toulouse house."

"Exactly. I've experimented with it, but I was wondering. Since you're so powerful, could you see if I'm right? Could you search my mind for that kind of link and break it?"

"The author of a mind-link has to break it."

"That's what Antony said but I'd still like you to see what's going on."

Endelle sighed. "You'll have to lower your shields. All the way. Can you do that or do I have to kiss you, too?" Her lips actually curved. So besides cursing, and wearing outrageous clothes, Endelle could sometimes make a halfway decent joke. Nice.

At that, Parisa laughed. "No," she said, still smiling. "For you, I'll lower my shields."

"Huh," Endelle said. "Looks like you might even trust me a little."

Parisa shrugged. "Maybe a little."

Endelle just shook her head. "You're one stubborn female, but I'll admit you've got some potential."

Endelle put her hands on Parisa's face. Parisa closed her
eyes. She took a deep breath and let her shields fall, all the
way.

Endelle traveled through her mind like warm water. The
movement was gentle—quite a contrast with the woman's
rattler-like temperament.

Parisa knew when Endelle found the voyeur link, because pain snatched at her, deep searing pain that caused her
to push at Endelle's arms and fall backward on her bottom
next to the railing.

She drew her knees up to her chest and tears flew down
her cheeks unbidden.

"Jesus," Endelle cried. "What did you do that for?"

Parisa looked up at her and scowled. Antony had dropped
down beside her. "You okay?" He asked that a lot.

But Parisa met Endelle's gaze. "That hurt like hell. What
did you do?"

"Nothing," Endelle cried. "Not a damn thing. I got to the
link and looked at it."

"It felt like fire inside my head."

Endelle shrugged. "You've just confirmed the truth that
only the author of the link can break it. I could barely get
near it without causing pain."

"Do you think it's Greaves?" Antony had a hand under
Parisa's arm, and she leaned on him as she scrambled to her
feet.

"I couldn't tell but from everything you've just told me
and from the burning sensation, I'd say yes, this smacks of
that pansy-ass bastard." She huffed a sigh. "Well, ascender
Lovejoy, there's nothing more I can do here and, unlike you,
I have to get back to work. But no more whining, goddammit." She lifted her arm and like that she was gone.

That was it? That was all the help she was going to get
from the most powerful vampire on Second Earth? Great.

Parisa was about to turn to Antony and say something to
him, but a wind came up with grit flying in her face that

stung, a wind that had Endelle's signature all over it. She cried out and Antony moved in front of her, muttering a string of curses.

"Fuck," he said. "She can be such a bitch."

"You know," Parisa said, "she really wasn't much help, was she?"

Antony chuckled. "She has her moments. This wasn't one of them. Let's get back to the villa, we'll do some flying then more work with the dagger and sword. I'll download a few more memories if you like." He paused and met her gaze. He still stood in front of her. She watched his chest rise and fall in a heavy sigh. "I won't force a mind-link on you. Even though it's a good idea and I really want you safe, I think this must be hell for you right now."

"Yeah, it is. But you know, I think Endelle is right about one thing. I've been feeling sorry for myself and I'm going to try to do better."

Antony put his hand on her shoulder, gave her a gentle warning, then she was flying through nether-space.

The stories told of Luchianne, the first vampire, always mention her royle *wings, which were said to produce inexplicable flames.*

—From *Treatise on Ascension,* Philippe Reynard

CHAPTER 17

When Medichi got Parisa back to the villa, he remained in the foyer with her. He drew his warrior phone from the pocket of his jeans and ran his thumb across the smooth black exterior.

"Carla here. How may I serve?" It was still daylight so Carla was on duty. Jeannie showed up at dusk, and for an hour or two their schedules would overlap.

"Hi, Carla. How's it going?"

"Hello, Warrior Medichi. Just fine. We're cruising the grid. I have two of my techs in here today just to keep the search progressing as fast as we can."

"Nothing yet?"

"Sorry. We have aerials of both the Burma anomaly and the Toulouse anomaly so we know what we're looking for but we really need to narrow the search down. We're over China, where it's light right now, but so far it looks clean."

"Parisa just did a quick voyeur. The sky is still very blue, wherever it is that Rith has the women."

"That's good. Right now we're looking at anything from Beijing to Sydney, anywhere that the sun hasn't set."

"That's a lot of ground."

"Yep. Thanks for checking in."

He thumbed his phone then slipped it back into his pocket.

He turned to Parisa. "The grid is somewhere over China right now."

"Good. We're getting closer. "

He nodded. "I'm trying to be sensitive here, so bear with me. I know Endelle was adamant about a mind-link and I think it's a good idea, maybe even a necessary one. But because of your voyeur-link with that bastard—" He clenched his fists then struggled to relax his hands. He took a couple of deep breaths. "Anyway, if you don't want to create a mind-link with me right now, I'd be okay with it. Honestly, with all that you're going through, I think this should be your call."

Her eyes widened. "Thank you for that, Antony. I really appreciate it." After a moment she added, "Why don't we hold off on that for a little while. The headaches—" She blinked and her mouth fell a little. "Wait a minute. Antony, I just realized we could play Greaves with the voyeur-link."

"How?"

"Well, so far it seems to me that Greaves never connects instantly, so there must be a slight delay for him when I open the link. I've been able to take these peeks at Fiona, but there's no flash of pain. The whole pattern is so obvious to me now. But I could establish my own pattern of voyeuring innocuous things, let him check in and watch, then get bored and leave. That might disrupt him just enough to ensure we get the slaves out."

"Damn, that might just work," he said.

She smiled. "I'm going to try it now."

She closed her eyes and for the next few seconds he watched her. She winced then took a deep breath, but he could tell she was sustaining a voyeur. The whole thing lasted a good long minute.

Finally, she opened her eyes and smiled once more. "I

panned your library that whole time. Right at the beginning, after a few seconds, I felt the usual sudden pain. But then I think *the master* got bored." She even laughed.

"Then we can use your knowledge of the process to our advantage."

Her smile broadened. "Absolutely."

Medichi smiled and something warmed in his chest. Here she was, stuck with a fucking voyeur-link to the vilest vampire on the planet, and she was laughing. She ought to be rewarded.

Though he considered taking her back to bed, he knew there was something else she loved doing, *a lot*.

He smiled at Parisa. "Well, how about a flying lesson?"

The sheer joy on her face tightened his chest. He loved that she wanted to fly, he approved of her drive to learn to use Second Earth weaponry, and he really admired the way she was putting her life on the line for Fiona.

She didn't have to do anything she was doing. No one had required her to ascend, but she had. No one demanded that she help rescue the blood slaves, but from the beginning she'd insisted on front-and-center involvement. The woman was game and *breh-hedden* or no *breh-hedden,* Parisa was revealing the truth of her character left and right and dammit, he respected her.

"Yes, yes, yes," she cried. "I'll need to change into flight gear. I'll be right back."

She started to head into the formal living room, clearly intending to walk to her room, but he called after her, "Fold, Parisa."

She turned back, a faint frown between her brows. He smiled as he said, "Dematerialize. Remember? You can do that now."

"Oh," she said. "I forgot."

"Work that muscle along with everything else. Rith knows now that you have dematerialization capacity, but he's fast. If he catches even the tip of your finger while you attempt a fold, he'll be able to take you with him wherever he wants to go and we'll be back where we started."

She nodded, closed her eyes, thought the thought. She vanished. She returned almost as quickly. She smiled at him then lifted her arm and dematerialized again.

That smile. Her smile. She seemed so pleased with herself. As well she should be. Damn, the woman could fold and she'd only been a vampire for how many hours? Christ, it hadn't even been a full day.

When she returned, she wore Havily's old flight gear. The tight black leather, which would have fit Havily perfectly, was just too small for Parisa and didn't he love it, perverted bastard that he was.

Without thinking too much about it, he folded off his T-shirt.

"What are you doing?" Parisa cried.

He glanced at her face and saw that her cheeks were flushed, and not from embarrassment as her gaze skated over his shoulders, his chest, his arms. He couldn't help but flex his biceps and pecs just a little. He smiled, way too smugly no doubt, as her lips parted and she blinked a couple more times than necessary.

He knew what he looked like; he'd had plenty of women over the years take delight in his body. He knew the effect he had. But when a swell of her tangerine scent, softened by a layer of scent that was just her, crossed the few feet between them, his body responded.

He lowered his chin and finished closing the gap so that he had his arms around her in a nanosecond. But her hand flew to his chest, not to welcome him or to touch him, but in protest. "No," she whispered. Yet the glitter in her eyes told another story.

He didn't try to push her hand away, at least not with his hand. Instead, he pushed against her hand with his chest. The movement caused his pecs to swell. She watched his chest then licked her lips. Her elbow gave way from the pressure and he enfolded her in his arms, her hands between them, her fingers plucking at his skin and at the fine hairs between his pecs. She seemed to like doing that.

He kissed her, a soft dragging kiss that elicited a girlish moan. *Antony* drifted through his head.

He loved the sound of her voice in his mind. He worked his arms a little farther around her. He eased one leg beside her so that his hips met hers. He ground against her and let her feel what he wanted her to feel, the hard length of him. She could blame the *breh-hedden* all she wanted, but she was beautiful and sexy as hell. What more did a man need?

One of the hands against his chest started moving down his abs, and he released her enough to let her go where she wanted. When she reached the head of him, her fingers stopped then began a light drift over the tip.

He groaned against her mouth, she parted her lips, and he drove inside . . . hard.

A sound between a cry and a moan erupted from her throat. She may have been insistent about moving into one of the guest rooms, but that had nothing to do with the strength of her attraction to him. She wanted him and right now, after all her protests about not wanting to feel so trapped, her desire, her need, felt very, very good to him.

He drew back and looked down at swollen lips and glittery eyes. She withdrew her fingers from his crown, then settled both hands on his waist, her fingers cool against his bare skin.

She was tall enough to fit him; even in her bare feet he didn't have far to go to kiss her. What would it be like to be inside her head, to move inside her head and take possession? He knew that completing the *breh-hedden* meant that all three things had to happen at once: penetration, sharing of blood at the same time, and deep-mind engagement, much deeper than mere telepathic communication. And as much as he might complain about it, he wanted to be with Parisa in just that way, wholly connected.

He'd once overheard Kerrick and Marcus talk about it, bits and pieces. Mostly, he'd heard the low guttural sounds the men made as they agreed about the experience. Kerrick had said that Alison released power, her abdomen to his.

Marcus had said that Havily often pulled them into the darkening and took them for a second ride right in the middle of everything.

What, then, would it be like with Parisa, with a woman so powerful? He'd always enjoyed sex, taking a woman, bringing her to a roaring orgasm. But this was infinitely more intense. How much of that was the *breh-hedden*? Shit, he'd never know. The *breh-hedden* seemed to be so different for those involved. How would it differ for them if they completed the act?

"What are you thinking about so hard?" she asked.

He blinked and she came into focus, a frown in her amethyst eyes. "Aren't you curious, even a little, with that scientist's mind of yours, what it would be like?"

"You mean the *breh-hedden*?" Her voice sounded low, a little hoarse.

He nodded slowly and trailed a finger down her cheek.

She drew in a ragged breath, turned into that finger, and licked the tip. Oh. God. "I've wondered," she said. "Of course I've wondered."

"You know what I wish?"

She looked up at him, her eyes smoldering. "What? What do you wish?"

"I wish we could do it without repercussions." He pulled her hard against him. "I want to fuck you with my mind buried in your mind, my fangs sunk into your neck, and my cock so deep inside that you'd feel me for a week afterward."

Her knees buckled. *Her knees buckled.*

He chuckled low as he supported her with his arms around her. He whispered into her ear, "I want you in my bed, Parisa. Fuck the guest room. I want you close so that when I get this hard, I can throw you on your back and plunge into you."

He felt her breath hot against his neck. Her tongue flicked over his throat. To her mind, he sent, *Imagine this, you riding me, your fangs in my throat, my fangs in your wrist, my mind moving into yours then you taking over and moving into mine. Imagine what that would be like.*

She was moaning now, her body writhing against his, her tongue arching over his vein, flexing, bringing forth what he could tell she wanted . . . right now.

He knew that if he wanted to, he had the power in his hands to follow through with this, to fold her to his bed and live out the fantasy. Her body was clearly in a state of surrender.

But that's all it was, a fantasy. If he seduced her right now, after all that she'd said to him so recently, she'd never forgive him afterward. If he understood things, the bond of the *breh-hedden,* once completed, couldn't be broken afterward except by death.

So . . . shit.

He trembled, actually trembled as he drew back from her. She whimpered her protest. He gathered her hands and kissed her fingers.

"What . . . what are you doing? Why did you stop?" Her cheeks turned crimson. "Is it me?"

"No," he cried. "Why would you say that?"

"Because I know I'm being difficult and I want you, Antony, I do. I've wanted you for such a long time, from the first time I mounted my wings and the voyeur window opened and there you were. I can still picture you. You were at the Blood and Bite standing next to Jean-Pierre. You were smiling and I thought, what a gorgeous man. But it wasn't just that you were so handsome." Her fingers touched his cheeks and there were tears in her eyes. "It was that I felt I could see into your soul as well. You . . . you have a light in your eyes you probably don't even know is there. I . . . I have always believed in you."

Of all the things he might have expected her to say after he'd shut down the passion between them, this wasn't it. He'd expected her to cry out, to complain, maybe even to shout at him—not to extol his virtues.

Again . . . shit.

He so didn't want this, need this, but something inside his chest began to fall, like a wall of clay against powerful ocean waves. The crumbling began in stages, but all those walls fell, the ones he'd erected thirteen centuries ago, the ones he'd thought were made of obsidian. Instead, just clay to the right kind of woman.

Double shit.

He drew her close and she opened her arms at the same time, wrapping them around his back. He felt a little sob against his chest. They were so fucked.

Neither of them wanted what was happening. He'd been crushed by life. So had she. He couldn't say he totally understood the difficulties of her childhood, of moving several times a year so that she never felt grounded, that she could never establish long-term friendships, but he did know what it was like to have life take a destructive turn leaving only one thought: *How do I keep myself from getting hurt ever again?*

But would it ever be possible for the walls of isolation she'd created for herself to crumble against the weight of his presence in her life? Could she love him?

Could she love him?

He held her for a long time, and she didn't move except to nestle into his shoulder. He felt her breathe in between his own breaths.

Finally, she said, "I can hear your heart beating. I love that sound. I think I could listen to it forever."

A heavy sigh rolled out of his body. He didn't know what to do. He didn't know what the fuck to do. Every second he was with her, he just sank deeper into these feelings that seemed a helluva lot like, yeah, love.

But there was something he could do for her that had nothing to do with whether either of them should surrender to the *breh-hedden*.

He drew back and once more took her hands. "You practiced flying in Burma, right?"

"Every day. Rith demanded exercise first thing in the morning, so I flew."

He nodded. "I want to take you someplace special right now to do our flying. It will be a challenge but I won't let anything happen to you. Are you willing?"

She smiled. No . . . she beamed. "Hells, yeah, Warrior. Let's do it."

There it was again. She was so game when she'd been dropped right into the middle of a war.

"And Antony—"

"Yes?"

"I'm sorry. I'm sorry that I can't—"

He shook his head. "It's okay. I can't, either."

"So we're stuck."

"Yep, but what the hell, let's fly."

Her smile broadened.

He closed his eyes. He thought the thought. The distance from his villa to the Mogollon Rim was over a hundred miles. But folding took only seconds.

When his feet touched down and he released her from the circle of his arms, she gasped. The canyon floor lay two thousand feet below.

"This is the Mogollon Rim," he said. "I don't know if you ever visited here or not. I know you can take jeep tours from Sedona, Mortal Earth, all the way up."

The small town of Sedona Two rested below, nestled at the base of the rim, bisected by Oak Creek. From where they stood, the town wasn't visible. There were too many twists and turns in the various canyon walls. "Both Thorne and Jean-Pierre have homes here. Did you know that?"

"Huh-uh," she murmured. "But I'm not surprised. Who wouldn't want to live here? Oh, smell the pine. It's heavenly. And it's much cooler than in Phoenix."

"We're not quite at seven thousand feet." He dipped down to look at her again, to once more catch sight of the eager glitter in her eye. "You ready to fly?"

"Oh, Antony, yes. More than anything in the world."

Parisa sucked in the dry mountain air, the resinous pine scent, and the sage that belonged to the man whose arms were still holding her from behind. She wanted to cry, then cry out.

This was where she belonged. Here. This was home. "I want to live here," she said.

He leaned close to her ear. "Then you should. You'd have two great neighbors."

"Yes, I would. I love the warriors, Antony. I love them. Does that sound strange?"

"They're my brothers so I love that you love them. No, it doesn't sound strange."

"I will never forget seeing all of them, *all of them,* in Burma. They were there for me and I want to be there for them, to repay them in whatever way I can." She turned her head to look at him. She kissed him on the lips. "Thank you," she said.

"For what?"

"For not holding on." She pressed the arms wrapped around her, which seemed ironic. *Thanks for not holding on.*

He nuzzled her neck. "It's both of us, Parisa. I never intended to take a wife again. I still don't."

She nodded. So they were both *inaccessible.* She smiled. "There's only one thing to do."

He smiled. He understood as though he'd read her mind. He stepped away from her and gave her space.

She closed her eyes and leaned forward just a little bit. She took in a deep breath. She felt the apertures all down her back dampen with moisture. Hormones flooded her veins, and the muscle and tissues of her back swelled. The feathers and attending mesh-like superstructure came next in an elegant erotic seamless flow from her body until they emerged in a powerful thrust into the air. She still didn't understand how her body could create such magnificence, but then how could she dematerialize or send her thoughts into someone else's mind or open her voyeur's window?

Ascended life, her new life as a vampire, was a mystery, complex, incomprehensible at times, and yes, like now, wondrous.

Her nipples were hard now and smashed against the inside of the leather vest. She couldn't help it and she hated to admit it, but desire swirled very deep. Why was mounting her wings so much like sex?

Whatever.

Just as she opened her eyes, a breeze blew from behind her, catching her wings before she could think to draw them into the close-mount position. Without warning, she was airborne.

She panicked but Antony was just there, his wings at full-mount and already in flight. He caught her hand and gave her a moment to assess and adjust. Her wings shifted, rippled, and played with the wind so that she grew steady in the air, confident. Yes, she'd been practicing, but there was also a part of her, a very instinctive part, that simply knew what to do.

We'll fly down, he sent. *Each intersection of canyon or narrowing of gorge will bring a shift in wind. Can you handle it?*

Parisa cupped the top of her wings, which kept her floating in place, not descending. He matched her with the ease of someone who'd flown for centuries. That knowledge added to her confidence.

Antony's wings were spread out above her and to her right. He hovered just as she did, making infinitesimal adjustments with each erratic current of air. She caught his gaze and nodded.

He smiled. Oh, how she loved that smile. Something around her heart began to peel away like paper touched by fire. What was left exposed was raw and yet hopeful, something she hadn't experienced . . . ever. Could she have a life with this man? How strange to be asking the question when just a couple of hours ago she'd all but shoved him out of her life.

Well, one thing she did know—she wouldn't have the answer right this minute.

She took a deep breath and let go, she let go of all that had happened; her captivity of the past three months, the struggle to understand the first mounting of her wings and the discovery of the world of vampires, of her recent ascension, of fending Rith off twice now, and her terrible fear of the *breh-hedden.*

She let go and savored this moment in time, as she lowered

her wings and began the descent into the twists and turns
and elegant beauty of Sedona's red rock canyon. She dipped
and turned, adjusting for each punch of wind, each stream,
each swirl of breeze. Sometimes she spread her arms to match
the movements of the wings; sometimes she kept them close
at her sides.

She forgot about Antony for a good long while. She saw
only the green pines, the manzanita, the ancient junipers,
the smooth-edged expanses of red boulders and small tree-
less mesas, the water in the creek as it made its way down
and down, the startled deer jumping below as her predator
wings and Antony's created shadows across the landscape.

She took in the fresh air, warm and dry. Very dry.

Antony was suddenly laying thoughts over her mind.
*Your wings are beautiful. In the sunlight, they dance with
unexpected color, almost like flames.*

She sent, *We have the same wings. Fly in front of me for
a moment and let me see yours.*

*I don't want to leave this position. I don't want to lose
sight of you, not for a moment, in case you need me.*

*I'm okay. Really. Please, Antony. I remember your wings in
Burma. I recall the flames. I thought it was the storm. Please.*

Okay, he sent but he sounded really reluctant. *But just for
a moment.*

He shot forward with a quick downward sweep of his
wings. There they were, the cream color of the feathers moving like flames. It was extraordinary, like wings of fire.

*Oh, Antony, they're so beautiful. But what makes them
like that?*

He laughed aloud then sent, *I have no idea.*

He dropped back immediately to fly beside her then
added, *Come this way.*

She glanced at him and watched as he dipped his right
wing and began banking to his right and down at the same
time.

She followed, dipping her wing as if she'd practiced for
years. She had just started making the turn when a wind shear
to her right caught her completely off guard and knocked her

sideways. She rolled; she had practiced rolling in the dome, way up high. When her back was once more to the sun, she brought her wings straight out and leveled her body.

She smiled but almost plowed into Antony, who'd brought himself into the parachute position to hang in the air in front of her. His legs dangled down like he was standing in mid-air, his expression stunned.

"What?" she called as she popped her wings into parachute position to match him.

"You're amazing," he cried.

"Oh."

"I expected you to need help, and instead you righted yourself like you've been flying for decades."

She couldn't help but smile. It was the best compliment he could have given her.

He shook his head, unfurled his wings, and rocketed toward a deep brick-red configuration of rock, flat and smooth and hundreds of feet across. A recent rain had left pools of water in some of the shallow indentations.

She followed him and landed easily. She pulled in her wings to close-mount so that the feathers were pressed against her body and random wind eddies wouldn't sweep her away again.

She faced the canyon below but also had a view of the curve of the rim off her left shoulder. They'd already traveled several hundred feet down.

She sighed as Antony drew up behind her and wrapped his wings forward to engulf her. She could not have been more content.

He leaned down and kissed her cheek. It almost felt like a date.

She smiled at the thought then let her gaze drift, rise and fall, shift to whatever object grabbed her attention, an outcropping, a hawk on the wing, the deep blue mountain sky over the rim. Why couldn't life be this simple always, a shared moment of the beauty of nature, the close comfort of another human being, okay, *vampire,* maybe even making simple plans, like where to have dinner.

Just as the question formed in her mind, unease descended. She felt sick into her abdomen. Her thoughts turned to Fiona. Without willing it, her voyeur's window opened and Fiona was just there. She sat on the edge of what looked like a camping cot, her hands in fists as she gripped the edge. She looked frightened, her lips set in a grim line, her eyes wide. Her chest rose and fell quickly.

"What is it?" Antony asked. "You've really tensed up. Is it me? Am I crowding you?"

"No," she cried. "It's Fiona. My window just sort of opened on her but I don't know why. Hang on. Let me see if I can communicate with her."

But as she reverted her attention to the voyeur window, another male voice broke over her hearing. Rith spoke in his cool demanding tone, "I said, summon her. Summon Parisa and do it now."

Fiona shook her head. "I can't. I don't have that kind of power. I don't know why you think I would."

Parisa gasped. Fiona was wrong. She did have the power to summon her, she just didn't know it. Aloud, she explained to Antony what was going on, ending with, "But Rith is there. What do I do?"

"Let it play out."

Parisa trembled. She was grateful Antony held her wrapped up in his wings.

Rith drew close to Fiona. Parisa knew what would happen and she wanted to warn her, but it was too late. She flinched as Rith struck Fiona hard across the face.

"I can't call her," Fiona said. "I don't know how. Why would you think I could call her? I'm not like you. I'm not fully ascended. I'm not a vampire."

Parisa heard a strange whimpering sound. She panned to the left, to a long row of cots. Bodies were huddled beneath blankets. Some shook, but more than one whimpered.

She panned up to the windows, but they were still full of sunlight. Good to know.

Just as she panned back to Fiona and Rith, a sudden twinge pierced her mind. Greaves. Shit. She closed the window as quickly as she could. Maybe she'd been in time. Maybe Greaves didn't know what she'd been voyeuring.

"Antony, I had to shut the window down. I felt Greaves. But I did see the windows and it was still light outside."

"Okay. Let me call Carla to give her the update."

Antony withdrew his wings and stepped away from her. He fluffed and retracted the wings in an amazingly swift and fluid movement.

Parisa had thought they would continue to fly, but even as the disappointment hit her, she realized that her surprise contact with Fiona had ended the simple joy of the flying experience. She'd be worried the entire time if they continued heading down through the canyon to the town below.

He held his hand out to her. "I'll support you while you retract. Go ahead. Full-mount first."

Parisa nodded but the process was difficult because of her inexperience and all the wind eddies. Rith's double dome of mist had protected his Mandalay home from storms, wind, and rain, so when it came to flying or in this case, drawing her wings in, she lacked experience with the elements. Still, within a minute she was fully retracted, and her back muscles were already thinning.

He pulled his phone from his pocket and called Carla. He relayed the update then thumbed his phone and returned it to his pocket.

"Rith struck her. He was trying to force her to contact me. I think she did so without realizing it. I really think Fiona has untapped powers."

Antony nodded. "Well, if she's Jean-Pierre's *breh,* then of course she would."

He glanced around, even up into the skies. She understood his thoughts and suddenly felt very vulnerable out in the open.

"Let's get back to the villa. I think we've been out here long enough."

It was always a risk, being in the open. Antony held her steady and with a smile and a nod, folded them both to the villa.

She felt the front pavers beneath her feet, but the sight of Militia Warriors now stationed throughout the property startled her.

"I know," he said, feeling her tension. "I almost drew my sword. I forgot they might be here. Endelle said she'd call Seriffe. But if Rith shows up again, uninvited, he'll have to face an army this time."

Rith felt his phone vibrate in the pocket of his white cotton trousers. He withdrew the Nokia and smiled at the word MASTER, which indicated the call's origin. He brought the phone to his ear. He felt pleased. "Yes, master."

"What are you doing over there, my dear Rith?"

"Experimenting." The woman Fiona had a bright red handprint on her left cheek. A small trickle of blood ran from her left nostril. It was actually rather pretty, that red stream on her creamy complexion. Fiona had very good skin, for a Caucasian.

"I felt Parisa's voyeur window open and I had a glimpse of the women in a long narrow room on cots. Was that your doing somehow?"

"Yes, I believe so, master. I asked the woman, Fiona, to contact Parisa. It would seem it worked."

"Interesting. Do you suspect Fiona of undeveloped powers?"

"I have for some time. How is that she has lived this long when no one else has?"

"I believe you may be right. I will read her powers the next time I come." He paused. Rith knew better than to disturb his master's ruminations. After a long moment, Greaves said, "Be prepared to move the donors again. In the meantime, you may want to stop further experimentation until we have command of Parisa. We would not want Fiona to develop the ability to communicate with our mortal-with-wings."

"Yes, master." Greaves was right. Parisa's ability to reach out to Fiona also allowed her to see his dying blood acquisition facility. What else she was capable of, who could say, but he didn't want to risk discovery. If he had to move the slaves again, he would disrupt the dying blood supplies he sent around the world.

As Fiona met his gaze, he really didn't appreciate the hard look in her eye. He lifted a brow. He pushed at her chest with his power, that physical power he used to command obedience. She resisted at first but after a minute fell back against the cot. For good measure, he sustained the pressure while he worked.

Into his hand, he folded restraint straps from a special chest he carried with him from place to place. He didn't touch her as he directed the straps through the air, around her wrists, and through the slots in the cot. He did the same to her ankles.

He ignored her after that but he kept the pressure on her chest until she was gasping for air. He didn't relent until she passed out. Only then did he let her breathe.

At the same time, he chose the next donor, the woman who had been whimpering. He really would not tolerate such pathetic noises among his slaves.

"You will be next."

"But I gave blood two weeks ago. I'm not ready."

He passed a hand over her eyes, and her gaze became blank. He left her in that state. He was debating whether or not to bring her back afterward.

Who is the true warrior
But the one tried in battle.

—*Collected Proverbs,* Beatrice of Fourth

CHAPTER 18

Medichi stood on the half-moon of pavers that formed the large patio in front of his villa. He watched Parisa throw her dagger with unparalleled accuracy. The target was now thirty feet away and still she nailed the bull's-eye every time.

An hour had passed since they'd returned from the rim. Parisa had done her voyeur window quick-checks twice now, but there was still a lot of blue sky at the window. Time was counting down, though, and he was ready.

She'd done her set-Greaves-on-the-wrong-path routine a number of times as well. That she experienced pain every time bugged the shit out of him, but there was nothing he could do and she was determined to see their plan through. Damn, he was proud of her.

He'd consulted with Thorne more than once, keeping him updated. This time, however, Thorne wanted all the warriors to go on the mission. Medichi wasn't certain why, but it didn't matter.

He felt a movement of air behind him. He whirled and folded his sword into his hand despite the dozen Militia Warriors stationed around the lawn.

Jean-Pierre shimmered into being.

Medichi released a breath. "Why didn't you call first?"

Jean-Pierre pushed a hand through his long, wavy, light brown hair that hung beside his face to mid-chest, and down his back. He wasn't wearing a *cadroen* and he looked like hell. *"Désolé,"* he murmured. Sorry.

"You look like fuck."

"I feel like fuck."

"You should be sleeping right now. Thorne will want you at the Borderlands tonight."

"I know, but I cannot sleep. I have so much fatigue. Medichi, I did not know how hard it was. The *breh-hedden*. It's like a torture in my head and a fire here." He circled his palm over his chest. He wore a navy T-shirt, jeans. Medichi glanced down. He wasn't even wearing shoes.

Medichi chuckled. "I'm sorry, Jean-Pierre, but welcome to the goddamn club."

"How did you bear it for three months? I have borne her disappearance for less than a day and I want to hurt someone very badly."

Medichi sighed. His gaze shifted to Parisa, who was heading toward the target to pick up the practice daggers. She still wore the flight suit and his gaze fell as always to the swell of her breasts. *Parisa,* he sent.

She stopped mid-stride and turned toward him. *Yes?* Her gaze shifted to Jean-Pierre, and she waved at him. He waved in return.

He felt like a pig speaking the words but he responded as gently as he could inside her mind, *Maybe a shirt? I hate to ask, but you're very voluptuous.*

She almost glanced down at her chest, but instead her hand came to the deep cleavage, her fingers resting on the push of her breasts beyond the leather. Her gaze shifted to Jean-Pierre and her cheeks fired up. She then glanced at the Militia Warriors who were at least some distance away.

Oh, you're right, you're right. I'll change now. Sweet Jesus, but Jean-Pierre looks wrecked.

She started to walk in their direction, but he added, *Fold. Right. Right.*

She lifted an arm, closed her eyes, then vanished.

"Mon Dieu," Jean-Pierre cried. "Did your woman just dematerialize?"

Medichi shouldn't have been so pleased, but he was. "Yes," he said. He crossed his arms over his chest. His pecs swelled. *His woman* was the only other known mortal to have born wings before her ascension other than Luchianne, she could communicate telepathically, she had a voyeur's window which was an acknowledged Third Dimension ability, and she could dematerialize. He felt damn proud.

"You are preening like a peacock, *mon ami*." Jean-Pierre smiled and nudged him with his elbow.

"Where's your *cadroen*?"

Jean-Pierre sighed. "What do I care for the *cadroen*? For anything, when *my woman* is held captive by that beast." His gaze fell to the nearby lawn. Back and forth his gaze flew as though hunting for her. "I do not know what to do, *mon ami*. I am desperate."

"Why do you sound so damn hoarse?"

"Because I have been shouting into the wind, calling for her. The *breh-hedden* is a terrible madness."

The air shimmered next to Jean-Pierre. Medichi leaped back and brought his sword into his hand once more. Jean-Pierre did the same, but it was Parisa now wearing a loose blouse over her flight suit.

Medichi groaned and got rid of his sword.

Jean-Pierre folded his away as well. This time he moved in a circle, his eyes closed, his hands once more pressed against his head.

"Did I do something wrong? I was practicing."

"You did fine. We're just on edge." To her mind he sent, *Fiona,* then gave a swift jerk of his head in Jean-Pierre's direction.

Jean-Pierre came to a stop next to Parisa. "Thorne said Rith tried to abduct you again. Is this true, *cherie*?"

"Yes, that's when I discovered I could dematerialize."

He nodded. "Have you tried to see the woman again, Fiona, with your voyeur window?"

She sighed. She explained what had happened, that somehow Fiona had opened the window while they were in the Sedona canyon. She didn't tell him that Rith had hit her and for that, Medichi was grateful. "Did Antony also tell you that I probably have a voyeur link with Greaves?"

"*Oui*. That you have headaches now when you try to see something."

"Yes, exactly. So we're being careful how we use the window. We're only opening it once every half hour, very quickly so that I can see the windows and judge the light. Once the sun sets we can really narrow the location." She turned to Medichi.

"How long has it been?" Jean-Pierre asked.

"Maybe five minutes. Sorry. Wherever they are, it's still light out."

He nodded. He looked up at the sky. "Well, there is one thing for certain. She is not in France. It has been night there for hours now."

"That's true."

Medichi met her gaze. "We could give it another shot, don't you think, Parisa?"

She looked at Jean-Pierre and nodded. "Why not?"

A sound erupted out of Jean-Pierre's throat, something between a huff and a cry. Before Medichi could stop him, he had grabbed Parisa and hauled her into his arms. He repeated, *"Merci"* over and over.

Medichi felt his nostrils fold inward and his hands bunch into fists. His brain shut down and all he could think was that another man had his hands on his woman. The sequence was irrational, but it didn't seem to matter.

"Take your hands off her," rushed out of his throat, a throat that felt too small for the words. At the same, time he grabbed Jean-Pierre by the shoulders and started dragging him away from Parisa.

"Stop that!" came from Parisa. He froze. He stared down at her, his entire body immobile.

"What are you doing, Antony?" she cried. "He was thanking me. That's all. What's the matter with you?"

But Jean-Pierre pulled away from her and started to laugh. He dropped to his knees and put his head in his hands and kept on laughing. This time, he repeated *"Mon Dieu"* over and over, finally ending with, "We are in hell."

Medichi just stared at him. Strange sensations flowed through his blood. He felt as though he'd just faced a dozen death vampires. His arms and legs shook. "This is a nightmare," he cried. "I was ready to kill you."

He walked in circles just as Jean-Pierre had. He couldn't look at Parisa for the longest time. When he'd calmed down enough, he turned to her to apologize, but she held her fingers up to her lips and he knew she was smiling, even laughing.

"What?" Medichi shouted. No man liked to be laughed at.

"Where's your *cadroen*?" she asked.

He reached back but it was gone. What the hell had he done with his *cadroen*?

Parisa approached him, smoothed his hair with her hands, then kissed him on the lips. He released a heavy sigh.

"I'm so sorry," he said.

"I hate to admit it but it's kind of sexy. You went wild there for a minute. I think you threw your *cadroen* so hard it landed in the pool, then you started tearing at your hair and growling. I don't mean to laugh. Really." She softened the blow of these words with another kiss on his lips.

Dammit, he'd forgive her anything if she just kept kissing him. He slid his arms around her, yet he couldn't help but glare at Jean-Pierre over her shoulder. "Just don't do that again, okay? Think what you would do if I hugged Fiona."

When a hard light entered Jean-Pierre's eye and he rose to his feet and lowered his chin, Medichi added, *"Exactement, mon ami."*

Parisa pulled back. She glanced at Jean-Pierre then rolled her eyes. "All right you two Neanderthals. Let me have a look."

She closed her eyes and opened them a moment later. She shook her head. "Sorry, Jean-Pierre, it's still really light outside."

The afternoon wore on Parisa, partly because Jean-Pierre stayed on at the villa. She always knew when half an hour had passed between voyeur-peeks because whatever she was doing, whether working out with sword or dagger, or preparing dinner, or even napping, he came to her with such a stricken look that she didn't bother even asking what he wanted—she simply opened her window, looked at the color of the sky, then shut it down.

At seven, Jean-Pierre finally left, folding to the Blood and Bite where all the Warriors of the Blood gathered before battling death vampires at the Borderlands. He had hated to leave, knowing that the hour was drawing close, but Thorne had made it clear that once Central had a fix on the women they would—for this one critical mission—leave the Borderlands as a unit, fold to the women, and take care of business. Colonel Seriffe was making arrangements to have large contingents of Militia Warriors ready to take their place until they returned.

Everything was set to go.

But by nine o'clock, the sheer waiting had stripped her nerves raw. She wore her weapons harness, black cargo pants, and Nikes and paced the foyer. She opened her window every ten minutes now. Central's grid had the area of search down to one strip of longitude, because eleven hours had now passed since Parisa had first viewed the sunlit window. The earth moved, the sun shifted, and every place that night had begun to cover became one less possibility.

It was just a matter of time, maybe even minutes.

At nine forty-five, Parisa stood beside Antony in the foyer. He, too, wore battle gear. Thorne had let the warriors know it would be anytime now.

She opened the window.

Antony had his phone to his ear, Carla at the ready.

And there it was, a beautiful violet and gray haze across the sky.

She smiled. "Sunset," she cried.

Antony spoke into the phone. "Sunset, Carla." He smiled, but then even Parisa had heard her squealing.

Antony phoned Thorne, exchanged a few words, then tucked his phone into the narrow pocket of his battle kilt.

"They're all waiting at the Cave."

"Already?"

He nodded. "About an hour ago, Thorne called Seriffe. Apparently there are now a hundred Militia Warriors stationed at every Borderland on Mortal Earth."

Parísa blinked. She was stunned. "That's five hundred warriors. Who's making the mist?" If there were that many hunky warriors, in leather battle kilts and black leather wrist guards, hanging around various Metro Phoenix access points on Mortal Earth, then someone had to create a protective layer of mist. One of the big rules between Second Earth and Mortal Earth was keeping Second Society a secret.

Antony laughed. "Leave it to you to be thinking about logistics. The truth is, I don't know. I'm guessing Endelle. Mist is one of her best things."

Parisa felt herself grow very still inside. "This is it, isn't it?"

He nodded. "Our best shot. You ready to bring Fiona home?"

"I hope so. I really do."

"Ready to fold to the Cave?"

This time it was her turn to smile. "Thanks for the warning."

The vibration began.

When her feet touched down, she glanced at all the men. One things was clear right away. The men had cleaned up. There was no blood spatter, no sweat among them.

Everyone was there . . . except Jean-Pierre.

* * *

Jean-Pierre was still at his house. Thorne had made it possible for each warrior to shower, a kindness extended to the several frightened women who would hopefully soon be in their charge. Such victims did not need to see the results of their battling at the Borderlands. War was a dirty, sweaty, messy business after all was said and done.

He remained at his home in Sedona, which he had built next to Oak Creek. He stood beside the small wood bridge he'd built. Stripped tree branches served as the railing, and hand-hewn planks for the curved arc of the base. His home was a rabbit warren, all wood and stone, with narrow connecting halls not much wider than the breadth of his shoulders. The entire house was built in sections from white oak. The floors were Brazilian rosewood because he liked the sweet smell when he worked the wood.

Alison would tell him the home was a form of therapy. Most certainly it was not a form of architecture. Probably just a look into his mind.

He shrugged. But he loved this home and now he had the darkest thoughts of all, that he would bring the woman here, the woman Fiona, the one he would meet in a few minutes, maybe hold in his arms.

He put a hand to his weapons harness just over his heart. He felt the hilt of one of the two daggers he carried. Within his chest, he felt a vibration, something holy and terrifying. What had been so empty for so long now filled with lightning. His heart jerked in response, and he couldn't breathe. *Merde.*

His knees felt weak, as if he'd lost the tendons somewhere in the past few days.

Fiona.

Fiona.

Now his chest hurt when he thought of her and his head throbbed. Already, he despised the *breh-hedden* and he had only been its victim for such a short time. He patted the Velcro pocket of his kilt and felt the treasure hidden deep within, bound in soft layers of velvet. The locket. The one he had found at the base of the armoire in Toulouse, the one that held the scent of his woman, of Fiona. He would return it to her, even though part of him wanted to keep it forever.

He was so fucked.

He needed time to think before he got the call from Thorne saying that Central had found them, a call he expected any moment now. How was he supposed to keep a clear head when his body betrayed him like this?

He planted a hand on the end post of the bridge and sucked air through his nostrils. The smell of damp sycamore leaves rushed through his brain, that heavy scent, aromatic, clean. His mind felt clearer, sharper. *Oui*, he could think again. *Un peu.*

He straightened his shoulders.

He felt like a fool because he had laughed at the other men, at Kerrick, at Marcus, and once upon a time at Medichi, but that was before Parisa's abduction, long before, when the *breh-hedden* had smashed the tall warrior into the ground. Medichi had been a walking open wound even before the abduction of his woman.

Jean-Pierre would laugh no more. He could not even laugh at himself, and usually that was not a difficulty.

He just had not expected so much pain and such a fierce drive to be with a woman. He ached deep into his soul. His mind was possessed and his body weak in the knees. Again . . . *merde.*

His phone buzzed against his waist. He slipped it from the narrow pocket of his battle kilt. His heart thundered, because he knew what was about to happen.

"Oui," he said, not thinking. He cursed again. He rarely answered his phone using any form of French.

"We have them." Thorne's voice, splintered like dry wood, grated his ear. "Come to the Cave. Now."

Jean-Pierre thumbed his phone and tucked it back into the pocket. He stared at his house, at the windows in various shapes and sizes, the backdrop of large sycamores. He had built the house in a grove of them. He had the horrible sensation, yet strangely exhilarating, that his life was about to change forever.

He closed his eyes and thought the thought. He moved through nether-space, through a fine rush of wind that wasn't wind. For a split second his body felt free, weightless, his mind at ease.

He landed in the Cave. Everyone was present. Parisa was armed for battle in a snug leather vest, buckled in places for fit, a single dagger hilt showing at her waist. Her breasts were too large to allow for more than one. Medichi stood close to her, his body touching hers, shoulder and hip, an arm across her back.

He looked intense and haunted, his eyes too bright.

Jean-Pierre had to look away. He understood.

Thorne was speaking but what was he saying? Yes. A battle plan.

New Zealand. The slaves were held in New Zealand. A place called Lower Hutt City Two, a rural location, very private, a few miles from Wellington Two, the capital, near the ocean. Same situation—a double dome of mist.

Thorne divided all eight warriors, eight because Marcus would not be left out of the mission. There would be two groups of four, one group to come from the south, the other the north because who knew what they would find. Parisa had voyeured seven slaves, including Fiona, in the Toulouse farmhouse. But Santiago had found one of the slaves dead, a woman whose bracelet had said DOHNA, a Tibetan woman.

"Unless Rith has added more females to his stable," Thorne said, his raspy voice cutting through the tension in the room, "we should find only six women." He met Jean-Pierre's gaze. "I want you on point." His gaze shifted to Medichi. "I don't like it that ascender Lovejoy is going. You know that. She may be good with a dagger, preternaturally good, but a sword can reach her as quick as lightning."

"You think I don't know that?" Medichi's voice had an edge.

Jean-Pierre shifted his gaze to Kerrick, who stood with a very stiff jaw beside Marcus. Both seemed uneasy, rigid. Neither looked at Medichi. Jean-Pierre understood. They were an emerging brotherhood now, men who had *brehs,* treasures it would be too painful to lose. Had Marcus argued with Havily about coming on this rescue? Havily was not here. Did Marcus win an argument? Maybe Thorne would not allow it.

"Let's go." Thorne's voice rumbled through the room once more.

Carla folded each group to opposite ends of the dome of mist. Jean-Pierre was with Medichi, Parisa, Santiago, and Zacharius. Thorne had Luken, Kerrick, and Marcus.

Jean-Pierre folded his sword into his hand the moment his feet touched solid earth. The sky was still partially light, which was good for battling. He spun in a circle, as did the other warriors. Even Parisa followed suit, her dagger in her hand, her shoulders hunched, knees bent. *Merde,* she behaved like a warrior, but then she had Medichi's battle memories now.

A strong breeze blew from offshore, carrying the smells of salt and fish. Medichi had his phone to his ear. He spoke softly then turned back to the group. "Thorne's in, near the barn. No sign of death vamps."

He gestured to Santiago, who inclined his head, disappeared through the mist, then came back. He drew close. "One death vamp asleep by the door. His sword is on the ground."

Jean-Pierre smiled.

Parisa spoke. "Let me do it."

All the men turned to stare at her. Medichi started to protest, but she glared at him then lifted her dagger. "In the throat," she whispered softly, "for all the women drained of their blood. Give me this."

There was not a warrior present who did not know exactly how she felt.

Medichi glared at Parisa, but his entire body froze perhaps long enough for his rational mind to move to the front of his brain.

Parisa added, "I'll use my window first. I'll be careful but I need to do this."

Merde. Medichi was trembling, his sword flexing up and down, his knuckles white around the grip. But he nodded. "You go in, let the dagger fly, then come back out."

Parisa inclined her head.

Parisa turned in the direction of the mist. Dusk was settling deep now, the shadows everywhere a dark gray. She closed her eyes and opened her voyeur's window. She saw the death vamp in profile, sitting in a chair. He was snoring. No one else was around.

She shut the window down. She moved through the first dome of mist, the one made up of white crochet-like filaments. The second was the elegant blue-green. She passed through and there he was, a beautiful glorious creature, pale of complexion, black hair hanging loose and wavy to his shoulders, his chin buried in his chest. He wore leather flight gear, but no weapons harness. His chest was bare. She forgot her mission for a moment at the sight of him. His beauty was meant to enthrall, and she felt the tendrils of interest and attraction reach out to her even while the bastard slept.

Eff that. She hoped he was having pleasant dreams because these would be his last.

She understood one thing about having downloaded Antony's battle images—to hesitate was to lose.

She felt Antony's muscles as she walked forward, the heaviness of them, in his tall warrior physique. The sense of him gave her strength and courage. Her fingers trembled, though. Too much adrenaline. She worked to breathe, to calm her heart.

She stopped as the bastard jerked awake. Something must have disturbed him. Then she heard fighting beyond the house, on the other side. The death vampire rose to his feet, and suddenly his sword flew from the ground into his hand.

"Hey," she called out. As he turned toward her, his sword still lax, she settled her gaze on his throat and let her dagger fly. She had speed and she had strength in her throw. Medichi was right—she had a gift for dagger work. The blade was long and sank to the hilt, which meant it pierced the spine and went all the way through. The vamp crumpled where he stood, his sword falling from his hand.

She turned and fled back through the mist.

She caught Medichi's eye. She nodded. "He's down."

Medichi put his hands on her arms. "You're sure."

"Yes, but there's fighting on the other side of the property." How calm she sounded even to her own ears.

He released her arms and spoke to the group. "Forward."

In a swift, preternatural flow, the warriors moved into the mist. Medichi waited for them to pass, keeping his arm against Parisa's back. "Get your dagger from the pretty-boy. Keep moving. Do you know where the slaves are being held?"

"Yes."

Once they were on the other side of the blue-green mist, she glanced up at the second story. She recognized the row of windows from the outside. She pointed. "Up there."

By now the warriors were running toward the back door of the house. She moved beside Antony until she reached the fallen death vampire. Antony bent down, but she touched his shoulder. "Let me. I'm the one who should do this. I killed him." She felt the imperative of it. She had done this thing. She had taken a life, however heinous it was. She needed to remove her blade.

She knelt down and had to push the death vampire's milky shoulder until he rolled onto his back. She moved to stand over him. His eyes were open but glassy. He was gone. So fast. She took the dagger by the hilt and withdrew the blade.

Her stomach turned. She shifted away from the body and almost threw up. She took deep breaths.

She felt Medichi's hand on her back. "It's okay," he said. "It happens to all of us, but we have to go. We have less than a minute to get this done. Do you understand?"

She took one last deep breath and felt her stomach settle back into place. She wiped the blade on her black cargo pants, a movement she'd seen in more than one of Antony's battle memories.

She rose up. Antony's gaze seemed to work in a complete circle, the upper half of his body whirling to keep track of the entire 360 panorama. She mimicked him as he moved to the back door, always checking her back trail.

She heard heavy battle sandals on the stairs. She followed the sound.

When she reached the steps, the front door was thrown wide and she had a view of the yard beyond—and of Thorne's blade slicing through a death vampire. Blood flew. She turned away as another wave of nausea rolled through her.

She ran up the stairs. At the landing, off to her right, Santiago emerged from a room and thrust his chin in the opposite direction. To the left she saw Zacharius in the doorway. He spoke into the room, "Jean-Pierre, you all right? Shit."

Parisa hurried to the door. Jean-Pierre held Fiona in his arms and he was weeping. "Is she dead?" she asked.

He shook his head rapidly.

"Hurt?"

"I do not know."

Parisa nodded. He was holding his *breh*, and overcome. Antony called from behind her. "Jean-Pierre, take her to the palace. Carla has Horace waiting for the women as well as a medical team. We'll follow. Thorne and his men are finishing up out front." Jean-Pierre vanished with Fiona. Parisa blinked—just like that, the woman she had met such a short time ago was saved.

Santiago went to the end of the row of cots. The last cot was empty, perhaps originally intended for Dohna.

Paris turned to Medichi. "Where's Rith and the serving women?"

He looked past her. "Zach, you see Rith?"

He shook his head. He had a woman in his arms. The insides of her elbows were taped up and her face was white, chalk white, ghost white. Oh, God. She struggled against him and cried out, "No . . . no," but her voice was slurred. Yep, the women had been drugged.

"Take her to the palace."

Zach nodded, then he was gone.

"How we doin'?" Thorne's voice boomed through the room.

Parisa turned back to look at him but Thorne's gaze shifted just past her shoulder then he cried out, "Fuck!"

Parisa had her dagger in her hand and didn't hesitate. Whatever was behind her was bad, the enemy. She whirled and thrust and there was Rith, a surprised look on his face as her blade slid into his stomach.

She withdrew, but not because she was squeamish. She withdrew to plunge again, moving into him this time, putting more force behind the blow. She withdrew the blade again. He stumbled backward, turned, and fell onto an empty cot. She followed after him and cried out, a harsh warrior cry. She started plunging the knife over and over and over until she felt gentle hands on her arms and Antony's voice in her ear. "Ease down, Parisa, he's gone. Ease down. That's it . . . ease down."

She blinked and realized her blade wasn't buried in flesh but in the thin padding of a fairly nice camping cot. There was blood, however; Rith's blood. He may have dematerialized but she'd hurt him.

She held her dagger up, her hand shaking.

Thorne's voice once more boomed the length of the room. "Luken, take the next one. Santiago, there's one more past Medichi. Kerrick, okay, you've got one. You're good. Back to the palace. Marcus. Good, you've got the last one. At least I think it's the last one. Do we have all six?"

Antony called back to him. "Yes. Jean-Pierre has Fiona. She went first."

He nodded. "Let's get the hell out of here. One of the death vamps sent for reinforcements."

The next thing Parisa knew, she stood in the middle of a rotunda, the one where she'd had her ascension ceremony. Her hand still shook, but she clutched her dagger hard in her fist.

The dagger was bloody and so was her fist.

The funny thing was . . . *the funny things was* . . . she didn't react the way she'd expected. She'd thought she would feel dizzy, feel a need to vomit again, become hysterical. Instead her heart had settled down, and little by little her nerves grew steadier.

She held her free hand out and pictured Antony's sink in his master bathroom. She saw the black washcloth and thought the thought.

A vibration passed first through her mind, then her body. The next moment, like magic, she held the washcloth in her hand. She'd accomplished another first—she'd folded something from one location to another.

"Jesus," Antony whispered. He now stood next to her. "You just folded that from where? My bathroom?"

"Yes," she responded. She wiped down the dagger very carefully. Santiago had given her the blade, and it was razor-sharp. She wiped until there wasn't a speck of blood on either edge or the point of the blade, then shoved it back into the space on her weapons harness. She stared at the hilt. The dagger had Santiago's signature, a small ruby embedded near the base of the hilt. She touched it, rubbed it, and was so glad she'd taken the time to learn a skill that apparently she was really good at.

But there was more, and she drew her shoulders back. She looked up at Antony. He stared at her hard.

"You aren't upset, are you?"

She shook her head. "No. I'd like to think that it will hit me later but I don't think it will."

"I've trained a lot of Militia Warriors over the centuries, tens of thousands of them. I've been with most of them after battle. Shit, Parisa, you're a goddamn warrior."

She nodded. She smiled. "Even though I almost threw up?"

"As I said, we've all done that a few times."

"Over the centuries."

"Yes." He took her hands in his and held them aloft, glancing from one set of fingers to the other then back. "You're as calm as anything right now."

"I know. Is it because I downloaded your battle memories? Am I feeling what you feel?"

He shook his head. "I don't think so . . . but I would never have thought this of you. You're a goddamn librarian."

She chuckled. "I know. With too big a chest to handle weapons with ease."

He laughed and then he drew her into his arms and hugged her. She released a sigh. Was this possible?

But as he kept his arms around her and she shifted her head, she caught sight of Fiona, who met her gaze. The woman's expression was . . . blank. She had her arms around another of the blood slaves, a small woman whose stomach . . . oh, God, she was pregnant. Maybe five or six months by the look of her. Tears streamed down her face.

"I have to go to them," she said.

"Yes. Go," Antony said.

She looked up at him and he nodded, a frown between his brows. He shifted his gaze to Fiona and the woman. He drew in a stream of air. "Shit. She's pregnant."

"I know."

Parisa approached the pair and dropped to her knees in front of them. She had forgotten how beautiful Fiona's eyes were, slightly upturned and silvery blue, the color of Christmas ornaments. Her chestnut hair hung past her shoulders. "You found us," she said, but her cheeks had a sunken appearance and her complexion was very pale. She had been drained and revived how many days ago?

"Of course we did."

"What happened the first time? Why were they waiting for you? I wanted to tell you but I couldn't. I'd been drugged."

"I know. It's okay. They knew we were coming because Commander Greaves has a voyeur-link with me but we figured it out and played him."

Fiona nodded, her hand moving in slow motion up and down the woman's shoulder.

Parisa glanced at her. "How long has she been in the facility?"

"Three days." She hugged her closer, kissed the top of her head. The woman burrowed her face into her neck. Her tears hadn't stopped.

"Can you tell me, Fiona, whether or not you're ascended? You said you were from Boston—was that Mortal Earth?"

"I was taken from Mortal Earth, and the best I can figure is that we're all partially ascended. We can survive on Second Earth, but none of the blood slaves has ever had vampire fangs." She looked around. "I was kind of hoping that there was another woman already here, waiting for us. She was Tibetan and she wore a bracelet with her name printed in English letters—Dohna? Did you find her in Toulouse?"

Parisa's shoulders sagged. "I'm so sorry, but she died that day. She was gone by the time we got there. I'm so sorry."

Fiona looked beyond Parisa's shoulder, but not at anything in particular. "I lost so many over the years," she murmured. "Hundreds over the decades." She blinked then glanced around. "So where exactly are we? What is this place?"

"Madame Endelle's palace?"

Her eyes widened. "You mean the palace of the Supreme High Administrator?"

Parisa nodded.

"Well, that is something." She looked around once more, still stroking the woman's arm. "She's not here then?"

Parisa turned and ran her gaze through the room as well. "No, but you won't mistake her when she arrives. She's very tall, imposing, and . . ." She struggled for the right word. ". . . fashion-challenged."

Fiona didn't smile, she just nodded. "Can you tell me something? What are these men exactly? They . . . well, they're all so *big*."

"Warriors of the Blood."

Once again her eyes widened. "You mean, *the* Warriors of the Blood, the ones known as Guardians of Ascension of Second Earth, came to get us out of that place?"

At this point, Parisa realized that the pregnant woman had finally grown quiet. She was watching Parisa carefully from red-rimmed eyes and a swollen nose.

Parisa couldn't help but smile, though, at Fiona's astonishment. Maybe Fiona could be awestruck, but Parisa's introduction to the warriors, especially Medichi, had been so, well, earthy, that she couldn't summon the same kind of hero worship. "Why shouldn't the warriors have come for you?"

"Well, I've known for decades that they were all that stood between Greaves and a takeover not just of Second Earth but of Mortal Earth as well. Knowing that they took the time to rescue us—that's something. I won't soon forget this."

Parisa thought of Jean-Pierre and of his certainty that this woman was his *breh*. She wondered what Fiona would say to that if she knew. She'd probably be stunned.

Still, it was hardly something she needed to share immediately, and she did want to tell Fiona about the Warriors of the Blood. "They're good men. Honorable. They didn't know, none of us knew, that Greaves was doing this, enslaving women to provide dying blood for his death vampires. Although it certainly makes sense. But though there have been rumors for decades, until you somehow escaped the basement that day and came to me while I sat beneath the tamarind tree, Greaves and Rith had kept his operation a secret."

Fiona nodded, tears in her eyes. "Thank you, Parisa. Thank you for coming for me. I would have died soon. I know that now. I really had lost all hope. But why were you there in that garden, held prisoner in that house? When I saw you, I thought you were Rith's wife or something."

At that, Parisa laughed. "Oh, God no. He abducted me from Warrior Medichi's villa three months ago. I was as much a captive as you. I just wasn't being used as a blood slave."

"A blood slave." Her gaze grew unfocused again. And once more she looked around. She frowned slightly.

Parisa turned to see what she was looking at. Ah, Jean-Pierre, and he didn't look happy. His arms were crossed over his chest, his brows low on his forehead.

Fiona glanced at Parisa then back to Jean-Pierre. She asked very quietly, "Do you know why that warrior is staring at me? He looks angry."

Yes, he was angry, and yes, Parisa knew why he stared at Fiona, but she wasn't about to start explaining the *breh-hedden* to the recently freed captive.

However, there was one truth she could relay. "We have all been so worried about you and the other women, especially when we found that your Dohna had not survived. Warrior Jean-Pierre took it especially hard. He was there when Rith folded you out of the back bedroom in France. He's been furious since that he couldn't prevent it."

"Where were we just now, that house I mean?"

"Would you believe outside the capital of New Zealand Two?"

For some reason Fiona laughed. "How strange."

"How long had you been in Burma? In that house?"

"Always."

"You mean all these years, all these decades, that's all you've ever known?" She was shocked.

Fiona nodded. "We were allowed exercise in the garden until, well, three months ago."

"When I arrived."

"So it would seem."

"Fiona, how on earth did you survive? I felt like I was going mad."

She shook her head back and forth. "I don't know. For a long time I held out hope that I would see my family again, my husband, my two children. The day I . . . begged for your help would have been my daughter's birthday. I went crazy. I knocked one of the medical technicians out cold and escaped to the garden and there you were. They put me through death and resurrection right after as a punishment. It was too soon, only two weeks, it was hard to survive—"

"I know. I watched. I didn't expect you to come back from that."

"You saw me?" Fiona asked. "Oh, yes, now I remember. You were there. I felt you."

Parisa nodded. "How did you find the strength to come back?"

She sighed. "I truly had made up my mind to die, but at the point of death I think I met an angel, albeit a rather strange one. His name was James. He encouraged me to keep going."

"James? His name was James?"

"Yes."

Parisa felt a shiver cross her shoulders. "Alison knows someone called James. He encouraged her in a very similar way." Was it possible it was the same man, the same ascender?

"Who's Alison?"

"Alison is only recently ascended. She's bonded with, um—" Parisa glanced around. Behind her, sitting on one of the terraces with Luken, was Kerrick. "There. Do you see the black-haired warrior? Alison is his . . . *breh*. That's another word for a special mate. More than a wife. A man can be a *breh* as well. Alison is . . . very powerful in this world. She's also . . . oh, there she is." She materialized next to Kerrick and soon after put her hand on her stomach and winced.

"She's very pregnant."

At that, the young woman beside Fiona lifted her tear-stained face. Alison was beside Kerrick, a hand on his shoulder. He stood up and put his arms around her. He appeared to be whispering to her, and Alison patted his arm and smiled at him.

"He's so tender with her."

"Yes, he is," Parisa said. "She's not doing very well right now with her pregnancy. The doctor assures her she's fine, but you can see she's suffering. She always has her hand to her stomach. She's a healer . . . of the mind."

"Of the mind?"

"Yes, she was a therapist on Mortal Earth."

Alison closed her eyes and appeared to be trying to relax. After a moment, she patted Kerrick and crossed the thirty feet or so in Parisa's direction. Parisa rose, weaving a little; she had been too long on her knees. The marble was hard.

Parisa introduced Alison to Fiona. Fiona introduced Kaitlyn, of Lake City, Florida, Mortal Earth. With Alison so close, Parisa drew back and gave her space to work. She asked questions of both Fiona and Kaitlyn, how they were feeling in general. There was something so kind in her tone that both women relaxed.

A minute later she called the healer Horace over, which

was Parisa's cue to return to Antony. There would be plenty of time later to get to know Fiona and perhaps all the women.

Jean-Pierre drew close. "How is she doing?" His arms were still crossed over his chest, the lean corded muscles straining. His hands made fists, released, then made fists again. He still scowled.

"She seems very calm. She was really surprised to learn that the Warriors of the Blood had come for them, and it's obvious to me that she's been a huge support to the other women. Also, she just told me that from the time she was taken from Mortal Earth she'd only known the Burma house."

"Jesus H. Christ," Antony muttered.

"Ditto," Parisa said.

Jean-Pierre responded with a low growl from deep within his throat.

The truth changes everything
But freedom comes through application.

—*Collected Proverbs,* Beatrice of Fourth

CHAPTER 19

Endelle never allowed anyone within her private sanctuary, her meditation room, that place where she hunted Greaves in the darkening.

Not even Thorne, her second-in-command, the man she trusted the most.

But here she was sitting on the edge of her chaise-longue staring at two men; one fucking unfamiliar to her, short, with gray hair, *gray hair!* And the other man she intended to slaughter with a quick snap of her wrist and a powerful roll of a hand-blast—Leto, the traitorous motherfucking-sonofabitch.

She didn't hesitate. Leto deserved to die so she flicked her most powerful hand-blast, not caring in this moment that according to Alison, he was a spy. A spy for whom?

"Die, asshole," she cried.

He flinched but for some reason, the stream of power that should have fried his ass hit the space around him and split into a number of elegant fireworks: blue, green, violet sparkles, really beautiful.

That Leto's eyebrows climbed his handsome forehead and his mouth opened in a big round O meant he'd expected to take the hit, maybe even to die.

Which meant . . .

She shifted her gaze to the short man to Leto's left and scowled. She rose to her full six-foot-five height, plus her five-inch stilettos, and stared down at the fucking bastard who had just robbed her of a very satisfying kill. "Who the fuck are you and why did you just protect this traitor and how the hell did you get into my inner sanctuary and why, if you have so much power, do you have gray hair?"

The man looked very strange—or at least his expression became quite odd, for a short man. His eyelids grew heavy as he stared at her chest then slowly lifted his gaze, up and up, to meet hers. Damn he was short—five foot seven if he was an inch. "Oh, I haven't been into your inner sanctuary . . . yet."

She could not mistake his meaning.

Her mouth fell open, flat open, almost to the floor. "You have got to be kidding me, *Shorty.* The day you see my inner sanctum is the day I mop the floor with your face—with one hand tied behind my back."

"I'd like to see both your hands tied behind your back. Then I'd have a good long look at your *inner sanctum.*"

Holy shit. This asshole was either really confident or really stupid. He smiled, and something in that smile made her uneasy. Well, she didn't think he was stupid, which meant . . .

She looked at him again. She pushed against his mind, wanting, needing to understand who the hell he was and why he had enough power to invade her space, bringing Leto of all assholes with him, and how he'd been able to deflect a hand-blast like that. "Who are you?" she asked.

"James."

Well, fuck! James at last! "Alison's James? Fuck. The one she dreamed about all those months ago? The one she still talks to mind-to-mind occasionally?"

"That would be a yes and another yes."

"You're from fucking Sixth Earth."

"I am."

"Then why the hell do you have gray hair? No one has gray hair, not even on Second." She knew there were much more important matters to be discussed but really, *gray hair*?

He sighed. "The only way the Council would permit me to intervene as I have—and yes, I only have a few moments left in this interview—was if I appeared as harmless as possible. And no, I did not design the appearance I currently display. It was designed for me." Shorty seemed a little bitter.

She nodded as though his explanation made perfect sense. Oh, hell, since he was from Sixth, he could probably appear in the guise of a troll or an asteroid if he wanted to. But right now she had one fucking question he'd better answer. "Who the hell has held up my ascension? I should be in Fourth by now, at the very least. Maybe even Fifth. Why have I been stuck in this God-forsaken, shit-eating dimension for all these millennia?"

That smile appeared again, the one that looked both bemused and pleased as hell. "I have a message for you from Braulio."

She couldn't have heard right. Braulio was the most powerful Warrior of the Blood ever to battle on Second Earth. He was a legend in his time and she had seen him die, struck down, sliced up by a death vampire. That had been five thousand years ago and Endelle had killed the vampire afterward, but Braulio was still dead.

"You need to get your facts straight, Shorty. Braulio died. I watched him die."

James shook his head but didn't say anything.

"You're telling me he's alive?"

"Yes."

At that, her knees gave way and she fell straight down, not onto the chaise-longue, but straight on her ass on the cold marble floor. "He's dead. That bastard is dead. I saw him die." Shit, her eyes grew stinging hot.

"He's not dead." James ground his teeth.

"I watched him die." If there'd ever been a man for her, he'd been the one. But when he'd died, she'd given up the hope that Second Earth could ever hold any joy for her, any real pleasure. She'd wised up, then she'd toughened up. But Braulio alive? Shit. Her head wagged back and forth.

"Luchianne pulled him into Third and healed him. It was against the rules but she did it anyway. She's only done it one other time . . . for me. So I know what I'm talking about."

She remained sitting on the floor, the marble cold through her linen gown. "Sweet Jesus, Braulio alive." She didn't want to think about him, not about him. He was the finest warrior who had ever lived and she'd grieved his death thousands of years ago. If she could admit the truth to herself, there was a small slice of her heart that still hurt. So, yeah, shit!

She stared at James for a long hard moment. "Let's say I believe you. What the hell is this message he has for me?"

"Here it is, word for word. *Hang in there . . . I'm coming.*"

"What the hell does that mean, *I'm coming*? You mean like the second coming of Christ?" She laughed at her joke, but James's blue eyes looked serious as hell.

"He's coming back for you."

"When? When the fuck *when*?"

"Near the time that Alison assembles her team and opens the pathway to the third dimension, he's coming back for you."

She'd been right, the second coming of Christ. She laughed, and yeah, her voice sounded bitter.

It wasn't that she didn't believe him, but she didn't fucking believe him. You didn't get to be nine thousand years old without understanding a lot about life and all this dimensional shit. Politics had always been, *would always be,* the order of the day—who could gain as much power as possible first so he, or sometimes *she,* could piss on everyone else. When Owen Stannett had stood in her office a few days ago and made his little speech about "taking it deep," she knew exactly what he meant. She might hate the bastard, but she sure as hell understood something of what he'd endured over the centuries.

So fuck her but she was just a little fucking skeptical.

"Whatever, Shorty." She used a little old-fashioned levitation to gain her feet since there was nothing pretty about trying to create leverage with a stiletto.

She planted her hands on her hips and stared down at James again. "No disrespect intended, but I'll believe the whole Braulio thing when I see him. Right now we have other fish-ass to fry. When Alison first told me about you and . . . him"—she jerked her thumb at Leto—"I thought maybe we were going to see some real action, get some real help. Hah. I don't know if you've noticed but according to the future streams we've got one assfucking coming any minute now and I ain't got the troops to pull off a win here. Then there's this whole thing about Alison leading a charge into the third dimension and right now she's turned into the pregnant-bitch-from-hell. You read history much? When has a pregnant woman ever been fit to beat down the gates of Hades?"

The expression that overcame James's face made her frown. She didn't understand what she was seeing. His light blue eyes seemed full of clouds. He smiled but it wasn't a smile. He looked lit up with a thousand lightning strikes. She almost thought she was looking at some bizarre version of . . . *affection* . . . but that was just stupid. He also didn't look like he was going to give an answer to what was for her a really serious question.

What-the-fuck-ever.

The clouds disappeared and the blue of James's eyes returned, but he shifted his gaze downward to the marble floor at his feet. He blinked several times. His attention seemed focused elsewhere. Maybe he was thinking or maybe someone from Sixth was shouting into his head. She'd like to shout. She'd like to shout at this Council he referred to until she was as hoarse as a nymph servicing Zeus himself.

Finally, he met her gaze again. "I can't give you a definitive answer. What I can tell you is that the Seers of Sixth still predict that Alison opens the pathway to Third—but other futures, darker possibilities, have been predicted as well. This is a delicate time in the history of the dimensional worlds, and the hour of fulfillment draws near. You must be careful, Madame Endelle. I beg above all things that you will be careful. Some of our Seers have also foreseen the demise of Second Earth, a fall to the Commander that will last longer than a hundred thousand years."

She leaned forward. "Then help us, goddammit! Give us what we need to get rid of this bastard forever!"

She felt the heat in her face. If she felt even a little more than she did right now, she was certain she would pop some blood vessels in her eyes.

James appeared to grow an inch or two, or maybe he was just lifting up on his heels. His nostrils flared. "Don't think for a moment I haven't considered it, not just for Second but for Third as well. The Council, for all its preternatural power, is weak, ineffectual. They can move mountains but they will not help the human soul."

Endelle closed her eyes. A great wind filled the room, emanating from the Sixth dweller himself. She took a peek and found Leto crumpled on the floor, shielding his head and face with both arms. More of that lightning had appeared in James's eyes, but he finally closed them. He grew calmer and the wind eased.

Sweet Jesus, Mary Mother of God, and all the Disciples thrown in.

"I'll be disciplined for most of what I've just said to you. I beg your pardon. I allowed my frustrations to speak." He gestured to Leto. "I want him kept alive, and that means that when the time comes you will offer your protection. For now, he goes back, but not without relaying to you the information he came to give." He turned to Leto. "Tell her what you told me then return to the Commander's Estrella Mountain compound. If you fear for your life at any moment, I have given you a trace back to this room, and no one will be able to follow you. But for God's sake, man, don't use it unless you are about to die."

The light blue eyes were now a strange brown color and

flashing wildly. He lifted an arm. The wind swirled once more through the room; thunder sounded as he vanished. Her hearing disappeared for a moment until her eardrums released a nice pop. Wow.

"What an exit," she cried.

She blinked a few times then turned her attention to Leto. He was a former Warrior of the Blood who had defected a century ago. His turning had put a hole in her heart, but now it would appear she really had been wrong about him all this time. Her first inkling had come when Alison fought him in an arena battle. Once Alison had subdued him, he had allowed her to dive into his mind. There she'd found this supposed truth about him: that he'd been serving as a spy for decades and he answered to James. If Leto was coming forward now, it put him in severe jeopardy. If Greaves ever found that he'd communicated with Endelle, he was toast.

He rose to his feet, a little unsteady, but he crossed the small rotunda and offered her his hand. She took it.

In her stilettos she was still taller than Leto so that she looked down at him. His gaze flew over her hair. From her peripheral she could see that it writhed.

She rolled her eyes and calmed the hell down. Her hair settled down as well. "Usually I can control it but I'm upset right now. So, Warrior, are you telling me you didn't desert me?"

He shook his head and tears filled his eyes. "I would never have done so without cause."

"I never understood."

"James approached me. Greaves is very powerful, and the Sixth Dimension Council needed access."

"Alison told me but I never stopped being mad about it. I didn't even believe it. Fuck. All right. Whatever. So what is it he wanted you to tell me?"

"First, James voyeured the extraction in New Zealand, so I know the first group has been brought safely here to your palace. But what you need to know is that Greaves has twenty-one additional death and resurrection facilities around the world. Rith heads them all. Essentially, Rith runs the organization. Also, Fiona was his first successful experiment during a time well before proper sterilization methods were employed or before electricity was used to revive the heart. Because of her ability to recover, she became his guinea pig.

"More generally, Sixth brought me on board because the Council needed to know the breadth of his power as well as the nature of his plans. Greaves apparently has some fourth dimensional abilities, one of which allows him to shield his operations from Sixth Earth. But in order to intervene, Sixth needs incontrovertible proof. I've been transmitting evidence for years." He looked weary, painfully weary. He had intense blue eyes but they were shadowed now. He was just short of Medichi's height, and his shoulders were as broad as Kerrick's. He had long black hair, which he still wore in the *cadroen*. All these years she thought he'd kept wearing it as a fuck-you to her and to the Warriors of the Blood. Now she thought it might have a different meaning altogether.

"But Sixth won't help us."

"I honestly don't know what they plan to do. James has let a few things slip over the years. Things are not well in the Upper Dimension. Apparently, if Greaves gains a foothold here and succeeds in dominating Second and Mortal Earth, he creates a domino effect that moves upward."

"How is that even fucking possible?" She moved in a circle now, around Leto. She pulled at her hair. "And how about we add just a little more pressure to this situation?" She shook her fist at the ceiling, "Thanks for nothing, assholes!"

Leto chuckled. "You really think that's going to help?"

She shrugged. "Well, it helps me."

Goddammit.

Fiona knew she should feel something other than what she did. She should be ecstatic, right? She should feel relieved, right? Happy, delirious, exhilarated? Right?

All she felt was numb, even cold.

Of course her blood hadn't entirely regenerated since the recent drain. There was always a lag time.

Still. She'd been rescued, taken out of the hands of that quiet monster, Rith, out of the service of the self-styled *Commander,* out of continued blood slavery.

The healer, Horace, had his hand on Kaitlyn's head; Alison held her hands. She was in shock and not doing well. Her abduction was only part of the reason she was listing in the direction of death. Her husband and young son had been murdered in front of her by death vampires. She had been next in line to drain, as well, and Rith hadn't withheld the truth; she would lose the baby once she completed her first D&R.

It was all too much. She honestly didn't know, despite the efforts of the healers, whether the woman would make it, but it didn't look good. The one thing Fiona had gotten really good at was predicting with fair accuracy the length of a woman's life as a blood slave.

She rose to her feet and moved to stand at the far terrace, far away from the other blood slaves and from the warriors. Looking back into the rotunda, she caught glimpses of other enormous round rooms, all sparsely furnished but made of beautiful white marble, streaked with gold, very much like a palace. Why were the spaces so empty? What did that mean?

Sconces lit each rotunda at four-foot intervals.

At least there was fresh air flowing in from the open walls, but because it was night, there was just an impression of blackness beyond.

September in Phoenix. She expected it to be hotter, but as she drew closer to the opening she felt the cool air blowing down from the ceiling, creating a shield between the heat and the comfortable indoors.

She passed through the shield into the starry night. She couldn't see very much, just open land for what seemed like miles, dark clumps, maybe cactus. In the distance there was the glitter of buildings, perhaps the center of this dimension's Metro Phoenix.

Rith had kept the women informed over the decades: where they were, what was happening in each dimension, how many dimensions there were. He'd at least provided them with books to read. She had wanted to marvel at all that she learned, but because she'd been a prisoner and her blood drained from her body every month, she fell short of being able to work up enthusiasm for things she believed she would never see, never experience.

Now here she was looking at the Sonoran Desert and thousands of stars overhead. Rith had allowed television once a month for half an hour, selected at random. Last month, the slaves saw a really weird cartoon featuring a character called SpongeBob; the previous month, half an hour in the middle of a movie starring a very handsome young man—*On the Waterfront.* She would like to see more movies, complete movies and definitely more television.

She heard a soft scrape of marble underfoot just behind her. She turned and hunched, her hands outstretched, ready to fight . . . but it was the warrior, the one called Jean-Pierre, the one who seemed so angry, the one who had brought her to the palace. Yes, she remembered now. She'd been dizzy with drugs, but now she remembered.

He held up his hands as if in surrender. "I would not harm you," he said.

He had a beautiful French accent.

She lowered her hands and straightened. "No, of course not. I'm not quite myself. I'm sorry."

She wanted coffee suddenly, a very strong cup of coffee with milk, maybe even cream. She shifted to stand beside him so that she could see his face. The light from the rotunda revealed the most beautiful eyes, not gray, not green, but a blend. He had thick dark lashes as well that enhanced the color of his eyes. His lips were very unusual. The lower was full and sensual and the upper came to exotic points. She had the strangest urge to run a finger over his lips, and for some reason the thought lit her body in a way she had not experienced in a very, very long time.

Oh, God. She *desired* this man, this warrior. She began to ache very low and a blush warmed her cheeks.

His nostrils flared and his lips parted. *"Mon Dieu,"* he whispered.

She returned to stand by the balustrade, afraid of what she was feeling. More than anything, such a reaction seemed completely inappropriate. She shifted her gaze back to the desert, the dark sky, and the stars. The air was very dry, which was so different from both Burma and New Zealand.

"Fiona," he said very softly, his voice a caress. He had moved closer. She could feel the heat of his body behind her. "I have something for you. At least, I am almost certain it belongs to you."

She turned back to him. The light from the rotunda cast his face in shadow. His hand was outstretched, and as he turned so that the light would cross his arm, something small and gold glinted in his palm. She drew in a soft breath. He held the one thing, the only thing she'd been able to keep, all these years, from her life in Boston in the late 1800s. She couldn't withhold a small cry.

Her gold locket.

She knew where she'd hidden it—behind the armoire, on the carpet. But she had been drugged when she left that house. When she awoke on the cot in the unfamiliar house, her first thought had been that she would never see her locket again. She had wept.

Now as if by some extraordinary miracle, the warrior called Jean-Pierre, who had a lovely French accent, held her only cherished possession.

She took it from him with trembling fingers. *"Merci,"* she murmured.

She opened the locket and there they were, portraits of her lost family, long since dead after so many decades: husband, daughter, son.

For a reason she could not explain, she drew close to Jean-Pierre, shifting to stand in the shadow of his shoulder. She flattened the locket on her palm and held it slanted toward the light so that he could see.

"My husband. He gave this to me the day before I was abducted. Our eleventh anniversary. These were my children. My son Peter—oh, that's your name, Pierre, isn't it? And this was my daughter, Carolyn." Her heart felt as if a stone had formed at the very base. She hurt.

"I always regretted that I did not have a family," he said. "I was married once, but it was not a good marriage. Then the revolution came."

"The French Revolution?"

He nodded, smiling faintly. *"Oui."*

"You're very old then."

He laughed and the gleam in his eyes, the humor, eased something in her chest, made the stone in her heart not quite so heavy. He turned back to look into the rotunda. "Do you see the warrior there, with hair just past his shoulders, dark brown hair, his eyebrows slashed over his eyes? Yes?"

Fiona saw him. *"Oui,"* she said.

He met her gaze and smiled. "Thank you for saying *oui*."

She smiled as well. She nodded. "I've always loved the French language. My grandfather was French, but I'm not fluent, unfortunately."

He held her gaze for a very long time, and for some reason a desire for coffee once more drifted through her. A very strange sensation. He seemed to give himself a little shake then said, "That man is Warrior Marcus. He is four thousand years old."

"No," she whispered. "How is that possible?"

Jean-Pierre shrugged. "Warrior Medichi, standing with his arms around Parisa, is out of Italy in the 700s. Warrior Thorne, who has his fist wrapped around a tumbler of vodka, is two thousand years old. I am the youngest of them all."

She felt her palm folding around the locket and glanced at her fist, the gold chain dangling down. The stone felt heavy again. "What am I supposed to do now?" she asked. She looked at the marble and saw splashes of water, single drops one after the next. It couldn't be raining. She hadn't seen a cloud in the sky. Oh, the drops were her tears. When had she started to weep?

She felt his arm slide around her shoulders. He pulled her close to his chest and she let him, though she couldn't say why. It just felt so right.

He smelled so wonderful, as though he had spilled some coffee on the leather of his weapons harness or on his skin. She was tall for a woman, and her nose nestled against his neck. How odd that she trusted him like this, without knowing him. But then he'd carried her away from that house of torture, away from Rith, and death, and slavery. Why wouldn't she trust him?

And he had brought her the thing she cherished most in the world—her locket.

She wept anew.

Jean-Pierre held heaven in his arms. His heart pounded in his ears. All he heard was *thump, thump, thump.* Desire flowed over his body, waves one after the other, washing over him, receding, only to crash again.

Was he holding her too tightly?

Was she falling out of his arms because he wasn't holding her tightly enough?

He could not tell.

He was lost in the sensation of her nearness, her quiet sobs, the grief she had lived with for over a century.

He heard voices behind him, gentle voices, the kind that belonged to healers. He wasn't surprised when Alison addressed him. "Jean-Pierre, Horace and I think the women should go to the hospital for a day or so. I've contacted Colonel Seriffe and he's going to send several squads of Militia Warriors to guard them in case Rith tries to reacquire them."

"Bon," he murmured. But he did not want to let the woman go.

Alison put a hand on Fiona's back. "We think you should go as well, Fiona."

"Of course."

Without another word, Fiona withdrew from him and moved back inside. She did not look back, which was just as well. She must still be in shock. Both Horace and Alison followed behind her. He did not wait too long before returning to the rotunda as well.

His gaze, however, remained fixed on the back of Fiona's

head. He watched her like a hawk after prey, except that she was not prey. She was the woman meant for him, his *breh*. Already the bonds were forming, tightening. He could feel them, and for a moment he could not breathe.

She returned to Kaitlyn, the young one pregnant with child. She helped her to her feet but the woman collapsed. They were both surrounded very quickly, healers anxious to help. Within less than a minute, a medical team had the pregnant woman on a gurney and was rolling her in the direction of the east entrance, where a long, long drive led to the valley floor below.

He did not attempt to follow. He remained in the center of the rotunda, alone, bereft, and angry, such a strange combination of emotions. But above all he did not wish to be with the woman Fiona, he did not wish for this entanglement and bonding. Whatever the *breh-hedden* might be, he knew in the depth of his soul that this was not the right path for him. He loved the company of women, a lot of women, and he was a warrior. Why did he need anything else?

Fiona would have a new life here, but that did not mean he had to be part of it. He was a Warrior of the Blood, and his duties would always keep him at the Borderlands, battling death vampires. Fiona's path lay elsewhere.

The difficulty seemed to be, as he breathed in through flared nostrils, he could scent her on his skin, the sweet smell of croissants, the heady aroma of a boulangerie.

But the scent would fade. In time, as she left his warrior world, he could forget her as well.

Medichi had his arm around Parisa's shoulders. He watched the last of the women being transported to the hospital, not by folding, but by ambulance. He felt peaceful and full, like he'd feasted at a banquet, an odd sensation, but it felt right.

They'd brought the women home. They'd done some good. Six women and a baby would survive now because of Parisa.

The healers departed.

Kerrick had his arm around Alison as they dematerialized

together. Then Marcus and Havily. Havily had apparently taken a break from her nightly darkening work with Endelle to meet the survivors and offer what comfort she could.

One by one, the warriors folded away, heading with Thorne to the Blood and Bite for a drink before taking up arms at the Borderlands again.

Endelle never did emerge from her meditation room. She hadn't stopped working in the darkening long enough to come and see the women.

Jean-Pierre was the only warrior left in the rotunda. He stood off to the side, his expression blank, eyes hollow, lost. He looked like a man with nowhere to go. He'd brought his *breh* back to safety, and now she was headed to the hospital.

Medichi whispered to Parisa, "Shall we try to comfort him?"

"Yes. Of course."

He let his arm slide off her shoulder, but not without his fingers catching and pressing her arm. He followed her to the Frenchman.

"Jean-Pierre," she said softly. "Thank you."

He turned toward her, his brow furrowed, eyes full of pain. *"Cherie?"* he murmured. He didn't appear to have heard her.

"Thank you," she said again, but before he could stop her, she slid an arm around his neck and hugged him.

Both of his arms found her back.

Medichi felt the deep growl form in his throat, an ancient response he tried hard to control. Earlier, at the villa, he'd almost gone mad when Jean-Pierre had dared to hug Parisa, but something in the expression of the warrior's eyes, so full of pain as though he'd had his heart ripped from his chest, stopped him. He didn't like that another man was touching his woman but the part of him that could think, that could recognize his warrior brother was hurting—well, that man crossed his arms over his chest, and hid his clenched fists beneath those arms.

Jean-Pierre met his gaze. He began to smile as though he realized what he was doing. Maybe it was something that he saw on Medichi's face, but Jean-Pierre flipped him off with Parisa still in his arms.

It was so Jean-Pierre. Medichi wasn't surprised that a moment later, he released Parisa, then without a word lifted his arm and vanished.

"Oh," Parisa cried. "I wish you boys would give a girl a warning. That just creeps me out. One minute he's hugging me and the next, poof, he's gone."

She turned to face Medichi but he still had his arms crossed. She looked at his arms, then up at his face, and rolled her eyes. "Are you kidding me? You're mad because I hugged Jean-Pierre?"

"Uh . . . yeah. New dimension here. Vampires. Warrior, caught in the *breh-hedden*."

But Parisa shook her head, chuckled, then walked toward him in a way that meant if he didn't unfold his stubborn arms she was going to bang her head against them. What do you know, his arms opened like automatic sliding doors. He wrapped her up and a wave of something very close to his earlier sense of peace flowed through his chest. He couldn't believe he was feeling like this—almost . . . happy.

"I'm so proud of you" were the first words that left his lips.

She wiggled to free herself enough to look up at him. "We brought them home, Antony." Then she smiled even though tears flooded her eyes. "We brought them home, out of slavery, out of certain death."

"*You* did. You put the pressure on, you kept your window open, you made sure it happened. Yeah, I'm really proud of you."

When his phone buzzed, he almost didn't answer it. But what the hell. "Give."

Thorne's voice rasped through the line. "Come over to the Cave and bring Parisa with you. Endelle's here with news." The line went dead.

Medichi scowled at the phone. What the hell was going on now, and why did Thorne have to be barking orders at this time of night? Besides, with Parisa tucked under his arm, he'd started getting a certain idea about just what they should be doing next . . . to celebrate their hard-won victory.

So, shit.

"Thorne wants us at the Cave."

"Why?"

"Endelle's there. Apparently she has some kind of announcement to make."

Parisa pulled away from him and looked around the rotunda. "She's not here?"

"I know, I know. But that's Endelle for you."

The heat of an argument
Brings truth rushing to the surface.

—*Collected Proverbs,* Beatrice of Fourth

CHAPTER 20

"What do you mean there are twenty-one more facilities like the one we just raided?" Thorne's voice held a dangerous edge.

Parisa stared at him then shifted her gaze back to Endelle. The woman's hair seemed strange, as though she'd been in a wind tunnel. She didn't seem to care.

She planted her hands on her hips. "Why the fuck are you arguing with me. Let's just say that my source is irrefutable and if any of you are guessing who it is don't say the name out loud and for shit's sake shield that thought."

Parisa didn't know who they were talking about. She glanced at Antony, who stood beside her. He met her gaze but shook his head. Maybe he would tell her later or maybe it just wasn't important.

"I want to take charge of this," Parisa said. She took a step forward almost without realizing that she'd just done either of these things: spoken aloud or moved toward Madame Endelle.

"You?" Endelle cried. Her upper lip curled.

"Why not?" Parisa returned. She planted her own hands on her hips so that she mirrored Her Supremeness. She still wore her makeshift version of battle gear, the buckled female weapons harness, the dagger with the ruby embedded in the hilt, black cargo pants. She could even mount her wings if she needed to.

Endelle looked her up and down. "You playing at warrior or what?"

"Yeah. I am. And in case you don't know, I'm entering the Female Militia Warrior Training Camps as soon as possible."

Endelle laughed. "Oh, I don't think so."

"Why the fuck not?" Parisa cried. She had mimicked Endelle's speech pattern without even thinking about it.

For the first time, Endelle narrowed her gaze. "You're serious."

"I'm serious."

"Why?" She glanced around at the men. When her gaze landed on Antony, she added, "You may want to think twice. Your man doesn't look very happy about this decision."

"He'll get over it or he won't," Parisa responded. No, Antony wasn't happy about it, but right now she didn't care.

Parisa had a mission.

"Tough words, ascender. But this won't be a fancy book-reading in an air-conditioned back room. Are you sure you've got the guts for it?"

"Truth? I don't know, but I know it's the path I want to follow."

"What the hell happened in New Zealand anyway?" Endelle shifted her gaze to Thorne.

Parisa could see that there was an exchange. She knew Endelle shared a mind-link with Thorne though whether he could share images with her, Parisa didn't know.

Endelle turned wide eyes back to Parisa. "You stuck Rith with your blade? More than once?"

Parisa's cheeks grew warm. "I confess I lost control and

did more damage to the cot he fell on than to the man. Rith dematerialized. But all the more reason I should enter a training program. I have a lot to learn."

"Huh." She glanced around. "Well, I guess nothing needs to be decided right this minute. Let me give it some thought, ascender."

"Of course." Parisa stood with her left arm slung behind her back, the way she had seen Antony stand when addressing Madame Endelle. It was a warrior pose.

Endelle looked her up and down once more. Her brows rose as she said, "Well, damn, ascender. Damn."

Medichi was just about ready to bust two pairs of balls.

Kerrick and Marcus stood in identical stances—arms folded across chests, grins spread over both faces as they stared back at him. Under different circumstances it would have been welcomed that both of them understood right now what he was going through. But those smiles made him want to clock them both. If they'd been closer, the hell he would have restrained the impulse.

He was just pissed off with a capital P.

Goddammit.

Parisa needed to be taught a lesson. A big one. He resented everything about her attitude right now, that *she* was going to take charge of finding the remaining D&R slaves, that *she* was going to become a warrior, that *she* was heading to the Female Militia Warrior Training Camps to train for battle. As though he had no say in the matter, as though he wasn't important to her, as though he could eat shit and die for all she cared. This wasn't a relationship. This was every man for himself—or woman in this case.

Inaccessible? Try *moved-to-outer-space-and-good-luck, asshole!*

What the hell was she thinking, *training camps*? The women there were butch as hell. They'd eat her alive.

"Medichi," Thorne cried. "Listen up!" Medichi blinked at him and ignored the way Marcus elbowed Kerrick and their fucking grins broadened.

"Yes, boss," he said. He glanced around. Where the hell had Endelle gone?

"Take Parisa back to the villa. You're still on guardian duty until Endelle says otherwise. Given the fact that Rith still seems to be captivated by our latest ascender, we're keeping her on emergency level. Got it?"

Even though Medichi wanted to argue, he said, "Got it."

"Good." His gaze skated over the rest of the group. "Well done, assholes. Let's have a drink and a toast, then we'll get the hell out of here. Time to take out more pretty-boys."

Medichi's thighs, heavy with muscle, shimmied. His arms ached from holding himself together. His throat was tight for all the words he'd jammed down to keep from spewing everywhere. He didn't want to yell at Parisa, but boy did she have a tongue-lashing coming.

Santiago moved to the back of the bar along with Zach. Together they pulled out a crowd of glasses. Zach opened the small fridge, and a bottle of Dom Perignon appeared. A pop followed.

"How nice," Parisa said. She left his side without even looking at him, as though she'd forgotten he was here.

If he hadn't been on guardian duty the fuck if he would have stayed in this room. All right, he would have drunk the toast with the boys then to hell with this female. *Inaccessible*. No fucking shit.

When the glasses were passed around, Luken held his aloft. "To Parisa, who kicked major butt today."

All the voices joined together, except for Medichi's. He drank and fumed. He ignored Marcus and Kerrick. He sure as hell didn't look at Parisa, though she turned back at him and smiled.

Then she frowned. Good.

He drained his glass and slapped it on the bar. "We need to get back," he stated.

She faced him now, her back to the warriors, a question in her eyes. One by one the men folded out of the Cave, heading to the Borderlands. Back to making war. Each time, a little breeze flowed in his direction, moving wisps of her hair forward around her face.

She glanced behind her and when the last of them left— Marcus offering her a salute—she turned back and said, "What's wrong?"

"That you even have to ask should give you some kind of clue, Madame Warrior."

Her pretty arched brows rose. "You're angry that I want to train as a warrior?"

"You don't even have the smallest clue what you'll be up against."

"You're right. I don't."

Okay, he hadn't expected that. "The Female Militia Training Camps are like Mortal Earth boot camp on crack. The women are hard-core. Simply put, you're not."

"You're right, I'm not."

He blinked and let out an exasperated sigh. "Then you shouldn't be going. You shouldn't even be thinking about a career in the military."

"I would have agreed with you yesterday."

He threw up his arms. "You saw a handful of seconds of military action and you think you can be a warrior? Look at you." He gestured with a hand up and down her body, his gaze pausing more than once on the size of her chest.

"So women with big boobs can't serve?" Now she scowled.

"I didn't say that."

"You were looking at my chest, though. Admit it."

"You don't look like a goddamn warrior."

She nodded, her lips pursed. "What do I look like, Antony? A vampire? An ascender? A woman who has to mount her wings at least once every ten days or she goes insane? A woman who just spent the last three months in captivity? A woman who before her ascension was hiding in a library because life had kicked her around too much? And exactly how many of those things make it bad or wrong for me to decide making war in a world at war is the right thing for me to do?"

"You haven't thought this through and not once did you ask, *What do you think, Antony?*"

At that, she released a small sigh. She even frowned a little. "What do you think, Antony?"

"Don't fucking patronize me. You don't give a good goddamn what I think. You already told Madame Endelle what you plan to do. That you didn't give me a second's thought summed it up for me."

"I didn't give you a second's thought? All I thought was—I want to do what Antony does. I want to lay it on the line every day or night of my life so long as Rith lives, so long as Greaves lives. I want to battle beside my man. I want him to be proud of me. I was such a mouse when I arrived here, when Havily and Marcus found me in my courtyard, naked and in full-mount and Crace arrived? There wasn't a damn thing I could do to stay alive in that situation. So, yeah, I did think of you, that I wanted to be just like you."

Shit. By the end of this speech, her eyes had filled with tears and she put three fingers against her lips in true Parisa fashion.

He took a step toward her but she lifted her other hand, palm flat out in his direction. "Don't." She lifted that hand a little higher, then vanished. He still couldn't believe she already had the ability to fold.

He traced her back to the villa. Thank God she'd had enough sense to go there and not anywhere else.

By the time his battle sandals touched down on the hardwood floor of his villa foyer, she was headed to the south rooms on a quick march. Now *she* was pissed. Fine.

He followed after her. By the time she'd passed through the formal living room and he was just about to catch up with her, she turned around and shook a finger at him. He stopped dead in his tracks.

"You don't want a long-term relationship with me," she cried. "You've told me you don't. Just remember that. "

Had he said those words to her? "You don't, either. You don't want the *breh-hedden*. You're *inaccessible*."

"Not like I used to be but you're right. I don't want to be

bonded to you. I don't want to be this close to anyone. But what's worse, what is killing me, is that I really, *really* don't want to lose you." Again, her fingers found her lips and her eyes filled with tears.

Ah, shit. "You don't?"

She put her hand on her forehead. "No. I really don't."

Just how far down this road were they anyway?

Oh . . . God.

"I don't want to lose you, either," he said. And that was the truth, apparently for both of them.

"Great," she said flapping her arms once up and down. "So what do we do? I didn't want this."

"Me, neither."

"Oh, Antony, what are we going to do? Everything is happening so fast and I'm still so raw about Rith and being held captive. I'm exhilarated that we brought the women home but now I'm horrified that there are twenty-one other facilities like Fiona's."

He moved close to her and put his arms around her. "Hey," he whispered against the top of her head. Even though they were fighting, that sweet scent of tangerines got to him all over again. "Ease down, Warrior."

She chuckled. Her arms slipped around his waist, finding a place beneath the center back strap of the weapons harness.

"You smell so good," she whispered against his chest.

Though desire rippled through him, he didn't act on it. Was this their first fight? Probably wouldn't be the last. Did he want to live without her? Could he bear her being gone day and night for weeks while she trained at the local camps?

Did she really want to battle as a warrior?

Shit.

"I don't know what to do," she murmured.

He sighed. "How about I hold you until you figure it out."

She chuckled once, a bounce against his chest. "That could be a millennium."

"Works for me."

How strange that he could look down the years, decades,

centuries and see himself holding her like this. What was it about Parisa that fit so well? Was it just the call of the *breh-hedden,* something outside them both forcing them together, or were they truly a good fit for this dimension, this world, this war?

He drew back and looked down at her.

She looked up. "You smell like sage." She smiled.

He didn't need more of an invitation than that. He dipped and caught her lips in a kiss that deepened swiftly. Before the thought had formed, his tongue was in her mouth and searching out every crevice as though he had never kissed her before.

She withdrew her arms from around his waist and slid them up his chest to encircle his neck. Her weapons harness and dagger collided with his. There just wasn't a lot of intimacy when three daggers and a lot of leather separated skin from skin.

"Antony," she murmured, meeting his gaze. "I'd like to go home, I don't mean permanently, I mean right now. I'd like to be with you in my home, the one I've lived in for the past several years, on Mortal Earth."

He had spent a lot of hours in her home. It was a unique house with a central courtyard, a private space that no one in the neighboring houses or the street could see into.

Everything about her house spoke of who she was: the muted hues of gold, maroon, and purple, the varying floors of carpet, wood, and tile, the heavy tapestry drapes in an olive green that flanked almost every window. In some ways, her house had a similar feeling to his own. And there wasn't a room or hallway that didn't have books in it, or on shelves, stacked on tables, locked away in glass cabinets as prized possessions. There had even been some left on her nightstand, a reminder that she'd had a life before her ascension.

Her love of books was just one more thing that bound him to her, whether he liked it or not.

"You know that I took care of your place."

She smiled. "You told me again and again, remember?

I know you couldn't hear me when I'd voyeur you but I heard everything you said to me."

"I know. At least, I thought that was the way it was for you. I hoped it was."

"It was. You told me you went to my Peoria home every Monday and made sure all the utilities were paid for, the mail collected. You said Endelle kept the house cloaked in mist to keep death vampires away."

"Yep."

"So the water's still turned on?"

He smiled. "You have a good-sized shower over there, though not as big as mine."

Her amethyst eyes darkened. "Antony, no one's is as big as yours."

He chuckled. She was so his kind of woman. His brother warriors might call him a gentleman but when it came to women he bedded, he'd always preferred everything to be open, erotic, even experimental. That she'd engaged in long-distance sex with him for three months still pleased the hell out of him, and when she'd agreed to use her voyeur window on them last time, he'd known bedtime between them would be just right.

He also loved never knowing what direction things would take.

"My bed is only a queen and you're definitely king-sized."

He met her gaze, his lids at half-mast. "King-sized, huh?"

An answering rush of tangerine scent, softened with a bouquet that was just her, tingled his nostrils. King-sized indeed.

She writhed against him, all of him. "God, yes," she whispered against his lips, which made his hips buck into her. "Fold me now."

He didn't hesitate. He thought the thought and the moment he felt the bricks of the courtyard beneath his feet, he kissed her hard. Small cries of approval drifted out of her throat and into his mouth. He wanted her to keep crying like that, louder and louder, until she was screaming against his lips and he could swallow her orgasms down.

He pulled back just a little. "I need this off." He touched her weapons harness and folded it off so that a split-second later, her pale flesh was a beacon in the night. His right hand caressed one of her full breasts. He was a big man and he had big hands. They barely fit around her, she was that big. Oh, yeah. He rubbed his thumb over her nipple and she cried out. He kissed her again.

He felt her hands give a tug on his harness. She drew back. "And I need this off."

He was about to fold it away, but she stopped him. "Allow me."

"Sure," he said, but he smiled. For some reason, this skill set had so far proved challenging.

She closed her eyes and he felt his harness give way, but it ended up hooked over his left shoulder.

She giggled as she manually pulled it off him and dropped it on the pavers next to the chaise longue. She looked down at it and laughed some more. "I'll get better."

"You did just fine," he said, his voice husky. He moved into her again and once more put his hand on her breast. He caught the nape of her neck with his palm and met her gaze as he slowly slid his hand over her breast, across, in a wide circle down, around, and up, a lot of beautiful territory to cover. She moaned.

He thumbed her nipple again, and her lips parted. He leaned into her and caught her mouth, driving his tongue deep. She whimpered and pressed her breast into his hand, grinding against his palm. The peaked nipple was a firm bead against his skin, and he needed more of it.

He drew back, dipped low, then caught her breast in his mouth and tongued her nipple, rubbing up and down in a sudden swift motion that brought little cries from her mouth. The rush of tangerine-and-woman scent rose like a cloud around him, which of course worked on his body like soft stroking fingers so that beneath his kilt he was hard as a rock. His knees felt rubbery the more he suckled.

He needed more.

He was breathing hard when he pulled back. She jerked

forward as though she'd lost that small bit of balance. Her eyes had darkened, even in the dim lights of the courtyard lamps.

He shoved a muscled thigh between her legs and stroked her. He wrapped his arm around her waist and lifted her onto his thigh. He held her tight against his chest. With his free hand he rubbed the side of her breast. Then he kissed her. He drove his tongue into her mouth over and over, letting her feel in that one pulsing movement what he wanted to do between her legs—tongue, cock, or fingers—to work her until she was screaming.

He drew back just enough to say, "First my tongue, then my cock."

She shivered, all the way down.

With his thigh still holding her up—even her feet were off the pavers—he walked her backward, then with an arm behind her shoulders and one on her buttocks, he laid her out on the chaise-longue, just shallow enough so that her hips came to the edge.

Oh, Antony, yes, yes.

I love you inside my head.

I love you inside me any way you can get there.

He chuckled, and the throaty sound rolled around the small courtyard.

With his knees on the hard pavers, he looked into her eyes, those beautiful amethyst eyes, and for a moment his desire became suspended in something more, something he couldn't explain, but he'd experienced it many centuries before with his wife.

Almost like, shit . . . almost like *love.*

But he couldn't go there.

He kissed her lightly. He felt disoriented, as if he'd been reading a book then suddenly lost his place on the page.

"What is it?" she whispered.

He shook his head. "I'm not sure."

She touched his face. "I think you're remembering other things. Come back to me, Antony. Save this time for me."

He nodded. He looked at her and drew back. He let his

gaze drift down her body, her extraordinary breasts, her belly button. He put a hand on her cargoes and folded them away.

The sight of her flat, smooth abdomen, her legs spread and waiting for him, the nest of her dark hair, sent a shiver down his body. A certain amount of pain accompanied the sight of her since he was holding back. He wanted to wait for her. He wanted to see ecstasy flow over her face and force more gasps, cries, and moans from her mouth before he came.

He calmed himself down and, with a thought, folded a towel from his bathroom into his hand. His kilt was long but not long enough to really maneuver and at the same time protect his knees.

He stretched the towel and settled his knees. Hey, a little preparation went a long way to getting his woman where he needed her to be. Still, he laughed at himself. God, he loved sex, and he really loved this moment.

As he situated his knees, he looked up the length of her body. She was propped up on her elbows, her face aglow, and it wasn't the landscaping lights. "What is it?" he asked.

"You. You're so beautiful, Antony. I know I should say handsome, but I think you're beautiful. Your cheekbones are sculpted. Sometimes my chest aches when I look at you and your long warrior hair." She sat up the rest of the way and ran her fingers from the top of his head down the entire length of his hair as though awestruck. "I never thought long hair on a man could be so erotic." A heady wave of tangerine pounded his senses but before he knew what she was about to do, she had launched herself off the chaise longue and onto him so that, even in his kneeling position, she now had her legs wrapped around his waist.

She kissed him hard and her tongue, so feminine, was a driving pulse in his mouth. He groaned and held her against him, her exquisite breasts against the flat plane of his chest. He squeezed and squeezed, his biceps flexing and releasing as he embraced her. He held her in a tight grip as though trying to press her into his body so that he could carry her around with him day and night.

His tongue dueled with hers, an erotic battle that lasted

several minutes until one of his hands was planted on her ass and pushing her hips in pulses against his hard-as-nails cock.

Sweet Jesus.

"I know you wanted this here," she said, panting against his lips. "But I think I want you upstairs in my shower. Okay?"

Okay? Hell, she could have said, *I want you to set your feet on fire,* and right now he would have agreed to it.

So much for the careful towel on the pavers, but truth? He loved it.

He gained his feet with his woman still wrapped around his body, her heels digging into his ass through the kilt. He thought the thought and carried her through nether-space into the master bedroom shower upstairs, a large walk-in shower, a good eight feet deep. He could make it work.

She unhooked her legs and dropped her feet to the floor. She stepped away from him a little and looked down at his kilt and battle sandals, his shin guards—and yeah, he still wore his silver-studded black leather wrist guards.

He was ready to fold off the rest of his clothes but she stopped him. "Let me practice."

He smiled because he loved the excited glitter in her eyes. They fit in this way. He was powerful and had known many of his powers from almost the day of his ascension. She was the same.

She worked at removing one piece of clothing at a time. She got his battle sandals off just fine. He nodded his approval. Even the shin guards came off. She put her hand under his kilt until she touched his flight briefs, snug Calvin Kleins, and she thought the thought.

"Not fucking bad," he said with a smile.

But she looked past his shoulder and laughed. When he turned around he saw them hanging from a nozzle.

He laughed and kissed her nose. "Still, not bad." Besides, it was incredibly sexy to have a naked woman undressing him like this.

"Now the kilt," he said.

She nodded and again closed her eyes to concentrate.

But the kilt ended up just below his knees, which knocked him off balance. He dropped to his ass on the cold tile. He laughed up at her. She joined him for a split second, then her gaze fell down the line of his body and her laughter faded. In its stead was a ferocious darkening of her eye and a wave of tangerine that once again took his breath away.

He leaned back on his elbows and spread his legs a little more by lifting one knee and shaking the kilt to his ankles. He was fully erect, his cock stretched out on his abdomen. He wanted her to take a good long look.

Parisa had been laughing at her stupidity but now she wondered if just maybe she was some kind of genius. God, Antony looked gorgeous spread out on the floor like that, leaning up on his elbows so that his stomach had small ripples near his belly button. She'd like to put her tongue there because at the same place was the crown of his cock and she wanted her tongue on him, all the way down.

Damn, he was king-sized. Yes . . . he . . . was.

When she had said she wanted to be in the shower, she had meant standing up, the water on, his body pushing into hers, all that good stuff. But honestly, this was going to be better. A very specific image popped into her head.

"More tangerine," he groaned.

She shivered in response because his sage scent swirled around her, licking at her body from her nose to her toes.

But as her gaze fell to what waited for her down low, her tongue tingled in anticipation.

She knelt. She could have practiced her folding technique a little more, but right now she wanted the pleasure of stripping his kilt off. She took her time, easing it past his ankles and feet, rubbing his shins with her hands, his hair teasing her palms.

She laid the kilt out between his legs so that she could stretch out as well. She settled onto her hip and smiled, her heart rate escalating. She wasn't sure where all this boldness was coming from but after all, they'd been making love together, even if it was a long-distance affair, for over three months.

She'd also voyeured him so she knew the things he would like. Her mouth actually watered as her gaze roved the heavy sac of his testicles and the firm length of his cock. She reclined so that her head rested on his leg. Sage rolled.

"Antony?"

"Yes." That one word was a husky drawl that filled the shower space.

"Will you do something for me?" Very lightly she drifted the backs of her fingers over his sac.

His back arched and he groaned. "Sweetheart, right now if you asked me to launch into outer space, I'd give it a try."

She smiled up at him, met his gaze, and her heart squeezed. Yes, he was so beautiful and some of his hair hung down both sides of his chest. He was in every way a treat waiting to happen. "Touch yourself while I tend to you."

He leaned back on his left elbow and said, "Is that what you want? You want to watch my hand move over my cock?"

She drew a deep breath. Desire played over her body. Shivers traced up and down as his hand moved lower and lower, teasing her.

She nodded. His fingers took his crown in his hand. He stroked lightly.

"Yes, Antony. I want your hand moving over your cock while I tend to you. Will that make you happy?"

He smiled then he sighed. "Just having you here, with me, and very naked, makes me happy. But if this is what you want, I'm in."

He took his thick stalk in his fist and worked himself up and down, caressing the crown with his thumb on each upward pass.

She turned her head into his leg and shifted forward to get closer. Her tongue touched his inner thigh, and he groaned. She licked him over and over, first on the inside of one thigh, then the other. She kept moving forward and inward with each pass, until her tongue played with the rippled skin of his sac. She sucked the skin in and he groaned. Her tongue found the testicles, and she rolled and played with them. The sound of his hand working over his flesh filled the short distance between her head and his hand.

His breathing grew rough.

Parisa, he sent. *Take my mind right now.*

She drew back and looked at him. "You want me to enter your mind?" The thought troubled her. Whatever sex was, however intimate it was to be enjoying his naked body, somehow the thought of being in his mind changed things.

He sat up. "Are you afraid?"

"Won't that mean going one more mile down this road toward the *breh-hedden*?"

He shook his head. "Not necessarily. Remember, with the *breh-hedden* all three things have to happen at once." He smiled and waggled his fingers over his cock. "This isn't even close to the kind of sex we'd need to be having to take the ritual all the way."

She smiled and nodded. Then her body betrayed her because somehow the thought of being inside Antony's mind made her clench. "Oh," she whispered.

He leaned close to her, his cock barely a kiss away, as he cupped her face with his hand. "I know you haven't done mind-penetration before but it's fantastic during sex. I want to do it to you as well, just not right now. What do you say?"

She wanted to. "I really want to."

He nodded then leaned back on his left elbow and once more touched himself, deft fingers that knew what they were doing.

She let her head rest on his thigh and wiggled to get as close as she needed to be, to do what she wanted to do to him. She drew the sac and one of his testicles into her mouth and tongued him gently. At the same time, she closed her eyes and concentrated.

She pushed against his mind. She could feel his shields, so powerful, protecting his mind. *Even in your shields you're so well muscled. Do I push, or do you let them fall?*

Try pushing.

She felt the seductive intent behind those words. He wanted her to push against him. She did, and he groaned aloud. *So damn sexy.*

She could hear the swift strokes now, the perfect rhythm of his hand, and she realized this was going to bring him off, which in turn set all the nerves of her body on fire. Moisture dampened the well of her body. She slung a leg over his, her hips rocking against him.

Ready? she asked.

God, yes.

She pushed until the shields crashed around her. She had barely dipped into his mind when the upper half of his body bowed and lifted off the tile.

Lift up and look at me, he sent. He was breathing hard when she left the cradle of his body, releasing his sac and testicles so that she could look at him.

On a quick downward stroke of his hand, while her mind was falling farther inside his head, she leaned forward and licked a combination of his fingers and cock.

"Oh, God," he shouted. She watched him erupt, his come spurting all over his chest, his face twisted in ecstasy.

His pleasure exploded over her mind. She had thought she might take some time to explore his memories, but all that sensation brought her body into a tight state of readiness. Need filled her, his body on her, in her, any way she could get him. She hadn't expected this. She rolled on her back then her side.

She was in agony. *Antony, help me. Oh, God.*

Her body knotted up in about a hundred different ways.

Help me, she sent, but he was already in her mind, she could feel him, which only further drew her into knot after knot.

I'm here. Look at me. Open your eyes and look at me. She felt hands on her arms. He was pulling her up his body.

"Parisa," he said aloud.

She opened her eyes. She was on top of him, face-to-face, but she was inside his head as well.

"I'm here. I know what you need." He turned his head.

Her eyes bulged. He was offering his neck, and she knew this was exactly what she needed. Oh, God, she really was a vampire now, wasn't she? Her heart pounded in her chest. Her fangs emerged. Saliva dripped in her mouth. All the knots relaxed.

She was panting and she was instantly addicted to being within his mind. She never wanted to be anywhere else, but her body was on fire.

She knew other things she should do first—like lick the vein and urge it forth—but she was too far gone. Some kind of cavewoman need had taken her over.

Yes, that's it, he sent. *Take me. Take me hard.*

She struck quick, like lightning, and began sucking at his neck as though she'd been dying of thirst for about a decade. She pulled in deep draws, savoring the sage taste of him.

Her internal muscles spasmed again and again. She ground her hips against him and found him . . . *hard.*

Antony, I need you.

I'm ready. I don't know what you've done to me, but I'm ready again. Take me, Parisa. Take all of me.

He held her tight around the shoulders, anchoring her against his neck. He groaned as she sucked.

With his other hand, he dipped low and cradled her entire pelvis—yes, he had big hands. He lifted her up, positioned her over his cock, then impaled her in a single hard thrust. She was so wet for him, so tight, so ready.

She screamed around the seal on his neck, but kept her fangs buried and continued to pull. As soon as he'd pushed himself in, though, her hips began to work. Her body felt so strangely powerful—maybe it was Antony's blood—but she rode him. She rode his cock hard and fast, his arm a vise around her shoulders, his free hand cradling the back of her head and keeping her pinned to his neck.

She drank and drank.

The orgasm began to build, like a huge tidal wave in the distance. She felt the pressure coming, coming. His hips suddenly took over. He moved the hand from the back of her head to her buttocks to hold her in place as he thrust deep, hitting the end of her and it hurt and it felt wonderful and hurt and the sensations got mixed up together until he was driving so fast, so very fast, hitting just that spot and suddenly the orgasm barreled down on her with the force of a tsunami.

She released his neck, arched her back, and screamed. She screamed and screamed as he stretched the orgasm out. Between her screams she heard his low grunting noises, spitting the sounds from behind clenched teeth.

The orgasm receded but it was like wave-sets at the ocean: The next one came and still Antony pumped into her, hard, grunting, animal, vampire.

Parisa. Oh, God, Parisa. I'm coming again and oh . . . shiiiiit.

A third orgasm pounded on her, rushing through her as he jerked inside her and pumped and jerked and filled her with his seed.

Then she saw stars, dozens of them, spinning and spinning, a full galaxy in motion, then they all winked out.

When she woke up, she was lying on something very soft, a bed, but she couldn't quite make her eyes open. But she was smiling. Why? She was giggling. Why? Soft little things dotted her nose, her cheeks, her lips, her chin. Ah . . . kisses.

"Parisa? Parisa?"

She heard Antony's voice from a great distance.

She giggled again. She was so happy. Was she on some kind of drug?

Oh, yes, Antony's blood and his cock and his lips and his tongue and his massive pecs and the fine hairs between his pecs, and his muscled thighs and the way he walked like a tremendous thoroughbred stallion, all quivering muscles, and she had been inside his mind when he came and he had been inside hers.

"Parisa, Parisa."

More soft little moist touches now, just on her lips again and again, then a delicate swipe of something wetter.

She parted her lips and she felt . . . Antony's tongue.

She giggled and woke up the rest of the way, her eyes

opening. He was over her now, kissing her. She was in his bed in the villa. He'd brought her back.

She was still connected to his mind. She leaned up and kissed him. *Did I pass out?*

He smiled and nodded.

"It was . . . unbelievable. We have to do it again only this time . . . oh, Antony, I didn't know it could be like that."

"I'm a little worried."

She smiled. "You ought to be pleased. You made a woman faint with pleasure." His neck was bloody and a little torn up from her efforts. "Are you okay?" Well, that was the first time she'd asked him that. He was always asking her if she was okay, but this time she'd asked him.

But he just smiled again and kissed her. "I'll heal."

He was a vampire, of course he'd heal, and fast.

She touched his neck. "Well, now there are *two* things I need to work at."

After getting both of them cleaned up in the shower, Antony took Parisa back to his bed and held her against him, his arm around her shoulders.

He'd come close to asking her to complete the *breh-hedden,* which required that each of them take blood, during intercourse, with a full exchange of deep-mind engagement.

What had stopped him? The sex had been mind-blowing, but sex was . . . well, it was just sex except that he'd been inside her mind. He'd picked up this memory, then that one. He'd lived much of her time in captivity, seen her despair, watched her watching him stroke himself morning after morning. He'd felt the depth of her feeling for him. She was in love with him, but how much in love with him? How far gone was she?

He knew that feeling. He'd had that same one thirteen centuries ago. He couldn't go through it again. He couldn't. If he completed the *breh-hedden,* if he went the distance with her, if he fell that far in love with her, what happened if she died . . . no, not if she died, but *when*?

He couldn't go through it again.

Her voice cut into the tangle of his thoughts. "Do you really think taking the warrior training is a bad idea?" Her fingers tugged at the hairs on his arms.

How did he answer that?

He wanted to shout and rail, to tell her to stay away from the camps, to stay in the villa, to hide here with him. They would hide together, forever, live like hermits.

But he didn't want to lose her. "You should take the training if that's what you want to do. Become a warrior."

He stared up at the ceiling, the words of his wife's poem running through his mind. *Love rises on wings of fire . . .*

She shifted in his arms so that she could look at him. She leaned up on her elbow. "You sang a very different tune before the sex." She smiled, but it dimmed. "What's wrong?"

His gaze was still fixed on the coffered beams overhead, the ceiling like a chessboard. "Everything. Nothing. The hell if I know what to do."

She turned and followed his gaze, dropping back down on the bed, setting her head into the well of his shoulder. "Tell me what it says."

He pointed straight up. He took his time and translated each line for her.

"That's beautiful and it does, doesn't it? Love rising like that, like wings of fire?"

"I can't do this," he whispered.

She didn't even tense. "I know. That's why I'm going to train as a warrior. What chance does love have between us so long as there is a Rith, a Greaves, and a war? We've already been separated once."

He turned into her until he was on his side. She faced him on her side as well. "I'm already in love with you, maybe not all the way, but almost," he said. "But I can't go any farther. I'm sorry. I'm so sorry."

She traced his lips with her finger. "I know. It's okay."

She looked as serious as he felt, her brow puckered slightly. "How do the others do it? Havily and Marcus? Alison and Kerrick?"

"I don't know." He leaned forward and kissed her.

"I love you, too, you know, as much as I can."

"I know."

"I want to go back to the guest room tonight. Tomorrow, I'll talk to Endelle about the training camps."

"Good." He expected her to pull away, to draw out of his arms, to make good on her word. Instead, she snuggled closer.

Just a little longer, she whispered through his mind.

Yes.

But after maybe only a minute, he felt her sigh and begin to rise up. She leaned over to kiss him, a soft press against his lips.

His head slid against his pillow, pulling on his hair. He watched her leave. He worked to keep his arms immobile. He wanted to reach for her, grab her, drag her back down to the bed, but what good would that do?

This was for the best.

Really.

The lesson ignored twice then thrice,
Creates chaos in the lives of many.

—**Collected Proverbs**, Beatrice of Fourth

CHAPTER 21

Parisa stood on one side of Fiona's hospital bed and Havily on the other.

Fiona had the bed raised in a full-sitting position. "I want to get out of here. I'm not sick. Just drained."

Parisa smiled. "Was that a joke?"

Fiona glanced at her, arched her brown eyebrows as if in question, then smiled. She even chuckled softly. "Yes, I guess it was." She sighed. "I slept well last night, and no drugs in my system anymore."

She wore a gold locket around her neck, the one Jean-Pierre had given her. Apparently, he'd found it in Toulouse behind an armoire but how he'd found it, Parisa couldn't imagine. Didn't matter. Fiona was safe.

Havily turned away from the bed and drew a chair forward. She sat down. "So, we're actually here for a reason, not just to pay a social call. We've been talking about the D and R refugees, for want of a better word. I hate using the word *slave*."

"But *slave* is accurate, believe me. Even though we had daily exercise and a healthy diet, full of iron, naturally."

Parisa didn't leave her post by the bed. She had an uneasy sensation about Fiona. The woman had an aura of dry brittle leaves. "This must be so disorienting for you," she said.

"Yes, I suppose it must seem that way." She lowered her gaze to stare at her clasped hands. The thumbs touched, rolled against each other. "I'm glad to be here. Let me at least say that. I am glad to be alive and to no longer be in that place or under Rith's command."

Parisa glanced at the doorway. The hospital was buzzing with activity. Antony was talking with Colonel Seriffe, and several of the Warriors of the Blood were here. She had seen Alison pass by once or twice as well.

Outside the building, a number of Militia Warriors could be seen through the street-side window, patrolling the hospital grounds.

Parisa had felt uneasy all morning. She had slept in the guest room, alone, the bed cool after Antony's warm presence. As tall as he was, as muscled, the man created a lot of heat. She had awakened more than once, forgetting where she was, reaching across the bed and patting cold sheets.

She would get used to it. She had to. They'd decided together that this was for the best.

Earlier, they'd met with Endelle, and she'd agreed to permit Parisa to enter the Female Warrior Training Camps. It seemed strange to have settled on that course, but of everything she'd been through in the past year and a half, warrior training was the one thing that felt completely right to her.

"So, what's going on?" Fiona asked.

Parisa glanced at Havily. "Well," Havily began, "it may be early in the process here, but the bottom line is that we've learned there are twenty-one other D and R facilities around the world."

"Yes," Fiona said her clasped hands coming loose. "Yes."

"Yes, what?" Parisa asked.

Fiona looked up at her. "I want to help get them out, all of them. Whatever it takes. But I'm not sure how we're going to do that and not cause even more problems. Even if we break up the D and R program, what happens next? Greaves will want to set up more of them, and in the meantime where will all the death vampires get their blood?"

Havily met Parisa's gaze. "She's right," Havily said. "If we disturb all twenty-one nests at once, two things will happen. More mortals will be abducted to replace them, and a lot more women will die. She's absolutely right. We have to battle this more extensively."

"How?" Parisa asked.

"Well, I've been thinking," Havily said, staring hard at Parisa. She shifted her gaze to Fiona. "The three of us have one thing in common. We've all been abducted. We all know what it feels like to be helpless, in the grip of someone more powerful. And the reason this hospital is crawling with Militia Warriors is because we are all still in danger. Rith will want his slaves back as well." She glanced at Parisa. "So, are you headed to the camps?"

She nodded. "Medichi's here talking with Colonel Seriffe about security at the training camps for me. No one really knows what to do, but I'm determined to go."

"What are the camps?" Fiona asked.

"Warrior training. I'm becoming a warrior." She laughed. "It feels so strange to say that out loud."

Havily rose from the chair. "Did you know that Endelle wanted Alison to go the camps, to train as a warrior, when she first ascended?"

"No, I didn't," Parisa said. "Do you mean Alison didn't want to be trained?"

Havily shook her head. "You know what she is . . . a healer. She couldn't even kill her opponent in the arena battle and it was supposed to be a battle to the death. The warrior was intent on killing her, but Alison . . . you won't believe this . . . cut off his arm then reversed a pocket of time so that he got his arm back."

"No," Fiona cried. "Is that possible in this dimension?"

Parisa glanced at her. "I had wings on Mortal Earth. That was supposed to be impossible as well."

Fiona turned to Havily. "What of you? What is your power that makes you a target?"

"Well, I have two actually. My blood has special properties and tends to act like dying blood in some respects. It made Crace maniacal. He was a High-Administrator-turned-death-vampire who wanted my blood more than anything. He was the one who orchestrated my abduction.

"In addition, I work with Endelle in the darkening. Yeah, I know . . . well, it's a nether-space thing, a place that exists between dimensions. When she and I do darkening work, we hunt for Greaves all night because he uses that time to travel around the world to ship death vampires to this area, to Phoenix Two. You know how the Warriors of the Blood battle all night? Greaves has been building an army of death vampires throughout the world by turning High Administrators and in addition making one of their tasks the creation of more death vampires through the taking of dying blood."

Fiona leaned her head against the mattress. She covered her face with her hand. "And he supplies the High Administrators with our blood, with the blood we died for every month."

"Yes," Havily said. "But yours no more."

Fiona's hand shot out and grabbed Havily's arm. "But Rith will acquire more women to meet the demand. And if not, the death vampires must feed. I've heard that to go without dying blood creates unbearable abdominal cramps."

Parisa turned and settled a hip on the bed. She took Fiona's free hand and held it tightly in hers. "That is not your responsibility," she said. "Your job is to get well quickly and to serve on our committee to free the rest of the slaves."

Fiona shook her head. "They will feed on mortals because they're weak. There has to be a better way. Something more permanent. The blood is packaged and distributed all around the world. What if we followed that trail and eliminated the source that needed the blood."

"You mean the death vampires."

"Exactly."

"Are you aware that Greaves has an antidote and that more ascenders partake of dying blood than we know of? It's rumored that a third of COPASS uses dying blood and the antidote."

"COPASS?" Fiona asked.

"The Committee to Oversee the Process of Ascension to Second Earth. No one checked the acronym, which is probably also an indication of the intelligence level involved. It's all political."

"What does COPASS have to do with anything if they just oversee the ascension process?"

"Over the decades, the governing body gained more and more power. It now has the ability to establish all kinds of laws. The one that hinders Endelle the most is that she is not allowed access to her own Seers Fortress at the Superstition Mountains without the permission of that Fortress's High Administrator."

Fiona frowned. "But I know for a fact that Commander Greaves uses Seer information to plot his course."

"How do you know that?" Havily asked.

A blush suffused Fiona's cheeks. "I can hear telepathic conversations." She whispered the words.

Parisa glanced at Havily. Havily returned her stare and into her mind, sent, *Is she lying?*

"I wouldn't lie about something like this," Fiona said. "And I only mentioned it because I trust you both."

Parisa laughed, then Havily. "Can you communicate telepathically? I'm just learning to do it myself."

Fiona shook her head. "I don't know."

"How did you discover you could do this?"

"Generally I can hear everyone's thoughts, though I've learned to block the noise really well. The first time I met Greaves and Rith all those decades ago, it was like hearing a symphony in full orchestral mode. I thought I would go mad." She shuddered at the memory.

"You must know way too much about everyone."

"More than I'd like to."

"What about Jean-Pierre?" Havily asked.

Fiona smiled. "I don't know French. He blends his French and English together in his thoughts. Besides, the minute I know I'm hearing thoughts instead of spoken words, I close my mind down."

Parisa blew air from her cheeks. "That's probably a good thing where Jean-Pierre is concerned."

Havily laughed.

"What am I missing?"

Havily said, "Well, he's a man and he's a warrior."

Fiona laughed, first a little then a lot. "You're so right. I forgot what it used to be like when I would listen in accidentally. Men do think about sex a lot." After the shared amusement subsided, she said, "I wasn't that way before I was abducted, on Mortal Earth, I mean. I couldn't hear everyone's thoughts until I arrived on Second."

"But how did you survive?" Havily asked. " Mortals can't, you know." She jerked her thumb at Parisa. "Except this one, but she's the only exception . . . ever."

Fiona shrugged. "The first thing Greaves did to me was ascend me. I know that's not the right phrase but he has the power to bestow immortality though he withholds the fangs, thank God. Vampire fangs would have been too much to deal with."

"As if the D and R process wasn't enough all by itself. You know, Fiona, what we don't understand is how you lived as long as you did."

She stared down once more at clasped hands. "I really don't know, but the worst of it was that I got really good at reading the women. I knew how long each one would last to the year, often to the month."

"Jesus," Havily whispered. She put her hand on Fiona's shoulder. "We've all been through it one way or another, because we're ascended and this is a world at war. My fiancé was killed by death vampires and he was a powerful Militia Warrior. Later Crace, who used to be High Administrator of Chicago Two, *turned* and got a taste of my blood and abducted me. He drained me, not to death like you, but he kept me drugged and chained to a wall. Sometimes I have night-mares, but Marcus is there for me now and it helps."

Fiona grabbed her hand, the one on her shoulder. "We're sisters then, in this kind of suffering."

"And power," Parisa said.

Another feminine voice flowed from the doorway. "And compassion." Alison moved forward, her gaze fixed on Fiona. "You have compassion for the other women. I've been talking to them this morning. You were the hub, the counselor, the comforter. You got most of them through longer than they would have survived otherwise."

Parisa turned toward her. Alison had spoken evenly enough, but now her hand was on her stomach and her nostrils flared. Was she in pain all the time? "How's the baby?"

Alison took in a deep breath. "I'm actually here for a so-nogram in a little while, but I thought I'd check in with our latest arrivals." After a moment, she seemed to relax, and she moved forward to put a hand over Fiona's hand, which still held Havily's. She smiled. "I like this. A real sisterhood. When I ascended I was alone except for Endelle. Believe me, that was no picnic."

Parisa and Havily burst out laughing.

"What?" Fiona asked.

Havily chuckled. "You'll find out soon enough."

"I hear she's fashion-challenged."

All the ladies shouted their laughter this time.

"To say the least," Havily said.

Alison broke the spell and hissed as she once more pressed her hand to her belly. She stepped away from the bed then cursed, a very long string of words hooked together that made Parisa stare. She had never heard her talk like this, but Havily didn't seem especially surprised.

Alison closed her eyes and breathed, her hand at the top of her belly as though trying to press the pain away.

"Okay," she said. "Enough of this. I'm going to track the doctor down right now."

She turned and hurried from the room. She headed to the right so that Parisa watched her pass in front of the glass windows that ran the length of the bedroom wall. Long vertical blinds ran the width of the window, but right now they were kept open just enough.

"God, I hope she's okay," Havily cried.

When Parisa glanced at her, she was dabbing careful fingers beneath her eyes. After a moment, she turned back in Fiona's direction and said, "Her sonogram will take a while so how about we focus on you. I suspect you have a lot of questions about Second Earth and about Endelle's administration, so if you feel up to it, fire away."

Fiona blinked. "Well, who makes the best coffee in this dimension? All I've had for over a hundred years is tea. I'm sick of tea. I used to have coffee every morning in Boston."

"Starbucks," Parisa and Havily said in unison.

Parisa thought the lightness of her tone and of the question was the best sign yet that Fiona would adjust.

For the next hour, both she and Fiona pelted Havily with dozens of questions on all sorts of subjects—about Endelle's administration, about the Warriors of the Blood, and about the organization of Territories. Spectacle became a lively discussion as well as horticulture, which was one of the highest art forms on Second Earth.

When another half hour had passed, Havily glanced in the direction of the hallway windows. She looked down at her watch then back to the windows. "I really thought Alison would be done by now."

Kerrick suddenly appeared in the doorway, a crease between his brows. "Hey, Hav. Just to give you a heads-up, Alison's headed this way and she's crying." He looked really worried.

Parisa knew that the bonding of the *breh-hedden* allowed Kerrick to know Alison's external sensations, anything she touched or anything that touched her, but it didn't translate into emotional understanding. No doubt he could feel the tears on her face.

But this so wasn't good.

"Why weren't you with her?" Havily asked.

"She was supposed to wait because I was out at the Militia Warrior Training Camps. Shit. I wanted to be here for her."

He was just short of Antony's height. He had dark arched brows over striking emerald eyes. He was built, too, and looked especially yummy in his battle kilt and weapons harness.

His expression shifted, a lift of the arched brows and widening of his eyes as he looked up the hall. He took a few steps so that Parisa could only see him through the hall window if she leaned backward, her gaze partially obscured by the blinds.

Alison came into view and the next second he took her in his arms, though her belly made it an awkward angle. Parisa felt tears touch her eyes. Alison's chest rose and fell in what had to be a series of sobs.

Fiona whispered, "Oh, no."

But it was Kerrick's face she could see.

"It can't be all bad. Look. Kerrick is smiling." His laughter suddenly boomed up the hall. He pulled away from her and laughed some more, then he hugged her and laughed again.

Havily said, "Maybe she's having twins. She looks big enough to be having more than one. She's only seven months and she's huge."

He put his arm around her shoulders and turned her in the direction of Fiona's door. Havily now stood at the end of bed.

The next moment, Alison appeared, wiping tears from her cheeks and grinning from ear to ear.

"What?" Havily cried. "Tell us right now or I'm going to throw my shoe at *you* this time, Lissy."

That made Alison laugh. "Oh, that was so bad of me but I've already promised Kerrick I won't do it again." She compressed her lips and tried to restrain what was a combination of a new smile and the beginning of a fresh bout of tears. Her relief was obvious.

Kerrick tightened his arm around her shoulders and met

Havily's gaze. "Well, first, nothing's wrong . . . at all. But you're not going to believe this. The baby has wings."

"Wings?" Havily cried. "That's not possible!"

"Apparently, it is," Alison said. "That's why there's been so much discomfort. The baby's healthy and she's right on schedule, but apparently the release of the wings has caused an increase in amniotic fluid in order to create more space and that's been the problem all this time. Well, that and the movement. Essentially, the flying." She wiped her eyes. "The baby has wings. I can't believe it. I just can't believe it."

Parisa stared at Alison's stomach. She tried to picture the fetus within, twirling, tumbling, practicing with wings. She couldn't imagine a finer beginning for any human—ascender—vampire—whatever.

Havily turned toward the couple a little more. "But does this mean you have two more months of this kind of agony?"

Alison stood up straighter and wiped a little more at her cheeks. She folded tissues into her hand and wiped some more. "No. The good news is that the doctor thinks I can begin communicating telepathically with the baby to get her to start bringing her wings in and hopefully keeping them in. It's a rare phenomenon for a Second Earth baby but there's anecdotal evidence that says it occurs in the Upper Dimension all the time." She drew a card from the pocket of her slacks. "There's a woman whose specialty is telepathy and infants. Her name is Tazianne. Now, why does that name sound familiar?"

Havily gave a brisk shake of her head. "Oh, I know why. She's the talented horticulturalist who designed the magnolia centerpiece on Medichi's foyer table."

"That's right, I remember now. Well, looks like she has more than one gift. Anyway, I'm going to give her a call ASAP and get Helena to calm the hell down." She chuckled. Kerrick hugged her again and kissed her forehead. They looked at each other for a long moment. Parisa knew they were communicating telepathically, and it was a beautiful thing to see the love on their faces, one for the other.

Parisa's heart hurt looking at them. She thought of Ant-

ony and of having spent the night in the guest room. For a
sudden hard moment she longed to have exactly that kind of
relationship with him.

Fiona didn't know whether it was Parisa sitting on the side
of the bed next to her, or that Havily and Alison and even
Warrior Kerrick were in her room with her, but somehow
she started to relax. Tears touched her eyes. The sight of
Warrior Kerrick so tender with his *breh* was so normal that
she felt maybe, *maybe,* everything was going to be okay.

The disaster that had been her life for over a century, the
suffering she had endured, began to fall back into the past.
She could take a step forward now, maybe two. She knew
this sensation, but it took her a moment to realize that what
she felt was hope, that her life even after so many horren-
dous decades, could start making sense again, could be something she could manage, perhaps even direct, even *enjoy.*
What would that be like, to be able to direct her steps, to order
them, to choose her path, to decide when she arose and when
she went to bed, to never again be at the mercy of monthly
needles, tubes, bags, and the presence of Rith and his medical staff?

She drew air into her nostrils and she smelled coffee. "Oh,
what I wouldn't give for a cup of coffee right now. When I
kept my house in Boston, I had my housekeeper bring me
a cup first thing. It was decadent, I know, but it was so
lovely."

"We can certainly get you some coffee," Parisa said.

Fiona looked past Alison through the long window onto
the hall. The blinds made it a little difficult to see, but she
couldn't mistake the man who came into view: Warrior Jean-
Pierre. Her fingers moved to the gold locket.

She shouldn't do it.

She really shouldn't do it, but for someone reason she had
to know his thoughts. Did he ever think of her?

She lowered her shields, just a little. At first, all she could
hear were the thoughts of the women closest to her. Havily
wondering if she should purchase the new Ralph Lauren

skirt she saw online and Parisa trying to figure out how to save all the D&R slaves. Alison needing Kerrick to take her home. Fiona pushed past all these thoughts, shutting them down.

Her telepathy moved into the hallway and as she let Jean-Pierre's mind flow over her, his eyes lifted to meet hers. *She is so beautiful,* belle. Mon dieu, *I cannot breathe. Sex. All I can think is sex, wanting to be inside her now. How lovely she is, her lips parting. I want to kiss her.* Ça suffice! *No more.*

He tore his gaze away and started walking up the hall. *Jean-Pierre,* she sent, panicked for some reason. *Don't go. Please don't go! You calm me. Stay with me.* She had no hope that he would hear her. No one ever heard her telepathic messages.

But he froze, his back stiff where she could see it through the blinds. Oh, God, had he heard her? She hadn't meant for him to hear.

Did you really speak to me, Fiona, into my head? I am here, if you want me. I will stay, if you need me. Did you really speak to me?

Yes, she whispered.

He turned around and started moving again, slowly, until he appeared in the doorway facing her. His eyes were wide, stunned. So he had heard her. She wasn't imagining it.

"*Allo,* Kerrick," he said, as the warrior turned in his direction. The word sounded like *Kareek.* He didn't meet Fiona's gaze. "The nurses have been talking. Congratulations to you both. Having wings, quite extraordinary." Oh, the way his accent caressed that last word.

Both Kerrick and Alison shared the news with him in turns, but Fiona couldn't exactly hear them. Instead, she felt strange ripples pass over her, like icy bits of water that left her shivering yet not cold, more like . . . *desire* . . . oh, dear.

After the happy parents finished explaining their latest news, Jean-Pierre moved up beside Kerrick. He met Fiona's gaze. "I was wondering if I could get you something?" he asked.

She met his gaze and for just a moment saw no one else. But she nodded and said the only thing she could think of. "A really hot cup of coffee with sugar and cream, but just little of each. All right?"

He smiled and the heavens seemed to part. He had the most beautiful smile. His eyes seemed to dance with life. His hair was wavy and in parts curly, almost unkempt, but it gave him such a look. Most of his hair was light brown but there was an outer layer of sunny-blond streaks that made her think of summers at the beach. *Charming,* she thought. The man radiated charm in every way.

"*Mais oui.* But yes, of course. I will bring you coffee." Then he smiled, inclined his head, lifted his arm, and vanished.

"Wow," Fiona said, but she wasn't certain if her reaction was to his sudden dematerialization or to *him.*

She became acutely aware that all three women, and one powerful warrior, were watching her, their expressions wary, thoughtful, although Havily smiled.

"What?" Fiona asked.

"Nothing," Havily said, but her smile flowed into a grin. "He's very handsome."

Fiona shrugged. "They all are, even the Militia Warriors." Her fingers plucked at the thin blanket on her bed.

"Well," Alison said. "We're going to take off. Again, welcome home, Fiona. If you need me for anything . . ."

Fiona smiled and nodded. "Thank you, Alison. You've been so very kind."

Alison gave a little wave before she turned away. When she reached Kerrick, he gathered her closer still and kissed her flush on the lips. Together they vanished, still kissing.

Fiona gasped—not because of the fold, but because Kerrick had been kissing her when they left. The tenderness brought tears to her eyes. Her husband had been tender like that, so kind, so protective. He hadn't wanted her to go shopping that day, all by herself. They'd had many disagreements over her independent spirit, but she had felt it absurd not to do her shopping alone. The streets of Boston, in their part of town, had been perfectly safe. That is, until she'd come across what she now knew to be a pair of death vampires, two glorious creatures shrouded in mist that only she'd been able to see.

Her natural confidence, which she now considered her supreme stupidity, had caused her to approach them. Despite all the strange looks various passersby gave her—she must have appeared to be speaking to the air like a madwoman—she had carried on a conversation with the monsters. But how could she have known what they really were? A few moments later, before she knew what was happening, she met Rith for the first time.

She blinked and forced the memories away.

Havily's voice broke through her thoughts. "Alison has suffered for weeks. I'm just so glad she has some answers now."

She glanced from one woman to the next. "Do either of you have children?" she asked.

Parisa shook her head, but Havily couldn't quite hide a sudden stricken look.

"I've caused you pain," Fiona said quietly. "I didn't mean to."

Havily smiled and shook her head. "It was a long time ago. I guess all this trouble with Alison's pregnancy has brought it back to me." She turned to face Fiona. "I had three little girls when I was a young wife on Mortal Earth. They died of scarlet fever, my husband as well, but that was at the turn of the last century. Like I said, it was a long time ago."

Fiona looked away and suddenly her heart hurt, maybe because Havily would understand. "I don't know when my children died. I know nothing about them or their lives, how they grew up, *if* they grew up, whether they married, had children, grandchildren. They were ten and eight when I was taken from Boston. There is something hideous in not knowing, and of course after all these years neither of them would still be living."

"We could find out for you," Parisa said.

Fiona sighed. "I've thought about it, probably one minute

out of two since I arrived at Madame Endelle's palace. Now I'm afraid that I'll have to live it all over again."

Havily moved to the side of the bed opposite Parisa and put her hand on Fiona's, giving her a reassuring squeeze. "Nothing has to be done today. Look, Jean-Pierre is back."

Fiona turned toward the doorway.

And there he was, holding a steaming brown ceramic mug in his hand.

She felt dizzy suddenly, such a strange reaction. Well, he was terribly handsome, and he seemed to always be looking at her, focused on her, which added to her dizziness.

Where had he found such a nice mug in the hospital?

"I went home," he said as though having read her thoughts. *He went home.* That translated into a quick dematerialization, but it also meant he'd made an effort. "It took no time at all. There is also a very nice coffeehouse in Sedona. They were very obliging. I hope the cream and sugar is to your taste."

She drew in a deep breath. Havily's hand slid away from Fiona's and Jean-Pierre took her place beside the bed. Fiona's gaze fell as it so often did to the shape of his lips, the two soft peaks, the full lower lip. Her breathing pattern changed, and she forced her heart to please slow down.

He handed her the mug, handle first, supporting it from the bottom. "Careful. It is quite hot."

She nodded but then she caught the scent of the coffee in the mug—and then the smell of him. It was so very wonderful, very male, and was that just a hint of coffee coming from him?

She now held the mug in her right hand. He was about to pull away when she caught his hand and drew it to her nose. She took an unladylike sniff then buried her nose in his skin. "It's you," she cried. "You smell like coffee. Did you spill some on yourself?" She looked up at him. His lips parted and the scent of him began to roll in heavy waves so that she was surrounded by his scent. The smell of fresh-roasted coffee beans flooded the space.

She released his hand with a gasp.

"I must go," he said, his voice barely a whisper.

"I wish you wouldn't." She felt suddenly desperate to keep him near.

"Actually, Jean-Pierre," Parisa said. "We were hoping that you would stay with Fiona for a little while. I need to speak with Antony, and Havily needs to get back to the admin offices."

"Bien sûr," Jean-Pierre said. He sounded strange, like he was in shock.

Fiona didn't know what prompted her but she lowered her shields and at the same moment shut out the mental exclamations emanating from both Parisa and Havily as they left the room. She focused on Jean-Pierre's thoughts.

Elle sais. Maintenant, elle sais. *She knows. She knows. I can see it in her eyes. I ache for her. I must leave but I cannot make my feet move. I want my mouth on her, on her lips, her breasts, between her legs, sucking . . .*

She drew back and realized her mug-holding wrist was growing lax. She righted the mug before she tipped the steaming contents on her lap. She drew the brown ceramic to her lips. She shored up the shields of her mind. Had she even said good-bye to Havily and Parisa? No. Had she really taken the warrior's hand and pressed it to her face to *smell* him? Yes.

She shook her head then sipped her coffee. She didn't understand what was happening. After a moment, she asked, "Jean-Pierre, what's going on? I . . . I'll confess I just read your thoughts."

"You did? But how? I did not feel you in my head."

She glanced at him over the rim. She sipped the coffee, careful not to burn her tongue. Oh, how to explain? She met his gaze and thought she would drown in the sight of him. He was so beautiful and his eyes were the color of the ocean and his smell an aphrodisiac.

Desire flowed over her now as though some floodgate had been released in her, something she had not felt for a man in decades. The blood tonic she had been forced to drink following each drain had always resulted in a powerful orgasm, but this was different.

From the time she could remember, even as a child, the eldest of eight siblings, she had been a woman of decision. When she saw what she wanted or what needed to be done, she took action. That she had been enslaved for over a hundred years was a circumstance she viewed as a terrible inconvenient breach in her life.

She understood that she would need some form of healing and therapy; that was a given. And as soon as the doctors released her from the hospital, she would get all that set up—not just for herself but for the other slaves as well.

But this was a new world and a new life. She desired this thoughtful warrior who had given her back a precious locket and asked, *Can I bring you something?*

Yes, she would begin her new life now, and she would begin by taking something she wanted.

She set the mug on the table beside her. She knew what she had to do. "You should shut the blinds," she said. "And close the door." She watched his face. His sensual lips were now set in a grim, determined line, even the points flattened . . . a little.

"I should not," he said, lowering his head, his gazing falling to her lips. Had he read her mind?

"Please," she whispered.

She heard the blinds close from across the room. The warrior had not even moved. So much power in this dimension. When the door closed as well, she leaned back on the pillows. "Will you kiss me now, Warrior? Will you let me thank you for carrying me out of that terrible place?" Her breaths were high in her chest. She had not felt the touch of a man in decades, not in over a century, not in this way since the night of her eleventh anniversary.

"I should not kiss you," he said. "But I think I cannot help myself." His voice was hoarse and his gaze was fixed to her lips, but he moved very slowly, a kind of lingering fall as he lowered himself to her, planting his hands on the raised bed to either side of her pillow, his hips suspended just above the side of the bed.

She saw only his mouth but coffee swirled around her in

decadent enticement, until she was dizzy and so warm and wet between her legs that she was ready for sex without even having touched him. How strange was this? How mysterious? How extraordinary?

As she closed her eyes, his lips met hers, and his breath was all coffee and sweetness with an undertaste of maleness that clenched her deep within and made her gasp. She hadn't made love in so long yet here she was, *remembering the how of it,* as though it had been yesterday.

But there was something more, something she didn't understand while he kissed her. She felt a pressure on her mind and knew it was Jean-Pierre's touch. Yet it was more than simple telepathy, because no words formed; he was just there and very present. It was so strange, yet wholly erotic. So erotic that she felt very close with just his lips pressed in a gentle kiss. Her breasts ached and her lips felt swollen and needy. Internally, very deep, she felt movement within, her body trying to pull at something that wasn't there yet, getting ready, so very ready.

Then she realized that she was a touch away from the pinnacle of pleasure. And all he'd done was press those sensual lips against her mouth.

The moment his tongue touched her lips she grabbed his arms above her, opened her eyes, met his and held on. She cried out, stunned because of what was happening to her. The orgasm was a quick ride over her tender flesh, and a pulsing inside that went on and on. She panted against his mouth.

He drew back, just a few inches. His eyes flared, "Are you—?"

She nodded.

"Mon dieu," he whispered.

When the spasms ceased she lay back against the bed, staring up at him. Her hands still gripped his arms. She couldn't seem to let go of him. She didn't want to let go. "How did you do that?"

He shook his head and smiled that beautiful smile of his. "Well, I am French—"

* * *

Jean-Pierre savored the hands still gripping his arms, the swollen lips, the flush on Fiona's cheeks, the startled surprise in her eyes. So his woman, who was not *his woman,* had just fallen into *le petit mort,* the little death, a beautiful climax. *Mon dieu.*

She was lovely, a great beauty with hair like dark rich wood, deep brown with glints of auburn. It hung almost to her elbows in elegant waves. But her eyes, a silver-blue like fine silk, now glittered with passion. Her nose was straight, very pretty, her cheeks round, high, and lovely. Her jaw was a smooth line.

Her complexion was very light, almost porcelain, but then she had been badly used, her blood taken from her, her life nearly stolen from her just a few days ago. There would be more color soon, although the blush on her cheeks just now was exquisite.

He smiled down at her. He wanted to kiss her again, but it seemed redundant.

She smiled in return, her row of even teeth returning. His heart swelled in his chest. Finally, she released his arms and he drew back. But he didn't move very far away.

Her gaze shifted to the window suddenly and she frowned.

"What is it?" He turned to look outside as well.

"I thought I saw something, a shimmering out there on the lawn."

A shape materialized. At first, Jean-Pierre couldn't make it out but after a moment, he realized he was looking at the back of Medichi, in kilted battle gear. Yes, Medichi, although what was he doing out on the lawn? He'd just been in the hallway talking to Colonel Seriffe, but hadn't he been wearing jeans?

The hairs on his neck lifted and he rose upright.

"What is it?" Fiona asked. "You seem tense all of a sudden. Is something wrong?"

He could not keep his gaze from the sight of Medichi on the lawn. *Oui,* something was wrong.

He glanced at Fiona. "Please excuse me. I need to speak to one of my warrior brothers. This is not right."

"Of course," she whispered.

He did not want to leave her. The urge to remain beside her, to have his sword in his hand as he watched over her, was profound. But he had to go.

He took a deep breath and forced himself to move.

Once in the hall, the hairs rose again: Medichi was still in the hall talking to Seriffe, and yes, he wore his jeans. So what was that on the lawn? Jean-Pierre called sharply, "Medichi, where is your woman?"

He frowned. "What? Parisa? I'm not sure. He looked around. I think she was headed toward the lobby with Havily."

"Find her at once. Something is wrong. I saw you just now on the front lawn."

"You what—?"

He shook his head. "I do not know what I was looking at, because here you are."

Medichi looked the opposite direction. "Hologram," he cried. He did not say a word to Colonel Seriffe but began to run.

Jean-Pierre, his instincts burning, hurried back to Fiona's bedside. He moved between her bed and the window.

And yes, he folded his sword into his hand and stared at what must be an imposter—or a dreaded hologram—out on the lawn.

Parisa left the hospital by the front sliders because she saw Antony halfway down the greenbelt, his hands on his hips. He had changed into kilted battle gear and looked around as if trying to figure something out.

"Antony," she called to him. "What are you doing?"

He turned to face her and waved her forward.

Strange.

She had an appointment in half an hour with the officer in charge of the Militia Warrior Training Camps, Female Division, and she didn't want to be late. She decided to work on her folding skills instead of just walking to Antony's position.

But as she thought the thought and entered nether-space, she could have sworn she heard Antony behind her crying out, "Noooo!"

As she touched down, another thought skidded through her mind—where were the scars on Antony's back?

She blinked at "Antony," who wasn't smiling and who looked *odd*. The hairs on the nape of her neck rose. No. Oh, no.

She lifted her arm to fold, but she wasn't fast enough. "Antony" smiled and put his hand on her shoulder before she could think the thought. The image of her warrior dissolved before her eyes. Rith appeared, smiling, a dark light in his eye.

He had deceived her again and just like that she was flying through nether-space, at his mercy. She had no time to respond and she felt like such a fool as she landed hard, stumbled, and fell to a hard, dusty terra-cotta floor.

She tried to rise but couldn't. A powerful field held her pinned down.

The air barely moved through the stuffy, dark building. She looked around. A single torch burned at the far end. The walls were also terra-cotta in color and carved with symbols she didn't recognize.

She felt a slight breeze, but Rith was nowhere to be seen.

"Parisa." Antony's voice drew her to lift her head up. The field barely allowed her to do that. She could hardly see him from her position on the floor. But there he was, standing with his hands pushing at an unseen barrier.

"Did you trace after me?" she asked. Dust got in her nose, and she sneezed.

He nodded.

"Oh, God, what have I done?" she cried.

And where was Rith?

Medichi's instincts had overrun his good sense. A vampire, capable of appearing in the form of any other Second Earth ascender, would have more plans in place than just taking Parisa away again.

So he'd followed a trace that in previous encounters *had been blocked*. And now he was trapped. He stood in the middle of what looked like some kind of religious shrine. And just like Parisa, he was boxed in by a preternatural field.

Air movement made him automatically flex his wrist as he attempted to draw his sword into his hand, but—surprise—it didn't work. In the distance, in an adjoining room perhaps, he heard the rattle of a cart. At that moment, he knew fear, the kind that drew his stomach into a knot.

The air in the chamber was stifling—the smell of a room that hadn't had a window opened in *years*. He glanced around. Centuries maybe.

A single torch burned at the far end of the space. An opening led to another part of whatever hell this was.

"I can't move," Parisa called out, but she coughed again and dust billowed up around her.

"Lie still." Was that the best he could do? Tell his woman to lie still?

He spent the next several minutes testing the shield around him. He'd seen this kind of shielding before. Alison had been able to create it during her one-on-one arena battle with Leto. This was not one of Medichi's gifts, but apparently Rith excelled at it.

He mentally pushed against every boundary but found the composition impenetrable.

A man appeared at the open doorway near the torch. He was pushing a cart that carried medical equipment. He wore a mask and green scrubs.

Medichi felt his heart give way as he recognized the tubing. "No," he shouted, but the man, with dark skin and Asian features, ignored him.

The cart stopped beside Parisa.

Medichi battled the field, punching at it, throwing himself against the invisible wall. He aimed high, he aimed low. He levitated but the swift movement caused him to hit his head on the top of the shield and he fell onto the floor . . . hard.

The man knelt beside Parisa, waved his hand, then propped

her up to a reclining position. The field seemed designed to restrain Parisa exclusively, because the man had no trouble reaching her. He could do whatever the hell he wanted. He had control over her, but she couldn't move, even if he shifted her position.

He elevated Parisa's arm and strapped it down to a flat board. He inserted a needle attached to the tubing, and immediately the blood started to flow.

Medichi shouted but got no reaction at all.

Parisa stared at her arm for a long moment. She tried to wiggle, to move, but couldn't do anything. Her beautiful creamy complexion was covered in orange dust. Her dark hair had a fine coating as well.

After a moment, as the first bag filled up and the man clamped the tube in order to change out the bags, tears began to stream down her face. "No," she cried. "No, no, no." Only then did her gaze turn to Medichi.

In a terrible hard flash, he traveled back thirteen centuries, only this time the blood was draining from between his woman's legs because she'd been raped.

Medichi blinked, trying to clear the images but couldn't. He couldn't meet Parisa's gaze because he didn't even see her. He just saw his wife's pleading expression as life drained out of her, the white cotton gown torn, bloodstained, her breasts bared to the room.

How the hell was he back here *again,* after all this time?

He sank to the floor, his knees bent, his arms clasped around his legs.

How the fuck had he ended up here . . . again?

He closed his eyes and drew a long deep breath through his nostrils. He'd failed Parisa as he'd failed his wife and even though his mind understood that life couldn't always be controlled, what stupidity of his had brought him back here? This couldn't be an accident that he sat on this floor powerless to help the woman he loved.

Death is a mirror.

—**Collected Proverbs,** Beatrice of Fourth

CHAPTER 22

Parisa had been counting. The med tech was on the third bag. How many bags of blood could the human body supply? Already she was feeling funny, a little faint, light-headed, even . . . happy. She had heard euphoria was a sign of blood loss.

The roll of another set of wheels on terra-cotta sounded behind her. She craned her neck to look. A second cart approached. This time a woman arrived wearing blue scrubs and a mask, yelling in a foreign tongue. The med tech sat back on his heels and flipped her off.

The rattling of her cart got really loud, and the next thing Parisa knew her other arm was being strapped down to another board. But a bag of blood, not her own, hung from the side of the cart. The needle punctured her arm. The blood flowed . . . into her. Thank God.

She looked from one arm to the next, her mind refusing to make sense of what was happening to her. Only when a third technician entered with a defibrillator did the pieces of the puzzle finally fit.

Images raced through her head of seeing Fiona drained, filled, shocked. Drained, filled, shocked. A century of death and resurrection. A century of seeing other women come and go, giving blood one last time and unable to make the journey back.

This couldn't be happening. Even though she knew that death vampires hunted mortals and ascenders alike, she had thought herself safe because she was ascended. Wrong.

What had brought her here to this place? Because she'd seen Antony on the stretch of lawn in front of the hospital? Because she'd trusted him? Because she'd been too quick to act?

She blinked. She'd started to feel so safe and in control of her life. She'd started to believe that all would be well. She'd been laughing with the other women, powerful women, in Fiona's hospital room. She'd plotted her course. She would go to the training camps and become a warrior, make a difference in the war.

She stared at Antony, sitting on the floor with his arms clasped around his knees, his jeans now dusty. What had he said to her? *You keep yourself apart.*

She'd started to change that, she really had, or thought she had. But as her mind drifted over her decision to enter the training camps she realized she would be learning skills but probably not encouraging friendships. Her body would become tough and she'd learn martial arts and the ability to defend herself, to make use of the sword and dagger and the ability to attack the enemy. She'd learn major flight skills as well.

But that was all external activity and skill-acquiring.

It came to her in the strangest flash that all she'd be doing is switching one controlled world for another. The new world just involved making war. The previous one involved reading and shelving books, keeping her world tight and controlled. But there was something very tight and orderly about a library, not unlike the military.

She would have no real friends, no real connections, not even a true relationship with Antony.

Air movement off to her right, just beyond the first tech, brought her gaze to . . . Rith. He smiled. "This is where you always belonged. Keeping you like a beloved pet in Burma sickened me every day. Now you no longer fill the future streams. Your ribbon has disappeared." He laughed. "You must thank me, you know. The Commander suggested you be removed from this world . . . permanently. Dear Parisa, there was a time when I wished for that as well but then a new plan occurred to me, a more complete plan." He waved his hand over the medical equipment.

"I don't want this," she screamed. She tried to lift even one of her arms but both were secured in place. "I'd rather be dead."

He shrugged. "I believe that is your choice. Didn't Fiona tell you it's a matter of will?"

"Why do you hate me so much?" she asked.

"Because *he* favored you."

"He? As in Commander Greaves? The one who wants me dead?" She couldn't have heard him right. He was making no sense.

Rith nodded. "He forged a link with you, remember?"

Enlightenment dawned. Rith was jealous. "You call that *favoring* me?"

"What else? I'd seen you in the future streams and I told him you needed to be destroyed, but he wouldn't have it. He wanted to make use of you. Only now, after his voyeur-link proved ineffectual and you succeeded in taking some of my blood donors, has he has decided you must die.

"But your service here is a much more fitting plan. Your blood will command an excellent price on the market."

She didn't understand. "Why?"

A black brow rose. "I keep forgetting that you aren't well versed in our world yet. The drinking of dying blood always relates back to the mortal or ascender whose blood is being imbibed. You're very powerful, you're the mortal-with-wings, as you will always be known, and your blood will have exceptional qualities that in turn will enhance the powers of the recipient. The more powerful that recipient, the greater the benefits of the donor blood. Do you understand?"

Since her heart had started to sink, she could only dip her chin. Oh, God.

He laughed again, a hollow sound in the dim light. He was standing with his hands clasped behind his back, his expression calm, almost disinterested. "But I suppose none of this was truly your fault. You could not help the level of your power, and unfortunately Commander Greaves's flaw is his desire to flaunt his victories. He truly enjoyed having possession of you and letting all his allies know.

"I am not encumbered by such a flaw. My purpose in life is but to serve him." He looked away from her as he spoke, as though talking only to himself. He sighed. "Life can be cruel in a great variety of ways. His will must be my will, in all things." He shifted his gaze back to her, his stare cold and quite indifferent.

His logic was so perverted, his intentions so vile, that a new kind of horror gripped her chest making it hard to breathe. Rith had no intention of letting her live for very long, despite his claim that he intended to profit from her blood. His purpose was deeper, more nefarious. He wanted to punish her because she had been "favored." No doubt when he was satisfied, he would simply let her die.

"What of Warrior Medichi?" she asked.

His gaze flicked in Antony's direction, then returned to her. "He will be executed at the hour Greaves wishes. It will not be long."

He lifted his arm and vanished.

Dizziness drifted through her mind yet she felt strangely relaxed, even sleepy. What bag was the tech filling now? Four? Five?

Medichi had remained silent. There was no point in shouting at a man who had him locked in a preternatural cage of energy.

He had to figure this out.

He sat on the floor, his arms still slung around his knees, his eyes closed.

When Rith had appeared, all he'd wanted to do was rage at him but what good would that have done? Rith held all the cards and right now Medichi needed to think.

He sent a telepathic cry for help out to Endelle. If anyone could hear him, she could. But his thoughts hit a shield and bounced back to him, a lumbering sensation that rolled through his head. Another shield, another dome of mist or two, Rith's specialty.

He had no hope of finding Endelle or one of his warrior brothers or of being found, not shielded like this, not caught below the mist. So how the hell was he supposed to get out of here, Parisa with him?

He doubted that even a telepathic link would work in this environment.

He opened his eyes and looked at Parisa. She lay quietly now, her eyes closed. He scooted closer, to the point that the field stopped him. He was only three feet away from her, three feet and completely impotent.

The blood leaving her arm filled the bag swiftly. The blood entering her body moved at maybe a third of the pace, enough room to allow for death. Of course. She had to die in order to produce *dying blood.* Then be brought back to life to sustain Greaves's operation. All twenty-one facilities around the world did indeed have to be found and destroyed.

But that was a job for the future.

He rose to his feet and started to pace what amounted to his cell.

Antony, Parisa sent out to him. He paced to the end of the narrow shield and pressed himself against the unyielding boundary.

I'm here, he sent. *I'm trying to figure this out. There has to be a way.*

I'm sorry, she said. She opened her eyes, barely.

For what? he cried within her mind—too strongly, because she winced.

I was reckless and stubborn. I thought I understood what

I could do on Second Earth to help, to make a difference, to become a warrior like you. I was fooling myself.

You wanted to serve in the Militia. It's an honorable goal. Now he was defending her choices?

But I hadn't changed anything, not really. I hadn't changed. Her voice drifted away. What did she mean?

He felt panicky. He could feel her leaving him. *Parisa,* he called to her. His heart thumped in his chest. Oh, God. Oh, God. The techs were moving around now in choreographed precision. They'd done this before.

"What are you doing to her!" he shouted. He already knew but the feeling of impotence crawled over every inch of his skin like a sudden burning. Shouting was all he could do.

The techs ignored him.

He couldn't hold the rage back. He paced the small five-foot length of the shielded box in which he was trapped. He roared at the ceiling at the knowledge that his woman was being drained for her dying blood so that she could feed a thousand addicted death vampires and that she might or might not make it back to him.

That last thought brought him to the dusty brick floor. His knees banged hard but the physical pain was the least of what he was feeling. He lifted his hands to the heavens and roared long and loud.

He felt her die.

He felt her die.

The roaring changed to a keening sound and he wrapped his arms around his chest and rocked back and forth. What had he done? What had he done?

Even if she made it back, what could he do for her? For himself?

He was trapped. They were both trapped.

And there wasn't a damn thing he could do.

Medichi came to an awareness that his pattern of keeping a safe emotional distance from the rest of the world, and of using brute strength to get a job done, wasn't enough in this situation. He thought it a poetic piece of irony that he was separated from Parisa by two powerful force fields.

He'd lived unto himself, not making connections for thirteen centuries for fear of getting too close to anyone again and risking the pain of loss should they die. When he ascended and experienced his initial onset of power, he felt invincible as he exacted his revenge.

Invited into the Warriors of the Blood soon after, he'd taken on the new mantle. He had felt born again, a new creature birthed in blood and power. He was good at making war, at fighting and killing death vampires, and the rest of the warriors were the same. They were a band of brothers, eight strong.

But with all that power, here he stood, trapped and separated from Parisa, unable to help her or himself. He served as her Guardian of Ascension. He was supposed to protect her, but he couldn't. He couldn't protect her because he'd kept his distance. When he spoke of completing the *breh-hedden* it had never been about caring for her. No, he'd spoken in practical terms, that the natural bonding that occurred would make it possible to know where she was at all times, to feel what she felt, and to come to her aid with a mere whispered thought. Both Kerrick and Marcus could do this as a result of completing the *breh-hedden* with their mates.

But he had never wanted the connection and maybe for that reason she had so easily separated herself from him, moved to the guest room where she'd spent the night.

Now he was paying for it, paying for all the ways he'd held back from her. Would she have been more inclined to complete the *breh-hedden* if he had just opened his heart to her, really opened his heart, loved her, made her feel safe, that he would never leave her, walk out on her as her fiancé once had?

The defibrillator wound up, a scream in the dim torchlight. The female tech called out. Hands flew back. There was a loud thump, then another and another. His stomach turned.

Live, he shouted within Parisa's mind. *Live, dammit.* What would he do if she died? How could he live without her?

The defibrillator cried shrilly again. Another shout. Another thump. Parisa's body jerked against the dusty floor. Another dusty cloud drifted around her.

Live, he sent. *Live, live, live, live.* The chant grew in his mind, expanded and grew until at last her chest rose, she drew a breath, and one of the techs put a stethoscope over her heart.

When the pair leaned back and started tending once more to their equipment, when he saw Parisa's chest rise and fall in the dim light even if her eyes didn't open, only then did he draw a breath of his own.

He released a heavy groan. He rocked some more.

Parisa opened her eyes. Her chest hurt. She felt as though she'd had big rocks thrown at her rib cage, one after the other, for about a year. She saw the green scrubs of the male tech. He was packing up. His job was done.

She shifted her head to the other side. The woman, with her sour black eyes and furrowed brow, met her gaze for a split second then looked away. She, too, was packing up her supplies, impatient to be going.

So, she'd made it back.

She felt ill. Her chest really hurt and she was so dizzy. She wanted to sleep but something was left undone.

Her gaze moved around the room.

There. Opposite her. *Antony,* she whispered softly in her mind. She couldn't have opened her mouth to speak if she'd wanted to.

I'm here, he sent.

She had trouble seeing him. She squinted. Antony's dark eyes glittered in the dim torchlight. He looked angry.

Sleep, he sent.

Her eyes closed. *Yes.*

When Parisa awoke the second time, she had no way of knowing how long she had slept. The room was now pitch black, the torchlight having gone out. She thought it fitting. Why waste light on slaves?

She sighed. She listened hard. She heard Medichi breathing,

long and regular. He was asleep. She had a moment of panic and almost spoke aloud to wake him then she thought better of it. Time to think, to make sense of her new reality, to let him rest, to figure this out. She had to get out of here. She couldn't let this be the end and she didn't want Antony to die because she'd allowed Rith to trick her . . . again.

From the first time she'd mounted her wings, from the time she'd felt that strange tingling in a V down her back, her life had been an odd series of experiences, like scattered glass pieces. She'd kept trying to put those bits together into a picture, but before she had time to finish, something would knock all the pieces out of the frame. She'd have to begin again, just like now.

This time, the glass pieces had arranged themselves according to Rith's orchestrated pattern and she'd become something horrible, something she had never thought she would be—a blood slave.

The question was, what could she do about it?

Her analytical mind kicked into high gear. She was flat on her back, on a filthy, dusty floor, in a room without light of any kind. She had no idea where she was, which part of the world she was in, or even whether she was on Mortal or Second Earth.

At least both arms were free now, free to move the few inches up. She touched the field. For some reason, of all the things that had happened to her, feeling this field, which kept her imprisoned *again,* sent fury writhing through her, compressing her chest, swelling her neck, causing her throat to seize, especially since she wanted to scream but she wouldn't, not when Antony needed his sleep.

After a long moment, when her heart had calmed back down, she drew deep calming breaths. It was time to think, not to freak out.

She had power, a lot of power, that much she understood. She had thrown a hand-blast at Endelle before she had even ascended, without even knowing what a hand-blast was. She had sent the Supreme High Administrator of all Second Earth flying over and behind her desk. She had done that.

All her life she had felt powerless. Now she had an abundance of it yet was still trapped. What on earth did this mean?

Something needed to change, something she didn't understand, not yet.

She drew more deep breaths, one after the other. From what she understood, Alison had also ascended with a phenomenal amount of power, and she had created similar restraining energy fields during her arena battle with Leto.

Huh. Parisa began pushing at the field over her. She held her palm flat and released a small pulse of energy, a tiny hand-blast. Thank God she hadn't gone full-bore because the energy caught on the field and traveled like lightning in a thousand directions at once above her, leaving her covered with small burns. She could smell singed fabric as well.

Okay, no hand-blasts.

She breathed some more, one breath then another.

She recalled being in Fiona's hospital room with Havily and Alison. A sisterhood.

Never had Parisa felt as close to other women as in that moment. Their sufferings, their shared power, their difficulty with mate-bonding had given them much in common.

As a child, she had never stayed in one place long enough to develop friendships, real friendships. She had always been the outsider, never quite fitting in, always the object of jealousy in the friendship twosomes that dominated schoolyards. Having boyfriends during those years had been equally impossible.

Her life had been colored, shaped, pummeled by her early experiences and her parents had been just flighty enough that they hadn't recognized or understood her suffering, or that her development was being warped. They had shared a love of moving around and experiencing new places but she had been left to tag along without either of her parents recognizing there might be repercussions.

She had fallen into a pattern of survival that had always required that she remain . . . *aloof.* And yes, *inaccessible.*

She felt defensive suddenly because the person she'd grown up to be wasn't her fault. She wanted to wrap her arms around her chest but the field wouldn't allow it. In this hateful captivity, she couldn't even comfort herself.

There had to be some reason why she was stuck here. Something she needed to learn. She was convinced that even the worst situations could provide some opportunities for self-knowledge and growth.

God help her.

Tears trickled down the sides of her face. She had done her best, she truly had, to make the most of her life. She felt she had succeeded admirably in terms of her career. On Mortal Earth, she had loved being a librarian. Now, here she was in another dimension with plenty of power but apparently not the ability to access it in a way that would allow her to free herself or Antony.

Again her thoughts returned to Fiona's hospital room and to that feeling of *belonging*. Then she'd seen Antony—who was really Rith—on the greenbelt.

Being grouped around the bed, she'd felt like she belonged.

But running then folding to Antony had been so rash, so separate from the group, so foolish.

She knew better. That's what popped into her head. She knew the level of Rith's power. Why had she run out onto the lawn, folding to the false Antony, without so much as a whisper of anxiety?

At the very least, *at the very least,* she should have looked around, even asked Havily to accompany her outside. Militia Warriors had surrounded the building, protecting those inside, but she had hurried out, separated herself from the group, without a single thought. She had been so used to making decisions on her own behalf for so long, that it hadn't even occurred to her in that split-second before she folded to Antony that she ought to be careful about leaving the security of the building.

Her body stilled as her thoughts heated up, as the truth of what she was thinking sank into her bones. Maybe independence was a wonderful attribute, but what had her level of independence, her *extreme* of independence actually won her?

She rocked her head back and forth. What had it won her? Well, it was pretty obvious, since she was trapped beneath a field of energy with no way out and that she'd ended up in Rith's clutches again.

Her situation suddenly seemed fully of irony. That which she had relied on for so long was in this moment her complete undoing, and not just hers, but the undoing of the man trapped in a separate field opposite her. He had followed her to try and save her and now he was trapped as well and destined to be executed on Greaves's whim.

Holy shit. This was all her fault.

If she had it to do over again, what would she do? She would have paused. At the very least she would have waited to see why Antony was out there. She would have contacted him telepathically. She would have consulted with ascenders who had been on Second Earth a helluva lot longer than her own sweet self.

Her thoughts took a leap, an important one. Could she turn to the group now? Could she consult with others, say, *with Endelle,* to help her get out of this fix? Did she have enough power to do that?

Maybe.

Air whooshed into her lungs. She opened her voyeur's window and thought of Endelle. The next moment there she was in one of the palace rotundas, surrounded by all the Warriors of the Blood.

She was about to attempt a communication with Endelle when she heard Thorne cry out, "We have to assemble the army at once, Endelle. For fuck's sake, we don't have a choice. Greaves has just folded another five thousand Militia Warriors and another hundred death vampires to the South Rim."

Parisa faltered and her window wavered, a preternatural form of stumbling. Greaves was attacking? The South Rim was at the Grand Canyon. He was bringing an army to Arizona to attack Endelle's forces? She wasn't sure, but she thought her situation may have just gotten worse.

Oh, *whatever.*

And here she was with one of their best warriors locked up behind an impenetrable field.

Parisa moved her window close to Madame Endelle.

Hey, boss lady, she sent. She wasn't about to try for subtlety. *Parisa here. Are you registering this telepathy?*

Endelle turned to face her off her left shoulder. She stared straight into Parisa's window and in that moment the Supreme High Administrator opened her own voyeur's window and met her face to face. It was the weirdest sensation, like two lap-tops facing each other.

Well, what do you know. She'd done it.

Endelle turned to the warriors. "I've got Parisa in my voyeur window. Hang tight, men."

Parisa heard the shouting and whoops of excitement behind Endelle, but Her Supremeness called out, "Shut the fuck up! Let me talk to her." She turned back to Parisa, *Okay, so where the hell are you, ascender?*

Trapped in some kind of temple beneath an energy field. Antony is with me trapped under a separate field.

I'm going to pan back. Don't fucking move.

Endelle did just as she said. Parisa watched her window move away from her.

It's pitch black, the Supreme High Administrator shouted, which of course was like knives through Parisa's head, but hey, she'd made contact. Endelle could shout all she wanted. *I can't see a fucking thing.*

No shit, Parisa responded. *Can you get a fix on me, on Antony? Can you fold us the hell out of here?*

Endelle closed her eyes but after a moment opened them. *No can do.*

Can you tell me how to get out of these fields then?

Endelle shook her head. *Not my power. Let me bring Alison in.* "Kerrick," she called out. "Get Alison over here, on the double."

"You got it."

Parisa panned back and watched Kerrick whip his phone to his ear. She looked from one warrior to the next. They looked wrecked, stunned, and a little confused probably because she'd made contact and because, oh, yeah, Greaves was planning what sounded like a major offensive at the Grand Canyon. She also recognized Colonel Seriffe, head of the Militia Warriors.

Thorne drew a little closer. "What the hell is going on, Endelle?"

"Parisa and Medichi are trapped somewhere beneath energy fields, the kind Alison created in the arena battle. So, yeah, they're alive." More shouting went up, quieter, but Endelle scowled at her warriors. "Celebrate later. We're in trouble here. Energy fields. Got it?"

The boys settled down.

Parisa saw a shimmering beside Endelle, then Alison came into view. A few seconds of explanation and Endelle put her hand on Alison's forehead, which allowed the powerful ascender to see Parisa, window-to-window. She made eye contact with Parisa.

An energy field? Alison sent.

Yep. I'm flat on the floor. I can't even lift my arms up. How do I get out of this? I haven't tried to work with energy fields before but I thought maybe since I could throw a hand-blast and dematerialize . . .

Right, Alison sent. She took a deep breath. *The first time I erected a field, I just thought the thought. And you're right, it's not unlike folding or throwing a hand-blast, just another aspect of power.*

This wasn't very helpful. Alison looked behind her. Parisa panned back to see what Alison was seeing. The warriors were talking.

Oh, dear God, Alison murmured inside Parisa's head.

What? What's going on?

Have you heard this stuff about Greaves and his army?

Yes, that he's gathering his troops at the Grand Canyon.

He's challenged Endelle to a battle. Thorne just said that Stannett checked in earlier and said unless there was some kind of miracle, she'd lose today.

Parisa's heart sank. She needed her own miracle to stay alive and to keep Antony alive, but she needed to let Endelle and Alison go right now so that they could work on this much bigger issue. She searched through her mind and had a thought. *Alison, I know you need to leave, but is there a chance you could download your "field" abilities straight into my head? I can take it. I know I can because I've had Endelle in my head and Antony as well. Will you do that for me?*

Alison turned back to look at her.

Endelle butted in. *Of course she'll do it but hurry the fuck up. Get yourself out of that hellhole and would you please fucking complete the* breh-hedden*?*

Alison didn't miss a beat. *Ignore her, Parisa. Just take your situation one step at a time, okay? Are you ready?*

Yes. Do it.

The images of the arena battle from seven months ago began to flow through Parisa's mind. She knew enough about taking someone else's memories to keep her shields down. She saw the battle with Leto in an instant replay: the cutting off of his arm, the reversal of the time-pocket, Leto's counterattack, then Alison erecting the energy field, effectively trapping the warrior on the black mats of the battle zone.

It was over in seconds.

Parisa blinked into the pitch black for one, two, three seconds. She smiled. *Thanks, Alison. I think I've got it. Tell the warriors I'll do my best to bring Antony home.*

You go, girl.

Parisa closed her voyeur's window.

You go, girl. Was there a sweeter, more sisterly thing Alison could have said?

Parisa closed her eyes and let Alison's memories flow once more, feeling exactly how Alison had built the field. But could it be done in reverse and with someone else's energy creation?

She turned her hand palm up and held her hand against the field. Removing a field meant taking the energy in, not releasing it. But it was Rith's energy. Could you take someone else's energy into your body?

She almost thought the thought, but held back. Maybe some sort of "ground" would help. She planted the fingertips of her left hand onto the terra-cotta bricks next to her just in case the energy needed someplace else to go.

She thought the thought and as though she'd opened a valve, the energy started flowing into her hand in a terrible numbing sensation. Just as she'd expected, it traveled up her arm, across her shoulder, her chest, to her opposite shoulder, down her left arm, and began to flow through her fingertips and into the bricks.

It took only a matter of seconds but by the time she was done she was panting and her chest hurt. Too much energy, too soon after being brought back to life with those fucking defibrillator paddles.

She reached up a weary hand—and *no more field*. The sudden relief eased the physical pain.

But she still couldn't see a damn thing despite her preternatural vision. Apparently the eyes needed some light to work with.

She crawled on her knees in the direction of Antony's strong, even breathing. At least the warrior had gotten some sleep.

When she reached the field around him, she groaned. It was much larger than hers—more a jail cell than a coffin. She thought maybe a different pathway would help, so she stood up, put her left hand on the field, and kicked off her shoes.

She refused to think about how uncomfortable this was going to be. Instead, she just let the energy flow. She tensed then relaxed and realized her decision had been a good one. The energy moved straight down her left side, missing her heart altogether.

When the last of it was gone she called Antony's name.

I searched for you
In the wilderness
I called your name at the darkest hour
I broke every promise
And shattered the unknown
I called your name when my heart was open
And you were there, Beloved,
You were there.

—*Collected Poems,* Beatrice of Fourth

CHAPTER 23

Medichi awoke to the sweetest sound in the world—Parisa speaking his name.

"Parisa? You sound so close, but I can't see you."

"I didn't want to startle you."

She was closer now, closer than she should be, like really close. Was he dreaming? He sat up then gained his feet. He put his hands out in front of him. "Where are you?"

"Right here. I . . . well, how do I say this . . . I contacted Endelle through our mutual voyeur windows. She brought in Alison, who sent me a nice little download all about energy fields. They're gone. The fields are gone."

Relief washed through him like a flash flood during a monsoon storm. His knees buckled but he caught himself.

"You're kidding" came out of his mouth. "I mean, that's fantastic." He grabbed for her and the next moment she was in his arms and flat against his chest, stuck to him like a wet autumn leaf. A series of sobs bounced her beautiful breasts against his. "It's okay," he said. "It's okay. You did great. It's okay. I can't believe it. You're amazing."

She laughed and cried but after a moment she took a deep breath. She pulled back but only far enough so that her hair brushed his chin. His nose started itching, and a second later he sneezed.

"I'm covered in that awful dust. Antony, what do we do now?"

Just as the words left her mouth, a distant light flicked on and Rith's voice echoed across the room. "Ready for the next round, my dear?" The rattling of wheels sounded at the same time.

The field was gone. Was it possible he could fold? Would it be this simple?

One thing was for sure, he wasn't going to wait around to find out.

Medichi clutched her close. Just as Rith appeared in the doorway, he thought the thought. The next moment he was holding Parisa in his arms at the foot of his own bed.

Holy shit, they'd done it!

"Did we actually make it out?" she asked.

"Yes. We did." He looked down at her, still clutching her hard against him, afraid she would vanish straight out of his arms.

"What if he follows your trace?"

"He tried that once before, and I almost had his head. Remember, he's not a warrior. He'd never be that foolish to come here again although I'd love for him to try."

She blinked up at him. "Antony, we did it."

He nodded, still stunned. "But how did you come up with using the voyeur window?"

At that her expression softened. "I figured something out: I don't have to go my own path alone anymore. I got us into this mess by chasing Rith's illusion outside the hospital because all my life I've acted independent of everyone. I had to let that thinking go, to think differently. And the moment I had that thought, I remembered that Endelle also had a voyeur's window. And now here we are."

He kissed her hard on the lips and she responded with a low cry in her throat as she threw her arms around his neck. His hand drifted low and caught her buttocks in his hand. He pressed her hard against him.

After a moment, she drew back. "Oh, God, I almost forgot."

"Why the frown? What's wrong?" He had the worst feeling.

"Greaves is mounting an attack. He's been amassing his forces on the South Rim of the Grand Canyon."

"Shit. Oh, shit. I've got to get over there."

She grew very still as he pushed her away. He reached for his phone then caught sight of Parisa's expression. "What's wrong?"

She shook her head. "I'm not sure." She put her fist between her breasts. "Antony, be careful right now. Be careful of the choice you make."

"What are you talking about?"

"I was so sure you were on the lawn that I rushed into harm's way without knowing it. I realize there's a battle taking shape, but don't rush. I'm here with you now. Take a moment to think what it is you really need to do, what perhaps you and I need to do . . . together."

He lowered the phone to his side and stared at her. "Something has changed for you, hasn't it?"

She smiled, a very soft warm smile. "Yes, it has. I'm willing to do things I wasn't so willing to do a few hours ago."

He knew she referred to the *breh-hedden*. A shiver crossed over his shoulders. "Parisa," he said softly.

"Just think about it, then make your call. I'm going to take a shower, here, in your bedroom."

"Okay." He lifted the phone and thumbed. "Hey, Jeannie, can you—"

"Patching you through to Thorne."

Yeah, they were in deep shit for Jeannie not even to greet him.

"Give," Thorne's gravel voice barked at him.

"We're out."

A long silence, then, "How?"

He glanced at Parisa who stood next to the shower attempting, not altogether successfully, to fold off her clothes. Her shirt hung off one arm. Not bad for a beginner. The terracotta dust clung to her hair, her arms, her pants.

"Parisa used Alison's memories about field construction and somehow disrupted the fields."

Thorne whistled. "That's one boatload of power but can you hold on for a second?"

Medichi frowned. "Sure."

Thorne's phone went dead. What the fuck? After a moment he came back online. "We have a sitch over here at the palace but Endelle said she wants the two of you to take some recoup time then check back in, maybe an hour or two. Can you do that?"

Two minutes ago, Medichi would have argued with Thorne. But two minutes ago, Parisa had seemed so very different. *Willing.*

"We can do that," he said.

"You know what's going on?"

"Parisa told me."

"And you're not gonna bust my balls about this order?"

Medichi smiled. "Nope."

"Well, fuck me. I'll be in touch." The line went dead.

He glanced in the direction of the bathroom. steam billowed from the shower.

He swallowed because right now his woman had to be naked. Her pants were hanging from the mirror frame, the empty mirror frame. Jesus, he really needed to get that replaced.

When the steam started carrying a light whiff of tangerine, his body responded. He started to pace.

He glanced at the ceiling, looked into the bathroom, and maybe it wouldn't make a damn bit of difference but he created a shallow dome of mist inside both rooms.

"That's so pretty, Antony. I don't think I've seen your mist before. You know, it has almost a golden hue."

For whatever reason the very feminine tone of her voice,

and the compliment she'd just delivered, brought a rush of affection, even love, flowing through his chest in a warm wave. He put his hand between his pecs and worked at breathing for a good long minute.

He understood something in this moment—he loved this woman. He loved her. *He loved her.* He loved being with her and he especially loved that even though she'd just been through one helluva trauma, she could take her shower and say nice things about his mist.

His heart swelled, pushing his ribs and chest out and out until the whole damn thing broke, a breach in a dam, and love poured from him, a rushing river full of life.

He was dizzy and struggled to keep his balance, then he fell. He fell onto the Oriental rug. He rolled onto his back, his cheeks rising, his lips curved. He must have looked like an idiot and he knew terra-cotta dust was getting on his fine antique carpet but who the hell cared?

Love had come to him, had found him, had battered the walls of his heart and his life and had pushed through despite his unwillingness to open himself. He had felt protected, and maybe a little self-righteous being part of the Warriors of the Blood. He'd committed to them, to his brothers, and he'd pretended that this made him all that a man ever really needed to be; powerful, in control, master of his world, a warrior.

His gaze became focused on the coffer beams overhead, the ones burned with his wife's poem. Directly above him, the final phrase, *Love rises on wings of fire.*

Understanding spilled over his mind and body. He knew what needed to be done. He understood the greater meanings of the *breh-hedden* for him and for Parisa. He understood the purpose, at least in part, of the shared *royle* wings.

"Antony?"

He looked over at the opening to the bathroom. Parisa stood in the doorway, naked, water pouring from her long wet hair. Her usual dark brown waves looked black. The shower had stopped running.

He leaned up on an elbow. He couldn't help it. He was a

man and his woman had the most beautiful breasts. They were large and peaked from the water and the cool air of the room.

Oh. God.

But why was she standing there like that. "What's wrong?" he asked.

"I *felt* you." She put a hand over her heart. "Here, as though you were speaking to me. Were you? Were you trying to say something?"

He rose to his feet, still feeling off kilter, his mind uneven. He drew close and tried to keep his body calm as he approached so much femaleness. He took her hands in his, then bent down and placed a kiss on each.

His heart started to ache. He lifted his head and met her gaze. "I love you, Parisa." His voice had sunk low. He was almost whispering. "I love you so much. I didn't think we'd get to have one more minute together." He swallowed hard. "Sorry, I'm having trouble breathing."

Her amethyst eyes glittered in the soft light of the room. She rose on her tiptoes and kissed him. His heart constricted a little more. "You love me?" she asked.

"I love you," he said. "I do." His voice sounded laced now with rocks and thorns. "I love you. I love you. I love you."

"Oh, Antony." He still had hold of her hands so once more she rose and kissed him. This time her lips lingered and his heart tightened a little more.

"I don't know how this happened," he said, "but I'm grateful, so grateful. I never thought I'd feel gratitude for the *breh-hedden,* but I do. I could never have reached for you otherwise, never drawn this close to you without the demands of that *myth* beating the stubbornness out of me." He smiled. "Some myth, huh?"

She nodded. Her gaze moved back and forth over his as though searching for the truth. Didn't she believe him?

"Parisa, when I watched you die earlier, and I was unable to do anything about it, I wanted to die, too. The sooner the better."

She frowned. "Wait. But you came to me when I was near

death, perhaps even when I was clinically dead. I heard your voice in my head, *Live, live*. You repeated it over and over."

He had.

"You brought me back. I know that now. There was a part of me that wanted to die as well and I remembered what Rith said, that coming back is an act of will. So, what happened? What changed?"

"You came to me."

She closed her eyes. "I don't understand."

"I have not given my heart in all these centuries because I didn't believe I had a heart to give. I buried my heart in my wife's and son's graves. When I met Thorne, and learned I had a permanent place in the Warriors of the Blood, I was done with everything else forever.

"When the *breh-hedden* struck I was enraged because I'd felt the first shattering of the walls I'd built around myself. Truth? I'd convinced myself there were no walls, I'd become a more sensible man. I was a vampire, I had powers, I knew how to make war, so war I would make and everything else could go to hell. I was in good company, too, until Alison arrived and turned Kerrick's life upside down. Although I think I was even more affected by Havily. I'd already been experiencing affection for her, even at times inappropriate desire."

"Oh, really." Parisa's eyes darkened.

His heart gave a little cry of joy. "Jealous?" he asked. He slid his arms around her back and pulled her close, even though he was still dust-laden and she was wet. She'd end up muddy but he didn't care.

"You just stay away from Havily Morgan, vampire." She kissed him again, only this one involved a lot of tongue and hard probing until his lips parted and she could force her way into his mouth. He groaned to see *his woman* intent on staking her claim.

She put her hand on his shoulder. He felt the vibration of a clothing-fold, but her powers in this area were still clearly lacking. His shirt was now plastered over his face. He was laughing as he sent, *Try it again.*

"Oh, I'm so sorry, I'm so sorry." The vibration began and yes, his shirt was off but now his cargoes were caught around his ankles. He fell backward, pulling her with him.

She was a laughing, muddy mess as she saw what she'd done. He didn't care. She was in exactly the position he wanted her as he said, "Complete the *breh-hedden* with me, Parisa, here and now."

Her brows rose and her body stilled on top of his. He thought the thought and got rid of his pants and steel-toed boots, even his socks.

"I want to," she said. "But there's something I need to know."

"And what's that?" he asked softly. He didn't want to spook her.

She smiled, a very soft smile, and put her hand on his cheek. He turned into her hand and put a kiss in the center of her palm. She wiggled her hips against his in response. He groaned.

"Wait," she said, breathless. "The sex is always great with you. But something has troubled me for days now, since I learned we had the same kind of wings, *royle* wings. I know that something extraordinary happens when the final link of a *breh-hedden* settles into place but, Antony I have this *feeling*"—she leaned sideways slightly to put her fist between her breasts—"right here. I'm worried."

He sat up and drew her onto his lap. They were naked and a mess, but whatever this was it had to be settled first. "You're worried about our wings?"

She nodded. "But I don't know why."

"I have the same heavy sensation as well. This could be an extension of the *breh-hedden,* I just don't know. What I do know is that I don't care. I want this with you more than anything in the world. I want the added responsibility, and I want the increase in powers. I want you in my life now and forever, no matter what comes, no matter what difficulties emerge, no matter what powers come to us as a couple. I want this because I want you."

Tears shimmered in her eyes. "I was so proud of my independence." She shook her head. "But not until I collided with your warrior world did I start to understand that I'd built walls, just like yours, to hold the pain of the world at bay.

"I never got close to anyone because it hurt too much to leave people behind and to go through the pain of starting over. Now here I am and when you were asleep in that strange place, I awoke trapped but I found my way out by realizing that if I was going to have any hope of living and of getting us both out of there, I would have to find some way of reaching out for help.

"That's when it dawned on me that I might be able to reach Endelle with my voyeur's window because she has a window as well. When it worked, when I contacted her, I was so not surprised. Our waging an effective war will only work if we join forces.

"After we brought Fiona and the rest of the blood slaves home, I'd been so puffed up in my new abilities that I'd missed the whole point—we'd brought them home as a unit." She kissed him. "Do you see? My independence had become an excuse not to get close to anyone. That was why I fell for Rith's deception—it never occurred to me to question what I was looking at, or to seek counsel from anyone else, or to even contact you mind-to-mind. It was just me, acting alone."

She relaxed against him. "Now I'm here. With you. And there's nowhere else I want to be."

He put his hand on the back of her neck. "You still want to be a Militia Warrior?"

She shook her head. "Truth? I don't know. I don't know if it's the right path for me or not." Then she smiled. "I think I need to seek counsel on that one, you know, not make the decision all by myself."

He laughed. He kissed her. "So you think you love me?" The question had just slipped out and his chest seized. What if she didn't or wasn't sure? Shit, he should have kept his trap shut.

But she stroked his cheek. "Oh, God. I'm sooo in love with you. I'm bewitched. If you weren't a good vampire, I'd say you had enthralled me. I think about you all the time, I crave your body, and when I see you my heart aches. How is that even possible? Antony, I love you."

Relief was another dam breaking and spilling. But he pressed on: "Will you complete the *breh-hedden* with me?"

She nodded. "Yes. Right here, right now." She glanced down at her naked breasts and grimaced. "Is that mud?"

"Yes." He laughed. "We made mud."

"Why don't we fire up the shower again and take care of business."

Shivers rained down his body and his cock responded, hardening, twitching, seeking.

"Sage," she murmured. She groaned and fell on him, kissing him as she once more forced her tongue into his mouth.

Her hips were connected low, just in the right place. If he shifted just a little, moved her up then down, he could impale her on him. If the tangerine scent flooding the room meant what it always had before, she'd be ready for him.

But like hell he was going to do this on the floor covered with mud.

He surrounded her with his arms, holding her against him, then with a good old-fashioned piece of levitation he rose up. With her feet dangling off the floor and her arms around his neck, he smiled down into her beautiful face and carried her into the shower.

He hit the lever and got all eight heads to blasting on them both. She took soap and worked over his body. He turned his back to her and had the pleasure of her hands soaping him from head to foot. It felt *cleansing,* even healing.

But when he turned to face her and she started lathering her own chest, he grabbed the bar of soap and growled, "My turn."

She giggled but the resulting wave of tangerine told him exactly how happy she was about his possession of the soap.

Okay, he was a man, so sue him. He lathered up, let the soap drop to the floor, and put his hands on her extraordinary breasts. She arched her back and his mind spun. His gaze narrowed to the sight of the foamy bubbles drifting over the swell of her skin and parting at the peaked nipple to flow down either side. Oh, God. He pushed her back just a little so that one of the nozzles could aim over her chest and get rid of the soap and the mud and make her skin ready for his mouth.

Two seconds later he bent low, and with one hand supporting her behind her back, the other holding her very large breast, he took the peaked tip into his mouth and sucked.

Parisa cried out and clenched deep between her legs. Oh, God. She ached just about everywhere, all around her heart and chest, her nipple, her labia, and in the deep well of her. She hadn't felt this way before with Medichi and she realized that the decision to let go of independence and embrace love had changed her body's reactions to the man she'd chosen to be her *breh* . . . or was it the man the *breh-hedden* had chosen to be her *breh*. Somehow, none of it mattered, only that she belonged to this man with her entire body, heart, and soul.

For that reason, each sensation felt doubled, tripled in intensity. Her body cried out to be filled.

He cradled and suckled her breast and brought little gasps from her throat. She smoothed her hand over his head, the hair beneath her fingers fine and silky, if a little dusty still. He was a feast for her heart, her mind, her hands, her body. And she loved him.

"How about we get cleaned up and move to your bed. I want to be in your bed, Antony, when we go all the way." He looked up at her, lips sliding away from her breast. A gasp caught in her throat at the sight of her flesh leaving his mouth.

"So, you want to go *all the way*?" he asked.

"Yeah." She giggled. For a moment, they were like teenagers again. "But you have terra-cotta dust in your hair and I could use one more shampoo."

Getting clean took a lot longer than it should have. Parisa kept getting lost in Antony's arms, primarily because he couldn't keep his hands off her.

She finally escaped him and left the shower. If he wanted her he'd have to get the crème rinse out of his hair.

She dried off, wrapped her hair in a towel, then moved to the bed. She practiced more of her folding as she worked to get the comforter peeled back to a thick bundle at the end of the bed. She almost broke a sweat. She wasn't sure why this particular power was giving her grief. How the hell could she open a voyeur window, download shield-creation abilities, then destroy a shield, but not be able to fold a stupid comforter off a bed?

Whatever.

Just as she'd gotten the top sheet separated from the bottom sheet—even if it did hang over one of the bedposts—Antony came up behind her and encircled her in his arms. "I think you're getting better."

"Right," she cried. But she turned in his arms and wrapped her arms around his waist. "So where were we?"

"Straight to the point. I like that about you."

She looked down, down his chest and beautiful pecs, down the indentation of his belly button, down the erotic narrow line of hairs that drew her eye lower and lower. He was a hard ridge against her abdomen, and as she leaned back she could see the crown of his cock. Her lips tingled.

"See something you like?" His voice was once more at the bottom of the sea.

She drew back just enough to drift her hand up the length of him. He gasped and hissed.

Then he stepped away from her. "We'd better get down to business or my feet won't have the power to move in about five more seconds."

She pivoted on one foot then launched into the air, turning mid-flight so that when she landed on the mattress, she was on her back. Thank goodness she had been quick about it, because he was on top of her at vampire speed, pinning her flat to the bed before she could take a breath.

Time slowed and she took a moment to register everything, the cool of the sheet behind her back, the heat of his body ready to take her, his long wet hair dragging over her warm breasts, the smile that suffused his oh-so-handsome face with love and laughter.

Her heart tightened as she reached out to drag her fingers over his high, strong cheekbones. Was she truly going to do this? Was she going to seal her fate with a warrior-vampire?

"Are we really doing this, Antony?"

He nodded. "Scared?"

"A little but then I look at you and there's nothing I want more. But what will happen to us? This will change us, won't it?"

He shrugged as much as he could propped on his forearms. "I don't know. Kerrick is the same, and so is Marcus, but they both seem better focused as men, as warriors. As for the women, maybe you can answer that better than I can. What I do know is that their powers are stronger and they've each made more of a difference in the war. They also have a constant awareness of where the other is physically."

She nodded. She could see that and accept it. "So we do all three things at once?"

"Body, blood, deep-mind engagement."

"How do we start?"

He smiled again. "Like this." He lowered himself slowly onto her and kissed her.

Parisa forgot about her worries over this new thing happening to her. She gave herself to the kiss, to Antony's beautiful, sensual lips, to the love she could feel in every drift.

I love you whispered through her mind, confirming what she could already feel.

I love you, too, she sent.

The weight of him was like heaven. She had always been uncomfortable with her height but not right now, not with Antony stretched out on top of her, his lean muscular thighs pressing into hers, his thick pecs stroking her breasts. Her fingers played with the grooves, swells, and planes of his back.

She shivered when the tips of her fingers found the apertures of his wing-locks moist.

He groaned as his lips plucked at hers. His tongue slid

inside and he searched through her mouth. She sucked his tongue as his hips rocked against hers. He was so hard and so big. She slid a hand low and wiggled her fingers beneath his hip. He lifted slightly, giving her room.

She released a heavy sigh as her hand found him and stroked him and loved him. He drew back and looked into her eyes.

"That's it," she whispered against his lips. She drew back and met his gaze. "Your eyes. You have a light in your eyes that I adore. I love you Antony, with all my heart. I think I have from the moment I first voyeured you."

Medichi's chest expanded . . . again. Her fingers had closed around him, touching him, loving him. He never thought to be undone in this way again. How magical this was, lying against her beautiful body, seeing the admiration in her eyes, knowing he was loved, knowing that his heart had been pierced wide open so he could love again.

He wanted to show her what he felt.

He slid a knee between her thighs and pushed. She opened for him, letting her legs fall wide and his hips slide between. Was there a more vulnerable position for a woman? More open? More trusting? That she trusted him so much pierced him once more.

He guided himself down low and thrust against her opening. She drew up her knees as her body rolled upward in a slow wave of desire.

"Yes," she whispered.

Such an excellent word. No better in the English language.

He pressed into her, just a little. So wet. So ready for him.

He closed his eyes, savoring. Everything would change from this moment on. But he was ready. He pushed a little more.

Her fingers dug into his shoulders and she whimpered. He leaned down, kissed her closed eyelids, then drew back. She smiled and looked up at him. "I want to be in your mind as I do this," he said.

She nodded. His gaze met beautiful amethyst. He settled his mind against hers and gave a little shove.

She smiled as she released her shields so that they fell in one quick tumble. He poured over her mind in a swift, flowing stream. She cried out and even though he had only a couple of inches buried inside her, he felt her clench.

He grunted in response. He was hard as a rock, his balls pulled up tight.

Shit, he could come in a heartbeat.

He took a few settling breaths . . . then, as he made his way into her body, he began a journey through her mind. She had only lived twenty-nine years, so young, but he saw her life and for the first time truly understood her pain.

He saw the release of her wings for the first time, the panic followed by wonder. He let all the love and compassion he felt for her flow through his mind and layered it over hers. He kissed her and found that her face was wet.

"So much love," she whispered. "Antony, you make me feel so *full* in every possible way. Antony, my Antony."

He drew his hips back and pushed and pushed. She cried out and clung to him. She dug her nails into his back. "Yes, yes." Her hands slid lower and she grabbed his ass hard, pushing as he pushed. A sound like a cry and a groan came out of her.

Antony, Antony, Antony, swept through her thoughts, which he felt and heard at the same time since he was within her mind. He felt how much she savored him deep. *I could keep you here forever.*

I want to stay here forever.

Her eyes opened. To look into her eyes yet be within her mind was a wondrous thing. He kissed her again hard and began to rock into her, pushing, driving, thrusting.

Her cries filled the space between them and he drank them down his throat one after the other.

My turn, she whispered within his mind. *Let me in.*

Yes. Oh, such an excellent word.

Parisa didn't want to take her hands away from the firm yet erotically movable flesh of his gorgeous ass. But she did, putting her hands on his face as she looked into his eyes.

Such beautiful dark brown eyes, almost black in the dimness of the waning afternoon, but always full of that wonderful light.

She had never thought she could love someone so much.

She was *inaccessible* no more.

He smiled and reminded her of what they were doing with a firm thrust of himself deep into her. Her eyes fluttered as she clenched unbidden, as she felt the supreme hard length of him, as pleasure rippled over her abdomen and sent delicious shivers down her thighs.

"Oh" swept out of her lips. He kissed her and took the rest of her breath into his mouth. His sage scent, roughened with a note that was all male, sent more shivers over her body. His presence was a delectable weight in her mind.

Focus.

Yes, she must focus.

Withdraw from my mind, she sent, *and I'll follow.*

Yes.

Yes, oh, yes.

She felt him begin to pull back and what might have ended in emptiness became a sense of complete penetration as she surged into his head. She felt herself crash over his mind like an enormous ocean wave. She pounded hard then spread out to see, to absorb, to embrace all that he was in his memories.

His body responded. He moved into her harder now and grunted. He no longer kissed her, his head was turned away. He was sweating.

So good, he sent. *So damn good.*

It was her turn to take the ride. She knew she was crying out, her body almost spasming with pleasure as she began to catch glimpses of former battles, former times at the Blood and Bite, even making love with her in the turret room. She wanted to pause and savor but she pressed on, back and back through time, back and back through centuries.

She became lost in the purity of moving through his thoughts, his memories, his experiences, and at the same time feeling his body push into hers. Alternating waves of cold and heat washed through her. Pleasure built on pleasure.

She was panting.

Her mind was flushed with endorphins. She was over-whelmed, overcome. His memories were too much, too wonderful, too horrible. She cried out, uncertain how to continue.

I'm here. And just like that the confusion dissipated. It was as though in the middle of his mind, he appeared right in front of her. She couldn't see him but she felt him. She calmed, grew still, rested within his mind.

You okay?

She could hear herself as she laughed. *How many times have you asked me that? Yes, I'm okay. We're close, though, aren't we?*

Yes.

She drew in a deep breath. *Give me your wrist,* she sent.

He unhinged his elbow. The moment she felt his skin beneath her mouth her fangs emerged. She didn't think. She struck. As his blood touched her lips and moved into her mouth she cried out and began to suckle. Any pleasure she had been feeling was a fraction of this. She was engaged with him in all three ways—mind, blood, and a cock buried as far as it could go.

She drank and drank and for a moment knew nothing else but that in this way she had taken possession of him, bringing into her body all that he was, his life force, that which flowed through his heart, that which gave him life.

She tasted sage and earth, man and fire. She tasted life.

She rolled her head, offering what she could give as well.

He groaned long and low and his tongue raked up her neck over and over until her vein pounded. She felt the tips of his fangs first. She cried out even before he struck. He sank his fangs and her hips jerked, her mind seized, and her whole body shivered.

Oh, dear God, what had they done, what had they begun, by engaging like this? She felt something coming, some-thing enormous, but how on earth was she going to be able to handle more?

* * *

Antony tasted the sweet succulent flavor of tangerines in the blood that slid down his throat. He also tasted Parisa, a flavor of woman and life and energy, tremendous energy. He felt her doubt, as well, but he let that go, at least for now.

For now, he drank and drank and though he could feel all the other sensations at once, that she was stroking his mind, and suckling his wrist, that she'd taken a thick rope of his hair in her free hand and that her hips were jerking against his and pulling his cock in deep, the forefront of his mind was focused on what he took from her neck.

He loved her so much. That she was willing to give of herself like this pounded him within his mind and her energy became his energy. He felt determined and almost wild. His hips became a dedicated surge and pullback, surge and pullback, a heavy piston working the well of her body, working her pleasure, pumping and pumping.

He felt his release building and suddenly he could feel hers as well. He felt what it felt for her to have his shaft buried inside her. He trembled because the dual sensation of pleasure was too much, too much.

She pulled on his hair and he felt the texture of his own hair in her hand.

He tasted the flavor of his own blood in her mouth.

Yes, it was too much, too much, yet not enough.

Antony, what's happening?

He couldn't respond. He felt a wave of energy begin to flow through him, up from his feet, to his knees, his hips, his chest. The apertures along his back began to flood with moisture. He could feel her wing-locks as well, wet, so wet.

Then he understood. He had to get them both off the bed.

He slung one arm under her hips and the other securely around her shoulders so that he could continue to drink.

We're off the bed.

Yes, let it come now, all of it.

My wings. Oh, God, they're coming.

Yes, yes, yes.

As her wings mounted his did as well, a simultaneous release that launched the other release. He withdrew his fangs from her neck and cried out. She screamed and he felt her pleasure, the lightning of ecstasy that streaked over her most tender flesh and flew up the well of her body and gripped him—and as she gripped him, he pumped into her that other fluid of life, that which had the power to create life. He pumped and pumped. His wings stretched and reached, wafted to keep them both floating in the air.

Oh, God, oh, God, oh God.

Pleasure continued to flow in waves, deep pulsing waves, and he orgasmed a second time, heavily, his hips working her body. He felt her pleasure again as once more she screamed, her mouth no longer connected to his wrist, her arms holding him, her legs wrapped around his legs.

But if he felt her pleasure, what was she feeling?

Parisa screamed at the ceiling at the beautiful coffer beams that went in and out of focus. Orgasm had her in a powerful grip and it kept rolling through her. When her wings had released, she had climaxed as though there had never been an orgasm before in the entire course of the world. She had felt Antony's release at the same time. When her wings came forth and his at the same time, she felt not only all those delicious sensations that had always characterized her wingmounts, but all of his as well. The combination of experiences had been overwhelming.

And now she felt the pleasure building again. Even though Antony had already orgasmed more than once, already filled her full to overflowing, because they were involved in deepmind engagement, and because his experiences were her experiences, she could tell he was going to climax again.

The exquisite pressure kept building and building. The release came. She threw her head back and screamed as the pleasure flowed—and then she felt it, a tremendous wave of energy that began at her feet, up through her hips, her chest, her shoulders, until it seemed to pass through the very top of her head.

At the same time she felt Antony's pleasure, the pull of her well along his pulsing cock, the extreme pleasure of his orgasm as he once more spent his seed, the heady rush through his abdomen, chest, and head, pleasure upon pleasure.

Panting, sweaty, her wings wafting, slowly, his wings sustaining them in the air, his hips quieting, at last the sexual pleasure began to dim but was replaced by something new, a kind of warm exhilaration, a different kind of ecstasy.

She opened her eyes and met Antony's gaze. His eyes were full of light, even more than usual. But her gaze was drawn away by colors playing over his shoulder. His wings flapped very gently, very steadily to hold them aloft, several feet above the bed.

She blinked. "Your wings are on fire."

"Yes," he whispered. "And so are yours."

She turned her head to the side and saw the expanse of her wing, and Antony's. Swirls of energy rose off both. The colors dazzled—gold, amethyst, blue, and green.

She shifted to meet his gaze once more. He seemed different. His hair danced around his shoulders as though the energy they had created blew it around like a soft breeze.

He was smiling. She was still in his mind and she knew his thoughts—he'd never been so happy.

Me, too. He nodded and smiled.

But the energy transformed suddenly. Antony winced, his back arched, and she felt him struggle. She knew, however, that she had to hold him in place.

She took the jolt next. It made her want to pull away but she forced herself to remain. Then she realized that this time he had kept her from moving, from disconnecting.

The click happened right there, chest-to-chest, a deep bond and joining. She stared into his eyes. He returned it.

The next moment, Parisa arched and cried out. "The pain. Oh, God the pain."

"Oh, God. In your mind. So deep. The voyeur-link." She knew he felt her pain because they were connected. "Is this what you've been experiencing?"

"Yes," she whispered, tears tracking down her cheeks. "I

can feel the link straining, almost trembling." She arched again. Once more she cried out, then opened her eyes to look at him.

The pain stopped, an ending so sudden that she gasped. "Oh, my God. The *breh-hedden* just broke my link with Greaves."

"Holy shit." He smiled. "I can feel it, too. He's gone. The bastard is gone."

Another unexpected benefit of the bonding experience.

She was ready to embrace him, to speak of love, to explore what this bonding might mean for both of them, even to make love again. But a sudden, terrible understanding arose: Something bad was about to happen to Endelle, to Thorne, to all the Warriors of the Blood, to Colonel Seriffe and his contingent of Militia Warriors.

"Do you feel that?" he asked. "The danger, to everyone?"

"Yes. What do we do?" It was not an expression of doubt but a concern about strategy.

She flowed through Antony's mind and picked up on the drift of his thoughts. He was riffling through all the books and articles he had read, and all the anecdotes he had ever heard about *royle* wings.

She began to peruse his memories at the same time, an amazing download of material. He then released all those thoughts and looked into her eyes once more.

He smiled.

She smiled.

So they both knew what needed to be done. But dear God, it seemed quite impossible.

Worse, if this failed, they would both be dead along with all those they loved, within the next hour.

Would this be it, then? Would their lives and their love be over so very soon?

"How about you open your voyeur's window and have a look."

Parisa nodded. She took a deep breath and thought of Endelle. The window opened and Her Supremeness came into view. She was dressed in a light blue flight suit, at full-mount. "Her wings are dark blue."

"She has the power to change the colors of the feathers at will."

"Wow."

"So where is she?"

Parisa panned back. "At the Grand Canyon . . . and she's not alone."

There is some anecdotal evidence from ancient times to suggest that royle *wings form the basis of the concept of the modern-day spectacle. However, more recent historical records do not corroborate oral traditions.*

—From *Treatise on Ascension,* by Philippe Reynard

CHAPTER 24

The Ascension Liberation Army.

Greaves.

What a fucking poser.

Endelle stood on the rim of the Grand Canyon, at one of the narrower points. A late-afternoon glow had settled on the land, bringing all the sharp and rolling contours of the canyon into beautiful relief. It wouldn't be long before dusk descended. What the hell was Greaves up to?

A mile below, the river was hardly visible, a distant blue-green line. On Mortal Earth, because of all the dams, the river looked mossy green. But rushing all the way to the Sea of Cortez, untrammeled by dams as it was on Second Earth, it looked a little different.

Whatever.

What didn't look different was Greaves.

She extended her vision—in her case real Third Earth shit—and she could see him, plain as fucking day, seated on a dais, *lounging,* sipping a cup of tea, the saucer in one hand and in the other, his white delicate teacup with pinkie held high. Well, weren't we just so damn pretty this afternoon?

If she could put metaphysical fingers around his throat and squeeze, she would. But that was Fourth Dimension shit and she wasn't there yet.

All this, an army of Militia Warriors and death vampires spread out on the opposing rim, and for what? Why couldn't some men just let people raise their babies, their crops, a few farm animals for sustenance, and live? Why did it always come down to some asshole needing to take over the world?

Jesus H. Christ.

So Greaves had announced to the world today that he was *saving* Second Earth from *the tyranny of an oppressive administration that must be stopped.* That's what Greaves had called her Phoenix Two operation in which her primary function was to keep death vampires from making it down to Mortal Earth and, yeah, to prevent assholes like Greaves from taking over the world. Other than that, her allied High Administrators ran their Territories however the hell they wanted to. Yeah, real fucking tyrannical.

Perfect.

Starting this morning, he had mounted a massive television and Internet propaganda campaign against her administration. He'd used every hideous photograph he could find of her, that showed her enraged—imagine that, pictures of her enraged. At least her clothes looked sweet. She particularly liked the one of her in a banana python floor-length evening gown, knees lowered and wide so that it stretched the skin out, her back arched, and her arm lifted high in a one-fingered salute. Okay, so maybe she didn't exactly look like the ruler of Second Earth. More like *the ruler of Second Earth gone wild.* She was even showing some fang in that photo.

Okay, really . . . *whatever.*

Unfortunately, the ads were being shown around the world, in every Territory and every language. Marcus's team had been monitoring global broadcasting around the clock.

He'd been cursing nonstop for the past several hours. So . . . fuck.

And today, Greaves had a hundred television crews, also from around the world, already filming him and his army. Remote-controlled video air-bots zoomed back and forth, from her army to his. If one of those damn things even got close to her, she was throwing a fucking hand-blast.

Ascension Liberation Army.

My ass.

That lying fucking bastard.

Greaves was just one big lie from the top of his bald head to the tidy break in the cuffs of his fine wool suits.

She flapped the great breadth of her wings, a rich cerulean blue for the battle, and rose into the air a slow couple of feet at a time. Her flight suit was a lighter shade of blue. On principle, though, she wore a leopard headband and a pair of leopard-print flight slippers. Hey, a woman had her standards.

And the fuck she was going to take that pansy-ass bastard Greaves seriously. Especially since beyond the assembled Militia Warriors serving on his side were communications tents with satellite dishes. He was up to something.

The question was, how much of this was for show and just how serious was he about challenging her administration today?

Still. She was thong-climbing-her-ass pissed.

On the other hand, one of the advantages of living so long was that the phrase *Now I've seen everything* had been her mantra for millennia already. If she flat-out panicked every time some little flyspeck of a prick flexed his muscles, she'd have stroked out a helluva long time before this. Not that a vampire could stroke out, but still.

Besides, something had shifted within her since Shorty showed up in her life. Maybe it was his speaking of Braulio, or maybe it was learning that Leto, one of her dearest friends from olden times, hadn't been a traitor after all, or maybe it was just knowing that the Upper Dimension hadn't completely buried its head up its ass all these centuries, but she'd gained a little confidence. There must be a way out of this morass.

Also, she had one ace up her sleeve that no one knew about. She had no idea if she could count on Parisa and Medichi coming through for her, but from the moment she'd learned that they both had *royle* wings, well she'd sort of had a hard-on. She was the only ascender on the face of the planet who had actually seen what *royle* wings could do. Luchianne had had *royle* wings, and on more than one occasion she'd used them.

Talk about *spectacle*.

What a sight those times had been. But whether she could call such an untried pair into battle—well, who the fuck knew. She was just employing a little bit of faith that even though she was a profane bitch, the Creator might somehow help her inadequate troops stand against a sociopath and an army that outnumbered hers three-to-one.

As she rose higher and pulled back somewhat on her preternatural vision, she could see the breadth of Greaves's assembled forces. His ALA was all in black with the occasional maroon slash of color for effect. Black leather kilts were the order of the day on both sides, but just to keep things simple Greaves's army wore maroon leather weapons harnesses, which she thought was a nice touch although some contrasting embroidery would've livened things up a bit. If she got out of this alive, she'd tell Stannett to give Greaves a few pointers.

She rose up even higher. Off to the southwest she saw something else, something in flight, something massive.

"No fucking way," she murmured as it came into focus. Just like that, she was worried. What people might dislike in war, they doted on when it came to display.

She drew her wings in slightly and floated back to the ground. Colonel Seriffe and Thorne flanked her. She turned to face them both, her back to the canyon.

"You're not going to believe what *the little peach* has done."

The men spoke in unison. "What?"

She shook her head. "If this doesn't fucking take the cake. Tell you what, boys. Fly up about forty feet and take a gander off to the southwest. I want you to see this for yourself. Tell me what you think."

The men stepped several feet apart. They'd already mounted their wings; now they unfolded them from close-mount into full-mount and in an almost choreographed movement flew straight up and out to hover above the maw of the canyon.

Thorne's voice pierced her head through their shared mind-link. *Are you fucking kidding me?*

Nope. Looks like Greaves has thought of everything.

So that no matter what happens today, he can't lose. No wonder he chose dusk. I thought it was because the canyon just looked prettier at this hour.

She rose into the air again and flew behind the men. *At your rear,* she sent. It was the proper form of flight protocol address, but it always made her laugh.

Thorne dipped a wing and shifted so that he could meet her gaze. "When do you think the fireworks will begin?" he said, his voice gravelly but loud.

"Any fucking time."

But as Seriffe turned to her, she saw the sudden raw state of his emotions and recoiled. He had three small boys and a wife. He adored his family and here he was facing the end of it all. If he died today, what would become of Carolyn and the little ones?

Aw, shit.

Almost on cue, yep, fireworks launched into the air and all the little video-bots floated into a variety of static positions to best capture a sky suddenly full of splashes of blue and green, purple, yellow—and every color under the sun.

She ordered the men back to the ground and followed suit. With her leopard flats on the soil again, she once more stretched her vision across the maw of the canyon. There he was. He even met her gaze and lifted his cup to her.

Goddamn fucking poser.

* * *

Greaves preferred a win–win, which was exactly what he had this afternoon. The fireworks were charming—not the most complicated designs and patterns he might have chosen, but he'd made this decision at the last minute so naturally there would be compromises.

Still, how could one ever go wrong with fireworks?

He sipped the last bit of tea. As squadrons of geese, swans, and ducks, as well as their magnificently costumed handlers, moved into position exactly between the rims of the canyon, he gestured for his aide to take the cup and saucer.

The young vampire didn't look at him as he hurried to his side, bowed, then performed the task.

As the servant moved away, Greaves rose to his feet—the prearranged signal. All his generals moved back into the ranks, all with the exception of Leto, his second-in-command, who took up the position on Greaves's far right. He kept Leto close, as always. Something wasn't right with his favorite defector but he hadn't had the time to pursue it yet.

He loved how swiftly the men moved, each disappearing into the ranks, barking orders until both divisions thrummed with battle energy, all to the pounding of the fireworks and the great flashes in the sky.

As he faced south, away from the canyon, he watched his death vampires rise into the air, a long glorious line of matched killers, stark white complexions with a faint bluish hue to the skin, huge glossy black wings and the fierce presence of muscled warriors. The promise? With the Coming Order, he would provide dying blood for all.

The sun was now almost set.

Let the fun begin.

Endelle shook her head.

Shit.

Fireworks were now blasting from both sides of Greaves's forces, so that the sky above the canyon was full of light and sparkle. Yeah . . . *spectacle*.

The squadrons of fowl drew opposite and very near to Endelle's forces. Their corresponding handlers wore enormous gowns, men and women alike. The costumes hung down into the air at twice their height. Each wore a massive head-piece; their wings were at least warrior-sized to support the weighty attire.

Endelle shook her head and exchanged a roll of the eyes with Thorne. Whatever she thought of Greaves, this whole fucking presentation was goddamn brilliant.

For the next fifteen minutes, the spectacle parade passed, performing to music blasted from a new set of air-bots, heavy orchestral music, which she recognized as Holst's *The Planets*.

Jesus H. Christ.

Well, this might just be a little payback for her last spectacle event at the Ambassadors Reception at White Lake. Despite the incendiary bombs that had disrupted the fireworks display, killed eleven people, and burned out a number of famous public gardens, the ensuing press had resulted in a staggering response of support for Endelle's administration. Both sympathy and accolades had flowed in from around the world.

Maybe tonight's little display would twist the world around Greaves's pinkie. Fuck. What the hell was she supposed to do to combat this? And just how many of her male and female warriors were going to fall to their deaths in the canyon tonight?

And—God forbid—would she lose any of her Warriors of the Blood?

She scowled up at the series of firework dragons that now flowed east over a dusky sky, above the final act of a thousand snowy white swans, moving in elegant wave-like patterns below.

She sent a message to Thorne. *Get Medichi on the com.*

Medichi stood with his arms wrapped around Parisa, waiting, his gaze fixed to the skies as several new dragons appeared, all moving toward their position at the farthest left flank of Endelle's forces. The swans were almost opposite them now.

"So beautiful," Parisa murmured.

Dread filled him. His face had that tight, drawn sensation he got so rarely. The last time he'd felt this way was the moment he realized that he hadn't been looking at Parisa at all, but a hologram.

His gaze fell to the army on the opposite rim, so far away yet so damn close. Once in flight, the far side of the canyon was only a few wing-flaps away. Though the Grand Canyon seemed to separate the two armies, it was nothing but an illusion.

He felt his phone vibrate and he released his right arm to fish out the black card. Must be showtime.

He thumbed the surface. Though he felt Parisa try to pull away, he didn't want space; he met her gaze and tugged her back against him. She smiled, turning into him and falling against his chest. She was feeling it, too. So, not good.

"Give," he said, his voice quieter than he had meant it to be.

A bunch of gravel came on line, "So you're here." The music blasted from both sides of the conversation.

"Yep. North end."

"Endelle wants a word."

"Hey asshole," Her Supremeness said.

Damn that made him smile and shake his head. "Where do you need us?"

"Well," she drawled as, the music faded out, "that depends. You complete the *breh-hedden*?"

"Yes." He gave Parisa's shoulders a squeeze.

"Anything notable happen?"

Now, there was a question. He could have answered that about a dozen different ways. Instead, he told her what he knew she needed to hear. "Our wings flamed—gold, amethyst, blue, green."

He wasn't sure, but he thought he heard her murmur, *Thank God.* "Good" snapped through the line. "I want the pair of you to mount up and do what you need to do. The truth is, I haven't seen this done in millennia so your guess is as good as mine. Got it?"

"Yep."

"And Medichi?"

"Yeah?"

"I think it's all up to you right now." Then she laughed. "But no pressure."

The line went dead.

He shook his head.

"What?" Parisa asked. When she drew back this time, he let her.

"Showtime and we mount our wings."

Parisa gave him a grim set of her lips then moved several feet away. He waited as she mounted her incredible, impossible wings, so massive for her body, all cream with beautiful bands of black, amethyst, and gold. Because of the wind eddies, she drew the wings into close-mount.

He smiled at her. His wings emerged in a sudden burst of power. He, too drew them in close.

"What now?"

He took her hand. "We wait." But for what he wasn't sure. Oh, God, how would either of them know what to do?

He glanced at his woman once more.

Worse, what if he lost her tonight after having just barely begun his life with her ?

Jean-Pierre headed one thousand Militia Warriors at the southernmost flank of Endelle's army. His heart thrummed in his chest, heavy now, almost painful.

The enemy was in the air across the canyon on the south rim.

Merde.

He lifted his sword and at the same moment mounted his wings. He heard the responding mounting of wings behind him, like a great wind.

This was his job to perform right now, as despised as it was. The enemy was better prepared in every sense. Camera crews were filming every moment of what Greaves most certainly intended to be a complete rout.

But, as was always said among the warriors, *fuck that.*

Very precise.

The enemy breached the side of the canyon and hit the open air. The distance might still be great but wings moved the body swiftly, so swiftly.

He opened his mouth and, with his sword lifted high, let out a roar. The Militia Warriors behind him echoed it. He flapped his wings in long downward thrusts and rose into the air. He did not need to turn around to see if he was being followed. The anger and the power and the energy of Seriffe's men pushed at him from behind.

He breached the North Rim wall and was over the canyon now, pulsing forward in slow, exact movements. From his peripheral vision to the left he saw that his warrior brothers had done no less. Closest to him was Luken, the most physically powerful of the brothers, plowing the air, moving forward just as he did.

All that he was as a warrior moved in him now, flooded his veins. The surface of his skin flushed hot. He was ready.

Leading the charge opposite him was a long, terrible row of death vampires. They began to break away in fours, some flying higher and higher, others lower. The ranks behind him would do the same, higher and lower to form a multiple-layered front line, offset so that if anyone fell into the canyon below, other battling pairs and groups would not be impacted.

But battle was chaotic and always the worst happened.

His peripherals closed down.

All he saw were eight death vampires in tight formation aimed at him. He would have expected no less.

On they flew, three hundred yards, two hundred, one hundred. He struck parachute-mount and hung in the air, his heart now hammering. Thirty feet. He did not wait but drew both daggers swiftly from his weapons harness and let each fly. The blades struck home. Two death vampires clutched necks, spun, and fell from the sky, tumbling down and down.

The remaining six were on him. He slashed, spun, levitated at lightning speed, whirled, cut, and the entire time kept his senses fixed on the location of each pretty-boy.

A battle haze consumed him now, the rage of serving for over two centuries, of facing an enemy that drank women to death. He became more animal than man, more flexing muscle and growling instinct.

He sent vampire after vampire into the abyss below, again, again, again.

Every few seconds, his peripherals registered the battle around him and down the line. Militia Warriors on both sides of the canyon fell in fading screams to the rocks and river below.

But when he heard his name called out, and recognized Luken's voice, he flew high in the air and slaughtered within seconds the warriors who dared to follow. He stretched his preternatural vision and saw Luken tumbling to his death, one of his wings sliced through.

One glance at the battle showed Greaves's numbers overwhelming the Militia Warriors.

He had a choice to make: to stay and support the Militia Warriors all around him, or to save Luken. But there was only one choice he could make.

He pulled his wings into close-mount, which made a rocket of his body. He headed to the bottom of the canyon. Within seconds he landed below Luken's falling body. He sent a hand-blast upward beneath him, slowing the warrior's fall.

Luken still hit the earth hard. He was stunned, shaking, and part of his left wing hung at a painful angle.

Jean-Pierre wanted to fold him to safety, but neither pair of wings would handle the trip.

Only at that moment did he see that Luken's weapons harness had been sliced high in the abdomen as well and that blood poured from him.

He looked up. Greaves's forces had pushed Endelle's army a third of the way back to the North Rim. Yes, there were times when numbers mattered.

He took the warrior's hand in a tight grip.

Luken's face was pale. "Go, my brother. Save all that you can."

It was a death sentence for Luken since his wounds made him open to attack. Yet Jean-Pierre had to return to the more vulnerable Militia Warriors.

Jean-Pierre nodded when a sudden breeze, very warm and strangely soothing, came from the east portion of the canyon.

"Do you feel that?" Luken cried. He blinked several times, a hand pressed to his stomach.

"*Oui*," Jean-Pierre responded. "But what is it? I do not understand and it is getting much stronger."

Luken cried, "Holy shit. Jean-Pierre, lengthen your vision. Do you see them? Do you see them flying? Together? Their wings are on fire."

"Who?"

"Medichi and Parisa. Oh, my God. They did it." His teeth chattered now and he was pale, so pale.

Jean-Pierre kept his hand around Luken's. He engaged his vision and stretched. "*Oui*," he cried. The breeze had strengthened to a strong wind, heavy pulses of great power. "I see them. Then it is true, not a myth."

"Not a myth," Luken said, his voice quieter.

Peace descended on Jean-Pierre, the likes of which he had never known. He watched above as every battle ceased, the opponents falling back and back toward each respective rim, divided now by what could only be called a *benevolent wind*—one that brought peace, great peace.

He kept his vision long and sharp as Medichi and Parisa passed overhead. They were but an enormous elongated shape of flames: brilliant gold, amethyst that leaped in rolling flares, an underbelly of blues and greens, and a tail perhaps half a mile long of deep purple and burnished gold.

So beautiful.

Parisa flew beside Antony, separated only by the span of each of their wings but bound by the *breh-hedden* and the phenomenon that was their *royle* wings.

The colors spun out in front of her, above her, beside her, and below her. She could not imagine what she and Antony looked like as they flew through the canyon and parted enemy from enemy, driving both sides back, Greaves's forces to the South Rim and Endelle's to the North.

Her heart was unbearably full, full to overflowing, of heat, of exhilaration, of peace. Yes, so much peace.

The moment they had launched off the North Rim, the process had begun. With each few seconds the sensation grew, so that she was fulfilling the myth as she flew beside Antony. Even she could sense the power that forged a wedge between the armies.

By the time they completed the run, the entire distance through the ranks, which had to be at least five miles in length, she was breathing hard. She wasn't certain how to stop the flames and the wind, but when Antony dipped his wing once in her direction, she met his gaze and slowed as he did. The flames diminished more with each gradual cessation of forward speed.

After less than a minute, she hung in parachute position in front of him, her wings cupped at the apex. She was jostled back and forth in gentle motions by the early-evening breezes.

He nodded to her and sent, *Let's find Endelle.*

He launched the opposite direction—but at a much slower pace, so that eventually her breathing calmed down. All along the banks, Militia Warriors from Endelle's ranks cheered them with loud shouts and fists thrust through the air one after the other, thousands of grateful voices rising to the stars above.

Parisa had seen so many warriors fall as they flew through the midair front lines, down into the now black abyss of the canyon below. The memory would haunt her for years to come, softened by the knowledge that many warriors had lived because of what she and Antony had done today.

As she plowed air beside Antony in search of Endelle, Marcus took up a wing position on her left flank; Thorne took up Antony's opposing wing flank. By the time they reached Endelle, other Warriors of the Blood had met them in the air, all shouting their victory—Zacharius, Kerrick, and Santiago.

They, too, fell in formation behind Thorne and Marcus. Luken, however, was nowhere to be seen, nor Jean-Pierre.

Antony called out in a strong voice, "Banking left?"

Parisa followed suit, dipping her left wing slightly then straightening to fly forward.

Within a few flaps she was drawing her wings in, slowing then popping her parachute configuration right beside Antony, to land six feet from Her Supremeness.

But Endelle merely nodded to her then to each of the warriors. Colonel Seriffe was on her left and Thorne, now landed, moved to stand at her right.

She was somber as she said, "Luken's been hurt. He's in the canyon below. Jean-Pierre is with him and apparently saved his life. I've already sent Horace to him."

And with those simple words, whatever peace and exhilaration had defined the last fifteen minutes of Parisa's life dissipated. An evening breeze carried moans from every quarter, and a terrible hush had settled over the Militia Warriors who were alive and uninjured.

"The losses have been *unacceptable*," she said. "But we thank Warrior Medichi and ascender Lovejoy for having the courage to work together this evening and create something I have not seen since Luchianne flew the air currents of Second Earth. May you be blessed by the use of your gifts in service to our great society." She paused and swallowed hard. "And now, let us tend to the wounded and to those we lost today."

I have only one regret in my life—that I turned my only son over to the system of fostering prevalent among the ancient tribes of Europe, Mortal Earth, so long ago, for nothing but destruction has followed that decision. Will I ever be forgiven for bowing to the custom of the day against my every proper maternal instinct?
Perhaps. But I will never forgive myself.
God help me. Effetne!*

—*Memoirs,* Beatrice of Fourth

From an ancient language, meaning "an intense form of supplication to the gods, an abasement of self and self-will."

CHAPTER 25

Five days after the battle, Endelle stood on the North Rim where so many of her Militia Warriors had died, where Luken had once again almost died. She was sobered and alone.

She had been in memorial services for four days now.

The loss of over a thousand men and women had pared something away from her, some laxity in her attitude toward Darian Greaves.

The enemy had suddenly become *her enemy*, despised of old, yes, but now she felt something more, something deeper, something she had never known in all these millennia. She wanted revenge, deep, abiding, permanent revenge.

And she had the power to set anything in motion she wanted to.

She felt the air stir beside her, but she already knew the signature.

"Hello, Shorty."

"Good morning, Endelle."

She was both surprised and not when he slipped his hand into hers. She felt his Sixth power flow through her, and her chin came up. For a moment, she couldn't breathe. A moment later, she felt . . . comforted.

In any other circumstance, she would have made a joke, teased him about his height, how his hand was actually smaller than hers—that sort of absurd hilarity.

But it would take some time for her sense of humor to return.

Instead, she spoke of recent events. "Greaves has been running his extremely well-edited footage of the battle, calling it an enormous victory for the ALA. Of course none of those clips shows Medichi and Parisa's affect on the battle."

"Did you expect something different?"

"I never believed it would come to this. I thought I had time to keep building and working. I never thought he would attack."

James didn't say anything, just stood beside her staring out at the quiet battlefield. But his comforting stream of power continued to pulse through her hand and up her arm.

As she stared out at empty airspace to the rim opposite, nothing looked changed. Of course, the environmental teams had already been through repairing horticultural battle damage. Second Earth's version of tree-huggers. Whatever.

"He attacked because of the future streams," James said. "You need better Seer information."

"Yes, I do."

"You must make a change. You know what I'm referring to."

"It will break Thorne's heart."

"Yes, it will."

Endelle had been avoiding this moment for over a century, from the time she'd first seen Thorne's woman hidden deep within his mind. She hadn't meant to invade such a private space, but the memory had glowed bright, the way the ribbons of the future streams were said to glow.

So she had pushed her way into the memory and seen what she was never meant to see.

Thorne's woman was a Seer with third, perhaps even fourth dimension capacity, well beyond anything she had ever known before, and Thorne had been protecting her from Second Earth involvement all this time.

But dear God, what would it do to Thorne if she used his woman as a pawn in this terrible game of war?

Greaves sat down in a chair covered in crushed purple velvet. He repressed a shudder. The vampire opposite him had the fashion and decorating taste of a pimp from a few decades past. Greaves deeply disliked him, the way he lounged so casually, several lines of cocaine splayed out in precise order on a glass coffee table in front of him. All he needed was two half-naked women draped over his shoulders to complete the absurd portrait.

"You've always hated my hedonistic inclinations," Casimir said. He smiled. He had large, beautiful teeth, the body of a god, the appetites of Lucifer. His booted foot swung up and back. His snug white pants concealed none of his considerable assets. If Greaves had been otherwise inclined, he would have thought Casimir was trying to seduce him.

"Not your hedonism. You of all men should know that I share your proclivities." He waved a hand around the room. "But I do find your outward expression quite ridiculous."

The vampire leaned his shoulders more deeply into the black leather of the couch. "What do you want, Darian? I take it this isn't a social call . . . unless you want it to be."

Greaves ignored the invitation. He swung many ways but he drew the line at sex with the Prince of Darkness. Even a sociopath had his standards.

He sighed.

The moment had come.

He had been dreading this interview for a good number of centuries. He had believed he would never be required to make the request because his plans had been going so very well. But then, he had hoped against hope that the Upper Dimension would not become involved, that his seizure of smaller realms would have lulled it into believing that his ambitions were negligible—until too late, of course.

However, now that three of the Warriors of the Blood had completed the *breh-hedden* and increased their powers exponentially because of the women involved, the hand-writing had simply appeared on the wall in a way he could no longer ignore. If he'd had any doubts on that score, they were settled by the fact that the most recent bonding had resulted in the loss of his voyeur-link with Parisa. Then there were the wings the happy pair shared. Not to split meta-phors too heavily, but the use of *royle* wings had been the nail in his coffin.

God, what a show that had been, and such a peaceful sensation. Talk about *spectacle*. It really was too bad that he hadn't been able to use the footage in his propaganda cam-paigns, but the energy the couple used showed up on film only as strange flashes of light.

It had been no accident that his minions had failed to kill them all. Forces were at work, some based in destiny and accompanying misfortune, some in the fulfillment of myth, some by the hand of an Upper ascender. It was because of the latter that he'd orchestrated this unfortunate meeting.

He had no choice now but to speak words that brought bile rising from his stomach. "It would seem I need your help."

The large white teeth made another appearance. "The cost will be high."

He nodded. "Naturally."

Casimir glanced at his well-manicured nails, buffed to a gleam. "I saw your mother recently in one of my visits home." Casimir was a Fourth ascender.

"And how fares the great philosopher of Fourth Earth?"

"Beatrice is lovely as always. She has not aged a day." He laughed at his little immortal joke. "She is as sanctimonious as ever, though, quite judgmental—I despise her for that—but beautiful. You have her eyes, you know. Sometimes it is most unsettling to see you, my friend, and at the same moment to recognize Beatrice's large round eyes. Yes, very unsettling."

"Is she still *building* things?" Beatrice had always had a passion for architecture.

He waved a hand, a sensual, delicate motion. "Her latest project is some sort of rehabilitation center surrounded by a lake. The lake is supposed to have healing properties, and the inmates are baptized in it. Can you imagine? I've dubbed it *the lake of fire*." He chuckled, but the sound had resonance and floated around the room until it settled on Greaves's shoulders, a heavy weight.

The time to negotiate had begun. "So tell me your price."

Casimir's teeth gleamed once more in the dim, dim light. "Oh, I think you know what I'll require, at least at the beginning."

Greaves felt his mind slide around loosely. How stupid he had been. He had thought perhaps wealth, or an endless supply of mortal women, or the right to half his kingdom, but he should have known better. Casimir always went to the heart of things. He preferred to draw blood at the outset.

"So you want Julianna."

He shrugged. "I have gazed upon her, so yes, of course."

That was a lie. Casimir may have actually *seen* Julianna, true, but her beauty was not what drew him. Greaves's unfortunate attachment to Eldon Crace's former wife was what Casimir had noticed.

Greaves sighed. His left hand twitched, but he didn't bring forth his claw. There would be no point. A Fourth ascender had advanced powers and would not be intimidated by anything so vulgar.

The question in life was always the same: *What are you willing to do to get the things you want?*

Oh, damn.

Rith trembled on his chaise longue in the underground cavern of his St. Louis Two blood donor facility. He pulled himself out of the future streams, sweating and nauseous.

Not only had his plans with Parisa failed, but his future had taken a terrible turn.

He had been such a fool from beginning to end where

Parisa Lovejoy had been concerned. She had been the cause of this new horror. He should have gone with his instincts and killed her at the outset. Even if he had secured her death later—while he had her in his control at his temple, say—his future might not look so bleak.

Instead, like a complete novice, he'd ignored the rising level of her powers and assumed his energy fields would keep both of his prisoners trapped so that they couldn't dematerialize. By the time he'd lit the torch at the end of the room, they were gone.

Now the ribbon of light belonging to Parisa had combined with Warrior Medichi's ribbon to forge an impenetrable prophetic signature, which he could no longer read. The couple had completed the *breh-hedden*. Whatever their futures might be, whatever roles they might play in the war, were now lost to him, lost to most of the Seers of Second Earth.

Still, Fiona, the one who had been the Commander's first blood slave experiment, had risen to prominence in the future streams, a glowing light that he had been unable to resist reading.

He had picked up her ribbon of an intense silver-blue and ridden her prophecies. What he had found there made him rise from his chaise longue and head into the makeshift lavatory. He threw up into the bucket of water.

He had seen his death in glorious Technicolor at the hands of Fiona. Then he had seen his death at the hands of the Warrior Jean-Pierre. After that, he had seen Greaves himself, his beloved Commander, plunge a blade straight through his heart.

How was he to forge a life from the future streams when his own death had been foretold in three different ways?

A week after the battle at the Grand Canyon, Fiona sat in a large conference room at Madame Endelle's administrative headquarters. The wall of windows to the east gave a view onto an expansive stretch of desert. It never failed to surprise her, since all she'd known for most of her hundred-plus years on Second Earth was a green garden and a large tamarind tree. Her eyes welcomed the change, surprisingly. But she supposed that from the moment of her rescue, when she was brought to Madame Endelle's palace, which overlooked miles of the same Sonoran Desert, she would always think of vast blue skies, clumps of cactus and creosote, and tall stately saguaros, as the representation of her freedom.

Alison sat beside her. She looked very pregnant but very relaxed now. Each time she tensed up, she closed her eyes, calmed her body, and ran a soothing hand over her swollen abdomen. She was communicating telepathically with the infant now, getting better every day at helping Helena draw in her temporary wings and keep her sloshy amniotic haven from spasming.

Fiona had loved being pregnant, carrying her children— lovely Carolyn with her soft honey-brown curls and Peter who came out charging forward, ready to take on the world.

Fiona smiled at the blond beauty. Fiona was tall but still two inches shy of six-foot Alison. Height was a good thing when a woman was attached to a Warrior of the Blood— better kissing distance.

Parisa had made an effort to discover on Fiona's behalf the basic events of her family's lives. Her husband, Terence, had remarried five years after Fiona's disappearance. He'd had a second family to whom he had been utterly devoted. She could smile at the thought. Terence had been a good man, a wonderful loving husband and an excellent father, his hand neither too heavy nor too light. Of course he would have married again.

Her adored children had not fared so well. Her son had died in a trolley accident at the age of twenty-five while pursuing a law degree. Her daughter, Carolyn, had drowned while out yachting two years later, but her body had never been recovered.

Fiona had shed a few tears that neither of her children had been able to live their lives, that each had died relatively young, neither having married or borne children. But in truth she had already grieved her losses for so many decades that a few days after receiving the news, her sadness had dimmed appreciably. More than anything, she needed time to recover and to gain a solid footing in this new world. That the fate of the blood slaves in the remaining twenty-one facilities weighed on her mind gave a strong indication in just what direction her first service to Madame Endelle's administration would go.

Alison opened her eyes. "Sorry about that but it's getting better."

"Good," Fiona said. "I'm so happy for you. There is nothing so wonderful as carrying one's children."

She felt a thousand years older than the therapist beside her, and perhaps in terms of experience and suffering she was. But the woman had a gift. There were moments when Alison reached out to Fiona, put a hand on her arm or her shoulder, and oh, such peace would flow, and some of that deep sense of being so very old would lighten, even disappear. She could even breathe more easily for a time.

She lived with tension constantly—that she would be taken again, spirited away, used for another century. She believed the sensation would go away in time, but how much of it? A decade? Two decades? She was a relatively wise woman, but damaged in her spirit. Who wouldn't be after an ordeal that had lasted longer than a century?

"Now. Let's talk about your future," Alison said. "For the moment, Madame Endelle would like you and the other women to stay at the palace, at least for the next few weeks for security purposes, while you get your bearings. She'd also like you to consider taking charge of the remaining captives. We can see that each has turned to you for leadership and guidance since you've been here."

"They'll need counseling, a lot of it. I will as well. I want to be up-front about that."

"Of course."

Fiona's gaze fell to Alison's belly once more, but she looked away, her gaze skating back to the window. Fiona was still young because she was partially ascended. She could remarry in this dimension. Vampires took husbands, or wives as the case may be. They had weddings and bore children—Twolings. The thought appealed to her. She had always loved being married, having a family to look after.

The memory of Jean-Pierre, the night of her rescue, was suddenly within her mind, the full glory of him in his leather kilt, heavy sandals, and shin guards; the silver studs of his leather wrist guards, the brace of leather over his chest. She recalled her desire for him, which returned to her in a quick flush that almost brought a gasp from her lips. A sudden craving for coffee burst in her mouth and she swallowed hard.

It was the strangest thing and yet she'd already been told all about the infamous and troubling *breh-hedden*.

She shuddered. That couldn't be her fate. Yet she had to admit that even a thought of the powerful French warrior sent shivers in places she'd ignored for, yes, longer than a century. These were modern times and sex had certainly transformed into a strange yet wonderful public conversation.

But in her day, the days of her marriage, it had been intensely private, a thing never discussed even between husband and wife. Fortunately, her husband had been generous in their marriage bed, and she had enjoyed what most women of her day were taught was a painful duty to be endured.

And Jean-Pierre had already proven to her, albeit unwittingly, that even his kiss could bring her to a place of ecstasy. Again she suppressed a gasp. What would lovemaking be like if just a kiss ignited her?

Alison frowned. "You seem distressed. Will the palace be all right with you? The security there is unequaled and we want you off the enemy's radar, especially since it would seem you are Warrior Jean-Pierre's *breh*."

The *breh-hedden*. Even though she could be intrigued by the concept of sex with the warrior, she knew she was no more ready to be anyone's *breh* than she was to take up a sword and battle Commander Greaves all by herself.

She met Alison's worried gaze. "The palace will be fine, of course."

"Good. For a moment there, you seemed upset, and that is not what I want." She began to talk about completing the ascension ceremonies for each woman to make sure they would become fully acclimated to this larger world; it was thought this would be done after a few weeks of rest. She talked about several counselors she knew and trusted. She even spoke about possible vocational training, all sensible things.

Laughter sounded from down the hall and for a reason she couldn't explain, a sudden chill traveled over Fiona's shoulders, as if she were getting a virus. She could hear a woman's voice. Two voices. Parisa, perhaps? Laughter again. No, not Parisa. Havily. Yes, Havily, the one who worked in the darkening with Madame Endelle, the one bonded to Warrior Marcus.

Now she could hear Colonel Seriffe's booming masculine voice. She liked the colonel very much. He headed the Militia Warriors in Metro Phoenix. He was a tough, commanding man but there was always a warm light in his eye, as though he lived with a constant sense of hope no matter how bad things got. Yes, she liked him very much.

He was laughing now, and as she listened to his words, she realized he was bragging about his little boy, who had walked at nine months.

"Do you hear him?" Alison said, smiling. "He adores his children, and his wife can do no wrong."

"In other words, he's the perfect husband."

Alison laughed. "You are more right than you know. He is one of those rare men who combine great strength at work with compassion and love at home. I'm afraid I tend to hold him up as a model too often to Kerrick. I have only to mention Colonel Seriffe and Kerrick bristles. Although, to be honest, sometimes I do it just to watch him pace a little, scowl, and glare at me. I can be very bad sometimes."

Fiona laughed and something inside her started to relax as well. She and Alison had both turned slightly toward the doorway to listen. Havily's excited chatter rose above even the colonel's voice. It was so great to be hearing what would have been normal conversation when she was a young mother.

Is he walking? Cutting teeth? Picking the wrong things up and throwing them? Havily's three little girls had died before her ascension.

So much sadness in life.

Yet so much joy.

"Why don't we go chat with the colonel? It sounds like he may have brought his entire family in today. Would you like to meet them?"

"Yes, I'd love to."

Alison rose, all stately six feet of her.

Fiona heard another woman's laughter, and that earlier chill once more caught her across the shoulders. What was that? Maybe she was getting sick. Then she remembered—ascenders never got sick.

"Yes, he brought his wife. She's a joy. I think you'll really like her. In some ways, oddly, you remind me of her. Probably because your eye color is very similar, a lovely silver-blue."

Fiona heard the rippling laughter and was transported back more than a hundred years. Her mother had had a laugh just like that. How strange.

Sadness crept in at the reminder of something so familiar to her, yet something she had lost when she'd been abducted. She felt an urgent need to remain where she was, maybe crawl under the conference table and stay there, oh, for a year, maybe a decade. She wasn't stable yet. Her knees shook as she stood. For all her strength all those decades, of being killed and brought back to life month after month, for some reason coming to a place of safety at long last had robbed her of her staying ability; she felt almost unequal to meeting the colonel and his family.

But she wasn't about to give in to such weakness. She'd always squared up to life, even when it was hard.

She moved next to Alison down the hallway. Colonel Seriffe came into view first. His wife was somewhere behind him, as was Havily. He had a little boy in his arms, dimpled fists, light brown hair in soft curls at the nape of his neck. So adorable. The sight of him, of a child thriving in this world, filled her heart with . . . joy.

But at the same time, a sense of knowing began a slow march down her spine. Again she had an impulse to run away and hide, but she didn't know why. What was it about the presence of this family that threatened to undo her?

Still, she stayed the course. She straightened her shoulders and took a couple of deep breaths. She focused on the child, the little boy, the one seated on the colonel's left arm.

Suddenly, she felt as though she knew that little boy, but that was impossible. Yet the feeling remained.

Behind the colonel, Havily spoke to Seriffe's wife. She could hear them chattering as Havily gestured in small wild movements with her hands, but the colonel's broad shoulders and six-five frame hid most of his wife.

Two older children moved up next to their father, both with Seriffe's dark hair and eyes. The toddler in his arms turned in Alison's direction and held his arms out to her. He looked achingly familiar to Fiona. Surely she had seen this child before, somewhere. But she'd been in Metro Phoenix Two barely a week. Alison took him easily and started speaking softly to him. He put his little hands on her face, and Alison kissed his fingers.

Her mind swam with images from long ago. Her daughter had looked just like this child, from the large silvery blue eyes, to the light curly brown hair, to the sweetest smile in the world.

Her gaze slid from the little boy, to Seriffe, then his wife joined him. Fiona met her eyes. She knew this woman. *She knew her.* She couldn't place her but another set of chills chased down her back, and this time her shoulders and arms as well, until her fingertips hummed with unsuspected power, even recognition. She knew her, but how? Had she been a blood slave who had escaped at one time, maybe decades ago? But that was impossible. Fiona would have remembered if any of the slaves had escaped.

Weirdest of all, tears started spilling from Fiona's eyes and the woman's eyes at almost exactly at the same moment. Fiona wept and the woman wept. But why? Fiona gave a little cry and the woman shook her head back and forth. She put her hands to her mouth and cried out behind her fingers.

"What's wrong, Carolyn?" Seriffe asked. "Darling, what's wrong? This is . . . Fiona. Oh . . . dear . . . God. You have the same eyes. I didn't see it before."

Havily drew up beside the young mother. "What is it, Carolyn? What's happening? Fiona, are you all right? Why are you crying? Why are you both crying? What did I miss?"

Alison just looked from one woman to the next then echoed Seriffe. "Oh, dear God. It can't be!"

The young mother, Carolyn, the one with the silvery blue eyes, finally said, "Mother? Is that you? After all these decades, you didn't die? You ascended? Oh, God, Mother is that you?"

"Carolyn? Carolyn Gaines of Boston?"

She nodded.

"You didn't drown in a yachting accident?"

"No. I ascended in 1913." She gestured with a graceful hand to the toddler in Alison's arms, to the older boys beside the colonel, then to Seriffe himself. "This is my family. The colonel and I . . . we married a few years ago."

Fiona's gaze hadn't left Carolyn's beautiful silvery eyes, her light honey-brown hair, the slight angel-kiss in her chin. "My daughter," she whispered. "Dearest Creator in heaven . . . my daughter."

She lost all sensation in her feet and before she understood what was happening, she fell into a black abyss of shock and disbelief and something more, something wonderful, something, yes, very much like . . . *joy*.

Parisa Lovejoy, newly appointed Guardian of Ascension, tried on the ceremonial *royle* robe. It had been designed for her based on portraits of Luchianne, done by historical artists about five hundred years earlier. The renditions had been created as a combination of Endelle's descriptions and anecdotal evidence provided by scholar Philippe Reynard.

Despite all that she had been through with Antony, especially the role she had played beside him during the recent

Grand Canyon battle, she felt ridiculous wearing the floor-length garments. Viewing herself in the mirror, she looked like something out of ancient Rome. *Who are you, what are you doing wearing such elegant robes, how can you be this person, this woman?*

She felt panicky. To go from librarian, to the bonded *breh* of a Warrior of the Blood, to a Guardian of Ascension, to an ambassador of Second Earth with *royle* wings was all way too much. To say the least, she felt inadequate.

The outer garment was deep purple with a soft but very large curled collar. Heavy wide sleeves were embroidered all around the bell-like cuffs with an intricate pattern of swirls meant to represent wind.

She turned to the side and lowered the outer robe to her waist. The shimmery gold silk of the under-robe felt right to her, though. It was cut in a T down her back, similar to her weapons harness, and was intended for wing release.

She let the outer garment fall in a purple puddle to the floor. Beneath all the gold silk was a fine mesh that secured the fabric of the skirt to her soft leggings. It had felt so strange when she'd first put the garment on, but she understood the purpose. When she was in flight, the mesh would keep the gown close to her body. Nothing had been left to chance.

Antony appeared behind her in the mirror. She turned to him. He wore a similar getup, leggings and all, but he looked magnificent. His hair was pulled back tight in the *cadroen,* which of course showed off his high strong cheekbones and his overall beauty. Her lips parted as she looked at him. And he was all hers? What miracle had brought so much man, so much warrior into her life, to savor, to love, to enjoy forever, God willing.

The gods had smiled on her. There could be no other answer.

Antony smiled. Her heart ached at the sight. She put her hand on his cheek. "I love you," she murmured.

He put his hands on her arms and drew a deep breath. He released it slowly. "Why are you fretting?"

"I thought I would be a warrior. I was going to enter the training program."

"I know."

"I still want to. My heart yearns for that, to be a warrior like you. But I think what I've come to realize is that every ascender is a warrior, no matter the occupation."

Antony kissed her. "So much wisdom for one so young. And remember, nothing is fixed. Right now we both have this job to do, but it's conceivable you could enter the program later."

Her spirits lifted. "That's true, isn't it? I keep forgetting that the ascended life has the potential for immortality."

She looked down at the purple linen pooled around her feet. "How am I worthy of any of this?"

He shrugged. "We aren't. Neither of us. No ascender can be, and the minute you think you're worthy, you're in trouble. Besides, I think you need some perspective about what's going to happen. Madame Endelle is sending us on a one-hundred-day tour of one hundred Territories. By the time we return I have no doubt we will both want to burn these robes, and we'll have a whole new set of really bad words to describe Her Supremeness."

"Oh, God, you are so right. We should plan a bonfire ceremony before we even leave. Why don't you hire a contractor to build a pyre near the pool?"

He chuckled and pulled her into his arms.

Parisa now stood on the purple robes but she didn't care. She pressed her nose into his neck and sniffed long and loud. He smelled sooo good, sage and earth and man all in one. Certain unfortunate thoughts began swirling through her mind. She felt him tense.

"Stop that," he whispered. "The scent of tangerines is so thick in my brain right now I can hardly think."

He pressed his hips against her and let her feel his response, but she already had. One of the results of the *breh-hedden* was the strange way in which she could feel his physical body, in an external sense. She could feel what her hips felt like pressing back at him, the pleasure she gave.

She could feel from his perspective what it was like to have her large breasts smashed against his chest. She could feel his body respond, his cock thicken, lengthen, harden.

Shivers chased over her body in response, and in further response, his own body quivered. It was such a hot, dangerous back-and-forth. *Oh, yeah.*

She drew back and looked up at him, but didn't break contact. "So how much time do we have?"

He growled. "We are not due at the palace for Endelle's costume approval for half an hour."

She shivered, he quivered. She started to fold off the clothes but he stopped her and laughed. "Allow me, please."

She giggled. They so did not have time for her to practice more of her folding skills, which still sucked.

Within a split second she was flush against him flesh-to-flesh. She sighed and melted into his arms. The *breh-hedden* lit her up, and he was fire on her skin. The apertures down her back wept, and her fingers felt the ridges of his wing-locks. She flicked them gently and he writhed heavily against her. He turned her in the direction of the bed. She heard the swish of the comforter and top sheet. The next moment she was flat on her back and he was entering her, all those weighty inches of him, pushing into her, making her back arch, her wing-locks seep and make a mess of their bed. The silk sheets would have to go. Silk didn't like moisture. Maybe a terry-cloth sheet . . . at least for times like these.

An hour after the meeting with Endelle, Medichi had his woman under the curve of his arm. He stood on the lip of the Grand Canyon, in about the same spot he'd been more than two weeks ago when he'd chased a rogue death vampire down, down, down to the raging river below, when he'd flipped him into the water then hauled him onto the rock that had broken him, when he'd pierced the bastard's mind and taken the one piece of information he'd needed to find Parisa.

Now he was back, to look, to remember, to ponder.

Parisa shuddered. "Why did you bring me here?"

The recent battle was still fresh, for both of them.

But so was the miracle that had followed, their miracle, which had emerged because they'd each had the courage to swallow their fears and to complete the *breh-hedden*.

"We were born here," he said, not looking at her. His mind was fixed in the distance, the vastness of the canyon, the beauty, the impossibility of it all, the breadth of time that had carved out the abyss, and his wings that could breach it all.

"Yes," she whispered. "We were born here, that part of you and me that became an *us*. You're right, we were."

He felt how solemn she was. He knew her mind now, all of her intricacies, her fears, her shames, her triumphs, her loves, and just how much she admired him. He thrived on that, her respect for him, her willingness to stand beside him because she believed in him.

He held her closer. Fear rode him for a brief arctic moment. A shiver passed through him. Bad things were coming, terrible things for the Warriors of the Blood, for those women bonded to them. He knew it in the hard hateful way that he had started *knowing* things.

But at the same time, peace descended.

This was life, ascended life, good, bad, indifferent, terrifying.

But it was also grand, huge, magnificent, full of unbelievable joys and, yes, on occasion triumphs.

He let these pleasures flow through him. He looked at Parisa, and she turned from admiring the beauty in front of her to meeting his gaze. Her smile reached her beautiful amethyst eyes, so much the color of the banding on their shared wings.

"I love you so much," she whispered.

He drew her into his arms. He kissed her, his tongue plunging and savoring. He loved all the connections he had to her, his tongue, his cock, his fingers, his arms wrapped around her, his body pressed to her, his wings, tip-to-tip, his fangs, but mostly his mind. God, yes his mind.

He felt her chest rise and fall in a deeply drawn breath and sigh. He felt her pleasure that he held her.

He pulled back from her then kissed her. "I love you more than I can say."

Her smile, always her smile.

He stroked her cheek with his finger. He was blessed, so very blessed.

"Do you know what I want right this moment?"

He smiled, and the smile crept over his face. Of course he knew, and that knowledge delighted him. "You mean besides my fearsome body?"

She giggled against him. "Yes, besides your fearsome body."

He kissed her again, then, without needing her to explain the desire of her heart, he stepped away from her. With an incredibly quicksilver movement he had not known before the *breh-hedden*, very much a third dimension ability, he released his wings as swift as lightning. She followed suit equally fast.

"Let's fly," he cried.

Yes, Antony, she laid over his mind.

Yes, he returned.

A most perfect word.

ASCENSION TERMINOLOGY

ascender (n.) A mortal human of earth who has moved permanently to the second dimension.

ascendiate (n.) A mortal human who has answered the *call to ascension* and thereby commences his or her *rite of ascension*.

ascension (n.) The act of moving permanently from one dimension to a higher dimension.

ascension, call to (n.) A period of time, usually several weeks, in which the mortal human has experienced some or all of, but not limited to, the following: specific dreams about the next dimension, deep yearnings and longings of a soulful and inexplicable nature, visions of and possibly visits to any of the dimensional Borderlands, etc. See *Borderlands*.

ascension, answering the call to (n.) The mortal human who experiences the hallmarks of the *call to ascension* will at some point feel compelled to answer, usually by demonstrating significant preternatural power.

ascension, rite of (n.) A three-day period during which time an *ascendiate* contemplates ascending to the next highest dimension.

ascension ceremony (n.) Upon the completion of the *rite of ascension,* the mortal undergoes a ceremony in which loyalty to the laws of Second Society is professed and the attributes of the vampire mantle along with immortality are bestowed.

Borderlands (pr. n.) Those geographic areas that form dimensional borders at both ends of a dimensional pathway. The dimensional pathway is an access point through which travel can take place from one dimension to the next. See *Trough.*

breh-hedden (n.) (Term from an ancient language.) A mate-bonding ritual that can only be experienced by the most powerful warriors and the most powerful preternaturally gifted women. Effects of the *breh-hedden* can include but are not limited to: specific scent experience, extreme physical/sexual attraction, loss of rational thought, primal sexual drives, inexplicable need to bond, powerful need to experience deep *mind-engagement,* etc.

cadroen (n.) (Term from an ancient language.) The name for the hair clasp that holds back the ritual long hair of a Warrior of the Blood.

Central (pr. n.) The office of the current administration that tracks movement of *death vampires* in both the second dimension and on *Mortal Earth* for the purpose of alerting the

Warriors of the Blood and the *Militia Warriors* to illegal activities.

darkening, the (n.) An area of *nether-space* that can be found during meditations and/or with strong preternatural darkening capabilities. Such abilities enable the *ascender* to move into nether-space and remain there or to use nether-space in order to be in two places at once.

death vampire (n.) Any *vampire,* male or female, who partakes of *dying blood* automatically becomes a death vampire. Death vampires can have, but are not limited to, the following characteristics: remarkably increased physical strength, an increasingly porcelain complexion true of all ethnicities so that death vampires have a long-term reputation for looking very similar, a faint bluing of the porcelain complexion, increasing beauty of face, the ability to enthrall, the blackening of *wings* over a period of time. Though death vampires are not gender-specific, most are male. See *vampire.*

dimensional worlds (n.) Eleven thousand years ago, the first *ascender,* Luchianne, made the difficult transition from *Mortal Earth* to what became known as Second Earth. In the early millennia four more dimensions were discovered, Luchianne always leading the way. Each dimension's ascenders exhibited expanding preternatural power before *ascension.* Upper dimensions are generally closed off to the dimension or dimensions below.

duhuro (n.) (Term from an ancient language.) A word of respect that in the old language combines the spiritual offices of both servant and master. To call someone *duhuro* is to offer a profound compliment suggesting great worth.

dying blood (n.) Blood extracted from a mortal or an *ascender* at the point of death. This blood is highly addictive in nature. There is no known treatment for anyone who partakes of dying blood. The results of ingesting dying blood include, but are not limited to: increased physical, mental, or preternatural power, a sense of extreme euphoria, a deep sense of well-being, a sense of omnipotence and fearlessness, the taking in of the preternatural powers of the host body, etc. If dying blood is not taken on a regular basis, extreme abdominal cramps result without ceasing. Note: Currently there is an antidote not for the addiction to dying blood itself but to the various results of ingesting dying blood. This means that a *death vampire* who drinks dying blood and then partakes of the antidote will not show the usual physical side effects of ingesting dying blood: no whitening or faint bluing of the skin, no beautifying of features, no blackening of the *wings,* etc.

effetne **(n.)** (Term from an ancient language.) An intense form of supplication to the gods; an abasement of self and of self-will.

folding (v.) Slang for dematerialization, since some believe that one does not actually dematerialize self or objects but rather one "folds space" to move self or objects from one place to another. There is much scientific debate on this subject since at present neither theory can be proved.

grid (n.) The technology used by Central that allows for the tracking of *death vampires* primarily at the *Borderlands* on both *Mortal Earth* and *Second Earth.* Death vampires by nature carry a strong, trackable signal, unlike normal *vampires.* See *Central.*

Guardian of Ascension (pr. n.) A prestigious title and rank at present given only to those *Warriors of the Blood* who also serve to guard powerful *ascendiates* during their *rite of ascension.* In millennia past Guardians of Ascension were also those powerful ascenders who offered themselves in unique and powerful service to Second Society.

High Administrator (pr. n.) The designation given to a leader of a Second Earth *Territory*.

identified sword (n.) A sword made by Second Earth metallurgy that has the preternatural capacity to become identified to a single *ascender*. The identification process involves holding the sword by the grip for several continuous seconds. The identification of a sword to a single ascender means that only that person can touch or hold the sword. If anyone else tries to take possession, that person will die.

Militia Warrior (pr. n.) One of hundreds of thousands of warriors who serve Second Earth as a policing force for the usual civic crimes and as a battling force, in squads only, to fight against the continual depredations of *death vampires* on both *Mortal Earth* and Second Earth.

mind-engagement (n.) The ability to penetrate another mind and experience the thoughts and memories of the other person; also, the ability to receive another mind and allow that person to experience one's own thoughts and memories. These abilities must be present in order to complete the *breh-hedden*.

mist (n.) A preternatural creation designed to confuse the mind and thereby hide things or people. Most mortals and *ascenders* are unable to see mist. The powerful ascender, however, is capable of seeing mist, which usually looks like an intricate mesh, or a cloud, or a web-like covering.

Mortal Earth (pr. n.) The name for First Earth or the current modern world known simply as earth.

nether-space (n.) The unknowable, unmappable regions of space. The space between dimensions is considered nether-space as well as the space found in *the darkening*.

preternatural voyeurism (n.) The ability to "open a window" with the power of one's mind in order to see people and events happening elsewhere in real time. Two of the limits of preternatural voyeurism are that the voyeur must usually know the person or place, and if the voyeur is engaged in darkening work, it is very difficult to make use of preternatural voyeurism at the same time.

pretty-boy (n.) Slang for *death vampire,* since most death vampires are male.

royle **(n.)** (Term from an ancient language.) The literal translation is: "a benevolent wind." More loosely translated, *royle* refers to the specific quality of having the capacity to create a state of benevolence, of goodwill, within an entire people or culture. See *royle* (adj.)

royle **(adj.)** (Term from an ancient language.) This term is generally used to describe a specific coloration of *wings:* cream with three narrow bands at the outer tips of the wings when in full-span. The bands are always burnished gold, amethyst, and black. Because Luchianne, the first *ascender* and first *vampire,* had this coloration on her wings, anyone whose wings matched Luchianne's was said to have *royle* wings. Having *royle* wings was considered a tremendous gift, holding great promise for the world.

Seer (pr. n.) An *ascender* gifted with the preternatural ability to ride the future streams and report on future events.

Seers Fortress (pr. n.) *Seers* have traditionally been gathered into compounds designed to provide a highly peaceful environment, thereby enhancing their ability to ride the future streams. The information gathered at a Seers Fortress benefits the local *High Administrator.* Some believe that the term *fortress* emerged as a protest to the prison-like conditions the Seers often have to endure.

spectacle (n.) The name given to events of gigantic proportion that include but are not limited to: trained squadrons of

DNA-altered geese, swans, and ducks, ascenders with the specialized and dangerous skills of flight performance, intricate and often massive light and fireworks displays, as well as various forms of music.

Supreme High Administrator (pr. n.) The ruler of Second Earth. See *High Administrator.*

Territory (pr. n.) For the purpose of governance, Second Earth is divided up into groups of countries called Territories. Because the total population of Second Earth is only 1 percent of *Mortal Earth,* Territories were established as a simpler means of administering Second Society law. See *High Administrator.*

Trough (pr. n.) A slang term for a dimensional pathway. See *Borderlands.*

Twoling (pr. n.) Anyone born on Second Earth is a Twoling.

vampire (n.) The natural state of the *ascended* human. Every ascender is a vampire. The qualities of being a vampire include but are not limited to: immortality, the use of fangs to take blood, the use of fangs to release potent chemicals, increased physical power, increased preternatural ability, etc. Luchianne created the word *vampire* upon her *ascension* to Second Earth to identify in one word the totality of the changes she experienced upon that ascension. From the first, the taking of blood was viewed as an act of reverence and bonding, not as a means of death. The *Mortal Earth* myths surrounding the word *vampire* for the most part personify the Second Earth death vampire. See *death vampire.*

Warriors of the Blood (pr. n.) An elite fighting unit of usually seven powerful warriors, each with phenomenal preternatural ability and capable of battling several *death vampires* at any one time.

wings (n.) All *ascenders* eventually produce wings from wing-locks. *Wing-lock* is the term used to describe the apertures on the ascender's back from which the feathers and attending mesh-like superstructure emerge. Mounting wings involves a hormonal rush that some liken to sexual release. Flight is one of the finest experiences of ascended life. Wings can be held in a variety of positions including but not limited to: full-mount, close-mount, aggressive-mount, etc. Wings emerge over a period of time from one to several hundred years. Wings can, but do not always, begin small in one decade then grow larger in later decades.

Coming soon . . .

Look for the next novel in the sensational
Guardians of Ascension series from

CARIS ROANE

BORN OF ASHES
ISBN: 978-0-312-53374-8

Available in January 2012 from St. Martin's Paperbacks